KU-465-150

WHITE MALE HEART

Ruaridh Nicoll

BLACK SWAN

WHITE MALE HEART
A BLACK SWAN BOOK : 0 552 99901 6

Originally published in Great Britain by Doubleday,
a division of Transworld Publishers

PRINTING HISTORY
Doubleday edition published 2001
Black Swan edition published 2002

1 3 5 7 9 10 8 6 4 2

Copyright © Ruaridh Nicoll 2001

The right of Ruaridh Nicoll to be identified as the author of
this work has been asserted in accordance with sections 77 and
78 of the Copyright Designs and Patents Act 1988.

The quotations on pp. 164–5 are taken from *David's Tool Kit: A Citizen's
Guide to Taking Out Big Brother's Heavy Weapons* by Ragnar Benson
(1996, Loompanics Unlimited, PO Box 1197, Port Townsend, WA 98368).

All the characters in this book are fictitious,
and any resemblance to actual persons, living or dead,
is purely coincidental.

Condition of Sale
This book is sold subject to the condition that it shall not,
by way of trade or otherwise, be lent, re-sold, hired out or otherwise
circulated in any form of binding or cover other than that in which it is
published and without a similar condition including this condition
being imposed on the subsequent purchaser.

Set in 11/13pt Sabon by
Kestrel Data, Exeter, Devon.

Black Swan Books are published by Transworld Publishers,
61–63 Uxbridge Road, London W5 5SA,
a division of The Random House Group Ltd,
in Australia by Random House Australia (Pty) Ltd,
20 Alfred Street, Milsons Point, Sydney, NSW 2061, Australia,
in New Zealand by Random House New Zealand Ltd,
18 Poland Road, Glenfield, Auckland 10, New Zealand
and in South Africa by Random House (Pty) Ltd,
Endulini, 5a Jubilee Road, Parktown 2193, South Africa.

Printed and bound in Great Britain by
Clays Ltd, St Ives plc.

Ruaridh Nicoll was born in Arbroath, Angus, in 1969 and raised in the Highland county of Sutherland. An award-winning journalist, he served as the *Observer*'s US correspondent and the *Guardian*'s Southern Africa correspondent. *White Male Heart* is his first novel. He currently lives in Scotland.

Acclaim for
WHITE MALE HEART

'At once both brutal and beautiful . . . The quality of observation is breathtaking . . . This is an absorbing and uncomfortable read, raising as many questions as it answers about what it means to be a young man in a territory where the roles are few and growing more limited with every passing year. But *White Male Heart* has far wider relevance than that. This is a novel that is both heart-rending and heart-stopping but which never loses sight of the importance of the blackest humour. It is without question a welcome and worthy addition to the growing sub-genre of tartan noir'
Val McDermid

'Eerily impressive. Like Sir Waltar Scott ambushed by Iain Banks, Nicoll produces prose both rhapsodically beautiful and red in tooth and claw, marking out this modern gothic tale'
Sunday Times

'Nicoll's first novel takes us to the Highlands of Scotland, but this is not a gentle land, it is a place with a dark and sinister complexion . . . Though Nicoll is a journalist, he has a novelist's eye for the beauty of the landscape and the shape of its contours . . . This is a novel of startling originality, an absorbing psychological thriller as well as a deft portrayal of friendship and betrayal. Nicoll conjures up the pain of rejection and abandonment as convincingly as he describes the way in which a stalker stands downwind of a rutting stag. It is a long time since we have had a writer who is so at home with nature and hunting, and who describes them so vividly and fluently'
The Times

'In Ruaridh Nicoll's *White Male Heart*, Hemingway's ghost would seem to roam the Highlands. This is a tale of male bonding and competition, full of animal killing and proofs of masculinity. The blood is all in the service of showing that love, maybe even love of women, is a truer path. What's more, this journalist knows something Papa didn't: rural Scotland'
Observer

www.**books**at**transworld**.co.uk

'Bracingly violent . . . beautifully told . . . this excellent, horrifying
first novel'
Evening Standard

'The juxtaposition of civility and barbarity is central to Ruaridh
Nicoll's *White Male Heart* . . . The structure of this novel creates an
overwhelming sense of portent . . . Nicoll recreates the Scottish
landscape with brilliance. He explores its latent violence and its
remarkable beauty in a language which at times will leave you
breathless. This is a bleak novel whose tensions build flawlessly
into a shocking denouement'
Literary Review

'A scintillating piece of literature . . . utterly accurate in its bleak and
isolated sense of place, *While Male Heart* comes on a latter day *Wasp
Factory*, but even more sting-y'
Waterstone's Magazine

'An explosively violent début . . . a natural-born writer'
The Scotsman

'Spectacular, page-turning . . . There are many highlights in Nicoll's
sweeping and assured narrative . . . But the real star of *White Male
Heart* is the Highlands, in all its glorious colours, with its mountains,
its glens and the magic of its storms and sunsets . . . It is his supreme
gift as a writer that he pulls this off on the page. He creates a
backdrop so vivid that it becomes integral to the action: the bigger the
country, the more suffocating it seems to be, the more intense its
beauty, the greater the ugliness of the beings crawl over it; the more
powerful it appears, the weaker its inhabitants. All this is evoked
magisterially and tenderly . . . until the terrible end, a moment of
inspired theatricality. Meaty stuff indeed'
Scotland on Sunday

'Powerful and passionate, this is an impressive fictional début'
Eve magazine

'Beautifully told . . . Here, among the glens and crags, every living
creature is either in pain or close to it; people are so achingly lonely
and savage that they're perpetually on the edge of insanity. And then
something dangerous and confusing happens – a young man, Hugh,
falls in love and tastes happiness'
Yorkshire Post

'Stark, uncompromising'
The Face

To my nephews and nieces,
Archie, Tom, Ramsay, Murdo, Hugo, Kirsty and Iona,
who each, in their own way, offer me a memory of my parents

ACKNOWLEDGEMENTS

I would like to thank the people who helped me along the way. Here they are, roughly in order of appearance.

Peter Jinks encouraged me to write *White Male Heart* and read the manuscript. Antony Harwood, my agent, added impetus through understanding and has proved the finest of comrades ever since. Bella Bathurst listened, read and advised.

Pat and Beth Wilson offered sanctuary in the Highlands for nearly thirteen months. Gill Devonport, Fiona Price, Ronnie, Dina and Kenny Ross, Sascha Burns and Sarah-Jane Fraser saw me through. Dave Gordon advised on steak, butchery and literature.

Norman MacLeod, Lizzie Francke, Euan Ferguson and Clare Longrigg offered liberally from their wide knowledge of culture. Kamal Ahmed added perspective. Alison Bell introduced me to Iomhar and Ruaraig Maciver, the foundrymen at the Beltane Studios in Peebles who showed me how to cast bronze. Duncan MacLeod checked the Gaelic. Carl Eastwood provided a thought I filched. Alex Linklater offered incentive and helpful bit-work.

When a five-week court case broke the writing of this book Camilla Nicholls, Siobhain Butterworth, Pat Burge and Rose Alexander made sure it didn't break my spirit.

They have my respect and profound gratitude. For the same reason my thanks to the editors and management of the newspaper involved.

Simon Taylor, my editor at Transworld, not only offered his belief in *White Male Heart* but has also, through wise and insightful reading, made it a better book. His many colleagues have also proved reassuringly good to have on my side.

My love to Angus, Rosie, Hamish, Penny, Katie and Andy. To Alison, my life.

PART ONE

PROLOGUE

Mac Seruant's fingers lay across the open page of a book, the text forgotten as he gazed out over the rock and shale landscape beyond his window. Behind him, beyond the kitchen wall, a car had arrived, the noise of its dying engine momentarily replaced by an ethereal church music before that, too, was killed. Mac smiled, his fingers flexing as he closed the book and reached over to adjust the lid on a vast stockpot that stood simmering on the range. He stepped back and opened a drawer, lifting out a thin, curved knife, a hacksaw and a cloth. Then he reached up and extinguished the lantern above his head, moving through the cottage as shadow, re-emerging as flesh only when he opened the front door and greeted his guest.

The visitor, a tall boy barely into his twenties, stood beside his truck, eyes almost translucent and deep-set in a narrow skull topped by dirty blond hair. His joints appeared to have been pushed out of shape by the confines of the pick-up's cab and he was stretching, shifting them back to order. Mac nodded and looked away across the surrounding landscape, a casual reconnaissance that slid across the floor of the corrie, then followed the shadow of a burn up to where its waters fell between buttresses that rose to the peaks of

11

soaring cliffs that enclosed the cottage on three sides. He was listening for a break in the silence and, once reassured that they were alone, left the doorway and walked quickly along a path that led in to the edge of the mountain, the boy following close behind.

They walked without speaking, following the thin trail as it crested a small rise and dropped away into a hollow where a wooden hut stood thrust into the cliff edge, its rusting corrugated roof hanging out, leached minerals leaving luminous lines in the grooves. Mac stopped at the hut's gate, pulled a set of keys from his pocket and opened the padlock. He placed his hand where someone, long before, had written, 'My Son, if Sinners entice thee, consent thou not,' and pushed his way in. A shroud hung on the right of the old mineshaft and Mac pulled it aside for the boy, who walked forward, hesitating in the staleness of the room while Mac struck a match and fired up a lantern that hung from the roof.

Around them stood the debris of another age. Rotted floorboards were covered with plywood, which in turn had softened and given way. The walls were covered with shelves, some holding lumps of magnesium and zinc ore, others disintegrating tools, tins, magazines and manuals. The boy lifted an old medallion, a St Christopher, from where it dangled on a hook, studied the image and spun it by its chain around his hand until it fell snug into his fist. He settled himself on a pile of straw bales stacked in the corner and watched as Mac carried the lantern to the far side of the room and hung it on the wall close to an ore-sifting tray on which the knife, hacksaw and cloth were laid out.

Mac picked up a long stick and used it to spring a hidden trapdoor in the roof, revealing a dark creature hanging by its haunches from a winch in the eaves. A glandular stench spilled out as he climbed into the attic and lowered the beast to the sifting tray and, as if

12

*comforted by the smell, the boy began to speak, slowly
at first, as if trying to order the recriminations in his
mind. As his words emerged Aaron Harding was gazing
into the creature's visible eye. Mac swung himself down
to the floor and began to work. He rolled the beast onto
its back and picked up the knife, cut into the flesh and
snapped off the lower extremes of the four legs. He sliced
the skin of the stomach in a smooth bow until the
creature's genitals came away in his hand, then skewered
them to a hook on the wall. Despite the chill he was
sweating. Aaron's voice grew more confident.*

*Mac moved along the carcass, running thick fingers
across the coarse hair, searching out the gash in the
beast's neck, feeling for the stickiness of its blood. He
drove the knife deep into the animal's throat, slicing
through the oesophagus and the jugular. The flesh was
still tender, and Mac allowed the weight of the beast's
head to tear the muscle. With a final slice he took the cut
to the spine, picked up the hacksaw and cut down, the
deep cord sound of splintering nerve filling the room.
The head fell, caught on a small stretch of skin, and fell
again. Aaron paused. The beast's eye was now covered in
a film of dirt, and all at once Mac was turning, looking
at the wall behind Aaron's head: another visitor was
approaching.*

*Aaron listened to the sound of the distant motor as
Mac returned to the sifting tray to check the block
running through the beast's haunches. He picked up the
severed head, lifted it into the rafters and tucked it away
before he winched the beast up so that it hung. Back on
the floor he pushed the tray to one side and left a bucket
under the severed stump of the creature's neck. The
sound of the vehicle grew louder, and Aaron stood up.*

*Mac's perspiration cooled and he wiped his sleeve
across his forehead, his skin reflecting the light of the
lantern. Outwardly, he showed little sign that he had*

heard the car approach the junction, only his brow moved when it failed to pass on. It had turned and was heading up towards the cottage.

He reached for the lantern, tightened the wick and killed the flame. Navigating in the darkness with ease, he pulled aside the curtain that covered the entrance, allowing a brief sliver of moonlight to flicker across Aaron's face, revealing troubled eyes. He slipped his hand through the gate and fastened the padlock, glancing up as the headlights showed. Then he turned and walked back into the room, adjusting the shroud and sitting down on the straw to wait.

Together, they heard the car rumble over the wooden bridge that brought it into the corrie's basin, then up to the cottage itself. Doors opened and shut, the sound of voices carrying across the small rise. The visitors knocked on the cottage door and, after a moment's pause, shouted from within. A drop of blood fell from the beast's neck into the bucket and Aaron flinched. There was silence and then their names were yelled from the top of the rise, the voice now recognizable. Mac began to get to his feet but Aaron reached out to stop him. Feeling the hand on his arm, Mac sat back, listening, as the shouting grew frustrated. A woman's voice mingled with the calls, attempting to soothe. It was the first time he had heard it, its tone deep, gentle and southern.

The visitors returned to the cottage, but Mac and Aaron remained in the dark, waiting as comrades for the vigil to end and the visitors to leave. Passing minutes existed only in the occasional drip of blood from the severed neck, and later, when time began to weigh, Aaron returned to his monologue. Now, though, he whispered, silent again only when the cottage door opened and shut, the car started and left.

Aaron stood while Mac refired the lantern, and when

14

the light came up he looked down at the palm of his hand to find the St Christopher had bitten deep. Unravelling the chain, he returned the medallion to its hook and pulled a shark's tooth from his pocket, which he began to roll between finger and thumb. Mac, who had been studying the boy as he adjusted the lantern, turned away and picked up the hacksaw. He swung the animal's belly towards him and cut deep into its sternum, the wet gristle falling away as the blade tore in. Aaron shifted to the door-frame and leaned against it as he finished his story, his words coming slowly now. At last he fell silent. The bone separated and Mac used a wooden stave to hold the animal's chest cavity apart so that its very core was visible. Inside, the beast's lungs hung down, like the wings of a diving angel, and he thrust his hand between them, pulled out the heart and held it in his palm. The muscle surface had been torn by the passage of a bullet, causing Mac to smile. He looked up at Aaron. 'So, you think it's love?' he asked.

ONE

'Show a little chutzpah,' whispered Hugh, and the Arab tensed. The boy straightened from where he was lying beside the mare's ear and ran his hand along the arched neck all the way back to the picked-up tail behind. On command Sandancer the Conveyancer struck out for the games at a skittish trot. Hugh pulled on the reins so that she veered away from the road and towards a grassy strip that ran between the floodplain's thick reeds and the riverbank. He could feel Sandancer cheered beneath him, the warmth of the autumn sun offering both horse and rider an easy joy.

'Chutzpah,' Hugh shouted suddenly, and Sandancer side-stepped into a canter.

Hugh inhaled. The sound of the hoofs and the glow of the day made him feel as if he were gliding over the turning world. His gaze fell on the shadow that horse and rider threw across the passing reeds and he placed himself at the centre of that fast-shifting darkness, looking up at his figure moving across the marshland on top of his Arab charger: the speed gave him a sense of power, as if he were freed from the dreary millpond of youth and launched into wild rapids of life. In shadow

17

Sandancer's shape seemed magical, her legs blurring into a perfect gallop, muscles bunching then stretching out with fluid ease. Hugh considered his own reflection and saw no less a creature: young, vibrant, in his prime. In the shadow he could see man and beast push forward, arms outstretched, grasping for the future. 'Nothing can stop me,' he whispered to himself.

With Sandancer at full gallop he balanced himself carefully on the balls of his feet, keeping his posture perfect by studying the shadow. He allowed the surroundings to pass ignored, mere beauty insignificant compared with the heroism in the shadow's dark flash. In the rhythm of his heart came the beating of the hoofs and the inhalation of cool Highland air, all in concert. Then the shadow changed. Hugh watched the darkness rise from the reeds, cross the grass and flicker back at him from the waters of the Kyle. He looked up and saw that Sandancer's forelegs no longer moved but were thrust out ahead. Then they hit water and he felt himself smash into the pommel of the saddle. He was flicked forward, his arms around the mare's neck.

The first surge of pain convinced him to dismount and he considered slipping forward but then he heard Sandancer's thrashing legs and instead rolled off her, adopting a foetal position as the water took his weight. For a while he floated, knees pulled in, chest and face upward, the sky revolving above his head. There seemed to be peace in the pain. The thought worried him and he struggled, finding that if he splashed hard enough the pain receded and he could avoid drowning. His feet hit gravel.

He climbed out to waist height, body bent over, hands clenched between his legs. Swivelling, he looked out over the waters of the Kyle for any other debris from the crash and was shocked to see, standing on a submerged sandbank a short distance off, a pearl-fisherman clad in black from his head to where he disappeared into the water. Hugh, feeling foolish, smiled as best he could, lifting one hand in a wave, but the man stood motionless, a hightide mark on his coat where the wave had hit. Hugh returned his hand to between his legs and turned slowly back to shore.

Sandancer had also hauled herself out of the water and stood cropping the grass at the river's edge as Hugh staggered up the bank. The horse seemed unconcerned but one slug pupil in an unblinking eye followed his approach, fuelling Hugh's irritation. When he was beside her he made to kick her in the shins, only to be bitten in return. They struggled for a moment before Hugh gave way and Sandancer resumed eating. With a sigh Hugh pulled himself up into the wet saddle, water bubbling out from where he gingerly settled his weight. He looked back at the fisherman. The man had resumed his search for the fresh-water oysters. With water dripping down his neck, Hugh glanced at their shadow. Christ, what must I look like? he thought, and pulled on the reins.

They travelled at walking pace now, moving along the edge of the big river, passing islands thick with birch, rowan and pine, crossing a shingle-bottomed tributary that flowed into the Kyle in an easy sweep, then trotting across the floodplain, apathetic cattle moving off in front of them. The village of Huil passed on his right, woodsmoke drifting from its small houses, and Hugh eased Sandancer into a canter. They made fast time into the south glen.

They crossed a road, stopping to let a fish lorry from the west roar past, then followed a track through a soundless pine and larch plantation. In the warmth of the sun Hugh's thoughts grew thick and lethargic, and it was only when the trees fell away that a breeze stirred him. He looked away over the sunwashed hillside, the heather a purple blaze, and found his eyes drawn to

19

the unfolding north, a landscape he had known for ever. At first his attention fell on the three great mountains to the north-west, the cliff-edged glens, peaks and jagged corries a kingdom in itself, and he would have studied them for longer, had not a flicker of movement at the point where road and river cut one of the ridges drawn his eye. A car caught the sunlight from the furthest extreme of the glen, so distant that it snagged Hugh's gaze only once and was lost.

He let his eye follow the river, the tributary he had crossed earlier, as it carried water from the mountains into a ribbon loch that sat above Huil, the great mass of water held back from spilling over the plain by a geological fault that had left a seam of thin, hard stone at its lowest end. Half-way along the loch, on the north shore beyond an island thick with Caledonian pine, a Victorian *faux*-castle stood in its gardens. To Hugh its imposing shape, with its outbuildings, gardens and wide-open policy woodlands was as familiar as the humble farmhouse he had left an hour or so before. This was Lochanthrain, which he had visited all his life. Unable to see his friend Aaron's pick-up, he used his knees to pressure Sandancer over the watershed. Huil and the field where the games were being held fell into view below.

Small figures, many recognizable even from a distance, circled a roped-off arena or paused at tents that stood on the outer perimeter. Other figures approached across a stone-arched bridge that led from the village or drove their cars down a rutted track. Hugh found himself watching the bulky, uniformed figures of the police sergeant, Simon Galvary, and his deputy, Morag MacPherson, known locally as Samson and Delilah, as they walked around the fair and passed into the car park. As they settled into their Metro and drove away, he saw Aaron's pick-up parked near the entrance, then spotted his friend fishing from a rock where the loch emptied through a series of waterfalls. He watched for a while, caught by the beauty of his friend's great circular rolling casts.

Hugh looked up the glen one last time then urged Sandancer down the hill. Aware that he was being watched, and knowing that any hope of a stylish appearance had been washed away by the river, the descent became a traverse. He crossed upstream of the games, climbing the bank where the grassland broke up in rocky and wooded ground reaching up towards the loch. Sandancer picked her route along the fishing path, the sound of the waterfalls filling their ears, moisture hanging from the autumnal leaves of the birch and reflecting in the sun. Aaron was out of view, fishing from a small ledge overhanging a deep pool at the bottom of one of the bigger waterfalls. Hugh slid to the ground and tied Sandancer to a branch.

'Down here, cowboy,' came the voice from below, and at Hugh's reply thirty yards of nylon and hook whistled through the trees, hung in the air then rushed back out over the water. Sandancer shifted nervously and Hugh nuzzled her mouth with his hand before making his way down to the ledge.

Aaron stood, foot against a rock, looking carefully at the ripples in the gully below, easing the path of the fly through the dark water. He lifted long fingers from the line to push a fall of blond hair behind his ear, his eyes on the fly. He was dressed in a canvas jacket fading to the colour of earth, cutting a figure more squatter than squire. Hugh looked down into the river, following a patch of white froth with his eyes, losing it in the eddy, then catching it once more as it made its rush away to the next drop.

'You missed me,' said Hugh.

Aaron roll-cast, sending the line in a spiral close to the

wall of rock before rushing it outwards to hover over the water, its fall causing barely a ripple. Hugh sat down and lit a cigarette.

'What happened to you?' At last Aaron had glanced towards him.

'Sandancer decided to take a swim. She dived into the Kyle at full gallop and I wasn't ready for it, nearly castrated myself on the saddle.'

Aaron cast again, small creases of amusement around his eyes.

Hugh allowed himself to be mesmerized by the water-fall. A salmon emerged fast and sleek, rising through the air before hitting the falling water and using its muscled length to power against the flow, its position secure for a heartbeat before it fell back, exhausted. He sucked the last drag from his cigarette and threw it into the river. The sun had reached around the rock and Hugh settled back in its warmth and let time drift by. He must have slept because when he came round Aaron had moved up to the base of the falls, letting his line take in the whole pool.

Hugh had been woken by the sound of a car approaching from the glen above, likely the one he had seen earlier. He sat up and looked upriver to where the road ran close to the edge of the gully. Aaron was doing the same. They both recognized the sound of the engine, the aggressive driving. Aaron threw a messy line but left it to float as a green BMW station-wagon rushed past, its windows reflecting a single strobe of light before it disappeared down the glen. Aaron was already reeling in his line as the salmon Hugh had seen earlier emerged once more in a streak of foam from the river by his feet. Reflexively Aaron punched outwards with his reel hand, catching the salmon half-way along its length and sending it twisting and spinning back into the flow of water. He looked at his fist in amazement, then shook it in triumph at Hugh. Both boys laughed and turned to scramble up to the path. They met at the top of the bank, and saw the BMW pass the entrance to the games then turn away up the Brae.

'Still, he must be up to something, to be down here at this time of day,' said Hugh, expressing their shared disappointment.

They began to walk down the path towards the fair.

'I was wondering if you'd got lost,' said Aaron. 'I couldn't have handled this thing on my own.' He stepped aside as Sandancer reached across to bite him. 'You're glue, horse, soon as I can convince Hugh to find sensible transport.'

Hugh lifted a hand and stroked the mare's long face.

They emerged from the wood by a cemetery. Hugh stopped to push open its rusting gates, led Sandancer in, then followed Aaron to the car park.

Aaron looked back as he approached. 'Best place for her,' he said. 'Among the dead.'

Hugh rested the saddle on the edge of the pick-up and hung the bridle from its pommel. He took the can of lager Aaron offered and leaned back against the car. 'You don't think that my being able to keep an animal without feeling an irresistible urge to kill it makes me a better person than you?' he asked.

'Not in this case.'

They looked out over the field. The arena consisted of an athletic track within which the big men, mostly from out of the area, tossed cabers, weights, and fought each other in the tug-of-war. A dog track had been cordoned off and a fishing competition was set up on another part of the field. At the river clay pigeons were being test-fired over the opposite bank.

'Citizens,' said Aaron.

Village ladies had laid out their cakes and pastries at stalls around the perimeter, ignored by the bulk of the crowd who clustered by the beer tent to be served by an ageing colonel or his assistant, a Danish student doing holiday work for the publican. The Colonel's laughter was audible across the park, punctuated by the squawk of a megaphone in the hands of the publican himself, Gus Houston. He had left his bar to run the games.

'Your father's standing alone,' said Aaron.

'I don't know why he comes to these things.' Hugh glanced across to where the old man stood, his two sheepdogs at his heel.

Many more people were milling around now than when Hugh had forded the river. Tourists wandered the stalls, peering at the Girl Guides' or the Women's Rural Institute's, or even pausing at a small, malnourished-looking church display, before the minister's unsettling presence caused them to move on. Hugh looked again at his father, was about to walk over and speak to him, but as he pushed himself off the car a tourist stopped and took the farmer's picture. Jamie MacIntyre seemed to shudder at the impertinence and set off towards the car park, his two collies, For and Sev, trotting half a pace behind. Hugh leaned back again and looked down to see Aaron sitting with his feet out of the car, rubbing an oily rag over a shotgun on his knee.

'Any fuckable *Fräuleins*?' Aaron asked, looking up.

'Nothing I can see, but give me the glasses.'

He was passed a fancy pair of field-glasses Aaron had stolen from a visiting fisherman's Range Rover several months before and lifted them to his eyes. He moved from face to face until he came to rest on a young Germanic-looking girl, perhaps fifteen, who was standing with her parents.

Noticing him pause, Aaron sat up and rested the barrels of his gun on the toe of his boot.

'Too young,' Hugh said. 'Way too young.'

'Young's the best you're likely to get, comrade. Make like a greyhound, get there before the hare.'

Hugh told Aaron to shut up and keep cleaning the gun, and his friend smiled as he resumed rubbing the stock with oil. Hugh flicked across more people. 'Is Alison going to be here?' he asked.

'Christ, I hope not.'

At last Hugh settled on two girls, not yet in their twenties, who were petting a whippet held by a third. One was leaning over and, through the beautifully tooled lenses, Hugh could see right down her front. 'Corn-fed and milky-white,' he said, not taking his eyes from her breasts. 'Aaron, there's a lovely pair of—'

'I don't think I want to know.'

Hugh dropped the glasses so that they hung on their cord. 'Hello, Dad,' he said.

'Mr MacIntyre,' said Aaron pleasantly. 'Don't look at me, I was just cleaning my gun.'

'I don't doubt it.' Hugh's father looked down at the field. 'But if you must examine the women in such an obvious manner, I think it perhaps better that you do it when you're not rubbing down a shotgun. People might worry.'

The boys laughed and Aaron slipped the gun behind the seat of the pick-up.

'What happened to you?' said the old man, looking at his son.

Hugh told him the story of Sandancer's leap into the Kyle.

'It's time you got rid of that animal. Ridiculous at your age, not having a car.'

'Too true,' said Aaron.

Hugh changed the subject. He asked what his father was doing there.

The older man grimaced. 'I'm going now. In fact

I came over to tell you that I'm away back to work. I don't suppose you want to come?'

'Wages aren't good enough.'

'You don't have to tell me that,' said his father, lifting a hand in parting and wandering off among the vehicles.

When he had gone, Aaron lifted the glasses from around Hugh's neck and scanned the crowd himself.

'I meant to tell you I saw a pearl-fisherman on the Kyle,' Hugh said. 'He got caught in the wave Sandancer sent his way.'

Aaron lowered the glasses but kept looking out. 'What did he look like?'

Hugh described the man: raw, weathered face, white hair.

Aaron shivered. 'Horrible,' he said. 'Fucking tinks. Mac calls them the beauty thieves.'

The boys looked at each other and laughed.

After Aaron had scanned the whole field he dropped the glasses to his chest. 'All it would take is two heavy machine-guns. You over there, me here, a crossfire.'

Hugh's mind wandered as he heard Gus Houston announce the forthcoming events over the Tannoy: 'And now for the tug-of-war, with the Tank captaining the blue end and wee Hairy Mary the red. Hang on, I've just been handed a note now. Yes, this indeed is the first pull Mary's had all year.'

Aaron looked at Mary through the glasses. 'Not fucking surprising,' he said.

'Time we got into the spirit of the thing.' Hugh dumped his empty lager can in the back of the truck.

'I think I'll do some more fishing,' said Aaron.

'The hell you will. Come on.'

They made their way down on to the field and through the spectators, Hugh nodding greetings to those he knew while Aaron ignored the few who acknowledged him. They were about a third of the way through when the

26

postmistress stopped them. 'Hugh, my dear, your father, is he all right? He looked terribly unhappy.'

'He's fine, Mrs Cameron. It's hard for him, you know. The games remind him of Mother.'

She reached out and took his hand. Hugh looked down at his enclosed fist in surprise. 'Yes, of course,' she said. 'And no doubt you too.'

'I never knew my mother, Mrs Cameron.'

'You'll recall it was Hugh who killed his mother, Mrs Cameron,' Aaron interjected. 'His head was too big when he came out.'

The postmistress ignored this and turned to pick up a Cellophane packet of flapjacks from the stall behind her. 'Well, you give these to your father with my best wishes.' She gave Aaron a hard look as they walked off.

'Do you think she fancies your dad?' Aaron asked.

Hugh looked at him. 'My head was not too big, cunt.'

Aaron laughed and asked for a flapjack.

They were sneering at the strongmen when the Tannoy squawked at them. 'And would you look at this, folks. Who should be gracing us with their presence but Huil's very own inseparable pair! Is it Jesse and Frank, Butch and Sundance or even Bonnie and Clyde?'

Aaron gave Houston the finger.

'Ah, yes, it's nice to see the more anaemic of the pair has lost none of his renowned charm – but, Master Harding, we're not here just to pass the day, we have a request that you proceed to the casting area where you can stun us all with your excellence at that other solitary art you practise so well.'

'I don't need this,' said Aaron, as Hugh tried to convince him that retreat would be folly. Better, Hugh said, to prove that he was still the best – after all, he had won the competition six years in a row. It was a perennial argument and, in line with tradition, Aaron

27

conceded and walked off to get his rod from the car. Hugh made his way over to the competitive area where an assortment of hoops lay spaced out in front of a line drawn in the grass marked 'bank'. The postmistress's husband, a local gillie, was acting as judge.

'Hey, Alfie.'

'Hugh.'

'I'm surprised you called him over, given his record.'

'It's a fair fight every year, Hughie, and what would it be without the young Lochanthrain?' The sarcasm was friendly.

'Bullshit,' Hugh said. 'So what's it all about, then, Alfie?'

The gillie gave him a tired look.

'It's humour, Alfie, like the time you put that eel down that woman's knickers.'

'That was different, Hugh, that was originality.' Then Alfie nodded to his side. 'It just might be that the Rod of God has scored twenty out of twenty, which if my mathematics are right should be just about unbeatable. Shame, really, if someone who, you know, can appear a little high and mighty now and again might get himself beaten by the minister, don't you think?'

'Don't get too excited,' Hugh said, and his gaze slid past the rocky face of the Free Church minister to snag on a woman he and Aaron had missed during their earlier reconnaissance. He couldn't believe they had overlooked her. It wasn't that she was particularly beautiful – although in the context of Huil she was stunning – but she carried herself in a way that caught Hugh's eye and held it. He spoke slowly, as if trying to remember the words: 'He can still draw.'

Aaron arrived and the gillie greeted him. 'Well, Aaron, the score to beat is twenty.'

Aaron failed to look impressed. 'What if I draw?' he asked.

'Cast-off,' said Alfie.

Hugh looked at the woman again, suddenly jealous of what he knew would be a perfect performance by his friend. She was with a shepherd from an estate up the south glen, Shiloch, he thought, a funny-looking gnome of a man, but there was no doubt she was from the south: the casualness of her clothes spelt expense, her complexion a good diet, her posture dance. As he eyed her, he noticed the shepherd watching him, a faintly unpleasant smile in his deep, puritan beard. Hugh brought his attention back to the action.

Aaron had shown no interest in the woman. Instead he readied himself to throw a line across the field, and with a quick flick of his wrist sent out his first cast. Slowly the gillie went out to check, filling in points as he returned. Then Aaron did it again, and again, and again.

'He's not planning to lose gracefully,' the woman said to the shepherd.

'No,' the shepherd replied, before giving a slow nod. 'Not even in the face of the Lord's servant.'

Much to everyone's annoyance Aaron took his twenty points. Hugh had heard the shepherd call the woman Miss Hume.

'Cast-off,' declared Alfie grumpily, and made a sign to Houston.

'Over at the casting field the tension is so high that if you plucked it, it would sing. A cast-off has developed between the moral core of our community and the six-times champion, folks. Roderick MacLeod versus Aaron Harding. Good versus Bad. The Lord's man versus the Devil's spawn. What more could you ask for? Get on down there.'

The gillie asked the two participants up to the line, the minister towering above Aaron and Alfie.

'Right, what we have here is a small hoop twenty-three yards out into the field,' said Alfie, pointing. 'You get

29

five casts, each of you taking a turn, and the one who gets the most in wins. Good luck, minister.'

Hugh noticed Miss Hume studying Aaron. He looked away then back, and caught her eyes on him. She looked at the shepherd.

'The Devil's spawn?' she said.

The shepherd did not reply but the minister caught the question and turned dark eyes to Aaron. 'I'll make you a deal, boy. If I win you have to come to church.'

Aaron laughed. 'And if you lose?'

The minister grimaced. 'That won't happen. I'm not asking you to gamble.'

'Not a very good deal, then,' Aaron said. 'But I'll beat you anyway.' He shrugged.

The Rod of God did well, but after three casts Aaron was up three–two. His concentration did not waver until he heard the green BMW turn down the Brae and accelerate up the glen.

The minister cast, throwing a perfect line out across the rough grass, letting it fall as straight as latitude, leaving the barbless hook to drop down dead centre of the hoop. He grunted and looked for applause but few of the spectators had noticed. The low-slung car, its metallic green nose low to the ground, rushed up the glen. The tourists turned to watch as well. For a moment it looked to pass; relief and mild disappointment touched the local faces. Then it slowed and turned, and Aaron and Hugh looked at each other, grins irrepressible.

'Let's finish this, Alfie.' Aaron threw a long cast across the field, his hook falling just beyond the hoop.

'All equal at three apiece,' said the gillie. 'One cast left, then it's sudden death.'

The minister took his shot and caught the inside of the ring but Hugh barely noticed. Instead he watched the BMW negotiate the bumps on the track down to the car park. Aaron, similarly distracted, was hauled back to the competition by the gillie. He nodded and threw his line.

And missed.

The minister barked in triumph, and Alfie made a sign to the commentary box. 'After seven long years there is a new casting champion,' Houston cried. 'Aaron Harding has been defeated by the Reverend Roderick MacLeod.' Even while he spoke the publican, like everyone else, watched the man get out of the BMW; a man with skin so dark-grey it looked as if it had been long soaked in brine. Mac Seruant heard the news of Aaron's defeat as he stood to his full five foot three and threw his protégé a look of disappointment and surprise.

As soon as he missed, Aaron, with Hugh beside him, had turned and walked off to meet Mac. As they approached they could hear a low, angry growl rising from the interior of the station-wagon. Mac reached in and emerged with a Jack Russell, its taut little body an explosion contained only by the poacher's enormous hands. Mac nudged the door closed with his heel and began to walk out onto the field, adjusting his route to meet the boys on his way. He was singing to the dog, a tune Hugh recalled from nights up at his mountain croft – 'Listen to my woeful tale . . . All is lost, my heart is broken . . . Death please sting me, my misery is complete' – and all the while the dog struggled, throwing about its muzzled head, releasing a continuous growl. Hugh thought Mac must be twisting its testicles in time to the tune.

'Afternoon, boys,' Mac said cheerily. 'I want you to meet Spot. Say hello to my good friends Aaron and Hugh, little hound.'

The Jack Russell yelped.

'Since it seems you managed to fail to triumph over the Lord's faithful servant at fishing, boys, I find it falls to me to uphold our good names. Gentlemen, our

31

companion here is going to be our entry in the terrier race.'

Aaron tried to stroke the Jack Russell only to have his hand pushed away by a muzzled bite.

As they made their way towards the track Mac nodded to acquaintance and stranger alike, a lack of discrimination grounded in the hostility of all but those who walked beside him. A familiar nervousness itched at Hugh's belly.

At the small table beside the dog-traps the Colonel's wife, a woman of world-weary elegance, jotted down the entries for the races on carefully drawn-up cards. She looked at the man standing in front of her then threw a disgusted look at the dog, which, Hugh now noticed, was covered in small scars.

'I presume that thing is to be entered for the terrier race,' she said. 'It is a Jack Russell, isn't it, Mr Seruant?'

'Indeed it is, Mrs Horne.'

'I didn't know you kept Jack Russells, Mac?' She leaned back, regarding him.

'That is because you haven't been to visit lately, Gladys.' She smiled at the impertinence and asked whether he planned to keep the muzzle on. Mac nodded.

'What name, then?'

'Spot.'

'Spot?'

'See Spot Run.'

She looked at him.

'I'm learning to read.'

'I've heard that you read too much, Mac,' she replied, writing out the entry ticket and handing it to him. She didn't look up, just left her palm outstretched. 'Two pounds, please.'

Mac had already moved on, and Aaron followed, so Hugh searched his pocket for two damp pound notes and paid.

She took them without comment.

The whippets were first to run, and Hugh, Aaron and Mac picked a place to watch the race. Of the five competitors, three were being led to the traps by people Hugh did not recognize. Aaron nudged him. 'That bloke there's English,' he said.

Hugh raised his eyebrows at this and offered his own, disconnected thought. 'They should hold these things in a shopping mall, with corners and polished floors.'

Aaron looked at him blankly. 'Do you think that guy's come all the way from England for this?' he asked.

Hugh shrugged and looked around for Miss Hume, but she had disappeared. Instead he watched the three girls they had ogled earlier fuss over their whippet; the dog was running in circles, ever more excited.

'Dogs, eh?' said Aaron.

Mac ignored them, concentrating on his own contender, and Hugh began to pick out a little of what he was saying. 'I know the hatred and envy in your heart,' Mac whispered. 'You may not believe me but in that hatred lies power. Don't be ashamed, embrace it, hold it dear, and use it to rise above all else.' Hugh raised his eyebrows at Aaron.

'You are the Nobill Boutie.'

At this Hugh could not help but laugh, and received a severe glance from Mac as his due.

The whippets were helped into the traps and began to yelp in concert. All three girls ran to the end of the course where they knelt by the finish-line laughing, ready to cheer on their dog. Hugh noticed Miss Hume take up a position near them. Almost everyone who was visiting the fair now stood along the course. Houston, at the starting-line, raised his hand then dropped it, and the man winding in the lure worked his machine at a furious pace. The hare, a tightly wrapped bundle of jumpers, bounced out across the rough ground, leaping madly past the boxes, which flicked open sending four whippets out onto the field, two immediately tumbling into a fight. The fifth walked nervously from the box, tail tucked between its legs, and looked around for its owner. The race was between the girls' dog and a black whippet belonging to the Englishman.

As the two dogs rushed past, followed by the fifth who had finally heard its master's cry from the course's end, Hugh noticed that the Jack Russell had stopped cowering and was now watching the race, Mac still whispering into its ear. The dog flicked back and forward between the man and the competition in an absurd show of comprehension. A huge cheer rose from the crowd as the girls' dog passed the post and ran straight for its friends, rolling in their arms, tail moving furiously, thin head rising up to be showered with kisses.

'The winner, by a head, was Plum, owned by the Havestock sisters of Bodley under . . . Wye, er, something Cheese, or some such place in Englandshire, a triumph of beauty and class I think you will all agree. Would those who have entered the terrier race bring their charges to the starting-gates now, please?'

Mac looked at the boys. 'Go up there and shout Spot on, then,' he said, and went off towards the traps.

This time all six gates were filled, Spot assigned an outside lane. When Mac arrived at the start, still whispering in the dog's ear, the owners who until then had been chatting to each other looked nervously at the creature in his arms. Mac offered them a horrible grin, which they received joylessly as they shoved their charges into the appropriate boxes. Most of the locals watched quietly. Hugh, walking up the track towards the finish line, noticed that the tension raised by Mac had failed to infect the tourists, who assumed it was either local racism against this strange black Highlander or part of the competition. The three girls were still cooing over their victorious whippet a few feet from the finish. Hugh nodded at them, smiling his congratulations, and they grinned back. Aaron gave him a look but he ignored it. He had seen that Miss Hume was watching him with a squint smile, seemingly aware of the atmosphere. He nodded.

'Sweet,' said Aaron loudly. 'I didn't know you were planning to follow in your father's footsteps and meet your true love at the village fair. It reminds me of a Van Morrison song.' As Aaron began to sing, Hugh felt the colour rise to his face and looked away across the river to the hillside beyond.

They reached the finish-line and stood looking down the course. While the other owners had loaded their dogs and stepped away, Mac knelt, presumably still whispering to the Jack Russell through the wire grille. Hugh reached for his cigarettes, tapped the end of one and put it into his mouth. He lit a match, cupping it in his hands while he inhaled, all the time watching the action at the other end of the field. Houston stepped forward, lifted his arm and dropped it again. Behind him, Hugh could hear the man wheeze as he pumped the handle on his winch, causing the hare to bounce down the line again, first right, then left, then high, maybe six feet off the ground at the moment the gate crashed up and the terriers emerged in a yelping, growling, howling mass, bumping and snapping up the field. Mac's contender, ignoring all else, flew towards the boys. Two of the other terriers noticed Spot pull away and made after him while the rest fell into a heaving battle further down the field. Neither Hugh nor Aaron chose to cheer Spot on: both had seen, as had all the spectators, the little dog's muzzle first slip then drag. Spot stopped, put one paw on the hanging leather and pulled his jaws free as the other two dogs came alongside and were about to attack, but through the silence that had fallen they heard their

35

owners' fearful cries from the line and came on, while Spot took up the race once more, moving so quickly he was up to the race leaders' flanks within moments and their owners' yells turned to panic but Spot came through, leading the field – but then he was pulling to the right, veering off his true line, slowly at first, then frighteningly, and all at once he was off the course and in one jaw-filled leap he had torn out the throat of the girls' winning whippet and, blood streaking his little scarred sides, was through and away towards the car park.

Hugh realized the cigarette had fallen from his mouth.

There were screams from the young women.

Mac, even at the distance of the course, could be seen shaking his head.

'Well,' said Aaron, pulling his shark's tooth from his pocket and beginning to roll it between his fingers, 'there go your chances of getting lucky tonight.' His down-turned mouth did nothing to hide the grin in his eyes.

People rushed towards the girls.

Hugh tried to clear his head by shaking it. He looked over at the catastrophe. The prettiest girl was holding the dying whippet in her arms, blood still pumping from its throat. Miss Hume was beside her, holding her. What can she say to her? thought Hugh. What the fuck do you say to that? He felt an unbearable urge to laugh, but looked up at the sky in an effort to capture and hold the feeling. People were already looking their way in anger.

Mac was striding up the field so Hugh and Aaron, taking very short steps, began to move towards the burgeoning crowd, aiming for simultaneous arrival with their man. To walk away would be to invite the crowd's wrath but, as yet, no one seemed to know how to react other than to offer comfort to the girls. Mac's approach was causing anxiety: heads flicked around as he drew in, and the crowd shrank away as if the sun had been blocked out by a malevolent shadow. It was Colonel Horne, fortified with whisky, who decided to stand up for the village and its guests. 'Mac Seruant,' he said loudly, 'while I hate to accuse you of releasing that monster in the full knowledge of what might—'

Mac was into the crowd and peering down at the bloody mess below, the girls looking up and recoiling at his vast head hanging like a boulder above them.

'—happen, but what the devil—'

'My dog did this?' Mac said, his voice heavy with fury. The crowd nodded, relieved that he had taken responsibility. He tensed.

'—did you mean by—'

'There's no room for killers in this county,' the poacher decided. He swept Aaron up, and made off in the direction of the car park. 'Aaron, I need you to do a nasty job of work for me,' he declared. 'I don't think I'm strong enough to do it myself.'

The Colonel gave up.

Most of those who were not involved in comforting the girls followed Mac, who sent Aaron to the pick-up, ignored the posse behind him and headed to where the little dog lay in the long grass at the side of the field. He stopped twenty feet from Spot and smiled as the dog chewed on a length of the whippet's windpipe, all the while growling at the crowd. There was a muttering about calling a vet, which rose in volume as Aaron approached, his shotgun opened and cradled, his bony fingers dropping two Eley SSG cartridges into the twin barrels.

'I don't think it is necessary to do this right here,' the Colonel said, his voice unsure.

'The dog knows no morality,' Mac declared, his words edgy and sharp. 'It has lived too long.'

The dog, its eyes questioning, raised itself. It looked

quickly at Mac, at Aaron, then back at Mac. It performed a small pirouette as if considering its options.

'Mac, there are children here.' A woman's voice from the crowd.

'Aaron!' shouted Mac.

In one long sweeping movement Aaron brought the gun to his shoulder and fired. The buckshot removed the skin, bone and meat of the dog's shoulder and neck, spinning the Jack Russell in a bloody Catherine wheel and leaving its carcass stretched out, head attached only by a thin strip of skin. For a moment Hugh thought he could hear the dog's last breath but he realized it was the joint exhalation from the lungs of the crowd. Mac nodded to the shooter, then turned and made his way towards his car while Aaron walked forward to pick up the remains.

Hugh was about to join him when he felt someone at his side. 'Interesting company you keep,' she said, before holding out her hand. 'I'm Rebecca.'

TWO

Hugh lay on his back watching the clouds – layered, frothy and oval – sit rooted in the blue above, a distant and soft eternity.

'You know, I think it's the character I go for in the end,' he said. 'All that shit about legs and tits and ass is fine, but it's a glance, an angled look, a laugh . . . That's what counts. Grace, that's what I'm attracted to.' He waited for a moment, received no reply and, encouraged, continued.

'Take Saturday. While everybody else went mental or burst into tears, Rebecca just had this little smile. She seemed to be amused by you and Mac – in a disgusted sort of way, of course – but she gave me a look that said, "You're all horrible but at least you're interesting." That's what got to me. And it wasn't just the disgust, I think she actually thought about it sexually, you know? As if perhaps there were sensual possibilities. She has grace, man, she has grace, character and beauty. Imagine what—'

'Oh, shut up.'

Hugh shifted his head to look across at Aaron. His friend had dropped his field-glasses and was regarding him with distaste. Hugh smiled. Aaron's face was smeared with peat, his hair covered with a woollen hat.

He laughed suddenly. 'Sensual possibilities bullshit. She was like the rest, wanting to kill us but unable to loosen her own tightly drawn arse so much as to fart out a rudeness.' He paused. 'Sensual possibilities? After that scene you've got fuck-all sensual possibilities around here. You're going to have to move to the next county if you hope to get laid.'

Hugh let Aaron's doubts float away by gazing back up at the sky and seeing the endless possibilities. 'Now that's where you're wrong. I saw her look when she said, "Interesting company you keep." She cocked her head, she smiled, and it wasn't a smile of disgust, it was of . . . intrigue.' He heard the snort he had expected but continued. 'Yes, intrigue. Interesting company, well, yes, I mean obviously she realizes you're repulsive but she knows I'm different. I'm sure she senses that in my heart I'm a nice bloke, you know.' He glanced across but Aaron was ignoring him, again looking through the field-glasses. 'It was the way she smiled, a little shy but, I mean, she's hardly going to be shy, is she? She's from London or something, so that must have been for my benefit and, well, she touched her hair and we all know what that means and—'

'Did she arch her back?'

'—and her handshake was warm, yes, warm and sincere—'

'Well, OK, at least that's positive for any forthcoming handjobs.'

'—and she listened to me as I said, "Terrible business, this," and looked sympathetic. I mean, clearly she was interested and if . . . if I had only fucking stayed there . . .'

'Keep your voice down.'

'Well, I mean, what a prick. Why the hell did I run away? Why didn't I stay and talk? Why, Aaron?' Hugh rolled onto his side and jabbed his friend with his finger. 'Why?'

Aaron's attention caught on something he had seen out on the hill. He dropped the field-glasses onto the peatbank. 'He's on the move,' he said, one hand on the Parker Hale .323 that lay beside him. Then he stopped to consider his companion. 'I'm sure she'll find your social ineptness endearing.' He looked back out at the hill. 'Violence?'

Hugh rolled onto his front and eased himself forward a few inches until the opposite hillside came into view. He lifted his own glasses and looked at the stag that had risen to its feet half a mile away, watching as it perused the countryside, great antlers swinging in the air. Hugh counted thirteen points. 'Not bad,' he said. 'Not bad at all.'

The two boys lay submerged in the deep, woody aroma that rose from the heather in the late-summer warmth. The blackness of the mountainside was broken under the blanket light of the sun, which lay softly across the heather, brightening the plants' heights while leaving the depths in darkness. Small purple flowers streaked the scene then faded where fire had broken through the mat and left coarse grasses in temporary possession. It was to one of these patches the stag moved, searching out moist tendrils left by the hinds. A faint breeze flowed towards the boys, and Hugh tried to scent the creature but it was too far away. He felt a twinge in his belly and thought about the possibilities of romance that had appeared from seemingly nowhere. Aaron nudged him and he looked across at the steep hill that rose away to their right, sheering on its forward side into a ragged cliff, then above, where an eagle circled. Hugh watched it for a time, losing himself in the azure beyond. 'How come blue is the colour of sadness?' he asked.

Aaron looked at him with pity, shook his head and motioned backwards with his thumb. The stag was moving his hinds to the north, harrying them with small nipping bites to their haunches, and the boys slipped away from the edge, pulling the rifle with them as they went.

Once they had dropped back they stood up, hunched in a small gully. Hugh looked again at the rearing outcrop at their side, conferred with Aaron, then started north at a fast, steady pace, staying low, following the path of a small burn as it trickled through a marsh. Their footsteps disturbed two snipe, instantly airborne, weaving their small bodies into the distance. Hugh and Aaron paused and watched their departure.

'You don't get opportunities like that every day,' said Aaron.

'So much to kill, so little time.' Hugh's tone was mocking, drawing a reproachful look from his friend.

Hugh glanced to the west and blinked away from the sun, which threw a white light from low in the sky. He could see the shadow from the outcrop ahead and soon they moved under the eaves of the rock itself. He felt the air darken and the breeze fall away. The hidden sun sent rays along the hillside above, lighting the higher levels in a hazy grey, while, below the absolute line of its beam, advancing shadow pushed upwards. Hugh shivered, feeling midges begin to bite his arms.

As they moved, their boots fell on the tufts of fibrous grasses that gave the best footholds. They crossed the burn several times to keep the lowest ground and whenever their cover fell away, exposing the hillside to the east, they would slow, searching, careful for any movement that might reveal a deer lying hidden in the heather. When nothing showed they moved on. They both knew this country as well as they knew each other, and instinctively they passed hidden through its depths.

To the west, beyond the outcrop, the stag would be moving its hinds to higher ground, into the stronger breeze to escape the madness-inducing attention of the midges. It had taken the boys three hours of waiting to discover whether the beast would go higher or choose instead to spend its evening in the pastures down by the lochside, and now they knew: the coming night would be calm and the stag had chosen the high tops. Once the boys had learned this, they moved from instinct.

Hugh paused to catch his breath and looked up. Above them, still in the full glare of the sunshine, the eagle circled, resting on the air that rose against the side of the outcrop in small thermals. The bird's flight seemed bored, as if this small drama would offer nothing new, just another version of an endless cycle. Aaron moved past Hugh into a gully that led up the northern edge of the outcrop.

Hugh followed, his feet placed where Aaron's step had fallen moments before, all the while watching his friend move effortlessly with the contours of the ground. He studied the bony, angular body that would better suit a city. On Aaron's back the rifle hung in its sleeve, its barrel downwards against the dark green of his old camouflage jacket. Others – the few others – who had ever seen Aaron moving in this type of country had told Hugh that even if he was only ten feet away he could disappear, walk in a circle around them and they would never know he was there, but that had never been true with Hugh. He knew, had always known, where Aaron was, even if they had been deliberately hiding from each other. It was Aaron's stride that helped him, the staggered lope that never altered however the ground was breaking beneath him, the distinctive gait of someone unused to conformity.

With his eyes on Aaron, Hugh tripped and sprawled over some loose rocks at the bottom of the burn, grazing his hands and hurting a knee. He cursed quietly, stood up and brushed grit from his palm. The pain brought tears to his eyes. Aaron stopped a few paces on but did not turn, and Hugh climbed up to him.

'Careful of that bit,' Aaron said.

Hugh ignored him and walked past. That, he decided, was why Aaron always knew where he was.

The gully began to narrow before it reached up towards the ridge, and they stooped to a crouch as they followed it. There were some boulders and a small cutting at the edge of the hill, the main bulk of the outcrop now to the south. They moved forward on their hands and knees, then on their bellies as they used the cutting to inch their way into the view beyond, slithering away from any horizon that might silhouette them against the sky.

Once again the sun fell on Hugh's back, its angle more extreme as the day bled away. The late-afternoon light touched the floor of the valley, leaving the thick bed of heather, rough grass and moss below looking warm and welcoming, the waters of the burn metallic. The boys paused behind a peatbank and scanned the ground below.

The stag had travelled only half the distance, the group of hinds proving unwieldy, and it would be another hour before they reached the waiting boys. Aaron and Hugh sought out a shooting position, and chose a small hollow at the bottom of the outcrop, then picked out the route they would take to reach it. They scanned the land around them and then, moving carefully, slid away down through the heather.

The ridges were often very slight and the boys pressed themselves into the contours, checking constantly that they were not breaking the horizon. Their progress took them down the base of the cliff, and as they crawled they occasionally passed a large boulder where they would rest. Looking up, Hugh noticed the eagle's nest, a mat of sticks in a rocky crevice high above. The going was slow and he felt the usual pain of unusual pressures upon his body, and with that pain came the small nausea at the coming kill deep in his stomach. Aaron, in the rare moments he glanced behind, displayed a look of complete happiness. He had never seen Aaron happier than this, but he had seen him as content many, many times before. It was always the same as a killing grew close.

They reached the edge of the shooting position and slipped into the heather-lined bowl, Aaron pushing the gun before him. Each of their movements was small and they shifted heather stems so slowly it might have been the breeze. Once inside they lay flat, the ridges around blotting them out to all but the view of the eagle above. Hugh relaxed for a moment, then eased himself forward to the lip of the bowl, looking out.

The stag was coming, pushing the hinds with him.

Both boys scanned the ground for any other movement that might disturb their wait. Hugh's eye was caught by a small hill loch that shimmered in the sun before it was drawn briefly to the shadowy outlines of the three great mountains in the distance. There were no other deer except those they waited for, making their inexorable approach.

'It'll be an hour,' he said quietly. 'I'm not sure I'll be able to stay awake.'

'Sleep then.'

'Wake me before you shoot, not with the blast.'

Aaron turned his face towards him. 'It's your shot. Are you saying you don't want it?'

'If it's my shot I'll take it,' he replied, to Aaron's disappointment. 'Just give me a nudge when you're ready to slip the safety off.' He made himself more comfortable in the bed of heather.

'I can't believe you can sleep at times like this,' said Aaron.

Hugh felt the sun's warmth slip drowsiness over him like a blanket and he was somewhere else a long time ago.

A hill vehicle, an Argocat, is churning its passage through a mist so thick that it clogs the air. A small boy sits, marble-faced, in the back, wanting to shut his ears to the roar of the engine, yet forced to hang onto the violently bucking machine. The Argocat stops and Hugh's father orders the boy to stay in the vehicle, before walking away into the fog, leaving him alone. He waits, listening, but the soaking air kills all sound and its greyness blinds him. He looks up into the sky but there is nothing. He tries to remember the way his father went as he feels the dampness reach out and touch his face. If he concentrates he can see a shadowy figure move at the edge of the wetness and he wills it to be his father, but soon it just shifts and disappears. He feels a calling, the friend just beyond vision who will bring this confusion to an end, and he climbs over the edge of the Argocat, calling for Aaron. He can hear laughter just out of sight and he walks towards the sound, a giggle rising in his throat, plans already forming. But as he searches the laughter seems to move away and Hugh hesitates, looking back, but the mist has taken the Argocat and he has forgotten to leave a trail and Aaron seems to be calling, but distantly, and from a new direction, so he walks that way, scrambling over rocks and circling a large pool of water, but there is nothing, just the dampness. He sits down to ponder but once again the small voice comes, the sound of Aaron's delight, on the other side of an outcrop in the mist, and he stands up and walks forward into the smell of death, at once surrounding and clinging to him as he clambers over rocks, and he looks around and then down into a small crevice, and he cries out at the decomposing skull of a sheep and the fright sends him into the foul remains, a mass of maggots and rotted entrails spilling over his trousers and filling his boots, half-dissolved flesh smearing his legs and his arms, which he had dropped to save himself. He retches and vomits and sobs so the bile flows up his nose, and he looks around with his tear-streaked face and feels a presence depart through the mist. Some creature has risen up from the earth and has gone, and all he can do is scream.

Hugh felt something on his arm and looked round. Aaron emerged out of the gloom, half-amused face peering from the blue sky beyond.

'Death's due in five minutes,' he whispered. 'You were sleeping ugly, old man.'

Hugh came awake and looked at the heather in the bowl where he was lying, then again at Aaron. 'OK,' he said.

His eyes took in the brightness of the now darkening sky, and he looked up and saw the eagle still high above. Then he rolled over and eased himself carefully to the lip of their hide and found the stag walking towards them, coming to within eighty yards, its hinds stepping easily behind or picking at the grass. Hugh looked for the gun and found Aaron had left it in front ready to be fired, the bolt up. He pulled back the metal ball, slipping the action towards himself until the leading edge of the mechanism caught the rim of the first of the four shells in the magazine. Then he slid back the bolt, pushing the bullet into the waiting chamber and pressing it home without a sound, flicking the safety-catch on. He glanced again at the stag and found it looking away, back at its fellows, so he shifted himself into the rifle's stock. He stared through the telescopic sights and saw the beast at close range.

The stag turned and pawed the ground, looking

beyond the boys. It turned and ran back to the herd circling the group, nipping the outsiders to keep them tight, before it returned to stop on a knoll close in front of Hugh and Aaron. It was big, its ears flicking forward and back as it listened, and below the long smooth snout, under the great dark eyes, its thick, coarse hair ran down the front of its neck to thin, powerful legs. Hugh centred the cross-hairs of the sights just behind the front haunch but the beast was filling too much of the sights. He switched to the base of its neck where he could make out his target better, where a hit would sever some vital cord: the vertebrae, windpipe or jugular. The stag stood and Hugh slipped off the safety with his thumb, feeling the smooth wood as he gripped the neck of the rifle's stock, the ridged trigger under his finger. His hand clenched, slowly applying a steadily growing pressure as he held his breath. The stag reared up, turned and bolted down the hill, its hinds bursting away in panic around it. Hugh released his grip and flicked on the safety-catch. He looked across at Aaron and then they were both rolling onto their backs, staring at the figure coming towards them over the horizon in a canary-yellow jacket.

Hugh felt the interruption in his belly and he let his body relax to fight the frustration. Aaron just stared at the newcomer.

The man was carrying a fishing rod and when he saw the running deer he stopped to watch them, not yet noticing the two boys lying in the heather. He was whistling a tune, 'Marie's Wedding', and he paused half-way through a phrase as he saw the two figures rise up, Hugh holding the gun to his side, fending off Aaron's attempt to grab it.

'It's that fucking Dane,' said Aaron, who had started wiping bits of undergrowth from his jacket. 'Let's shoot the son of a bitch.'

The Dane recognized them and, aware that he had spoiled their sport, seemed to opt for a conciliatory approach, walking down the hill in great strides, a big apology of a grin on his face. Aaron was still looking at the encroaching figure with malice so Hugh, in a friendly gesture he did not feel, put a half-resigned smile on his face.

'*Feasgar math*,' the Dane shouted as he closed. '*Ciamar a tha sibh?*'

The boys looked at each other.

'What the fuck's that?' Aaron said. 'Viking?'

'*Ciamar a tha sibh?*' he said, as he reached them, with a resigned laugh. 'It seems I have disturbed your hunt, I am very sorry.' He looked up again. '*Co dhiu, feasgar math.*'

'What?'

The Dane looked at Aaron in surprise. 'Gaelic for "good afternoon",' he said. 'You do not speak your mother tongue?'

'Gaelic?' Aaron shook his head. 'My mother's English.'

The Dane looked at Hugh, who had pushed the bullet in the breech back into the magazine and was now slipping the gun into its leather sleeve.

'No,' Hugh said, a little softly. 'It's no use, these days.' He noticed Aaron smiling at his self-conscious use of accent and turned back to the Dane. 'I thought you were studying land use?'

'Yes, land use, but the land is no use if it lies in the hands of rich foreign owners, as I am sure you know. I have decided to learn Gaelic and help in the fight against the settlers.'

There was a pause, then both Aaron and Hugh spoke as one. 'Gus Houston has got you to join Settler-Watch?'

When the Dane said yes, they looked at him and then

at each other in amazement. 'Well, *camerahatstand*,' said Aaron.

'Excuse me?'

'It's Gaelic.'

'Ah, really?' The Dane looked excited. 'For what?'

'Anything you like,' said Aaron.

Hugh shouldered the rifle while Aaron looked across at the falling sun, and they began to walk down the hill, picking out a track that would lead into the woodlands below. In the distance the deer had stopped, and for a while they were watched until the stag led the hinds off in a wide circle across the hill before heading north once again.

'I am, as I say, very sorry about your hunting.'

'So you should be,' said Aaron. 'What were you doing? What's with the trout rod? Have you been poaching up on the Coronach?'

'Poaching, no, no, of course not. Your father said I may fish up in the loch.' The Dane pointed to the north.

'The Coronach,' said Hugh.

Aaron thought about this. 'I thought you said you hated landowners?'

'Not the Scottish.' The Dane said this with finality but Aaron persevered.

'My mother's English. And they have only lived here for twenty-eight years.'

The Dane looked slightly exasperated yet determined to be polite. 'Your father is Scottish. You live on your land. It is enough.'

'Many of the absentees are Danes.'

'That is why I feel so strongly.'

Aaron gave up and turned to Hugh. He suggested trying for a Sika buck on the way down and received a nod in reply. 'Come on, Olga,' he said, cheering up. 'Have you ever shot a deer?'

'No, I do not think I would like to kill a deer. They are

too beautiful. And my name is Peter. Olga is a woman's name.'

'How do you know you don't like killing deer if you have never done it?' said Hugh. 'I used to say the exact same thing about eating spinach and now I can't get enough of it.' He saw the Dane's look of doubt. 'We'll start you off with a little one,' he added.

The doubt turned to disgust.

They were moving over ridges that increasingly gave them views of the glen below, following a stream that, once in a while, ceased its tranquil bubbling to roar angrily over a small cliff and into a dark pool. The hill, steep now, revealed the furthest reaches of the loch below.

Aaron picked a few blades of grass and let the wind take them. The breeze was still from the west, and the boys turned to look in its direction. At that moment the sun flared into a trough between two of the Three Great Mountains and lost its power. They broke away from the pathway. The Dane tried to leave them but was told he would ruin their sport once again by disturbing the deer if he walked down the hill. They moved in single file, Hugh behind the Dane, who had been relieved of his garish jacket and told to mimic Aaron, who was weaving unnecessarily between the small hillocks that covered the steepest ground above the woods.

Eventually they stopped, sank to the ground and, having left the Dane's fishing rod in the heather, crawled up a slight rise from which a view of the woods and the hillside opened out below. Aaron and Hugh scanned the view, letting their field-glasses travel from opposite ends. They saw two Sika does moving out of the woods to the west, and another almost directly in front. Hugh turned to the Dane and explained, 'Sika. They're Japanese imports, live in the woods but come out on to the open hillside at night. We'll wait for them here, then

51

see if we can get round them and into a shooting position.' He paused and smiled. 'It's great fun, much better than the red deer.'

The does emerged along the edge of the forest like a silent army, suddenly visible where a moment before there had been nothing. Long eerie whistles broke the silence, and Hugh explained to the Dane that this was the sound of the bucks beginning the rut. Aaron reached across and nudged Hugh, pointing to the west where a buck had appeared. Hugh looked at it through his binoculars. He dropped the glasses, turned and shook his head. 'Too small.'

The Dane was scratching himself – the midges were closing in. Aaron told him to keep still so he adopted Hugh's example of continuously, but slowly, running his hands over any exposed skin. Aaron never seemed to notice the insects, allowing them to settle and feed undisturbed. Hugh watched this, then picked up his glasses; he found his friend's self-control almost as much of an irritant as the midges. During the last long sweep of the treeline he saw a darkness move at the edge of the wood and swung the glasses back, but whatever he had seen had gone. He took the glasses away from his eyes and looked again for movement. A doe stood just out of the trees then looked back. That was enough for Hugh to catch Aaron's attention and nod down to the spot in front of him. Aaron scanned in and Hugh softly kicked the Dane so that he would stop his scratching.

Out of the woods came the buck, eight points above a big, dark face and a black, powerful body. Even the Dane had seen it and stopped his battle against the midges.

'Big,' Hugh whispered, passing across his field-glasses. 'For a Sika, very, very nice.' He gave an OK signal to Aaron, who looked away, already plotting the stalk. 'It'll look nice on your wall,' Hugh whispered to the Dane, who shook his head nervously then looked back to the animal, which had begun to make its way up the hill.

Aaron caught Hugh's eye and pointed his thumb backwards but Hugh shook his head. 'You take Peter,' he said. 'I'll stay here and watch.' Then he turned to the Dane. 'Aaron will take you in to the kill. Be sure to do exactly what he says and remember not to pull the trigger. Squeeze it softly, like a woman.'

Aaron looked open-eyed at Hugh while mouthing, 'Like a woman?' His expression was mocking. Colour rose on Hugh's face.

'It's better that I don't kill such a beautiful creature,' whispered the Dane. 'Let me watch.'

'You'll do fine.' Hugh put a hand on his shoulder. 'I'll look after your fishing rod. Just do what Aaron says.'

The Dane gave him a last, uncertain look, then Aaron was instructing him to inch his way backwards and into the gully where the rifle lay. Picking it up, Aaron turned and whispered in the Dane's ear. He seemed to listen carefully, nodding once in a while. Hugh eased himself back up to the edge, attempting to ignore the midges and raising his glasses to look down on the killing field below.

There were now pockets of Sika along the length of the hillside, each in various stages of their dusk-time advance. He looked to the east where danger for the stalkers would come: a doe had emerged from a tall stand of pine, making quick time up the hill. Aaron would have to get into a shooting position before she walked into his scent. Then there were those does the target buck had sent out. One had reached a small peak and was looking back down the hill; two more were just in front of the approaching buck. Hugh relaxed, and looked up to see real darkness blurring the horizon, the brighter stars showing in the firmament. He thought the eagle must now have returned to its nest.

He looked down at the gully to where the Dane crawled beside Aaron, watching the foreigner's nervousness and wondering what instructions he had been given by his guide. Hugh could see the spot where Aaron planned to take the shot, although his friend did not take the easy route to this position, instead choosing to crawl face down through thick bog. Hugh picked up the field-glasses and looked at the two figures. The Dane's face, when he lifted it, was covered in slime, but Aaron kept motioning him lower. Hugh looked down the Dane's body: his sweater, scarf and corduroy trousers were already an ugly mess of rotten peat. His wellington boots would be full. Aaron was in no better condition but he was dressed for this. Then the Dane lost his spectacles, and when he found them spent several moments trying frantically to clean the lenses. Hugh flicked his gaze over to the buck, which was still coming on. He looked up at the sky and reckoned on about fifteen more minutes of shooting time.

His thoughts turned to Rebecca Hume. He had never managed so much as to kiss a girl who was on holiday. As he watched Aaron torture the Dane, he realized his friend would amuse himself in derailing any attempt he made to sleep with her. Aaron would see it as a game, and the thought irritated Hugh. He wanted Rebecca: she was so thrillingly exotic. In the east the doe had not moved.

The stalkers below reached the shooting position and sank deep into the heather, the gun out in front. They had arrived just in time: the leading doe was two or three minutes away from walking downwind of Aaron and the Dane's scent. The buck, although further down, was now within range. It was a good beast, beautiful even, and Hugh sucked his lip in anticipation as it approached. The doe was very close. Hugh dropped his glasses and let the scene play out in front. The Dane was now on the gun but, even from this distance, it was clear he was scared of it, with Aaron doing nothing to prevent him breaking his shoulder at the recoil. The doe was looking nervous but the buck kept coming. Hugh wanted to tell the Dane to hold the gun in tight but he could do nothing except wait and watch as the doe reared up on its haunches to look for the danger it suspected nearby. It squeaked with alarm, bringing the buck to a sudden stop as the reverberating crash of the rifle spread out across the hill, an instantaneous whine and the sound of a high-velocity bullet hitting a peatbank.

Hugh picked up his field-glasses and looked at the buck. It had leapt back at the shot and stood shaking its head while every other creature on the hillside spread out and ran. He focused on its face and saw the white of bone across its snout and dark blood drip from its nose. The Dane had shot it in the face, grazed its snout. Suddenly the buck regained its senses, turned and ran towards the wood, but a figure rose out of the heather to its right, hammering the bolt of the rifle home and bringing the gun to his shoulder, swinging with a perfect ease, and then the explosion that, in the gloom, lit the barrel for a moment. The sick thud of bullet hitting flesh accompanied the careening fall of a large, dead animal.

Hugh looked across at Aaron, who was already throwing back the bolt to drive the third bullet into the chamber in case the beast rose again, but Hugh knew that even Jesus couldn't bring it back. He lit a cigarette, enjoying the high of breaking his day-long fast, then turned to pick up the Dane's fishing rod and jacket.

'Want me to go and kick it?' he shouted at Aaron. The Dane was standing a few paces behind Aaron but in the gloom Hugh could see nothing more than that he was nursing his shoulder.

To Aaron's affirmative Hugh made his way down the hill, aiming his approach so that Aaron had a clear line of sight to fire at the beast if it stood up. His legs were tired and he stumbled on the heather clumps and on slippery sections of peat. It was getting very dark, and once he was into the gully he lost sight of where the buck had fallen. He was directed in by shouts from his friend.

He caught the stench of the animal first, then saw it lying sprawled in the heather, neck stretched out in its desperate bid for the wood. He walked in a semi-circle around it then approached its head. He could see immediately that the light had left its eyes but to be certain he nudged an antler with his foot. There was no movement so he looked up towards Aaron. 'Dead on arrival to the heather,' he shouted. He knelt down and looked at the buck's face. The Dane's bullet had skimmed the surface of the bone, cutting open the skin in a downward slash so that the yellowy white skull was revealed below. Blood had spilled all over the creature's nose. 'That must have brought tears to its eyes,' he said, when he heard Aaron's approaching footsteps.

Aaron looked at the cut and then up at the Dane, who stood miserably pulling on his coat. 'What were you trying to do? Shoot it between the eyes? I told you to aim for its fucking neck.'

Aaron leaned forward and dragged the buck round so that its head was downhill. Then, taking a curved knife from his pocket, he stabbed the stag in the base of its throat. Thick blood flowed into the heather. Aaron scooped up some in his hand and walked over to the Dane. 'Your first deer,' he said cheerily. 'Well, sort of, we'll say so, and now you have to be blooded.' He tried to smear the blood on the Dane's face but as he lifted his hand the man flinched away.

'I should never have listened to you.' The Dane's voice was filled with self-pity. 'It is all right if I go now, I hope. I won't disturb any more of your sport.' He was looking at Hugh.

'Is your shoulder hurt?' Hugh asked.

'Bruised.'

When Hugh nodded, the Dane turned, casting a last hurt look at Aaron, who sipped at his palmful of blood, then walked away downhill, his fishing rod marking his descent. Hugh watched him go, waiting until he was out of earshot before turning to look at his friend.

'I know,' said Aaron. 'I know.'

Hugh said nothing.

'I thought he would miss,' Aaron said, shrugging his shoulders. 'I thought he would miss, for fuck's sake. I'm sorry, all right.'

'It would have been a bastard tracking in this light if you hadn't brought it down. I think I might have left you to it.'

Aaron knelt down at the buck's stomach, cutting backwards and pulling the guts out so that they fell into the heather with a long, wet thud. He looked inside to make sure it was clean. Hugh crouched down, and for a moment they both held their hands inside the empty cavity as if warming them against a fire. Then Aaron stood up, tied a rope around the antlers, threw the other end over his shoulder and took the strain.

Hugh removed his warmed hands as the beast began to slide, picked up the rifle and walked beside his friend. Their progress set off shrieks from the does at the edge of the wood.

'Perhaps we should take a drive tonight,' Hugh said.

'Would that be up the south glen past the farm where some woman is staying?'

'We could stop at the pub on the way back and have a game of pool.'

'In case she might have gone there?'

Hugh sighed. 'You know,' he said, 'last night I was lying in bed thinking about her, and you know how these things go, well, I imagined her naked and created a little scene and, well . . .'

'You did yourself a favour?'

'Yes, exactly, but the amazing thing is that at the end, I shot right over my head and onto the pillow, which I've never done before. I mean, it freaked me out as this dollop of come flew right past my nose; for a moment I thought I'd come in my hair but it went right past me.' He paused. 'Do you think maybe I'm in love?'

Aaron had stopped. 'Hugh, mate, perhaps you should tell her about it and see what she thinks. But first I want you to promise me that you will never tell me something like that again.'

It was dark and the moon offered the only light. In it the boys could be seen reaching the track that would take them down through the woods. It was here that Aaron passed the weight of the buck to Hugh and reverted to his loose-limbed lope, his arms swinging easily. He turned and spoke, and his companion laughed and pulled the rope he held across his shoulder tighter, hauling the creature with a practised ease.

THREE

To his own surprise, Hugh found himself reading a government notice-board planted at the tourist viewpoint in the south glen. He pulled a packet of cigarettes from his pocket, lit one and inhaled.

> *The prominent ter   ces to the west of Huil are glacial outwash deltas formed in an ic   ge about 1,700,000 to 10,   0 years ago. A large lake was dammed by glaciers to the west and by a lobe of ice in Str   hkyle to the east. Traces of this f   mer lake are evident in the form of faint shorelines along the hillside to the n   th, although they are not as spect   ular as the famous 'par   lel roads' of Glen Roy in Lochaber.*

Below the text, in a neat hand, somebody had written, 'loch not lake english bastards'. Hugh wondered if the Dane was responsible. It was not Gus Houston's style to be so uncouth but he might have put his protégé up to it. The bullet holes offered no mystery, and Hugh counted them, recalling the various journeys on which either Aaron or he had leaned from the passing car, using the sign as a target. All the holes were their own – there was, after all, nobody else, which was why the graffiti was so strange.

He turned to the view. The terraces ran down each side of the glen, broken by a gap through which a smaller river arrived from the south. With his field-glasses he studied the green depths, looking over the farm that lay sprawled on the floodplain below – Shiloch. Despite careful reconnaissance he saw no movement on the flats. He looked to the east, into the breeze, and shivered at the undertone of chill it carried. The Indian summer still hung a lantern in the sky, but winter was gathering around this small community. He yawned, tired from having spent a wasted, if amusing, night with Aaron, fishing for the last of the season's sea-trout, half drunk and splashing about in the river below the falls. It had only been three hours since he had bade his friend goodbye and returned to the farmhouse to sleep, although as soon as he lay down his mind wandered and so, in time, had he. He looked again. A track crossing the south glen bridged the river and led up to the farm but that approach seemed too obvious.

A late-season tourist pulled into the viewpoint, towing a caravan. Hugh turned and hoisted himself onto Sandancer in the hope that he could get away before the arrivals engaged him in conversation. He passed the couple as they walked towards the sign, nodding in reply to their accented hellos. A moment later Sandancer reached through the open passenger door of their car and grabbed the woman's cardigan from the seat.

'Oi,' came the shout from behind. 'Your horse has got my cashmere!'

Hugh winced, pulled the mare up and looked round. He didn't want to fight Sandancer for the cardigan: it would just turn into a humiliating tug-of-war.

'My apologies,' he said, smiling broadly. 'My horse has little to eat.' He spun Sandancer and they plunged down the steep slope at the edge of the viewpoint, the mare's hind legs bent and skidding in the loose shale.

He held onto his hat as they slid between the trees.

'You're some piece of work,' he said, when they reached the bottom. He patted her neck. Sandancer, still chewing, looked up and down the river, which now stood in front of them, and it was only with a split-second realization that Hugh stopped her from diving in. He pulled back the reins sharply, looked for a crossing, then turned up-river. The tourists were shouting from the viewpoint, their voices gradually receding as horse and rider threaded their way up the bank, Hugh ducking to avoid low branches. He turned Sandancer into the water when they came to a sweeping bend in the river, ripples marking out the shallows, the small round rocks green with slime, and then they were up the other bank, cantering over the floodplain, making for ground where the terrace had long since crumbled and created a path to the top. He followed a track up and stopped a hundred feet above the plain. The tourists had gone, and to the west Hugh could see their car and caravan disappearing. Then he looked ahead, drew his coat around himself and heeled Sandancer forward along the edge of the precipice. Walking gingerly, stepping carefully over fallen logs and weaving among the larger rocks, the horse held her head tight in, neck arched in concentration.

Hugh felt the itch of nervousness, excitement and dread. Despite its proximity to Huil, Shiloch was at the outer edges of Hugh's range, and he felt a freshness catch him as they threaded their way south. It was as if the ghostly presence of his ancestors left him as he moved onto ground on which they had rarely stepped. Moving outwards always thrilled him but now, as his excitement grew, so too did fear. He was all too aware that this game was virtually guaranteed to end in his humiliation. After all, there was no reason in the world that Rebecca Hume should like him. They had killed a dog in front of her.

He visualized her, attempting to set his desire against anxiety. He wanted suddenly to turn but as he lifted the reins his longing, fear and hope formed a tidal wave that threw him forward.

Every once in a while he stopped and studied the farmhouse below, scanning for movement. A car, an ugly sports saloon, was parked outside the back door, but he could not tell whether this meant the residents were at home or whether another vehicle was missing. As time passed his anxiety grew stronger, and he all but convinced himself that nobody was there. When he recalled that Rebecca was on holiday, and that soon she would be gone, he forced himself on. One chance was all he had.

Before he had left home he had shaved, studying himself closely in the mirror. The dark bristle that had begun to emerge in his early teens now blackened his chin almost as soon as he had scraped it away, joining at his ears with hair that lay thick across his skull and was straight and tough, cut short by his father in a long-held reciprocal arrangement. As he had gazed at himself, he had tried to imagine what Rebecca would see. His head was well proportioned on a stocky body, his forehead rectangular and as yet unlined, his eyes dark. His nose was straight before it flared at the nostrils. His mouth was his mother's, feminine, above his broad, hard chin. As he had finished shaving he knew that the first thing Rebecca would see was his youth; the ability of this face to absorb the passage of time only illustrated how little experience looked back at him.

What's more, he thought, as he rode along the terrace edge, with his jeans and heavy canvas shirt, he looked exactly as he should: every inch the hick farmer boy who had made too much effort in dressing that morning.

He ended another sweep of the floodplain by turning to look back at the road, shuddering as he saw Aaron's pick-up parked in the viewpoint. He stopped, surprised at his reaction, trying to overcome sudden guilt. He lifted his binoculars to look at his friend but the glass of the pick-up's cab acted as a veil. Then the vehicle reversed, turned and drove back towards Huil. Hugh followed it with his eyes before he turned back towards the depths of the small glen, looking at the way it rose into the low, midday sun. A bird wheeled, remote against the yellowing nucleus. He rode on.

Right there and then all Hugh wanted was to look at Rebecca moving across the farmyard, or to see her sitting in the garden at the edge of the house. At this distance she might see him; he was sitting on a horse, after all. He lifted his glasses and searched the yard again. Nothing. He allowed them to fall on to their strap and, disappointed, he looked down at the river. The stream had eroded the terrace below into a real cliff, creating a sweeping pool that shelved into a pebble beach on the other side. She sat on a rock at the edge of the bank, smiling up at him, a small trout rod by her side. Hugh felt the mortification of discovery ignite on his face. Sandancer stopped, unhappy at the proximity of the precipice. As the mare fretted Hugh tried desperately to think of something to say. Rebecca, who had the advantage, spoke first. 'Anything interesting happening at the farm?' Her voice was teasing.

Hugh's first urge was to spin his horse and flee, but the path was too narrow. Instead he sat still, shocked, his mind empty of things to say. He would have liked to ride down to her, but the cliff was impassable.

Her gaze had not left him, and the silence grew until Rebecca's patience failed. 'You could be a statue up there,' she shouted. 'Try to be a little more traditional, draw a sword or something.'

Hugh laughed and looked up the glen at the sun. The bird, an eagle, seemed to be circling close, its presence unnerving. His attention swung back to the woman by the pool below. 'Have you caught anything?' he called down. It was a start.

She looked confused for a moment, then remembered the trout rod. 'Oh, no, I don't know how it works.'

They looked at each other in silence again.

'Maybe you could show me?' she said, keeping the conversation going. 'If you're not too busy.' She pointed vaguely in the direction of the farm then smiled broadly at him.

He ignored the implication. 'I'll have to find a way down.'

'I think there's a track a few hundred yards further up.' She pointed, and Hugh looked, then turned back.

'I'll go and look,' he said. 'You'll stay there?'

'Can't promise.' She laughed. Then, seeing the look on his face, she relented. 'I'll be here.'

Hugh felt himself a poor Don Quixote as he urged his charger along the precipice. He cursed himself for losing all control of the exchange before it had even started. He tried to think of what he should have said but by then an exploding sense of elation spread out to annihilate all else. She wanted him to go down to her.

The track was tricky and Sandancer chose to move slowly. Hugh forced himself not to look back. He started to think about the next step, and felt his stomach all but collapse. All at once, his memory offered up his past efforts at lovemaking. He heard the mocking laughter of schoolgirls, took in the patronizing and inevitably wrong advice of his peers, then cringed at the horrible memory of a *ceilidh* when he had been drunk and . . . He looked over the cliff edge and thought about jumping.

He tried to restrain his panic by thinking of the great unspoken between Aaron and himself, his sexual ignorance in the face of his friend's experience. He had always been grateful that, apart from an initial burst of

64

enthusiasm, Aaron had managed the good grace never to boast of his visits to Alison MacGilvery in the town over the hill. Unfortunately these thoughts only took him back to the aftermath of the *ceilidh*, and he saw himself curled up on the bed of a visiting folk musician, a woman of seemingly limitless depths of compassion, who had told him it didn't matter that he couldn't get it up.

At last he saw the gully where a burn had cut into the terrace, forcing a rough track down to the plain below. He looked over the flatlands and imagined Rebecca watching him gallop away across the grass, mud flying up from the horse's hoofs. He would be free, filled with self-hate, but still free. But then, as he looked down towards Huil, he realized he was assuming a great deal: she had addressed only three or four sentences to him and he had said even fewer to her. He felt a little better, more in control, and he rolled himself off Sandancer and led her down the steep path.

Rebecca was where he had last seen her, standing as he approached, joining him as he tied Sandancer to the branch of an ageing birch tree.

'Hello, beautiful,' she said, blowing into Sandancer's nostrils. 'What's your name?'

Hugh undid the girth and slipped off the saddle, turning when he sensed Rebecca looking at him.

'Her name?' she said. 'I wasn't actually expecting the horse to answer.'

Hugh smiled, resting the saddle on a fallen tree. 'Sandancer the Conveyancer.'

'I like Sandancer,' she said, looking back at the mare, who was nuzzling her, 'but what's with the Conveyancer? That sounds like a lawyer.'

'Get to know her and all becomes clear.' He ran his hand along the horse's neck, feeling the familiar movement under the skin. 'Watch your shirt, she's big into the latest fashions.'

Rebecca caught Sandancer just in time to avoid a side-of-the-mouth attack, and pushed her nose away. Hugh wondered whether he should have kept his mouth shut. 'She is really very beautiful,' Rebecca said.

Hugh looked at Sandancer, who made another small attack on a laughing Rebecca, then walked to where the fishing rod lay, wanting to move the conversation away from the horse. He had always been irritated by women's affection for the equine and was pleased when Rebecca turned and followed.

'I told the shepherd,' she looked across to catch Hugh's nod of understanding, 'that after seeing the display at the games I wanted to try fishing for real.' She watched as Hugh picked up the rod. 'He put this fly on the end of the line, but as soon as I tried to cast it got caught in the top of that tree and the line broke and, well, I just gave up. It's such a nice day and I wouldn't know what to do with a fish if I caught one anyway.'

'I always like them grilled,' Hugh said, comfortable enough to try a joke, albeit a poor one. He picked up the fly box she had brought with her. 'With lemon and butter.' He chose a Butcher, a little black one with a red tail.

'Well, I never,' she said, all mock surprise. 'If I'd known you could catch them precooked I would have shown a little more enthusiasm.'

He looked up from the fly. 'Do you have any gut?' he asked.

'A fishing term, I presume.' She reached down into her jacket pocket and pulled out a roll of clear line. Hugh took the nylon and unreeled a length, biting through the filament. 'I might watch this.' She moved close beside him. 'I've already been shown once but I managed to forget.'

He made small loops and talked briefly, in mnemonics. He asked if she would remember.

'No shortage of wildlife involved, is there?'

'Give a man a fish and he will eat for a day, teach a man to fish and he'll grow very, very boring,' said Hugh.

'Super.' She smiled sweetly, and the skin around her eyes wrinkled. 'I was also given this. Can you use it?'

She had pulled a short length of polished wood and brass from her pocket, which Hugh took, smacking its heavier end into the palm of his hand. 'Not yet,' he said. 'It's called a priest. You hit fish over the head with it to kill them. A rock works just as well, though.' He handed it back.

She returned it to her pocket with a look of distaste. 'I rather hope we don't catch anything,' she said.

Hugh stood up and walked to the water's edge. He started at the top of the pool, sending the line like a streamer back and forth past his head until the fly fell perfectly, without a ripple, into the fastest water of the stream near the other bank. 'Just like that,' he said, and offered her the rod, but she shook her head.

'I think I'll just watch and learn.'

Hugh watched the end of his line swing round in the current, slowly stripping the cast until a loop hung down at his feet and the fly sat in the quiet water near the closer bank. Then, holding the line in one hand, he drew up the end of the rod, slowly at first and then, in one fast movement, sent the line back, allowed it to straighten behind him and effortlessly returned it out across the stream. It landed perfectly again. He took a step down the pool and let the line come round. 'You have to practise to learn,' he said.

She took the rod, holding it away from her. Hugh moved close behind her, adjusting her right hand until her long fingers grasped the cork handle. Then, with one hand on hers, he made to encircle her with his other arm. She turned, sceptical. 'Honestly, I can't show you any other way,' he said, colouring fast. He wondered how he had suddenly got himself into this situation.

She looked unconvinced but turned back towards the river. He encircled her again, taking the line in his left hand and pulling up her right hand before returning it to the horizontal. The line went out and, relieved, Hugh backed away. 'Just like that.' He was alive with the smell of her scent, the touch of her skin under his fingers, the texture of the skin on her neck, soft, papery.

She tried casting again, succeeded, and smiled with pleasure.

'So where are the charming friends today?' she asked.

'Which friends would those be?

'Oh, you know,' she said, playing the game. 'The Beemer-driving troglodyte and his blond junkie sidekick.' A pause. 'Or are you his sidekick?'

Hugh laughed. 'They're not my friends,' he said, the smile now in his eyes. 'I've always hated them.'

'Denying knowledge of your friends.' She sighed.

'If I denied them again would you like me better?'

'You want me to like you better?'

Hugh decided to answer the original question. 'Well, I last saw Aaron, the blond one, driving down the road back there, and Mac will be at his croft, which is up in that big group of mountains at the top of the north glen. He doesn't emerge very often.'

'I'm glad to hear it. I don't think people could handle the excitement.'

Hugh grinned. 'Mac's all right. He's a passionate man caught in a cold climate.'

'I take it that's his line?'

Hugh left his grin where it was.

He watched Rebecca cast, offering advice as they moved downstream. It was almost midday, and although there was still a chill in the air, the sun felt warm.

'So,' said Hugh, immediately realizing he had given the

word too much emphasis, 'how long are you on holiday for?'

'Oh, anywhere between three and six months, depending on how I feel.'

Hugh felt a jolt and couldn't tell whether she noticed. 'That's a long holiday,' he said, as evenly as he could. 'All the way through winter?'

'I expect to emerge with a well-laundered soul,' she said, casting.

'Good, we need interesting new people.'

She laughed, a rolling, open sound. 'Oh, I'm not so interesting. In fact, I'm planning to err on the side of dull.'

Hugh doubted it.

Hugh rode Sandancer through the Victorian outbuildings of Lochanthrain. The sheds were stacked loosely with long-abandoned machinery, the ancient pushed into the recesses while the less bizarre, and in rare cases still used, stood at the doors. He passed the game larder, and through the window's greasy glass could see stags hanging by their haunches, headless and illuminated by a naked bulb. Sandancer paused at the old pheasant pen, where she was usually left, but Hugh urged her on, passing workshops now damp and lifeless and entering a tunnel thick with rhododendrons rising up on either side. Then they were out on the long driveway, facing the vast granite façade of the castle itself. Although he was still several hundred feet away, the building's shadow reached towards him. To his right a lawn led down to the loch. Hugh noticed at once that the small rowing-boat that usually sat at the jetty was tied up to the pier on the island.

Sandancer flicked her head to rid herself of a fly, bringing Hugh's gaze back to the building. The architect's intention was obvious: Lochanthrain's proprietorial stance in such wild country was meant to astound with sublime beauty. The building's vast bulk rose vertically for three storeys on a broad front before giving way to a series of outcrops, the greatest placed at the western end – a dominant square tower, like the poop of an ancient warship, reaching higher than the great pines that clustered at its feet. The uniformity of the castle's front was broken only by a one-storey hall with two heavy wooden doors. Its roof provided a large terrace reached through floor-to-ceiling windows on the second floor, and as Hugh approached, a woman, lean to the point of aggression, emerged onto the terrace, a watering-can in her hand. Her greying blond hair was short and severe.

'Afternoon, Mrs Harding,' Hugh shouted.

'Keep that bloody horse off my garden,' she replied sourly. She began to water some plants that lay unseen beyond the parapet, Hugh's presence no longer of interest. He glanced up the loch to the mountains and above them the wispy streamers of high cloud that smeared the sky and heard the sound of oar strokes as Aaron rowed towards him. He turned Sandancer towards the pier and tied her to the handrail.

Aaron was turning the green and white boat when Hugh stepped in, and sat down in the stern. Aaron stood up, bracing his legs, and pointed a slim, black remote control at a box on the pier. He sat down again and began to row. The first blast rolled from the castle, an entire choir roaring '*Kyrie*' in the quiet of late afternoon, followed by the high yearning note of a soprano. Hugh kept his eyes on Aaron, whose smile lay content and unchanged on his face as he leaned against the oars. Eventually Hugh could not help but turn and look back at the castle. Aaron's mother was standing at the edge of the terrace, shouting wordlessly in their direction. She turned and disappeared into the depths of the building.

Aaron seemed relaxed at the oars and the boat moved swiftly through the dark waters towards the twisted grove on the island.

The 'Sanctus' – Hugh at once recognized Mozart's Coronation Mass – was closing when Aaron motioned with a finger and Hugh turned again to see his friend's mother throwing a large speaker from the high battlements. The box arced, showering music, its cord catching and forcing it to the side of the tower. She looked down the wall. She must have had her pruning shears because the sound gave out when the wires were cut and the box dropped to the ground. With less resistance the remaining speaker breathed its last, '*Agnus Dei, qui tollis peccata mundi: miserere nobis. Agnus Dei: Dona nobis pacem*,' then flew into space, falling freely until it shattered on the earth below. Hugh looked back towards Aaron, and from behind he could hear a distant shout filling the sudden silence with the words 'fucking' and 'arsehole'.

'Notice how she says it,' Aaron commented. 'She beats the vowels flat in "fucking". Like faahhking. Mac says he finds it attractive.' He seemed thoughtful.

'Were the speakers expensive?'

'I made them myself. I should be able to recover the cones.'

Hugh rested his hands along the high edges of the boat, silent until they approached the island landing, and then he spoke. 'Don't you want to know how I got on?'

'Did you faahhk her?'

Hugh laughed.

Aaron stood, holding the painter, and jumped from the edge of the boat onto the pine-needle-covered earth and tied it to a tree. 'Then, no, I don't,' he said.

Hugh sighed and made his way ashore. He looked up at the bars of a vast eagle's cage that rose away in front of him, their lines straight for thirty feet before they bent inwards to its apex where two iron sculptures of the bird the cage had once housed stood hunched, looking down. A welding gun and a small generator stood on the concrete floor beside a hole where the cage had rotted away. New bars lay nearby, and he noticed some had already been welded into place. Cans of black rustproof paint stood at the other side of the cage, just inside the doorway of the eagle's house, which itself gave on to the ornate keeper's cottage. Aaron was looking at Hugh. 'Thought I'd fix it up,' he said.

Hugh nodded, looked around and asked what he needed doing.

FOUR

Rebecca examined the soapstone eagle, turning it over in her hand as she walked to the till. 'I might take this,' she said, handing it to the postmistress and noticing the menu on the wall. 'Food as well?'

'All home-cooked,' said Mrs Cameron.

Rebecca asked Hugh if he wanted anything to eat. She ordered tea and sandwiches for them both. 'We'll have it outside.'

She turned, walked out of the shop, which served as post-office, café, craft shop and village store, and sat down at a wooden table in a garden still alive with flowers. She set the eagle down on the table-top. 'I studied sculpture at school,' she said. 'I was quite good at it, loved working with the different materials. It's been a while since I tried, though.'

'Get back into it,' said Hugh. 'Go into the craft business.' He looked without interest at the eagle. 'Long tradition up here among the settlers.'

She ignored the sarcasm. 'It's not a bad idea. I've looked around and there's a workshop at Shiloch. It's fairly well equipped, lots of electric saws and stuff.' She looked thoughtful. 'And I'll need a hobby or two, to pass the time.' She turned her assessing gaze on Hugh.

He flushed, and looked across to where Sandancer was

hitched beside her car. He felt uncomfortable being in the village, but had seen Rebecca arrive as he was riding through and decided to follow her. Her car was a Maserati, of all things, which was far uglier than he had imagined it should be but, then, he had never seen a Maserati before.

'So, do you ride everywhere?' She had followed his gaze.

He nodded, leaning back to allow the postmistress to set out the sandwiches. Rebecca turned and complimented Mrs Cameron on her garden, triggering a long colloquy on the difficulty of raising colour in such a landscape. She and her husband Alfie loved their gardens, both here and at their croft, to an extent that raised comment in the village.

As Rebecca listened Hugh's gaze wandered to her uncallused fingers with their long thin nails speckled with chipped varnish. He followed them up as she lifted her cup, transferring his gaze to her eyes, which flicked across to him before turning upwards once more, the irises sandy. Her ear was perfect, unmarked, the fading red hair tied tightly behind, pulled back from a broad expanse of forehead. The visible eyebrow curved from the centre, giving the impression of constant interrogation, and although he could not see the other Hugh knew that it was cut in half by a small scar. Her nose seemed full, almost indelicate but correct to the shape of her face, touched by freckles that led out across her cheek. Laughter, or perhaps stress, had worn the skin beneath her eye and this now rippled as the edges of her long lips rose, bidding thanks to the postmistress.

He shivered: there was a chill to the day, and he regretted the passing of the Indian summer as he looked out towards the north, where the sky seemed to have darkened. Rebecca turned back to him, the scar in her eyebrow showing, tiny but very white.

'Do you miss London?' he asked, picking up a sand-wich, inspecting the spread, then pushing the layers back together.

'Not yet.'

'I sometimes wonder what it's like.'

'You've never been?' She looked surprised.

'Never really had any reason to.' He paused and went on, 'I've been to Edinburgh twice.'

'How very cosmopolitan.' Again the assessing gaze.

He laughed and took a bite. 'There's no reason to go. Aaron and I shop for things with his computer now – you know, CDs, clothes, books and things. Aaron even gets electronics, chemicals, that sort of stuff.' He checked her expression but she showed none. 'He gets all this weird shit and builds stuff, stereos among other things, he's a regular engineer.' He wondered why he was telling her this.

She flicked at a fly that had settled on the plate. 'And you?'

'I just get books, some music too, rock – rebel music, Aaron calls it. He listens to classical, big church music. It's kind of strange.' He realized he was justifying his friend, repairing the damage done at the fair, ridiculous – after all, who was trying to get lucky here?

'You spend a lot of time together, you and Aaron?' She now propped up her chin on her palm, tapping her lower teeth with her fingernails.

'Yes. We're sort of inseparable.'

Rebecca smiled at Hugh, causing the little ripples to rise around her eyes once more, eyebrows arching fractionally. Her smile was so slight, so thoughtful that Hugh felt anxious in the face of it.

'So you plan to make sculptures then?' he said.

Hugh sat in the dark, a rifle held between his legs, one gloved hand out of the pick-up's window, shining a spotlight over the peatbog. Aaron, who was driving, kept the speed low while fumbling with a CD box, finally slipping the disc into the stereo. After watching this Hugh turned his attention back to the night and swung the beam over the ground again, in case they had missed anything, the light cutting a narrow tunnel through the darkness. They were looking for the reflective sheen of animal eyes and Hugh let the light run freely over the few sheep that raised their heads. Inside the car, over the sound of the fan blowing hot air, the strings of the English Chamber Orchestra rose to fill the space.

'Ah, a little singalong, then,' said Hugh.

'Take the chill out of the air.' Aaron steered with his knees while he sat on his hands.

They passed a stand of trees that reflected the beam back at them, and the hillside opened up once more. Hugh's mind wandered over his strategy for the conquest of Rebecca. He had asked if she needed a guide to show her the area in his hope that this would allow him closer, and she had taken him up. He thought about telling Aaron, but was restrained by an illogical sense of guilt. Outside, the light passed over more sheep and then some deer. Aaron muttered.

Hugh brought the light back and the truck rolled to a stop.

'Nice beast,' said Aaron.

Hugh looked at the stag, which stood broadside to them, a hundred and fifty feet away. Its head was straight up, holding a wide and heavy pair of antlers. 'Cups,' he said.

Aaron reached across and pulled his field-glasses from the glove compartment. On the stereo the Wandsworth School boys' choir adoringly addressed their sire, lord and master.

'Thirteen points,' said Aaron. 'And cups you could drink out of. I wonder where it came from.'

'Well, it won't be going very far if it stays there,' Hugh replied, holding the beam steady.

The car's horn sounded, but the blast rolled over the stag. Aaron got out of the car while Hugh flicked the light up and down to break the beast's trance, but his attention shifted to his friend who, now in the beam of the headlights, had begun to let out the most horrible howl. He looked at the stag. It had not moved.

'What the fuck is that supposed to be?' Hugh asked.

'It's the noise a hungry wolf makes. I just had it sent over from Canada.' He showed a small wooden whistle.

Hugh looked back at the stag as Aaron howled once again into the night. It stood completely still. Hugh opened his door, stepped out of the car, keeping the light on the beast by shifting the lamp from one hand to the other through the window.

'Fuck off, ye smelly great hoor,' he shouted. The stag jerked as if slapped, turned and loped off towards the hill. 'Wolves.' He got back into the car. A grinning Aaron joined him. They watched the stag disappear into the darkness, pushing it along when it turned with occasional blasts of the horn. 'I'm surprised Mac hasn't already got that one,' Hugh said. 'It seemed to be waiting for a poacher's bullet.' He waited in silence for a reply, looking out into the night, a grin on his face. Aaron was ignoring him and he was forced to speak again. 'Sorry, I forgot, of course Mac wouldn't poach on your land.'

Aaron said nothing.

'Not on his old friend Aaron's patch.' Hugh nodded into the blackness. 'I bet he's lying out there now laughing at us. He's probably got his cross-hairs on that lily-white forehead of yours. What colour do you reckon his eyes are at night?' He swung the light round, then imitated Mac's dirge: 'The weak creep into the hearts of the powerful and there they steal power.'

Aaron eased the truck into gear and they began to move forward. 'Mac spends too much time alone,' he said, after a while.

They rolled forward, letting Bach wash over them.

'So have you done her a favour yet?' Aaron asked.

Hugh smiled. 'No, but rest assured you'll be the first to know when I do.'

'What are you doing, then? You seem to be spending a lot of time sniffing around her.'

Hugh looked at his driver. 'Poor baby, have you been missing me?'

Aaron snorted. 'Don't try it. It's just it's the middle of the stalking season and you're pissing around with this woman.'

Hugh was now ignoring the hill, looking directly at Aaron, whose eyes flicked on to him then back out into the night. 'Sorry, I didn't realize that being your friend meant that I had to remain celibate.' He nodded at the stereo. 'You're listening to too much of this music, brother. It'll soon be the priesthood for you.'

'That's not what I'm saying.' Aaron sounded exasperated. 'I just mean that any normal man would have given her one by now.'

'She's not a normal type of girl.' It was meant to sound smug and Aaron sighed.

The loch was opening up now on their right, and the beginnings of a wood reached down towards the road from the hill above. In the distance the lights of Lochanthrain glowed through the damp night. Hugh could feel Aaron's wish to leave the conversation lose its battle against his inquisitiveness.

'So what's she doing here, then? What the hell does she want to spend a winter in Huil for?'

'She hasn't told me.' Hugh thought for a moment, before deciding to expand. 'I think she's burnt out, too much of the big city.'

'So she's going to get over it by screwing a yokel, then? A bit of Highland cock is what she's looking for?'

'Perhaps.' Hugh was laughing. 'And if that's what she wants then this here yokel is ready and willing.' He had glanced outside and tensed. 'There.'

As he spoke Aaron hit the brakes and grabbed the gun, pushed Hugh back and pointed the barrel out of the window. Hugh, hearing the click as the safety-catch was disengaged, brought the lamp into the cabin and held it alongside the telescopic sights, the beam steady through the manoeuvre.

'It was just beside that small bush,' he said. In the distance a ditch ran away from a birch towards the woods and Hugh followed it with the light. He picked up the two little red eyes turning to look at the car, and there was the crash of the bullet leaving the rifle. The cabin filled with smoke.

'Thanks,' said Hugh, wiggling his finger in his ear as if he were deaf.

'Oh, stop whingeing.' Aaron was smiling as he tried to clear the smoke with his hand. 'That was a beauty. Keep the light on the spot so that we can find him.'

Hugh looked out, and although he could not see the fox he knew Aaron had hit it, knew it would be lying dead in the ditch. Aaron was having trouble keeping a grip on his excitement as he got out of the car. 'I'll go and get it.' He laughed, leaning down. 'Then we can hang it from that pine tree beside the tourist cottages, scare the crap out of them.' He was still laughing when, on the stereo, Benjamin Britten gave Gwynne Howell the signal to ask, 'Whom seek ye?' prompting Peter Pears to comment, 'And they answered him,' which in turn caused two armed young men in the darkness of a midnight Highlands to shout with all the air in their youthful lungs.

'Jesus.'

'Jesus of Nazareth.'
'Jesus of Nazareth.'

Hugh's fingers hurt from gripping the warm leather of the seat below him. He felt his buttocks tense again, this time in response to an oncoming bridge. Beside him elegant fingers dropped to the wooden ball at the top of the gearstick and rammed it into third, forcing the eagerness from the car to ebb before massive power took over yet again and thrust it into the corner, then under the aged granite blocks, and finally out of the chicane. For a second Hugh felt his muscles soften and then the fish lorry appeared in front of and above him and he dug himself back into the seat, only to see it pass away to his right, Rebecca nimbly steering into a passing-place and back out onto the now clear single-track road. 'All I wanna do is get with you,' shouted an outfit called the Phat City Effect. 'Shake that bootie.' The noise was all-embracing. Rebecca shifted back into fourth, then dropped her hand onto Hugh's knee so as to get his attention. 'I just love these roads,' she shouted, and he nodded back dumbly, the lyrics refusing any opportunity to reply. 'Bouncin' that ass, bouncin' that ass, just don't ya stoppa.'

The scream of the engine drowned the sound of the stereo as the speedometer rose. Hugh leaned across and shouted that they needed to take a left turn, and then they were at the junction and the car was away on the new road, with Hugh feeling surprised he was still inside.

For the next ten minutes – 'oooo-eeee, bouncin' that bootie babeee' – Hugh sank deep into his misery, emerging only to shout warnings about the proximity of the really bad corners. Finally he pointed at a gravel car park and Rebecca reined in the monstrous car, stopped and turned off the engine.

'What a team,' she said. 'We should take part in a

proper rally.' He gave her a look and her smile turned to a vague concern. 'Are you OK?'

'I might have to kill you,' he said.

Her grin re-emerged and she looked up at the mountain above. 'I suspect you might,' she said. 'You really want me to go up that?'

They followed the path along the edge of a small river, Hugh looking every inch the native in big boots covered by waterproof leggings, thick moleskins and camouflage jacket, while Rebecca, three paces behind, had chosen instead to cover her long coat with an even longer silver waterproof with 'SorteD' written in gold on the back.

When he looked back for the fourth time she raised her hands in exasperation. 'Look, I'm sorry, I bought it at Glastonbury. I was stoned at the time.'

They wandered through tangled birches and past rowan trees, whose berries had turned scarlet in the last of the autumn. The sun appeared briefly between banks of cloud, and they took the opportunity to sit beside the loch before tackling the steep climb ahead.

As yet Hugh had failed to come up with a plan for how to make a pass at Rebecca. All his waking hours were filled with thoughts of her. He had decided she was fabulous in all ways – except perhaps her driving – and picked over her attributes one by one as perfections. Yet when he found himself with her he realized that in all the hours of thought he had created no strategy for taking his suit forward. Instead he felt he showed nothing but awkward youth.

'Can you use these for anything?' Rebecca asked, showing Hugh a bunch of the berries.

'Rowanberry jelly.'

She picked one off and was about to put it into her mouth.

'But they're inedible when they're like that.'

She regarded the berry for a while then dropped it

with the rest, and turned to look at the mountain behind. 'Why didn't we choose one that was closer, like one of the mountains at the top of the north glen?' she asked.

'Too nasty,' Hugh replied. 'You have to scramble along ridges and it's easy to fall, and I don't trust the weather enough today to take that sort of risk.'

He stood up, asked her if she was ready to go on, and she collected herself. As they left the woods they met an ageing man coming the other way. He was dressed in a purple and green Goretex jacket and Lycra shorts. He was using two ski poles to help him walk. 'Morning,' he said cheerily. 'Or is it afternoon?'

Hugh looked up at the sun but it had gone behind a cloud.

They climbed for an hour, the track getting steeper before it flattened out on to a plateau where Hugh slumped down in the heather, lying back, looking up. Banks of cloud had been rolling in and hitting them with the occasional shower, the latest breaking open to reveal a beam of light, while rain further out in the glen turned the opposite mountainside dark and obscure. He lit a cigarette and, when Rebecca arrived, asked how she was doing. 'You like to move fast,' she said, struggling to fill her lungs with air.

'You should have told me to stop or slow down.'

'I don't think so.'

They lay in the comforting bed of heather, watching the weather pull through the glen, sunlight suddenly slicing through the gloom, opening up the cragged features of a nearby mountainside before disappearing again. As the sky cleared, peaks showed up across the vast horizon, glens diving away into depths where trees hung in varying shaded forests and lochs fragmented light. Hugh pointed, showing Rebecca the whole scope of the west coast as, briefly, Raasay and Skye revealed themselves, before grimy tendrils of cloud licked down from the approaching weather to hide their faces once again. 'The majesty of Scotland,' he said, adopting the accent of an American video narrator and sweeping his arm in an expansive semicircle.

'Quiet,' Rebecca replied, clearly moved.

They traversed the plateau, their feet sinking into the peat, their legs growing cold, the track leading up between the ridges of the mountain's two highest peaks. As they approached the final climb heavy rain moved across the face, and Hugh sought shelter in the lee of a large boulder. He pulled a small flask from his pocket and offered it to Rebecca as she crouched down under the overhang.

The rain had turned to hail and they watched the small white dots bounce off the rocks. Rebecca had pulled the hood of her coat over her hat, tucking herself into her own warmth. He thought he might try to kiss her. 'Are you all right?' he asked. 'Do you still want to go to the top?'

She nodded, hardly moving her head. 'I think we should, don't you?'

He said nothing and they were quiet again until she exclaimed at a particularly violent burst of hail and he rubbed his hands in an effort to shift the blood. Now he had decided to make a move he didn't know what to say. He had never made a pass at a woman before, not properly, not soberly, not one that was accepted. He could not push himself towards her but he knew he had to do something so, with nerves raw, he muttered to himself about expressing his desires and suddenly he saw Rebecca was looking at him, gauging. He wondered if, inside, she was laughing at him. His muttering had been audible. 'Well, since we're here, we ought to get to know each other better,' he said quickly.

She smiled, but something in her eyes stopped him

moving towards her. He lost his nerve. Instead he asked, 'Well, what is it you do, when you're not spending months in the Highlands?'

She looked away. 'I'm a shipbroker,' she said. 'At least I was. And what is it that you do?'

He was surprised and embarrassed by the laughter in her voice. 'Oh, I don't do anything,' he replied.

'So I noticed.'

He sighed and tried again. 'What is a shipbroker? Do you get to sail the seas?'

'No, I sit – or, rather, before I resigned I sat – in an office in London and sent ships all over the world to pick things up and take them somewhere else. It's a bit like running a truck business, only bigger.' She looked around and then at Hugh. 'Are you really conducting small-talk on the side of the mountain?'

He ignored her. 'And you organized all that? Told sailors where to go?'

'Yup,' she said. 'I was in charge of all the non-oil business for the third largest shipping firm in Europe. Impressed?'

'I'm interested.' He meant it. 'So why did you resign?' The idea of this job fascinated him, so alien was it to his life in Huil. To speak of it in such surroundings might seem absurd to Rebecca but to Hugh the mountains disappeared around her words and, more importantly, it gave him time.

She had paused as if questioning the wisdom of opening her heart. Evidently she decided that she would. 'Well,' she said, 'I was desperately in love with one of my captains.' She was quiet for a moment. 'We were to be married. But he died. The ship sank. Off Africa.' She looked at Hugh. 'It was my fault. I sent him to the wrong place.'

They looked at each other for a long time before Hugh was shaken out of his stunned silence by sunshine once again licking the Highland landscape. 'God, I'm sorry,' he said quietly.

She thought for a moment. 'Don't be. It's not true.' She smiled broadly. 'What actually happened was that I was living with an insurance broker who dumped me when I was promoted and, well, I had a lifestyle crisis. I nicked his car, the Maserati, told him he was a jerk, moved into my own flat but I couldn't for the life of me decide what colour to paint the bathroom and I found myself weeping on my lush bombs and they were making scary whooshing noises and I realized I needed to take some time out.'

'What are lush bombs?' asked Hugh.

Rebecca studied him, smiled and, with infinite care, leaned over and kissed his cheek. 'Right question,' she said.

Carefully Hugh turned the wheel of the Hilux, easing its trailer backwards towards the loading bay. In the truck's wing mirror he watched the grimy hands of a man in waterproofs guide him. Aaron, who was sitting in the passenger seat, gazed at the passing farmers in disgust. 'Teuchter convention,' he said, nodding. 'I read the other day that one in a hundred Highlanders is mental. Inbreeding, I suppose. Or maybe the Americans wouldn't take the rejects. Come to think of it, you're probably one of them, you and your spastic teuchter cousins.'

'You didn't have to come.' Hugh eased his foot onto the brakes, bringing the car and trailer to a stop as the man lifted his palms outwards. He pushed open his door and walked back to the ramp, where the man was already lowering the gate of the stock trailer. The vehicle rattled as the heavy tups inside shifted nervously on its wooden boards.

'Not a bad day for it,' the man said, and Hugh looked up at the grey sky.

'Ay, if the rain keeps off.' He looked back. 'How're the prices this morning?'

The man laid the ramp flat on the concrete, and opened the two hinged gates. 'Not good,' he said. 'Where are these lot going?'

Hugh told him the number of the pen, stepped back and battered on the side of the trailer. The three tups tumbled out into the damp air. Hugh turned to ask Aaron to park the car, but the man offered to deliver the sheep to the pen himself and the boys slipped back into the vehicle.

'Fine day?' Aaron said. 'It's fucking drizzling. What an inbred cunt of a man.'

'You didn't have to come,' said Hugh.

By the time they returned a slight rain was falling and Hugh nodded from hunched shoulders at those he recognized. He pushed open a gate, let Aaron through and closed it again. They made their way down a sheep run beside a large wooden barn, and opened a door into the market itself. Men in a variety of worn jackets, fleeces and heavy sweaters stood leaning on the metal palisade watching the tups get pushed around the sawdust-covered centre. The smell of the sheep hung, oily, in the chill air. The auctioneer, a Borderman in an ill-fitting tweed suit and tie, was in full stream, his mumbled numbers spilling out over the arena, spreading out on to the players – the men competing in these quiet battles. On terraces around the ring families sat looking on, waiting to see what their year would bring.

'Buy healthy and stay healthy. Why buy in enzootic abortion?' said Aaron, and at Hugh's look pointed at a poster above the ring. Hugh turned back and watched the auctioneer drop his hammer as a sale was struck, and the tup was guided back out into the vast network of pens beyond. He knew, and nodded to, the owner, a friend of his father, who now stood just under the

86

auctioneer's pulpit. As the next tup entered, the owner turned and told the auctioneer its history, the quality of sheep it had sired, its prizes, and this was passed on to the spectators. Hugh tried to spot the buyers by the slight twitches they used to bid.

'No shortage of enzootic abortions in here,' Aaron opined. 'Look at that retard.'

'You didn't have to come.'

'Of course I did. I mean, when else would I get the chance to spend quality time with my old buddy Hugh now that he has a girlfriend?'

'Fuck it.' Hugh sighed. 'I'm going out to the pens. Are you coming?'

'No, I think I'll sit here and study the pastoral beauty that is the hill-country farmer.'

The three tups were in the pen the auction house had allocated. They stood in a pile of straw and turned their dull stares on the farmers who stopped at their gate. Hugh leaned on the rail and looked them over, making sure they had everything they needed. He hated sheep, but his father had been busy and had needed this favour, and given how little Hugh did, it was the least he could do. He wished he had asked Rebecca and he thought about their day on the hill. After a while he turned and leaned backwards against the fence, beginning a series of small conversations with men his father knew. He watched the auction-house staff start clearing the pens at the end of his row. Then they came closer and finally a man with a clipboard looked him up and down and asked if he was Jamie MacIntyre's son, and Hugh said yes and shook his hand. 'We'll take yours now,' the man said.

'Fine,' replied Hugh, and moved out of the way.

The sale went easily, all three animals fetching prices safely above the minimum his father had laid down. Afterwards he moved around the ring shaking hands and thanking the men who had bought them. All asked after his father and, on hearing of his absence, made the excuses that allowed Hugh to avoid buying any congratulatory drinks. He nodded at Aaron and they went for the car.

'You were masterful in there,' Aaron said.

'Thanks.'

'I think you'll make a fine farmer.'

'Do you now?'

'That'll be what Rebecca wants – to be a farmer's wife.'

'You think?'

'Making pancakes, wearing wellies, shagging you muddy.'

'Probably.'

'I think you need to do her, my friend. I think you need to get laid – you're too tense.'

Hugh opened the door of the truck and stepped in, leaning across to unlock the passenger door.

'Cunt,' he said, and Aaron smiled.

'Ah, yes, but no longer your cunt.'

'You see, that's it, isn't it? You're just a big, screaming, frustrated faggot, aren't you? The truth is you want to suck dicks.'

'I don't think I'm the one who has to prove their heterosexuality here, big boy. Maybe you can start throwing insults like that when you've at least touched her.'

'Fuck you,' said Hugh.

Aaron looked outside then pointed at the ignition. 'Let's go, these freaks scare me.'

Aaron looked at all the animated faces and sneered. 'No way,' he said, shark's tooth turning quickly between finger and thumb. 'Absolutely no way.'

'Come on, mate, you have to. I can't stay here alone.'

'She'll come.'

'Yes, but you can't leave. I'll look like an idiot standing here.'

'I'm sorry, I draw the line at this.'

'Maybe Mac'll turn up.'

Aaron laughed. 'Yeah. Right.'

'Oh, come on, just for once. Look at all the scum – we'll have a laugh.'

Aaron looked at him, serious. 'Hugh.' He was about to say more but he turned and walked out of the barn, stepping over the thick pile of cables that snaked up to the *ceilidh* band.

Hugh watched him go, then looked round the shed.

Huil was at play. Almost all of the village's forty or fifty residents were there, but the numbers were made up by others from further afield, brought in by the promise of a party. The room, with its bright overhead lighting and thick planked walls, was still filled with the usual Highland assortment of the landed establishment, folksy hippies, crofters, traders, foresters, fishermen and tourists. The elements shifted separately but soon the night would boil them all into a heaving broth. In one corner Gus Houston stood at his bar, dispensing drink with the help of the Dane. Hugh moved towards them.

He passed through the small crowds of people and felt the energy build up around him. The locals' determination to enjoy created an expectancy he could sense but not yet taste. He felt apart, and lost, without Aaron. He decided to drink, joining the queue at the makeshift bar. Two lines had formed, one to his right served by Houston.

Rob Munro, the bank manager from town, was pointing at the banner behind the publican, which read 'Free Bar' in big letters painted in the upper and lower blue of the Saltire. 'It says there it's a free bar, Gus?'

'You of all people should put your glasses on and read

89

the small print, Rob. Look, see the words there and there, which say "Scotland" and "paying". It reads "Free Scotland Paying Bar" so you better give me three quid.'

'Away with you! I can't see those words.' Munro turned away.

'Rob the Bank, if you don't pay me you'll not ever buy another drink off of me in your life.'

The bank manager stopped dead, turned, put down his drinks, pulled three pound coins from his pocket and placed them carefully in Houston's outstretched hand.

'You're a con-man, Houston, that you are,' he said, with no humour. 'And don't call me Rob the Bank. It's not funny.'

Two people were waiting in front of Hugh, a stranger and a known man. He shook hands with the local, and they were just about to mutter banalities at each other when they looked at the Dane in surprise.

'Sorry,' the stranger said to the Dane, clearly bemused.

'*An gabh thu balgam beag?*' the Dane repeated, with a proud smile.

The stranger turned to the crowd then back again. 'Sorry, do you speak English?' he asked.

'It is Gaelic,' the Dane said. 'Why do you not speak Gaelic?'

'Because I'm from Whitley Bay.'

'You're a settler?'

'No, a tourist, and I'd really like two vodka and tonics, please.'

The Dane looked at Houston, who nodded. He began making the drinks.

'Christ alive,' said the known man, stepping forward after the tourist had walked away. He waited.

'*Dé tha thu ag gabhail?*'

'What will I have? I'll have your fucking head, you stupid wee gobshite.'

Houston stepped in. 'What can I get you, John?' he asked. 'The lad's only practising his Gaelic.'

Hugh stepped around the arguing men and asked for a beer and a whisky chaser before the Dane could say anything else.

Having received his change, he turned back to the room and looked down at the stage where the three-piece band were tuning up. The keyboard player leaned forward and spoke into the microphone, the drone of a set of bagpipes acting as a dampener on the chatter, a fiddle cutting the air.

'I'm Andy Tagget, and this is Donald MacBain and Duncan Mackenzie, and we're the Glen Lyon Beggars.' A cheer went up, glasses raised in a mass toast, as they burst into 'Mrs MacLeod of Raasay'. The room began to move as most of the lights were doused. Hugh looked down as the beer was taken out of his hand.

'Hello, Mr MacIntyre,' Rebecca said.

Hugh leaned down and awkwardly kissed her proffered cheek. Rebecca turned to take in the milieu, which had erupted into dancing with the first skirl, and they sucked in their stomachs and held their glasses high as a speeding crocodile of children emerged screaming from outside and charged through the barn; its leader, a small boy with no front teeth, was holding a terrified rabbit in his hands, and as the children circled a number fell from the chase and into the dance, inspiring the others into yet greater energy. The beat was hammered out by a collection of the older folk, who stamped the barn's edges flat.

Rebecca had already rid herself of her coat and was watching the mayhem. Hugh, taking his chance, looked her over. Her hair was down over a dark-blue crushed-silk shirt, which fell in turn over a slip. Her legs were bare down to the flat shoes she had chosen for dancing. Keeping her eyes on the dance, she leaned sideways

91

until she was close to his ear. 'I think I overdressed,' she said.

'I don't.'

She looked at him, the smile never too far from her eyes. She offered him the beer and he took a slug, trying to calm his nerves. And then she told him she liked the *ceilidh* and he smiled as if it were his.

'Take me dancing,' she ordered.

Hugh knocked back half of the whisky, gave the rest to Rebecca, and then they were into the flow. The dancers spun, using the space in the barn that wasn't occupied by bales of hay, machinery or the elderly. In one place rotating couples broke around an outcrop of crusty rural punks, who pogoed to the beat, then came together again, accelerating or piling up as the chaotic clinches of the very young hurtled erratically through the stream. Rebecca grasped the moves as Hugh led them, and he took pleasure from her smile. He spun as they moved, turning her to where she needed to be, allowing her to roll in his arms with an extravagance that came with the knowledge of safety. Soon she could tell where she was going and Hugh relaxed, and they laughed with wide-eyed grins at their fellows, who crashed into them and then away. Then the drawn-out last chords of the music, and they came to a stop. He bowed slightly and laughed, and they brushed the perspiration from their foreheads. The next dance was announced and away they went again.

Once in a while they rested, got drinks from Houston's bar and crashed down in a pair of free seats. She would lean on him in mock-exhaustion and he would feel the thrill of her warm flesh on him. They discussed the dance and the music, laughed when tunes varied away from the staples and Elvis was played on the bagpipes and the fiddle. Then they would dance rock 'n' roll, in Hugh's case very badly. He saw that Rebecca could dance and he fell in love with her grace all over again and she, noticing it, used the full effects of her agility and told him it was the result of always having wanted to be a dancer and only having given up in her late teens, and he fell in love with that as well.

And then it was past midnight and the booze was still flowing and had spread to the floor so that its stickiness gave added grip, and all the children had exhausted themselves and had fallen in a great pile on top of each other in a hay-covered corner, where sleep had arrived as suddenly as the blankets their mothers threw over them. And still the band played on, the fever broken only briefly when the Dane leaped drunkenly onto the stage, took the microphone, broke into a slow, butchered mourning song of the Gaels and was hissed and booed, with cans thrown at him from the floor, until three fiddlers stormed the stage and erupted into a cacophony of movement.

Hugh and Rebecca danced on. In Hugh's mind lecherous hands reached for Rebecca but she saw them off with barely a sign and kept him at the centre of their blurring world. Occasionally a move would throw them close and he could smell her perfume and he went back into a world where only they existed. Then there was silence and the bagpiper laid down his instrument and stepped up to the microphone as Tagget put on full piano effect and broke into Robbie Williams's 'Angels', making Rebecca throw back her head in laughter.

To the bagpiper's shaking tenor, Rebecca rested against Hugh's arms, and they gazed into each other's eyes, and she smiled, they turned, and she whispered to him that this was their song. As the bagpiper crooned it was all that Hugh could do to keep laughing at himself because he was falling in here, really falling in, and he felt her move against him and he closed his eyes so that he could just feel the beat of the keyboard and move to the shifting sound of the tenor until they hung together as one, and he felt perfect and happy, with this woman who had all the grace of the world, and he couldn't believe what he was thinking, and he remembered to smile to himself. He was falling, falling.

They swung through the chorus, Hugh allowing his senses to focus on the scent of her, her hair against his cheek; she was holding him tight, her movements though effortless seemed disconnected and he knew she was a long way away. As the voice rolled over them Hugh opened his eyes and saw the musicians lost in their slipping irony, the man at the microphone using every breath while Tagget was himself playing the keys as if it were Rachmaninov on a Steinway and not Robbie Williams on his Roland. And as Hugh and Rebecca spun, the wreckage of the night passed Hugh's eyes, couples waltzing, drunks asleep, punters holding each other up and singing along, and then he closed his eyes again and fell back in.

His desire for her was complete, this woman who showed no signs of discomfort, of fumbling, of not knowing where she was and when. He wanted her so badly that his fears cowered back. At last he felt sure of her, and he felt the shock of seeing his own work bear her towards him, this comfort denied him by the cruel country.

He felt her head shift and he opened his eyes again and looked down at her. He sensed a slight tearfulness around the curling eyelashes, below which her smile had gone. He thought that now he should kiss her but she turned away to look at the band, who were consulting Houston, and again he lost his nerve. They separated slightly, but conscious that their dance had been intimate Hugh lingered, touching flesh.

Tagget returned to the microphone and told them the evening was coming to a close and would they please take their places for 'Auld Lang Syne'. The many who had survived the night began to form a vast circle. Hugh winced at Rebecca and pointed towards the door but she smiled and shook her head. 'We need to see it through to the end,' she said.

So they took their places and did the customary stamping of their feet, and afterwards the lights came up and Hugh felt cold air come in and the magic go out. He found Rebecca's coat, then his own, and they walked out into the night, which had cleared into a freezing sky. Under the icy pinpricks of the stars they walked with interlocked arms towards her car, but as they passed a large Transit van Hugh pulled her up and told her that she was the most lovely woman he had ever seen and made that terrible journey towards her lips.

She turned her head away, so slightly.

'Oh, God,' he said, self-pity bubbling up.

She looked at him and put a hand to his face. 'I'm sorry, it's not you,' she said, clearly trying to think of ways to calm his horror. 'I'm not ready for this . . . I've come up here to recover from someone who hurt me, I'm looking for fun, not to get involved.'

Hugh pulled away from her hand and mumbled, and she, still with a look of concern he could barely tolerate on her face, asked him what he had said. 'It's all right, it's me, I should be sorry for being presumptuous, I'm sorry.' He shook his head to clear his thoughts, trying to break through the humiliation and make a plan, a plan that suddenly must include what a few minutes earlier he had hoped to lose: his solitude. He looked at her briefly, that look of concern, then away. 'I think I'll go home. Will you be OK? Have you got your car?'

She looked down the hill. 'Yes, but I'll give you a lift home.'

'No, it's close, just over those fields. I'll walk.'

'Don't be ridiculous, it's too cold.'

'I'd like to walk. It'd give me time to be on my own.'

'Let me give you a lift.'

Hugh realized that he would look yet more foolish if he did not give in so he followed her to the car and they drove in silence back to the farm. He opened the door and looked out, away from her. 'Thanks for the lift,' he said.

'Aren't you going to kiss me goodnight?'

He turned and, almost angrily, brushed her cheek then stepped out of the car and walked up towards the grey shape of the farmhouse.

FIVE

The pick-up veered gently from the road, its deviation ignored by Aaron until a ditch threatened. With a sigh he turned the wheel. Ahead lay a junction.

'Which way?' he asked.

Hugh shrugged and Aaron wavered between the options, the car swerving lazily back and forth, before being guided to the south.

'So you came across this man?' Hugh prompted, resting his knees on the dashboard. 'He was painting beside the road?'

Remembering, Aaron continued his story. 'Yeah, he was painting.' He leaned forward and started to fiddle with the stereo, trying to get the balance right, cursing that he couldn't hear the choir properly. 'I should get a new sound system, this one's shit.'

'It was new three months ago.'

Aaron hit the machine with the base of his palm, then leaned back into his seat.

'Yes, so this guy was painting the mountains from that lay-by just beyond the woods. I had to pull over behind him to let another car past and I saw his picture. It's a big canvas and he's painted the mountains but on the mountains he's painted this entire fucking city, just covered it all with roads, houses, skyscrapers, cranes,

97

people.' He shook his head. 'I just sat there stunned, looking at this until the man turns round.'

'And?'

'Well, I drive off. I'd have given his painting two barrels with the twelve-bore if it wasn't a fucking Sunday. Painting in a city there. Can you believe it? Jesus . . .'

Hugh saw his friend's attention leave the road and fall on the heavy grey façade of the church. The pick-up slowed and they pulled into a gravel car park, stopping next to an Austin Allegro. Hugh looked the building over, running his eyes up its straight sides to where the roof sloped inwards to a small empty bell-tower. The structure had no whimsy to hold his attention so he read the sign.

Free Church of Scotland
Huil
Rev. Roderick MacLeod
Service First and Third Sunday of Every Month
12 noon

He checked his watch – seven minutes after noon on the third Sunday of October. 'Pub's open,' he said.

Aaron switched off the engine and started tapping his thin, colourless lips with his shark's tooth, then he put his other hand on the door-handle. 'The Rod of God,' he said. He had not yet opened his door.

'You never agreed to the bet.' Hugh kept his voice level. 'We're not obliged.' And then, hopefully, 'Are we really this bored?'

'That's not what we should be asking ourselves.' Aaron swung the car door open. Hugh at once smelt winter on the fields around them. 'It's more about whether we need some good old-fashioned morality – I mean, the way things have been lately.'

'You think we've been growing soft?'

'As puppies, my friend. But this'll straighten your head out.' He stepped from the car and leaned down to speak again. 'Make you remember why you should avoid those Pape bitches.'

Hugh shook his unstraightened head and got out. 'I don't need this right now.'

'But you do, you do, and anyway he won the casting competition, debts need to be paid.'

'That was ages ago and, anyway, you never agreed to it.'

Aaron walked up the path and tried the big metal handle. The door gave to allow them into a small hallway, musty and old, the taste lying unpleasantly on Hugh's tongue. He was handed a copy of the psalms and a small edition of the King James Bible, which his friend had taken from towering piles on the waiting shelf.

'Don't these things usually take three hours?' Hugh asked, as Aaron pushed his way into the interior.

Their entrance into the gloom of the church raised the heavy features of the minister, but only so far that his eyes appeared from beneath a heavily lobed forehead. There they held Hugh until the presence of the five parishioners looking at them from the pews grew uncomfortable. All were women: ancient, bent and twisted, their hair grey and knotted into tight buns on which rested small black hats. Hugh tried a smile but received no response. A sliver of sun broke through the small square panes of glass revealing clouds of suspended dust. Hugh's gaze returned to the minister, whose eyes stared back from a long pagan face rimmed by sprouting growths of coarse hair above each ear. Feeling other eyes on him, Hugh looked down to notice a younger man beneath the minister's pulpit, and recognized him as the shepherd from Shiloch, who had stood beside Rebecca during the Huil games.

The dust moved, but slowly.

The sun, as if shunned, disappeared behind a cloud.

'Finally.' The Rod's voice was quiet, but fell across the room like a javelin. 'Well, are you here to quake in honest terror before your God?'

The boys nodded.

'Sit down, then. You're late. Sit down there.'

They stood, uncertain of where he meant.

'There, there, in front of your God, over the souls of your ancestors.' The preacher pointed at the centre of the empty church and they moved down the aisle to the seats, Hugh looking at the ground as if souls were beached jellyfish.

'You can't see them, boy,' the minister hissed. 'They are suffering eternal torment.'

The Rod recovered his breath and turned his attention to the whole congregation. 'We shall sing,' he declared. 'Psalm six, verse six.' He waited for the small rustle of pages to die down, then read out the words of the psalm. ' "I with my groaning weary am . . ." '

Hugh sighed. He was about to stand but remembered the contrary Free Church etiquette in such matters.

'Psalm six, verses six to ten.' The Rod of God sat, disappearing from view.

The shepherd, who had been waiting below, now stood with his Bible open in his hand. Hugh laid a hand on Aaron's arm to stop him rising. The man's drone began in a voice cracked and ethereal, like that of a sailor lost in the depths of a thick fog. Still sitting, the other five members of the congregation picked up the dirge. At the final words, the Rod called the house to prayer and the worshippers struggled to their feet, copied once again by Aaron and Hugh.

'Lord,' the Rod began in an apologetic tone, 'we are rotten fruit, Lord, festering here in the midst of your creation.' His brow creased as he looked directly at

100

Hugh, as if some vital thought had come on him, a task that needed to be carried out. 'Lord, others might tell us lies about your forgiveness, but we do not heed them, we know that they are tricking us on to the short road to Hell. Lord, your commandments are set in stone, those precious stones Moses carried from the mountaintop . . .'

To Hugh, the minister seemed to be speaking from memory, his mind running along some parallel road.

'Lord, cause the Sabbath-breakers pain. We beseech you to mark out a special part of Hell for the men who live lives rich and arrogant, and hope you will send them there in the company of the whores who marry them for their wealth . . .'

That was for Aaron. Suddenly Hugh was reminded of the dog race, when Spot had slewed off his line, but this time the minister was the aggressor, Hugh and Aaron the target.

'Lord, we remind ourselves that evil stalks this land, that others come from beyond the mountains to tell us that Catholicism is acceptable, that it is acceptable for women to have children out of wedlock, even that buggery is not a crime. Our youngest leave us for the temptations of evil . . .'

Hugh allowed a smile to creep onto his face as he realized the minister was behind the times: the news of his failure to bed a Catholic had not yet reached the pulpit. He turned to Aaron, who, for some inexplicable reason, had written 'Violence is my Labrador' on his hand. With contact broken, the minister's attack seemed to slacken, and the prayer moved on to a call for divine help in achieving financial security for the church before barrelling to an end.

Another psalm passed and then the reading. Hugh mulled over the words. He had noticed the minister's harsh gaze falling towards them again, this time as he had read from the Bible. ' "Ye ask, and receive not, because ye ask amiss, that ye may consume it apon your lusts." ' The Rod of God had pushed himself up against his pulpit, ignoring the text that lay below him. ' "Ye adulterers and adulteresses, know ye not that the friendship of the world is enmity with God? Whosoever therefore will be a friend of the world is the enemy of God." ' So convinced was the minister's tone that even Aaron's attention had been caught.

Hugh couldn't believe he was here.

Another psalm passed, and the minister stood to exposit on the text. He allowed his eyes to sweep the congregation, dropping them on each of the women, for the moment ignoring the boys. There was the rustling of sweetie papers in anticipation. The minister's jowls smoothed, then rumpled into speech. 'Last week, you will remember, we looked at those unhappy souls who prayed to God for their own selfish ends. We looked at Betsy, whose prayers for her sister we decided were self-serving. She had asked God to spare her ill sister, for whom we all pray honestly, so that she would not feel lonely. Well, according to the doctors, things have in no way worsened so it looks like Betsy is no longer asking amiss.' Hugh watched as the minister paused, the congregation smiling at the old lady, the Rod's gaze falling briefly to the page in front of him. 'Today, we move on to the next verse, "Ye adulterers and adulteresses, know ye not that the friendship of the world is enmity with God? Whosoever therefore will be a friend of the world is the enemy of God . . ." '

Hugh looked back at Betsy but her face showed only the acceptance shared by her peers, the only movement the sucking of boiled sweets in the cheeks of all five. He began to try to let his mind wander from what the minister was saying but that only conjured up Rebecca. He wondered whether there was something in her Catholicism that had stopped her from returning his kiss, that had made her turn her head in that slight way that had shattered him, but he dismissed the thought at once. Her confidence, sassiness, assuredness all stood against any such cheap assumption. She knew exactly what she wanted and it wasn't him. He had misread the signals so he tried to put her out of his mind. Unfortunately she refused to budge.

'. . . are you an adulterer or an adulteress?'

The Rod had paused and Hugh turned to Aaron. His friend was sitting quite still, his eyes fixed on the minister.

'Perhaps you haven't betrayed your vows to a spouse, perhaps you haven't come between others' vows, perhaps you haven't had intimate relations with another out of wedlock. You may think this does not apply to you.' A pause and then a bitter laugh. 'Oh, you fools, you poor deluded fools. You've broken your word with God and that is adultery. Yes, you are all whores . . .'

Suddenly Hugh felt irritated by Aaron. Rather than find entertainment that would have taken his mind off Rebecca's rejection, his friend had dragged him into a church where he was being told he was a whore. Yet Aaron remained oblivious.

' "Know ye not that the friendship of the world is enmity with God?" '

The shout made Hugh jump.

'We lust after nearly everything. That is why the Devil is so entrenched, the culture of the world is now based on lust. The Devil is winning the war, my friends, winning everywhere, and the only place we can stop him is in our hearts. Friendship of the world is enmity with God . . .'

Aaron appeared to be enjoying himself. His unhealthy skin lay calm across his bony face, eyes directed up towards the minister. The only concession to his usual scepticism was an arm thrown along the top edge of the pew, a long finger tapping.

'Here in Huil we are, it is true, better protected than most. We don't have the constant clatter of neon billboards telling us what to think. Here we have our Church, our precious Free Church, standing guard against Satan's approach. But even here defeat is at hand, our congregation is low, our finances drained. Every day radio and television bring Satan into our very houses.'

At last Hugh realized why Aaron was intrigued. This was his language: the protection of their little world against the incomers, an argument against the painter with the vision – and here Hugh couldn't help but smile – of a city on the hill. The smile slipped, Hugh sighed and looked out through the murky window-panes.

' "Ye adulterers and adulteresses." Adulteresses. James, who, despite what Catholics try to claim, was Jesus' brother, pointedly referred to adulteresses, and that is unusual but very important. Men have the will, the power to remain moral, but women are weaker. Women must be extra vigilant. It is easy to be drawn from the path of righteousness by their very natures, their emotions, which so often overwhelm their better judgement. And down that road, my friends, lies damnation. "Thou hast destroyed them all that go a-whoring from thee." Psalm seventy-three, verse twenty-seven, as you will remember we sang earlier. And once fallen, a wanton woman, a Delilah, can draw even the best man away from the true path. For when a woman falls she falls heavily indeed. Beware that woman, my friends, beware that friendship with the world.'

Hugh looked back at the minister and found himself under the heavy gaze. He tried to stare back but failed beneath those eyes. At last they swivelled towards Aaron.

'Do not think that what James is saying here is that you shouldn't have any friends. Oh no, he is talking about friendship with the world, a different thing entirely. You will remember the friendship of David and

Jonathan in the Old Testament – "We have sworn both of us in the name of the Lord, saying, the Lord be between me and thee, and between my seed and thy seed for ever." Friendship is very important. Often the lusts of the world will draw you – or a friend – away from the True Path. Only true friendship will hold the bridge against the Devil. If you see a friend making an error, say, with a Delilah, don't take the modern route and say, "Let him make his own mistakes." No, you have to step in, make them realize the error of their ways, and if that fails, use whatever means necessary to draw them back. I promise you will be securing your friend's future . . .'

Hugh snorted, thinking he might be annoyed by this nonsense if he had managed to sleep with the woman who so clearly exercised the minister. He turned away from his friend and let the rest of the sermon slip past his ears, wondering how he was going to get over her.

At the door of the church, the Rod of God stopped them and said he hoped they had learned some valuable lessons.

'I shall beware the whore,' Hugh said, with an uncertain sneer.

Instantly he fell under the Rod's gaze, feeling the vast weight of the old man's judgement bear down.

Just in time, Aaron spoke. 'It was a good sermon, Minister,' he said.

The Rod did not take his eyes off Hugh. 'Thank you for coming, boys,' he said. They stood for a moment, as if expecting more, then turned and fled.

SIX

It was early and the first rays of sun shone hazily from the eastern horizon, throwing long shadows across the dew-covered grass and a warm light through the big kitchen windows of Lochanthrain. Aaron was filling a hip flask with whisky, while in the room's dark, vaulted depths a radio spoke of poaching in Africa. He placed the flask in a small canvas bag and followed it with a Thermos. Then he reached out to tap Hugh on the shoulder, shifting his friend's gaze from the dripping cone of rowanberries that hung in muslin, filling a bucket on the floor with blood-red juice.

'Stop looking so sad, comrade. I know it's the last day out but we'll make it count.'

Hugh smiled and pushed forward from where he leaned against a deep porcelain sink. He moved out of the soft beam of sunlight, and picked the rifle off the kitchen table. Aaron threw an arm around his friend's shoulder, releasing him only when they got to the door.

They walked in silence, one behind the other, out of the policy woodlands and up through the plantations, the sun behind barely lifting itself into the southern sky. They killed a hummel – a big, hornless stag – before they passed the last stand of larch. They watched it tumble into the stream below and then made for the Carach, a glen that led away to the north. It was midday by the time they reached the hunting ground, and they sat down by a large rock, turning their heads to the west wind to scan the mountainside for beasts. With the rut at its height, animals covered the landscape, filling it with movement, and groups of deer lay scattered across the face, single stags wandering between the bigger beasts and the hinds they held. Aaron unstrapped the canvas bag and offered Hugh a sandwich. Then he opened the Thermos and passed across a mug of sweet black tea. They planned their moves then leaned back and allowed the sun to warm them. For a while there was silence. Eventually Aaron spoke. 'It breaks my heart to see you like this.'

'Sure.' Hugh looked over the dark colours of the mountainside. It was four days since Rebecca's knock-back and the frustration still ate at him, each hour bringing further reasons for regret. The few moments they had spent together now seemed unbearably precious. He waited for Aaron to continue.

'That's what happens if you chase after these uppity English lasses. What you need is a nice Highland girl, someone who looks up to you.'

Hugh knew now that he had seen the possibility of a future with Rebecca. With these hopes now dashed all that was left was what he had always had: these hills, Aaron's companionship, the mockery.

'She was too old anyway, probably sagging in all the wrong places.'

His thoughts brought on guilt in Hugh that all that surrounded him was not enough. He looked at Aaron, who was grinning. 'I'm glad you're enjoying this,' he said.

'I'm not enjoying it in an unbrotherly way. I'm enjoying it because it's so, well, poignant to see a friend have his heart broken for the first time.' Aaron made a show of trying to find the right analogy. 'It's like watching a toddler fall at the first step.'

Hugh sighed. 'You know about getting your heart broken, do you?'

'Of course not. I would never let it happen.'

Hugh turned away, allowing the mockery to disperse, then swung back, now serious. 'It's not my heart that's broken, it's more my faith in my own judgement. I mean, we had shared intimacies, it all seemed perfect. Where did I miss the signals?'

'She's a tease, Hugh, a tease.'

Hugh spat, and broke a personal rule when stalking by lighting a cigarette. He looked again at the hillside. 'So where exactly are these nice Highland girls you were talking about?'

Aaron grimaced and suggested moving on.

By late afternoon they were lying on a plateau, the plants beneath them pale, arctic. A stag lay a little way off, looking down the other slope, its back a long dark line in the heather, the rifle sighted on its neck. It was only a matter of time now before the creature stood, and when that happened Hugh would kill it. He listened to its occasional roar, a lazy yawn from its prone position, all the while peering at the Three Great Mountains beyond. Hugh remembered the nights when as a child he would cry himself to sleep after killing an animal, and wondered at how, now, he felt only the vaguest regret. The wild and empty country seemed to tighten in on him, the mountains crowding him. Get up, he willed the stag with sudden anger, get up, and it did.

It lurched to its feet and turned, and as it did Hugh moved in and encircled the rifle. He felt pressure on his arm and looked across to Aaron, who was gazing out to the edge of the hillside. Moving across the slope was a younger stag, facing down its elder. Hugh kept the gun steady but did not shoot, watching as they came alongside, turned and locked horns, nine points to twelve, pushing down, each holding their place. With a click the antlers disengaged and then they came back on each other, the force greater this time. Hugh looked through the scope, seeing only a dullness in the eyes of the two beasts.

In time the old stag gave way, its muscles weakening, and as it did, Hugh fired, once and then again, victor first, vanquished second. With its heart blown apart, the old stag hunched its shoulders, the dull, wet thud of the impact rolling away across the hillside. Then it shuddered sideways and took two numbed steps, before seeming to sigh and, rear first, like a sinking ship, slipped into the moor. The hunters, who had been lying in the heather for over an hour, stood up and stepped in different directions to urinate.

A decision was made that Aaron would return to Lochanthrain for transport while Hugh gralloched the beasts and dragged them to the track that allowed the Argocat up on to the high ground. With Aaron gone, Hugh disembowelled them and then removed the thick rope he kept fastened around his waist and tied it around the head of the younger beast, throwing the other end over his shoulder. He pulled the animal across the flats, pausing only to change shoulders, at last making the edge of the plateau. There he untied the rope, and as the ground steepened he turned the stag so that he could hold its weight while letting it slide ahead down the hill.

He left the carcass where the undergrowth had been flattened by the little aquatic vehicle's eight fat tyres and slowly began to climb the hill again. By the time he had started to pull the older beast across the moor he was exhausted. He leaned forward, often stumbling, dragging the dead weight, cursing when peat-hags forced him to lift the animal up the slimy black banks, tearing the strength from his arms. Like a penitent sinner, he dragged his burden on. And with every footfall he felt himself take a further step into the emptiness of his life. This country, which was Aaron's cocoon, felt to Hugh like prison, and all the opportunity offered by Rebecca was drying up like the blood on his hands.

He left the second beast beside the first and sat down on a rock. A large black crow flapped its way up the glen, banking in to land beside a heaving mass of its fellows on the opposite slope. Hugh raised his field-glasses and saw an eagle hunched at the centre of the complaining crowd, eating the gralloch of a beast killed the day before, and he saw the crows surround then enclose the bigger bird until their presence grew tiresome; the eagle turned and sent them into the air in fright. Then the dance would begin again, the eagle tearing at the meat underfoot, then raising its head and eyeing the world.

Hugh moved so that he lay in the heather. He thought of his father, his dead mother and the farm. He hated the idea of farming, and looked again at the eagle as it turned on the crows. He thought about Rebecca and how she had deserted the world he did not know for this, the world he did, and he doubted he had the courage to do the same. This was what he had wanted, he realized, but the idea scared him. Rebecca would go. He would stay. He thought about the future and saw nothing.

The sun was slipping away to the west, and darkness infused the air. The shadow of the hillside reached the eagle's position as it finished the last of the gralloch and staggered into a laden flight with two large beats of its wings, turning to sail down the glen. The crows, rushing forward to find all the viscera gone, leaped into the sky and beat away after the great bird. Hugh followed them with his eyes until they had disappeared. He heard the faint scream of the argocat's engine on the steeps and looked the other way. Suddenly he was aware of the deer that covered the hillsides, making their way to the lower ground for the night. The roaring of the stags, which had died down in the middle of the day, had returned in force, filling the air. Hugh listened to it, and the noise made him suddenly uncomfortable, as if the sound was of a thousand wounded men screaming.

The first heavy frost of the year arrived in the night, and with morning came a delicate sun to tease out the autumnal colours with its quiet light. Hugh and San-dancer picked their way through sunbeam and shadow, the rider caught in the accentuated shades of the woods around them: frosted grass as pale as pistachio; rhodo-dendrons as sharp as fresh limes; beech leaves as golden as the morning itself. As Sandancer's hoofs pressed down on the crispy undergrowth, Hugh travelled through gently descending leaves, theirs the only movement beside his own in a landscape frozen to twisted sculptures. Melancholy still wrapped tight around his heart, the leaves reminding him of tears on this most beautiful morning. He allowed Sandancer to pick her way down the frozen, rocky path to where the river flowed and then, with barely a shiver, they were on the shale, and then the wide grasslands of Shiloch. Rebecca's call the night before had been brief, and Hugh had kept his tone distant. She had wondered at not having heard from him, and he had told her he had been busy. Perhaps if it were a nice day he might take her west and show her the beaches. He supposed he might. Twelve hours later there he was, confused.

He was hitching Sandancer to a post in the yard when she came out of the house, her smile broad, her long dark coat done up tight and her hands in gloves. He felt his need for her and lost any ability for hardness.

He looked at the sky. 'It was a nice day,' he said,

shrugging and making no attempt to greet her with a kiss.

She smiled, walked up to nuzzle Sandancer, and suggested he leave the mare in the paddock. They stood and watched as Sandancer rolled in the frosted grass.

She asked if he wanted coffee and he shook his head. He threw his small canvas bag into the back of the Maserati and sank low into the passenger seat. 'I'll go easier this time,' she said, as she sat down behind the wheel.

They drove west for an hour, the country rearing up and dying away as the car negotiated the watershed. After the bleakness of the high country they descended into the softer west, plunging down among the rivers and woods, travelling through a scraped, battered landscape, under towering boulders, beside brown waters turned white by the jagged grey rocks. And then they were out onto the sandy links seemingly at the edge of the world, an occasional croft dotting the slopes and the great grey Atlantic beyond the concave sweep of the smooth, blackish sand. The road ended, Hugh pointed up a small track, and Rebecca parked on a gentle bank. They stepped out into the breeze.

The air carried the sea and Hugh could taste it on his breath. He looked at Rebecca as she walked around the car to him. She had fastened her coat tight again and its soft material covered her figure in a way that moved him. He slung his bag over his shoulder as she flicked open the boot, revealing a wicker picnic hamper. With a smile he put his bag back in the car and lifted the hamper to his shoulder. They began to walk, ignoring the main sweep of beach, instead heading up into the dunes, careful to step on the sand and not on the delicate salt-grasses that pioneered this furthest edge. They slipped down into a gully where a stream meandered through a clean-sided cut it had formed in the sandy

112

floor and walked out between two high cliffs onto a beach all their own, the sand coloured like ageing white gold.

Hugh left the hamper beside a cliff and they walked to the water's edge, their footprints alone on the unmarked flats. The sun had found its winter apex and held them until the first fingers of a cloud reached out and caused it to glow. They turned and moved along the shoreline watching the tide, uninterrupted by waves, slink up the beach. Where the sand ended, the rock-face climbed away, black and infested with mussels and whelks, before returning to its natural cold steel-grey well above the high-water mark. A buttress of land reached out into the sea, then disappeared, returning at a distance then curving away through several miles of peninsula, its furthest reaches still out of shadow, causing its low outline to glow golden. Hugh stopped and looked straight out at a distant black island that, at its northern end, barely broke the horizon then reared up into crags and spurs. There was absolute calm under the growing wispiness of the sky.

'It's so quiet,' said Rebecca.

At Hugh's feet, small rivulets had begun to urge the tide on, tiny harbingers of change. The silence was a vacuum and out there, over the horizon, Hugh felt something shifting: an advance had begun.

'For now,' he said.

'We should take advantage of it while it lasts.' Rebecca peered up at the sun, which now shone from between the clouds' outstretched fingers. They turned and made their way back up the beach.

At the cliff edge, Rebecca opened the hamper and removed a rug, which they spread on the sand. She placed the sandwiches and cakes around its centre and handed him a bottle of wine, watching him as he pulled the cork and poured two beakers, handing one back to her. She held it up in toast. Resting their backs against the cliff, they looked out to sea. The sun had been muffled once more and Hugh shivered slightly at the acidic taste.

'You don't like wine?' she asked.

Hugh sipped again. 'I don't drink it very often. Aaron and I used to steal bottles from his father's cellar at Lochanthrain. He's got this big collection – it's a hobby, I think.'

Rebecca shifted, settling herself, close to Hugh. 'I haven't seen the castle yet, they say it's magnificent. I drove up there but all I could see from the road was an aviary on an island.'

'That's the eagle's cage. We've been doing it up.'

They sat in silence for a moment. Rebecca, legs pulled back under herself, leaned forward and offered him a sandwich. 'They used to keep eagles?'

Hugh nodded.

'He's a strange one, that friend of yours.'

'Oh no, he never kept eagles. It was back in Victorian times, when the castle was built. It was a hunting lodge, the eagles were like entertainment, you know, before television.' Hugh examined the sandwich in his hand; it wasn't very appetizing.

'Still.'

'You shouldn't judge him,' Hugh said, but without irritation. 'He's had a rough time. His mother's awful, hates him, and his father's very weak. He has grown up out on the hills. It's difficult to understand if you don't know him.'

She was looking at him. 'He has you.'

'Yes,' Hugh conceded, then smiled. 'But that's not very much.'

'Why does his mother not want him?'

'Way too long a story,' he said, holding up his hands. 'You'll have to ask him.'

114

'And what about you?'

'Oh, she hates me too.'

'That's not what I meant.'

Hugh told her about growing up on the farm, about his father, about how his mother had died during child-birth, and how his father worked so hard to try to keep the farm running, unfazed by his son's lack of interest. He explained how Aaron had always been there. 'He's in my first memory of life,' he said, noticing a breeze picking at Rebecca's hair and hearing the distant sound of small waves moving with the incoming tide. 'We were about three, I suppose, and he is standing there with his hair filthy with mud and his small boots thrust apart at the edge of the pond just behind Lochanthrain. He's smiling, I mean pure joy, and he has this frog impaled on the end of a small screw-driver – you know, one like clock-makers use – and I have no idea what he was saying but I remember looking at this mucus sheen on the end of the screw-driver and his great grin beyond.'

'That's your first memory of life?' Rebecca said. 'Jesus.' She shuddered.

Hugh laughed and took another sip of wine. He found he liked this new relationship: he felt no need to be on his guard.

They sat talking about the past, and as they did the wind got up and the separate clouds that had first appeared huddling on the horizon shifted forward. Cracks in this advancing mass allowed the sun to fall to the sea's surface in Jacob's ladders while in other places rain fell in perfect symmetry. Where its descent was touched by sun it burned white. Hugh watched one shower move across the face of the island, seeing the land grey before it disappeared.

After a time they walked. The sun had gone and cold clutched at them as they picked their way up through the rocks to where the cliff-faces fell into the sea. In a

115

sheltered bay, where the water had yet to be stirred up, they could see the sand below through the green depths, patches of seaweed shifting listlessly. They settled at the very edge of a spit, leaning back against a small concrete weather station, listening to the gentle beat of the wind-mill that powered the hidden instruments as it turned above their heads. Around them the grass grew in thick tufts, and Hugh gazed out to where the clouds now banked on top of each other in great cliffs, heaped and heavy. Waves rolled against their rock. 'Perhaps we should think about heading back,' he said. 'Here comes the storm.'

Rebecca said nothing for a moment, her focus on the infinite distance, and then she sighed. 'Can't we stay and watch it come, build a fire and sit here?'

Hugh looked at the clouds and tried to imagine the walk in the dark, the wet rocks, the lost pathways, the violence of the storm, their exposed position, the misery of the night. 'Of course,' he said.

He took the hamper back to the car, plotting the route they would have to walk in darkness, and collected his canvas bag with its tea, and her overcoat. On his return he found Rebecca collecting wood, which she added to the small pile she had raised while he had been gone. She seemed happy and knelt with him as he crushed up pieces of paper, surrounded them with small bits of wood and put his lighter to the kindling. 'Am I being silly here?' she asked happily. 'Is this a really bad idea?'

The flames took, rushing up to catch the wind and be thrown onto the wood behind. Hugh laid larger pieces of the flotsam against the heat. 'Yes,' he said.

She laughed into the wind, a rare display of open emotion, sat and drew her knees up towards her. 'Good,' she said, looking at him from the edge of her eyes. 'You'll look after me.'

Darkness came without a sunset, the light conceding

the drama to the coming storm. The wind increased steadily, and the fire feasted on its supply of wood. Hugh and Rebecca sat close, backs against the weather station, under a sky still half stars, and were at last lit by the rising moon, which emerged to show them the great wall of cloud, now thousands of feet high, that had come on in secrecy to hang menacingly overhead. Above them the windmill rotated, its gentle thump comforting. Rolling water surged onto the broken rocks below, sending phosphorescence up into the air, the waves reaching into the fissures, licking at the earth before being sucked away. In time Hugh and Rebecca's words ebbed and flowed with the rhythms of the great actions playing out below, a sense of security granted by the graduality of the increase in the rhythm of the windmill's rotor.

They hunched, keeping out of the way of the sparks that now rushed inland with the wind. Conversation existed only in eruptions, the salt hung heavy in their hair, the spray now reaching easily to their high perch. Hugh felt uncertain, happy to be there but unsure of what was expected, so he grinned at his companion with a sort of nervous excitement. He was beyond his own experience, on a precipice far more unsettling than the cliff that lay around them on three sides. She knew what she was doing; he knew where they were.

Rebecca had taken on a look of heightened calm. She sat, her hands thrown back as buttresses to her slim form, infinity holding her gaze until it was broken by the rain that arrived with the suddenness of a wave, soaking them instantly. She looked across at Hugh and said, almost shouted, that this was the moment when she needed him to kiss her.

PART TWO

PROLOGUE

Mac and Aaron worked in tandem, their punches falling onto the carcass, tearing back its skin with each impact, revealing taut, darkly marbled muscle beneath. After pulling ahead Mac paused, wiping the sweat from his neck, allowing Aaron to catch up. He watched the boy, studied his expression, only shifting towards the beast again when Aaron's pale eyes rose to meet his. Mac pulled hard at the loose flap of skin, driving his fist into the recess.

'So, the woman.' He raised his voice over the sound of the blows. 'Who is she?'

Aaron kept punching. 'Some fuck-up from London. Hugh says she's recovering from being dumped, said she has a "broken heart". I expect he thinks he can patch it up for her.'

'And she's here for the entire winter?'

'So she says. She seems to think she has everything she might need now that she has Hugh to keep her warm. She's got him convinced she's pretty sweet on him, from what he says. She's old enough to know what she's doing.'

'How old?'

'I don't know. Old enough. She's been around, I'd say.'

'And you don't like her?'

'I don't know her. The last time we spent any time with one another I was shooting that Jack Russell of yours.'

Mac sighed, looking down at the carcass. 'That dog.' He offered Aaron a small smile. 'It had no class. Despite everything, it still believed what it had done was wrong.'

Aaron, used to Mac's quirks, said nothing. The poacher pursed his lips. 'So why the problem?' he asked. 'I would have thought you'd be pleased Hugh is having sex. It wasn't too long ago you were telling me that his lack of success with women was becoming embarrassing. I seem to remember some theories about his mother's death.'

Aaron stopped punching the carcass. 'That wasn't my theory. My mother gave him some book and told him he'd never be comfortable sleeping with women after what had happened. I told you this.'

Mac nodded. 'So?'

Aaron stepped away from the beast and moved into the semi-darkness. He leaned on the rim of the rainwater barrel and ran his fingers across the dark surface, as Mac began to work his way around the whole of the cadaver, the loose skin now brushing across the floor with each punch.

'Hugh's desperate to get out of Huil,' Aaron said finally. 'I catch him looking south sometimes. He believes there is some sort of promised land out there. And it makes him unhappy.'

Mac pulled the last edges of hide from the beast.

'And this woman is encouraging him,' Aaron continued. 'I hate to see him unhappy.'

Mac held the separated skin in one hand and ran the other down the translucent membrane that covered the beast's rolling muscle. His smile was momentarily

122

unguarded, then he caught himself. 'And you think he's going to leave?'

'This woman's his ticket.' Aaron swept his hand across the water, sending a small wave over the edge and onto the floor. 'Don't get me wrong, I don't mind him going off – I mean, it's his life . . . I just feel that this thing is wrong, that this woman isn't what he should be doing right now.'

Mac leaned back against the sifting tray, the butchery, for the moment, complete. 'So you want to discourage him?'

'I think so, show him there's too much to lose leaving here.'

Mac ran his hand over his broad skull and showed a wide yellow smile. 'Then maybe you and I need to come up with a plan,' he said.

SEVEN

Hugh could see Aaron moving across the slope above him, his form weaving among the trees, disappearing, reappearing, ghostlike. He called up to him, asking where he had been the previous night, then switched his attention to the dog, letting his tone ease. 'Seek 'em, Fi, seek 'em in there!'

The coffee-coloured Labrador rotated, its tail beating, spun again and disappeared into a thick stand of gorse.

'Well?' he shouted up the hill.

A dismissive grunt was all that fell back.

Fi emerged from the other side of the gorse, her body rippling, and rushed uphill to search the ground in front of Aaron. The night had been clear and dawn had revealed an icy sky. The country was white with frost.

Hugh held his shotgun, a sixteen-bore Newton, across his pelvis, the carved lock cradled in his left and gloved hand while his right curled around the shank of the stock, a finger resting on the trigger, thumb ready to slide the safety-catch forward. The barrels were sticky with cold. He began to sing under his breath, a song taught to him by an Australian who had come to shear sheep one year, the memory triggered because Hugh was wearing a long duster stock-coat and an Akubra hat. Fi emerged from the spindly, wispish young birch, nose to the ground, following scents across a small stream. Hugh took his right hand from the gun, balanced it in the left and, gripping the trunk of a tree, swung himself down into a cut then over a burn's icy edges and up the other side. He picked his way through the rigid stems of dead and frozen bracken, careful to avoid fallen logs that lay slippery in the undergrowth. The grasses hissed as Fi pushed through.

'Seek 'em in there,' he told the dog.

Hugh's heart beat heavily under the effort of clambering over the rough ground, the rushing oxygen seeming to ignite his body into prickly good health. The innocence that had robbed him of confidence in the past had now left him and he felt bolder, stronger and happier. He felt Aaron's surliness jar uncomfortably against his good humour. Worse yet, his friend was being ungrateful: this was not Lochanthrain, the ground belonged to Hugh's father – they were in the thick brush at the edge of the MacIntyre farm.

Hugh covered his irritation by thinking back to Becky, the name he had been told to use when they were alone. Fighting a passage through the elastic young birch, holding out his hand to protect his face, he let his mind take him back to the early hours of the day. Before dawn he had fetched wood and built a fire at Shiloch then taken her the fresh strong coffee she liked. She had emerged from the myriad covers and quilts, yawned, sat up and looked at him with a slight squint that highlighted the small scar above her eye, her smile vital, emanating warmth, sleep and health. When he made to leave she wrapped herself in a dressing-gown and several blankets, picked up her coffee and followed him as far as the sitting room, collapsing into the sofa in a colourful heap of fabric, eyeing the fire, which had taken a hold in the hearth. Several minutes later, when he had returned from saddling Sandancer to kiss her goodbye, she had been asleep.

An icy birch struck Hugh in the face. He turned his head and saw Aaron standing at the top of the slope, waiting for him to straighten their line. Fi sniffed excitedly at the bottom of a stump, her nose pushed deep into the crevices. 'Seek 'em,' Hugh said. 'Seek 'em in there.' He watched the dog, his gun ready, but then she rushed up the hill towards a clump of rushes and Hugh took the weapon in his right hand, finger still on the trigger, and rested the barrels on his shoulder, his thoughts elsewhere as one eye lazily followed Fi's path.

The ride back to the farm had taken half an hour, despite his galloping across the open land, and he had arrived late, a cheerful apology greeted with only a shrug from the waiting Aaron. He had been ready to boast, to describe the pleasures of his night with Becky, but his attempts to raise his friend's interest received only a watery smile. When he told Aaron that they had looked for him the night before up at Mac's cottage, and asked where he and the poacher had been, Aaron failed to answer. Instead he had suggested that since they were so late they'd better get going . . .

Hugh threw the gun forward, catching the barrels in his left hand, stock rising to his shoulder, his left foot moving forward to square, and now he heard the sound, the birds' wings beating against the undergrowth, and felt himself hunch, his eyes picking up the tawny spurt, barrels shifting to darken the blur, and he felt the slap to the shoulder and saw the feathers . . . He heard a second bird and felt the excitement now, the bird weaving and his gun swinging fast, his finger on the second trigger . . . A blast, he missed, a second blast from above and the bird was dropping . . .

Hugh felt movement beside his leg, looked down and

found Fi wagging her tail, woodcock in her mouth. He ejected and replaced the used cartridges then knelt, took the bird and laid the gun down so he could rub Fi's ears. Aaron was standing on the slope above him.

'I can't believe you missed the right and left,' Aaron said, his voice the same flat monotone.

Hugh grimaced and stood up, looking resigned.

'Three or four times in a life you might get that opportunity,' Aaron continued. 'You blew it.'

Hugh said nothing.

'You used to care about these things, Hugh. You're allowing your mind to wander. You're not concentrating.'

Hugh felt sudden outrage at this lecture, fury that what should have been a perfect day was being soured. He made to snap back up the hill but Aaron had turned away, leaving him gazing at his back. After a few moments Hugh turned to his dog.

'Fetch it down there,' he said. 'Fetch the bird.'

Fi rushed down the hill until she crossed the scent of the woodcock where she tumbled to a stop, and in a swift meander retrieved and rushed back to Hugh. He knelt once again. 'Dead,' he said, quietly pocketing the little body.

They went on into the icy morning, each pushing through his own thickets, forty yards apart, a brooding silence growing physical between them. Once in a while Fi would dislodge a bird from hiding-places close to the icy pools of water that dotted the land. The woodcock would explode into the thick woods, weaving through branches, followed by a spread of pellets that wreaked noisy havoc in the trees ahead. Hugh alleviated his irritation by slipping back into his love of this shooting, revelling in its immediacy. When Fi arrived with a dead bird, he dropped it into his pocket without looking at the body. Above him Aaron walked forward to retrieve a bird from where it had been caught in a branch, and Hugh thought back to the previous night and Becky's curiosity.

She had sat looking at him, her head resting on one long-fingered hand, and had asked him about his childhood with Aaron. Finding himself increasingly uncomfortable in his attempts to explain his friend, Hugh had suggested they go and find him. She had grimaced, her interest roused only when a telephone call to Lochanthrain revealed that Aaron had gone to see Mac, her change of mind making Hugh smile. 'You're quite taken with the idea of Mac, aren't you?'

'I have little experience of hermits,' she said.

They had taken her car and driven through Huil and into the north glen, the night clear, the village lights fading behind them. The icy moon shivered light onto the Three Great Mountains so that they appeared to hang oppressive and ethereal above the earth. She had driven slowly, growing silent.

Soon they had swung up by the edge of the loch and passed the entrance of Lochanthrain, two great stone eagles sitting on top of the pillars that held the filigreed wrought-iron gates, the castle's lights flickering through the trees. Then the landscape grew desolate, rising evenly and treeless, the moon playing on the water. For a moment she had rested her hand on his knee, before a corner forced her to change gear.

The separate shores of the loch had pulled themselves into a thin yet powerful stream that intercepted then accompanied the road through a great cut between the high peaks. The one-lane tarmacadam strip wound steeply up into a pass, giant boulders hanging on the edges, under which they made their ascent until they had crested a lip. The flatness of the high moor spread out, the stream now close to its source. Snow pockets hung in the recesses of the slopes to either side, and as the road looked icy Hugh had suggested they drive with care, but she had already slowed further, her eyes wandering over the glacier-whipped landscape.

'He lives up here?'

'Higher yet.'

'On his own?'

'Yes.'

The road pulled through the pass in a long, shallow curve, marked only by a small cairn two-thirds of the way along its length. 'Here.' He had pointed out a track that led into the darkness, ice filling its gravel depths.

She had picked her way up the track, adjusting to his occasional suggestions, the gears straining as the way steepened into sharp bends, the Maserati clawing at the frozen stone. Overhead, the second of the Great Mountains had reached out as they continued into its belly, crossing the Bruch burn with a rattle on the log bridge and pulling up beside Aaron's pick-up. There had been no lights in the croft.

'Eerie place,' she had said, stepping out and looking at him over the roof of the car. 'It's so cold. Why would he want to live up here?'

'Solitude.'

'Surely Mac didn't build it?'

'A mine. They used to mine magnesium and zinc here. This is where the miners stayed.' He had knocked on the door.

The trees thinned then ended at a wall, Hugh following its course to intercept Aaron. The sun now dappled the ground under the branches and the air tasted cool in its freshness. Fi appeared at his feet, steaming slightly, before rushing off to investigate the wall. Aaron arrived just as a rabbit broke cover and, with a smooth swing, ended the creature's bid for its burrow, Fi tumbling over the body, grabbing it and bounding back.

'Nice,' Hugh said.

'How did you do?'

'Four, including your one.'

'Four?' Aaron sniffed. 'I must have heard at least nine shots.'

Hugh shrugged. 'You?'

'Six, including the one you've got.' Aaron ran his hand down his face, grimaced and looked up the hill. 'I shouldn't have had a go at you.'

Hugh didn't reply, preferring not to push his friend but allowing the apology to hang in the air between them.

'That's the eel's croft, isn't it?' Aaron asked.

Hugh looked at Alfie's cottage and its surrounding small-holding. 'The charmer himself.'

'You seen him lately?'

Hugh thought about it. 'Not since the games, I don't think. Remember, he judged the casting competition. But I saw his wife – I was in the post office the other day.'

Aaron seemed to consider the information, and Hugh followed his stare. The croft was tucked away, surrounded by an impressive garden suffering from the first frosts but still under careful cultivation. The house itself was new, covered in pebbledash, an older black-house behind it in an area given over to some sheep, a small flock of chickens and a large sow. As they watched Alfie emerged from the front door of the house, stepped into his car, waited for his collie to jump in over him, and drove away. Aaron's attention stayed on the croft as Hugh tapped his arm and handed over a hip flask. He took a slug and, without turning his head, handed the flask back. Hugh took a draught and screwed the top back on.

'Bastard needs taught a lesson,' said Aaron.

Hugh didn't say anything: his friend's mood seemed

set to remain unfathomable. He decided to humour him. 'What are you planning?'

Aaron finally broke from staring at the croft. 'I'm not sure, but let's go and have a look around.'

Hugh called Fi to heel and they turned north towards the croft, Aaron leading, picking out a path through vegetation now mottled by sun-stroked light and icy shadow. Hugh walked for ten paces before he asked what Alfie had done.

'You saw him at the games,' said Aaron, continuing to walk. 'He wanted me to lose, he mocked me in front of the crowd. Why should I put up with that?'

Hugh thought this over, trying to work it out. 'Because he thinks you're a hoity-toity wanker?' he asked, hoping to break Aaron out of his sulk. When his friend didn't say anything he added, 'And because he'd be right?'

Aaron kept walking.

Hugh held the barrel of his shotgun in the palm of his right hand, stock slung back across his shoulder. He said nothing more and Fi, sensing the requirement of obedience, hung close to his heel.

Hugh had stood on top of a small hill outside Mac's cottage while Becky held herself tightly against the cold, shouting for his friend. He had felt uncomfortable as he yelled at the cliffs: he had sensed Aaron's proximity and it had upset him. Against Becky's protestations he had insisted they wait for Mac and Aaron in the croft. Hugh used the moonlight to find matches and light a lantern, while Becky looked over the clutter of the poacher's life.

Aaron and Hugh now crawled up against the cover of the wall bordering the croft, Aaron lifting his eyes to a break where some rocks had fallen away. Hugh turned his back against the stone, shotgun on the ground, holding Fi's ears in his hands and scratching where the soft flesh met skull.

'There's nobody there.' Aaron checked his watch. 'She'll be at the post office for a while yet.'

Hugh continued to pet the dog. 'We're trespassing by being here, you know,' he said. 'This isn't my land any more. And we're armed.'

Aaron went back to the gap. 'Come on,' he said, climbing over. 'Leave the dog and the guns here.'

'What are you going to do?'

'Come on.' His tone displayed irritation.

Hugh sighed, attached Fi to her lead and tied her to a root. He stood and looked out over the croft. The house was now end-on, only twenty yards off. There was one window in the closest wall, the room beyond dark. The garden was beautifully landscaped, paths snaking away between the bushes and borders where flowers would rise come spring. Further off the pig stood in its fenced-off pen, regarding them with little interest. Hugh climbed over the wall, watching Aaron jog away along a path heading towards the house. He noticed that the shark's tooth was now between his finger and thumb.

Hugh walked after him. He felt his nerves warm him, the ticklishness of being on somebody else's ground, but he had decided that, on this of all days, he didn't want Aaron to feel he was letting him down. He wanted no arguments: he was so desperate to boast about the previous night.

He followed the path around the house and found his friend in the garden shed, running his hand along the well-ordered shelves.

'Sodium chlorate,' Aaron said, laughing, his mood suddenly new. 'Perfect.' He picked up the container and showed it to Hugh. When Hugh smiled obediently, Aaron pulled a bucket from the bottom shelf and pushed past, kneeling down at a tap-stand that rose beside the house. 'You're keeping a lookout, aren't you?'

Hugh checked the surrounding landscape for movement. Only the livestock looked back. He wondered what Becky would make of this. 'If you're planning on doing what I think you're going to do, then it's Mrs Cameron who is going to be upset,' he said. 'She's the one who does most of the gardening.'

'She's as bad as he is.'

Hugh grimaced.

'But then again, I suppose we could do something to the sheep as well.' Aaron was looking over at the pen.

'No,' Hugh said quickly. 'Do what you are going to do so that we can get out of here.'

Aaron stood up. 'What *we*'re doing, Hugh. *We*.'

He had emptied half the container of sodium chlorate crystals into the bucket and poured just enough water in so that they dissolved. He nodded towards the front of the house and began to walk, Hugh following until they reached the front porch. Casually Aaron emptied the bucket over the branches and roots of four big rose bushes that stood around the front steps. As he shook out the last drops he grinned at Hugh. 'I don't think they'll be winning any prizes next year,' he said.

Hugh stood looking at the sun-warmed earth absorbing the poison as Aaron went off to wash out the bucket and return everything to its place. He felt he should be appalled, but, rather, he found his thoughts wandering to Becky as she had stood studying an old sketch on Mac's wall in which an African pulled a gold chariot through the streets of Edinburgh. He had told Becky that it was James VI's chariot and that Mac was a direct descendant of the man in the picture. When she had scoffed he had shown her a pair of dark-barrelled duelling pistols, the surfaces hard, oily and utilitarian, one word, 'Seruant', scripted on the hexagonal barrels. His eyes focused on

133

the last of the poison seeping into the earth around the rose bushes and he imagined the name Seruant traced in the soil, before shaking his head and laughing to himself as Aaron returned.

'Aaron, tell me where you were when we came looking for you last night.' He was aware that he suddenly sounded tired.

Aaron inhaled, equally weary. 'Butchering a stag,' he said. 'We were in the mine with a stag but because that bird of yours was there, Mac wouldn't let me tell you. You know how he is about poaching – there's a good reason he hasn't been caught yet.'

Hugh had turned towards his friend. 'She wouldn't have told anybody. Who has she to tell?'

Aaron raised his palms. 'Look, Mac wouldn't have it, what can I tell you?' The statement was an end, final. 'What do you reckon to this?' He pointed proudly to the roses.

'I think it's a shitty thing to do,' Hugh said evenly, looking across. He had tried to make it sound non-judgemental.

'What's wrong with you?' said Aaron, suddenly agitated. 'Don't you get it? It's you and me against them. It's you and me against all of them.'

They looked at each other and Hugh, feeling more weary by the moment, turned and walked towards the woods. He could almost hear Aaron sag.

'So she's a good fuck, then?'

Hugh stopped. The question stripped away all other thoughts. He swung round, eyes bright. 'Mate,' he said conspiratorially, 'it was fucking fantastic. Let me tell you what she did last night.'

EIGHT

The shed door blew in and she turned, smiling at Hugh, who stood dripping under its mantle. Behind him the gale flicked leaves, sticks and rubbish across the yard; the air, carrying its full weight of water, swirled round and in, dousing him again, breaking over his shoulders and beating down on the floor.

'You should come in,' she said.

He turned and heaved the door closed, shutting out the tempest that raged on, hammering at the tin roof, assaulting the creosoted walls. Dim lights cut through the haze of dust thrown up by the wind's incursions and Hugh moved through it, swinging his sodden Akubra against his long coat. Dusty hair tied up, she lifted grimy hands to his face and they kissed. 'I missed you.' She was opening his jacket to see if he had been soaked. 'Wasn't it dangerous, riding over in this weather?'

Hugh put his hat down on the workbench and took off his coat. His legs were dark where they had been exposed to the rain. He kissed her again. 'It was worth any danger.'

She smiled, teasing him as he tried to kiss her once more, moving her head to the side so his lips slipped by her cheek and raising her eyes to his. 'I really did miss you, you know.'

He moved towards her and she slipped herself up so that she sat on the workbench, then took him in her arms.

His attention expanding outwards from Becky, Hugh looked about him. 'What were you doing in here?' His eyes passed over the workshop machinery, the circular and band saws, the welding kit, the lathes and assorted tools. Bits of metal and wood were scattered everywhere.

'Playing with the toys,' she said.

He sat up on the bench and looked at his leg. With great care he pulled a sliver of wood from the surface of his skin, wincing as it came. He examined the splinter then looked over Becky's semi-nakedness. '*Penthouse* meets Pirelli,' he said.

Becky frowned and hopped off the bench, adjusting her clothing, her expression changing as she ran her fingers through a drift of sawdust. 'I would have thought this would appeal to a country boy like you, all this machinery . . .' She tossed a leftover lump of pine into a bin.

Hugh sorted out his own clothing. 'It was no criticism,' he said, returning to the assessment. 'I particularly like the sawdust in your hair.'

'Hick chic,' she said. 'What do you think?' She shook her hair, the flakes falling away as she sauntered through the tables and machines in a sole-of-the-foot walk she had used since he arrived.

'Hick chick, certainly.'

She threw a gauging look over her shoulder, a thin-eyed smile.

Hugh watched her, bemused at how engaged she seemed. He hoped this meant a growing affection for him but then he recalled the first kiss on that rock a month before and wondered if she wasn't perhaps affected by storms. Following her, he rubbed the splinter wound through his sodden clothes.

She turned and presented him with a length of wood lathed into a series of curves.

'You did this?' he asked, and she nodded.

'What is it?' he asked.

'It's a start,' she said.

The lathed wood looked like a chair-leg. He widened his eyes to show how impressed he was. 'It's only a very small step from here to furniture to who knows? Religion, even,' he said. 'I mean, Jesus must have started like this.'

They were very close to each other.

'Careful. I'm a believer.'

He reached forward, using her necklace to pull her lips gently to his. 'Feeling guilty?' he whispered.

She pushed him away. 'I think we should get you out of those wet clothes.'

They walked across the room, Hugh laying her craftsmanship on the bench while telling her about Sandancer's skittish behaviour on the way across. 'She loves this stuff,' he said. 'You'd think an Arab would hate water.'

He opened the door and was nearly blown back into the room, the driving rain blurring the view, the few trees in the yard bent over so far they failed to spring back between gusts.

Holding each other, they rushed into the open space, and by the time they crashed through the door of the farmhouse their faces were streaming with icy water, Becky gasping as she leaned against the wall, sinking into the coats that hung from a roughly made rack. 'This place is going to be the death of me,' she cried. She shook her head, water dripping to the floor, and turned to go into the kitchen, making for the range where she put her back to the heat, leaning over to move the kettle onto the hotplate.

Hugh joined her.

'So how did you get on yesterday?' she asked.

They had spoken the night before by telephone but only briefly, and now Hugh made some quick calculations about how much he wanted to say. He decided to be coy. She would think Aaron's adventures against the Camerons childish.

'Aaron shot a bird over my head after I missed a right and left.'

'One each seems reasonable.'

He explained the rarity of the opportunity but she shrugged, unimpressed, uninterested. 'So did he tell you where he and Mac had got to?'

He thought about this too, aware that he was being watched.

'Apparently they were hiding.' A quick decision. 'They were butchering a poached stag and didn't want you to know. It takes a while to be trusted around here.'

She looked away to adjust the kettle. 'I'm glad I didn't see it, really. That sort of thing is a little too rural.' She paused. 'I'm going to put some food on. Why don't you go and run a bath?' She threw him a clean towel from the drying-rack hanging overhead.

He was out of the door when he heard her ask where Mac and Aaron had been hiding. He pretended not to hear.

He was submerged under a sea of bubbles when she walked in and handed him a whisky. He took the glass, sipped and put it on a chair beside the tub while she eased herself onto the edge of the ceramic, bubbles sticking to her. She leaned across to look at the bottles, her fingers behind her, resting on the effervescence.

'What did you use?'

'A little of everything.'

She read out the titles on the bottles – Vivacity, Surfeit, Exhaustion, Seclusion, Mal de Siècle, Desire, Fervour, Regret, Ailing – and then sniffed the air. 'Could be a

138

plot. Henry James, perhaps.' She looked down at him, lifting a handful of the bubbles onto his head, adding, 'He's a writer.'

Hugh's mouth opened in indignation. 'I did go to school, you know,' he said.

She laughed, leaned down and kissed his cheek, his eyes following hers. When she sat up again she frowned and looked around. 'So, I take it you can stay tonight? You're not planning to go back out into that.' She nodded towards the wall.

He realized he was pouting and she laughed again. 'Come on, I'll be all girlfriendy and make you supper.'

'Aaron was talking about going to look at the ducks this evening, but there's not a chance of that in this weather. Tonight I'm all yours.'

She lifted some more foam, put it in his hair then drew her hand across his face as she stood up.

'You've got foam all over your bum,' he said.

She wiped it off as she walked away, then Hugh heard music on the stereo. He sipped his whisky and sank back into the bath.

He lay among the bubbles and thought about calling Aaron, worried that despite the weather's preclusion of shooting his friend might suggest a trip to the pub. He scooped up two mounds of bubbles as if to weigh his choices. He had spent that morning – those short, cold, saturated few hours – moving sheep and cattle off the low country in case the river rose into flood. The water level had been high enough to force Hugh to use the bridge when he had ridden across, and he knew it was likely that he and Becky would soon be cut off. When the river broke its banks the farm building sat on a small island in the middle of the floodplain. They would be cut off from the world – the shepherd lived further up the small glen and would be stranded as well, but on high ground. Hugh warmed to the thought, conjuring up

Becky as worried and himself as the brave man, all the while knowing that the water had never yet come into the yard. He recalled a flood that had cut off Shiloch for four days. Four days. He thought he could cope with that.

He slipped below the waterline, his raised hands the last of him to submerge, all the while laughing the ease of his decision into the water.

When he emerged he took another sip of whisky then washed off the sweat that the heat had caused to form on his brow. Stepping out of the tub, water falling across the floor, he took the towel and rubbed himself down before wrapping it around his waist and walking through to the kitchen. When Becky turned and looked at him with an easy appreciation, he drew himself up to her appraisal but then she walked past him and down the corridor, returning with a floral dressing-gown that she threw over his shoulder. Despite the cold beyond the walls, the house was warm and he put on the robe and took the towel back to the bathroom.

Back in the kitchen Becky lifted a pan from the hob. Hugh opened a bottle of wine and set the table. They sat close to each other to eat, at first quiet, listening to the sound of the storm against the house, and then he asked if she would return to shipbroking. She said no, she didn't think so. 'I got into it just after leaving school. I was a secretary at first, during the recession, it was the only job I could find, but I got promoted so I never got out. So many of these jobs that sound interesting are quite mundane. When I get back I think I'm going to be looking for something else.' She picked at her food. 'I enjoyed the travelling, though.'

He asked her about the places she had been, a continuous stream of questions about the cultures she spoke of. She answered with small stories and smaller descriptions and, quickly growing aware of his frustration with

140

her generalizations, switched the conversation back to how she felt about the end of her career. 'If I look back all I can be proud of is that the British never ran short of rice, or some such.' She looked into her risotto.

'I think it's a fine achievement,' said Hugh.

They ate quietly until he felt her studying him. She was slowly turning the end of the fork on her plate. Her thumb had bruised where she had hit it with a hammer during her experiments in the workshop.

'You should travel, you know. You've got that in you. I can tell.'

'Would you come with me?'

She smiled. 'I'm just a tourist. I think you're the traveller. You should wander the world.'

'I haven't got a passport.'

'You should get one. I think you'd look good with a backpack, out there exploring distant shores.'

He thought about it, wondering how much to admit. 'I'd like to. All those places. But, you know, it's difficult . . . the farm, Aaron.' He stopped, not quite sure why he had mentioned Aaron, now embarrassed that he had.

Becky leaned back. She touched her thumbs together and Hugh found himself looking at her fingers again. He was aware that he had blushed slightly. He tried to think what to say, but she spoke first. 'Well, if you are so inseparable maybe you should go together.'

He leaned back and laughed, unconvincingly. 'It's not like that, it's just what you're used to. And anyway he hates leaving Huil, even on small trips. We went to a sheep sale in the autumn, just after you and I met. I wish he hadn't bothered, he whined so much.'

Becky was using the opening she had made. 'Then he demands your attention.'

Hugh laughed. Again he was aware that it sounded false. 'No. He's incredibly self-reliant. He has the land.

It's all he really needs; he's like the old farmers, he takes the idea of land to a whole new level . . .'

'Are you sure he's so self-reliant? Look at the two of you, both only children, growing up in the wilderness, having to rely on each other for all those only-child needs.' Becky was laughing at him.

'He's not an only child.'

'Oh.' She looked disappointed.

'He has two brothers, but they're both much older than him. He hardly knows them. One is in America, a banker of some kind, the other works in London and I think is quite a nice bloke but he never returns home. He lives with an Asian woman and Aaron's mother refuses to have her in the house.'

'Hence Aaron's friendship with Mac?'

'No, Mac would appeal to Aaron whatever colour he was. Mac is a bit of an outlaw and he's pretty unpitying and, well, he hangs out on top of a mountain, which is kind of cool. Still, I don't think his mother's fury at the friendship hurts.'

Becky regarded him quietly, head on the heels of her hands. 'Well it sounds as if he is effectively an only child.'

Hugh shrugged. 'I don't think it's that easy. It's a pretty weird family. His grandmother got eaten by a shark while fishing off the coast of Australia.'

Becky, who had been picking at her food again, stopped and looked up. 'A shark?'

'She was a great fisherwoman. This is his dad's mother, of course. She'd fish all over the world – the Arctic salmon runs in Alaska, tarpon in the Florida Keys, trout in Zimbabwe – and she left her amazing collection of flies to Aaron even though he had not been born. She bequeathed them to her son's last child, which is kind of spooky when you think about it. Aaron idolizes her. He's got her journals. It's practically all he's ever read but he knows them off by heart.'

Becky poured more wine. 'She was eaten?'

'She was on this big marlin boat down in Australia, which belonged to a client of the family company – the Hardings made all their money in textiles – and she had hooked a great white shark and fought it unaided for five and a half hours until she managed to get it alongside. The crew began to turn the thing round so that they could pull it backwards through the water and drown it. They got gaffs into it and she unstrapped herself from the fighting chair and went over to the side to have a look. The newspaper reports from the time are in the back of the journal – they're probably exaggerated but they say the shark saw her, broke the gaffs and God knows how many lines, came out of the water and grabbed her, rolling on the edge of the deck, the whatever they are called—'

'The rail?'

'Yeah, it rolled off the rail then disappeared back into the depths with her firmly clamped in its jaws.'

Becky leaned back and whistled.

Hugh grinned. 'The thing lost a tooth in the process. Aaron carries it everywhere. He rolls it between his fingers when he's thinking.'

The telephone rang, and Becky got up and went through to the hall. Hugh looked around, then stood up to take the kettle from where it burbled gently on the hotplate. He made coffee for Becky. Although he was in the dressing-gown he felt warm and the storm outside now seemed a protection rather than a threat. He walked through to the hall and gave Becky her mug. He was heading towards the sitting room when she put the phone down. 'That was the shepherd. The river has broken its banks and he was asking if I had enough food. He said he thought the farm buildings would be surrounded by the morning and suggested I might want to go and stay at the hotel, although there is no danger.'

'What did you say?'

'That I was fine for the moment but if I changed my mind I'd call. I didn't tell him you were here, I don't think he approves of our little romance.' She picked up her coffee and was about to join him when the phone rang again. She turned and answered it.

Then: 'Natasha! . . . No, no, it's a fine time, in fact I'm just about to be surrounded by water . . . Yup, the river is rising towards me.' She laughed, then turned and smiled at Hugh, who smiled back and walked into the sitting room, irritated at the intrusion.

He worked on the fire, bringing it back to vibrant life with a mixture of coal and wood from brass buckets on each side. Pleased with his efforts, he settled back into the sofa, picked a copy of a magazine from the floor and flicked through the pictures of the young couples in houses with no paintings. He thought that if he moved to a big city he should like paintings, probably landscapes. As he turned the pages he could hear Becky's voice. 'The autumn was stunning, truly amazing, all these colours you just never see in England, but now it's something else, brass bloody monkeys. Suddenly you knew winter had arrived and since then everything has been moving towards the bleak and black . . . It's going to take a while, though, we've not even hit midwinter yet . . . I hope I'm able to handle it.'

And later: 'No, not even a fucking letter and I'm damned if I'm going to call. Well, I know, but he's such an arse. Yeah, I heard, apparently somebody at his work, an assistant . . . it's such a cliché . . . Well, it's his fucking life and I . . . Yeah, I've heard what he's been saying but I'm not going to respond . . . If he doesn't get why I'm doing this he's more dumb than I thought. Unbelievable but completely typical, he thinks it's because of him . . . No, fuck him, I don't need that . . .

'Of course. Nourishing, I like to think. A bit tougher

144

than Champneys but, well, listen, it's way, way better than therapy. Out here you can really breathe. It really is a whole different place . . . Well, yes, it's dark and cold, but so what? Beautiful too . . . Yeah, well, there might be that too . . . I mean, what do you expect when the river floods and it's dark outside and . . . I'm not telling you, no . . . Yes, he bloody well is in his twenties, who said he was seventeen? . . . No, I'm not telling you but I'll tell you one thing, he's way more mature than fuckwit. Well, and that too. Yes, he's here, of course. In this weather I need someone to protect me, I'm a damsel in dampness . . . Let it rain, I say.' Her laugh crackled like a cough.

And later: 'Well, why don't you? It's really easy to get here, a flight to Inverness . . . Yes, I am aware that the countryside is grubby but it's also beautiful . . . No, there are no wild animals, merely untamed, and I'm working on that . . .

'I'm not really sure what I'm doing for Christmas, apart from coming under heavy pressure from my mother . . . No, I'm coming down, although I think it would be kind of good to ignore the bloody thing up here . . . Well, you don't hear a lot about it, thank God . . . Yeah, I suspect I'll have to go to my mother's first . . . Dad? Oh, he's in Mexico . . . Well, I'd love to go there but Mum would never forgive me and it's such a pain getting confused with one of his girlfriends . . . Yeah, he actually told me the other day that some friend of his had seen my picture on his piano and told him he was losing his ability to discriminate, i.e. I wasn't as pretty as his usual fare . . . Yeah, I know, he actually told me that, told his daughter that she wasn't as good-looking as his mistresses and he's surprised I give him a hard time . . . Yeah, too many little princesses, that's his problem – well, one of them . . .'

And later: 'Please phone more often, it's not like I'm on the moon . . . I am still alive and you can tell the

145

others they should call me once in a while at least until they hear for certain I've frozen to death . . . And I love you too, big kisses . . . night.'

When Becky came into the sitting room she leaned over the back of the sofa and kissed Hugh, smiling down, her hair falling onto his face. 'That was my friend Natasha. Apparently you are the subject of much discussion in London.'

'Oh?'

'But I'm afraid you've been reduced to a seventeen-year-old.'

Hugh smiled, not knowing what to say. He eased himself off the sofa. 'I think I should ring my father and tell him what's happening, and perhaps I'll call Aaron as well so he won't be too pissed off.'

She nodded and he went into the hallway. He felt small and, as he dialled, tried to shrug off a general anxiety.

The conversation with his father lasted all of two minutes, and the one with Aaron not much more. On dialling Lochanthrain he had been told that Aaron was out, so he called the bar. 'You at Shiloch, then?' Aaron said, when he came on. 'How's the water?'

Hugh told him it had broken the banks and now covered the road. Aaron offered to come and get him in the pick-up, but Hugh said it was better if he stayed with Rebecca, given that the farm would soon be surrounded.

'Fair enough.' The voice was level.

'I'll see you when the waters recede and the doves return,' Hugh said, but Aaron had already handed the phone to Gus Houston.

'So, Noah, you got enough beer to see you through?'

'We're fine, Gus, thanks.'

'Well, you be careful of those English girls, they carry disease.'

He returned to Becky and found her sitting on the arm

of the sofa, waiting for him. All at once he felt her warmth and softness include him, as if she was an alien core of humanity in this cold, grim place whose very boundaries began at the edge of her presence, extending to those icy people out in their icy world. Even Aaron, he felt, his oldest and only real friend, understood that coldness and had adopted it as if it were warmth. As Hugh looked at Becky, he imagined her as a spark, as he had always imagined Mac, another whose soul lit those icy depths with flames, but in Mac's case it was a passion of no compassion, an active loathing for what he saw as a society of the weak. Hugh stopped and felt his head cloud. Then she was there, her arms around him, concerned, asking if he was OK. He looked at her and smiled. 'I'm glad it's just you and me,' he said. 'I don't know what it is that I haven't got, what I'm missing, but with you here I feel better. I'm glad you're here. I'm very, very glad.'

Dawn arrived late, a greyness encroaching over the eastern edge of the glen a little before nine, the wind still throwing rain against the bedroom window as he sought her among the layers of coloured materials that fell haphazardly between the old wooden bedsteads. They made love quietly in the half-light of their own consciousness then slept longer until finally Hugh slipped from the bed and looked out of the window. Water covered the land from one escarpment to the other, its surface ruffled, its bulk waiting to be pulled back into the power of the main river almost half a mile away. The farm buildings were now an island with twenty feet or so of boundary before the water began, the rutted track leading out into oblivion. Gusts brought the occasional flurry of water through the yard, drowning the view across the valley floor. Hugh wrapped Becky's dressing-gown tightly around himself and, tiptoeing against the

147

chill of the floor, made his way down to the kitchen to make tea.

When he returned Becky was standing where he had been minutes before, a long pale-green towel wrapped around her. She took the offered mug, shook her head at the view, then turned to kiss him and suggested they go back to bed.

Come afternoon they were hungry. Hugh dressed to check on Sandancer, and Becky came along to see the watery limits of their new world. They emerged wrapped against the weather. The rain had died away and small arrows of light pierced the rolling grey mat above their heads. The ground was muddy, and by the time they reached the barn it was as if their boots were in fetters. Hugh opened the door, scraping the heavy gunk away onto the frame. Inside, the air smelt musty but warm and still. Sandancer looked at them from the door of her stable, tutting at their approach. Becky went up first and offered an apple, which was swiftly taken into the velvet of the horse's muzzle. Sandancer made to sniff for more, a tactic preceding a lunge with her teeth. Becky put her hands behind her back and the mare whinnied and shuffled her hoofs in the straw. Hugh walked up with half a bale of hay and Becky undid the latch to let him in. 'Are you sure you want to do this? She seems in a bad temper.'

'She won't hurt me.'

Hugh pushed his way in and Sandancer crashed around, slug pupil on her master. He stood until she calmed then walked past, dumped the hay in the feeder, turned and went head to head with the horse. Hugh didn't say anything, just refused to move when Sandancer attempted to pull her nose up. Then she backed off and turned to the hay. Hugh walked out, patting her on the rump, to which she replied with a small kick, aimed to miss. 'She gets like this when her blood-sugar levels are low,' he said. 'Do you have any oats?'

Their task complete, they took a turn round the buildings, checking on the small flocks of hens and ducks, the latter peering warily out at the great expanse of water from the safety of their small pond. They collected eggs and drove a peg into the ground at the water's edge to check for any rise or fall. Hugh said that a lot more water would have to arrive to flood their island, and Becky, looking out towards the mountains, said she believed it might be clearing.

They watched a heavy shower break over the furthest edges of the flooded waters, stirring up the surface in little eddies as it rolled towards them.

'I'm not convinced,' Hugh replied.

They ran, clutching their eggs close, only just making it to the door of the house when the squall burst across the yard. Becky was bent double, holding the eggs to her belly. 'Running through mud,' she gasped, laughing.

'It's good for your legs.'

Hugh began to cook an omelette, taking eggs and breaking them into a bowl, while Becky collapsed, exhausted, onto one of the kitchen chairs. He raided the fridge for other ingredients, aware that he was being watched from the table. When he was finished, he laid down the two filled plates and handed her a fork. She tasted it as he watched and she looked at him, impressed. 'Good,' she said. 'This is really good. You can cook.'

He smiled, and poured himself tea. 'One of the side effects of matricide,' he said.

They ate fast and cleaned their plates. As Hugh stood up to take them, Becky spoke. 'I've heard you make that joke before. Am I supposed to laugh?'

He had expected this, had already regretted his comment. 'I'm sorry,' he said, taking the plates to the sink where he began to wash them.

After a while she spoke again. 'Well, why do it?'

He shrugged, but said nothing.

'Do you feel guilty?'

He gave a short laugh, shook his head but did not turn.

'I suppose you don't want to talk about it?'

'I'm sorry.'

'You keep it all locked up. We're sleeping together. If you are not able to tell me . . .'

He heard her sigh. The omelette pan he was holding was dripping onto the floor – he had turned to look at her. 'It happened at birth, it was eclampsia,' he said. 'I think I was under the culpable age, I don't think it was my fault.'

'Obviously, but you must think if you hadn't been born . . .'

He didn't flinch: it was nothing to the cracks Aaron occasionally made, and he watched her eyes fall away from his.

'I'm sorry,' she said. 'I shouldn't have said that. I wasn't thinking.'

Hugh was feeling the usual womb-like darkness envelop his thoughts, sweeping in like a fog of blankness, meaninglessness, nothing and nothing again. He wondered if he should explain but how could he explain this emptiness, that this complete lack of feeling was all the feeling he had ever had about his mother's death?

Becky was on her feet now and close, holding him in an awkward embrace, his arm still stretched out with the frying-pan. He pulled away, put down the pan and lit a cigarette.

Her face showed sympathy, concealing puzzlement. He saw it and realized he loved her. 'That's OK,' he said, glad that this would mark the end of the conversation.

After building up the fire, they dropped cushions and rugs in front of it and opened a bottle of wine.

Cross-legged, they faced each other and played cards, letting time run by, hardly talking except to laugh and throw the occasional accusation of cheating. Hugh noticed that since her arrival her face had relaxed, the outdoor lifestyle, the peaty water and pure air were softening her, working the edges and pressures away. With his thoughts, desire came, rising in his belly, and soon he had crossed the floor to her.

Wrapped in blankets, they sat close together, their backs against the sofa, legs intertwined, feet towards the fire. On the other side of the windows rain still fell and night had returned but the wind came from the west and could not be heard here in the lee.

He told her he thought he loved her, and she turned her head and looked at him, eyebrows raised until her face fell to a frown. 'Do you?'

He smiled to himself and when he spoke there was an edge to his voice, which he attempted to make sound of sadness. 'But you still love this man in London.'

They were very close together, the firelight illuminating the soft down that was her hairline. 'You think so?'

'I think you were talking about being able to express your feelings a little earlier.'

'I can. I have a therapist . . .'

'Therapist?'

Now she had one arm on the seat of the sofa. 'You've got a problem with therapy?'

'Satan took the rapist and remoulded him as Therapist, a plunderer of women.'

Her head recoiled and she laughed, short and sharp. 'What?'

'Our local Free Church minister, the Rod of God, wrote that in his religious column in the Huil newsletter – I think it was after Diana died. It caused a huge fuss.'

'You've got a minister called the Rod of God?'

Hugh nodded. 'But you were telling me how you are still in love with someone else,' he said.

'No, I wasn't.' She picked at a small blemish on his neck. 'I can tell you, though, that I have an affection deficit in my life. Of this I am reliably and expensively informed. Personally I think it's a lot of garbage and that's why I've come up here, to prove that I'm self-reliant.' She examined her fingers to see what she had scraped away then looked him straight in the eye. 'And then you came along and fucked it all up. So, Hugh, go figure, because I don't know what it all means.'

'That you don't love me.'

She snorted. 'Well,' she said, 'if you love me and I have an affection deficit I think we're a perfect match, don't you?'

'You're mocking me.'

She looked away. 'Who knows? Maybe I do love you.'

'And this guy in London.'

'Forget about the guy in London.'

Their supper was brief, eaten in the sitting room, and after the plates had been left to the side Becky asked Hugh to read to her, making him choose from the books she brought from the south, books that she said she had been meaning to read for years. Hugh, who had not had to read out loud since his schooldays, chose Scott and struggled through Frank Osbaldstone's trip to Northumberland until Becky tired of the story and chose from the lighter reading left for tenants by the farm's owners. They settled on *Forbidden Fruit* by Jessica Haddow and Hugh found himself in equal difficulties with Chicory Lane, a firm-bodied American teacher involved in sexual meandering with a dark-eyed Colombian drug-runner called Calypso. This too came to an end when Becky decided one act was physically impossible and decided to try it out on Hugh.

It was even later and they were sitting nursing mugs.

'I'm impressed,' Becky said. 'Top marks for stamina.'

'Why, thank you,' he said. 'What about skill and daring?'

'Daring?' She considered this. 'Daring I don't know about but, with a bit of practice, I think we can enter the top ten in sensitivity. And you seem to be improving as far as inquisitiveness is concerned.'

'Thanks. Feel free to be as condescending as you like.'

She smiled and reached across to touch him but he jerked away. 'Don't flinch when I touch you.'

'I'm in pain.'

She laughed, and the sound made him flinch again.

Later, in bed and long after midnight, he asked her about her father.

'He lives in Mexico.'

When Hugh didn't say anything, she went on, 'He's a minor diplomat in the embassy there, cultural attaché, although he does bugger all except pretend to know his way around fine wines and cigars and try to sleep with, well, anyone who'll take him.'

'Is that where you grew up? Mexico?'

'No, all over the place but mainly in Angola. He was based there for a long time.'

'As cultural attaché?'

She laughed, the darkness holding the sound, making it distant. Their feet were touching but their heads apart. 'No, he was interested in the diamonds. I think he was some kind of spook – he always made a big deal of secrecy. He'd always shout at my mother when she fronted him up about being out overnight, saying she didn't understand that the nature of his job meant that he couldn't tell her anything without putting all of us in danger. The trouble was that even I could smell the women on him. My mother started smoking small cigarillos just to mask the smell. Although he smoked Havanas himself, he said he found her habit disgusting.'

She paused and then continued, 'Do you know anything about Angola?' Her voice was lost in the darkness.

'Lots of landmines.'

'It should be a paradise but it's been at war for ever. The left-wing control the oil and the right-wing the diamonds, and they both sell them to the West in return for weapons. I think my father's job was to make sure the balance that kept the war going was never upset.'

'That must have been horrible.'

'Not really. Angola has beaches to die for. But my father's womanizing became an embarrassment, and there might even have been a small internal Foreign Office scandal about some lost diamonds and he got pulled out of there and sent to Mexico. He told my mother she couldn't come and set her up in a small house in north London with very little money. So it has been ever since.'

'And how is she?'

'My mother just complains that nobody cares about her and has learned to live just above the poverty line, mainly because I give her money or at least I did until I came up here. I haven't been able to send her the cheques lately and now she's accusing me of throwing away my life. I managed to convince my father to take up the slack while I sort myself out and so . . .' here Becky put a hand out to Hugh '. . . a peace of sorts reigns.'

'I'm sorry,' he said, moving closer. She ran her hand through his hair and he fell asleep.

He woke late to a calm world, Becky lying beside him, the light from the window resting on her face, the slight lines showing around her eyes, the small scar in the eyebrow, her breathing slow and quiet. He had slept without dreams and felt himself emerging from the comfort of the depths. As he lay still, he found himself thinking over the previous day: his new closeness to another, which gave him a feeling of uneasiness. He thought about Becky and felt a desire to do her no wrong. She had been hurt and the jagged edges of her humour added to her perfection and he felt in himself the ability to make it better. Even the mother living in north London seemed somehow closer to glamour, nearer something he wanted, something that existed beyond the reach of his knowledge. Mexico and Angola: once again he felt the desire to escape the claustrophobia of his life; the awful prospect of farming the same earth he would see turned over year after year. He thought of his father's eyes on him, their recognition of his unhappiness, but his father was unable to offer any solution, never having seen anything but this place, his own honeymoon a fishing-trip to a nearby river.

Becky seemed tired of London, and perhaps she would take him abroad. She had the strength to take him out of this eternal orbit around Huil. He could be part of the famed diaspora, he thought; no more MacIntyre Junior of Huil, instead Hugh MacIntyre of the world. He smiled at the thought and at the woman next to him in bed, bringing one hand from under the covers to lift away a strand of hair that had fallen over her face. Then he leaned across and gently kissed her forehead and she made a small unconscious complaint before settling.

He eased himself from the bed and tiptoed to the window, pulling on her dressing-gown. The sun burned thinly from the horizon, its power as yet too weak to turn the sky blue. The great waters that spread away from their small island were calm, the wind had died and all the world seemed to be holding its breath as if waiting for either reprieve or apocalypse. A rooster crowed into the icy dawn, its voice as sharp as glass, and in the far distance to the south his eye snagged on a small movement, merely a dot in the sky circling at the head of the glen. He watched the lazy flight of the eagle until he shivered from the encroaching cold.

Hugh felt optimism rise with the winter sun and padded softly to the bathroom, where he urinated, wincing at the tenderness between his fingers. Even in this weather it was unlikely that the river would drain in time for him to ride out come darkness. The thought conjured up Aaron and he tried to remember the last time they had spent three days apart and he doubted they ever had. He turned back towards the room but stopped to brush his teeth. He felt a sudden desire to see his friend. Becky rolled as he slipped into the warmth of the bed, laying one hand over him, and he remained in this uncomfortable position for a while so as not to disturb her. Finally he relaxed into an embrace and slept again.

When he next woke it was to apocalypse. His eyes jerked open, looking up to where the sound of the heavens collapsing beat down on the house. Becky was bolt upright, hands to her ears, terror in her eyes, and Hugh turned towards the window. The wind had returned as a tornado, its force throwing dirt, rubbish and foliage into the sky.

Becky was screaming at him as he tried to come full awake. The thumping fell heavily on his hungover head.

Then a voice from above drowned the heavy beat, a Liverpudlian accent bursting through the roof beams. 'Hello, Shiloch farmhouse. Are you there, Shiloch farmhouse?'

Despite the noise, Hugh rolled into the covers, snorting with laughter in Becky's lap.

'Hello, Shiloch farmhouse. This is Her Majesty's Royal Navy.'

'The Royal Navy?' Becky was shouting. 'What the fuck is the Royal Navy doing above the house?'

'It's a helicopter,' Hugh yelled back. 'They've come to rescue us.'

Becky looked confused as Hugh threw on his clothes, the sound of the chopper easing slightly as it moved into a hover above the yard.

'Do we need to be rescued?' she shouted.

Hugh, still laughing, rushed out of the door.

He stopped in the hall to grab a jacket and a pair of boots then burst out into the yard, at once sheltering his face from the Sea King's downblast, which, as it now barrelled down into the water, instantly soaked him.

'Hello, Shiloch farmhouser,' the amplified voice greeted him. 'We wish to land. Is the yard clear of movable objects?'

Hugh staggered into the yard, pushing against the blast. He stopped and made violent gestures at the vast pug-nose of the enormous machine. It swivelled round and charged off to a position a couple of hundred yards away where it spun round once more, waiting, watching, reminding Hugh of an over-eager dog. He checked the yard but the storm had already blown it clear of everything that might endanger the rotors. He made the thumbs-up sign and waved the chopper forward before retreating to the shelter of the house. The Sea King rolled in and settled on the dirt, breaking through the crust and sinking a few inches into the mud. A man jumped from the rear hatch and Hugh went to meet him. He was holding a clipboard, which he shifted to his left fist so as to shake hands.

'Flight Sergeant Peachie at your service, sir.' He looked at his sheet. 'You can't be Rebecca Hume? We definitely had one lady all on her own here.' He looked up.

'I'm Hugh MacIntyre, better known as Prince Charming, and you're too late.'

The sergeant, who had dropped his earphones round his neck, grinned. 'Yeah, but I bet you didn't arrive in such style.'

Hugh looked over at the Sea King. 'Yeah, right. So

what's with this anyway? You practically knocked us out of bed.'

They had both turned their backs on the noise of the rotors.

'Bed?' The sergeant looked at his watch. 'It's eleven o'clock.'

'I don't know if you noticed but we're flooded in.' Hugh was feeling a bit hoarse from all the yelling. 'What else should we be doing?'

'What else indeed?' said the sergeant.

Hugh followed the man's gaze to where Becky stood looking on, her long coat held tight but still flapping around her legs. Hugh frowned at the sergeant, who quickly glanced at his board. 'There's still a lot of snow melting up on the mountains so it's unlikely you'll be able to get out today. We thought you might need supplies – we've got milk, bread, eggs and stuff. Oh, and also water. Has your tank flooded?'

'The water comes from up the glen so that's fine, but since you've come we'll take some milk and bread and fags, if you've got any; I'm getting very short.'

'The government's not allowed to give out cigarettes but I brought some along if you don't mind giving me cash for them, or if you're short you can send it by post later. Are you sure you don't need eggs? We've got plenty.'

Hugh pointed across the yard to where all the hens and ducks were hiding from the monstrous apparition.

'You've got ducks?' The sergeant was excited. 'I'm always trying to find duck eggs. I make a soufflé with them and my wife loves it so much that it usually ends in another child. You wouldn't swap a half-dozen for a packet of fags, would you?'

Hugh thought the offer over, mainly because of its oddness, agreed, and the sergeant ran back to the big door of the chopper, returning with a cardboard box.

'Here you go. I've put the smokes in there, a couple of packets, my treat.'

'I'll just give this to Rebecca, hang on.'

Hugh walked back with the box and handed it to her. 'He wants some duck eggs,' he shouted. 'For a soufflé.'

She nodded without comment.

Hugh made his way towards the duck coop, joining up with the sergeant half-way across the yard. It was quieter in the shed.

'Khaki-Campbells,' the sergeant said, still very loud. 'Fantastic.'

'I don't want to appear ungrateful or anything, but don't you guys usually call before you make these mercy flights? It must cost a fortune.' Hugh was on his knees among the huddle of grumpy ducks that objected to his presence in their protected bunker.

'Christ, no,' the sergeant said, from above. 'This is only the third day of floods, so nobody's going to ask for help and this is the only excuse we ever get to have some fun and not stay above the legal limit. Think of it as meeting the people.'

Hugh stood up with the eggs held in his jumper. The sergeant, who had brought an empty carton, began filling each of the little cups.

'So who else is getting the pleasure of a visit?'

The sergeant sighed.

'It's a drag but only four households are cut off. We've still got to go to the shepherd up the glen and to some people over the west. We've already been to see this hermit guy, Seruant – you know, the weird black bloke who lives up in the mountains.'

'Yeah, I know Mac.'

The sergeant finished taking the eggs and closed the box. Then he looked at Hugh. 'To get to him, right, it's real risky.' He waited for Hugh's nod. 'Well, I have to go down on the winch and I get down there and hand him the box and you know what he says?' He gave Hugh a nudge with his fist. 'He asks if we've got any marjoram, says he's run out and can't make a bouquet garni.' He laughed so loudly that the ducks were frightened and huddled deeper into the corners.

'That sounds like Mac,' Hugh said, accepting the open-handed slap on the back.

The sergeant wiped a tear from his eye. 'I said I thought the two of us would get on, and you know what? He gave me some stock. Man, I had a quick taste, it's a killer, never had anything like it in my life.' He paused and lifted the eggs. 'Thanks again, Hugh. If the next one's a boy we'll name him after you.'

'How many have you got?'

'Eight so far.' The sergeant grinned broadly.

They walked back out into the maelstrom. Hugh struggled over to Becky and put his arm round her as the engines began to roar. The sergeant hopped in just as the tyres freed themselves from the gunk. As they rose the amplified voice was back. 'So long, citizens. You have just had a genuine Royal Navy experience. Keep paying the taxes.'

Becky returned to the house, while Hugh fed Sandancer then raided the hen-house for eggs, unhindered by the birds who clustered together, cocking their heads nervously in case the much larger and more fearsome danger should reappear.

When he came into the kitchen, Becky took the eggs and began breaking them into a bowl. Once done she turned to where he sat at the table. 'That was really fucking weird, you know.'

Outside it was one of the rare winter days on which the world is so clear and frosted that it appears unachievably clean. To walk into it, as they did once they had dressed properly, was to enter a land where daydreams might

160

exist. The air seemed certain to shatter as they walked. Hugh took a deep breath, and with the sharpness burning his lungs, a vital feeling for life roared through him.

Becky turned to him, smiled foolishly and began to run, wine bottle in hand, across the grass at the edge of the yard. She stopped and held out her hand, and he joined her for a couple of steps until the two deck-chairs he was holding clattered so much that he let her go on ahead to the grassy edge where the flood lapped the shore.

Hugh set up the deck-chairs while Becky removed the cork from the bottle and produced wine-glasses from her jacket pockets. They were both padded with warm clothing and their breath left white clouds.

Hugh said he thought he might let Sandancer out for a run. He walked over to the shed and entered its twilight. Sandancer peered at him from the stall door. When he reached her, he ran his hand down her face and nuzzled her raised nose. Then he picked up the cord from a nail beside the door, attached it to the head-collar, opened the door and led her out into the sunshine. She raised her shoulders and shook her great head as soon as he unclipped the cord. He walked back to Becky, the mare following a couple of feet behind.

Becky handed him his glass and he looked at Sandancer. 'Well, go and have a run round, then,' he said.

Sandancer looked at the seats, at the wine, and at Hugh and Becky. Then she lifted her tail and took a long, loud piss. When she had finished she trotted into the water.

'Germaine Greer has nothing on her,' said Becky.

They watched as Sandancer walked out onto the flooded plain, lifting her front hoofs high to make her way through the water.

'She is going to stop, isn't she?'

'I hope so,' Hugh replied. 'I hadn't thought of that.'

'Shouldn't you call?'

'It would only encourage her.'

But it seemed Sandancer's nerve finally failed. She looked back then turned side-on, and began to make a circle of their small island. When she disappeared behind the wall of the kitchen garden Hugh and Becky sat down and toasted each other.

'Lovely out today,' Hugh said.

'Beautiful,' Becky agreed.

NINE

By morning the river had pulled the floodwaters clear of the plain. Hugh felt depressed as he rode out across the dirty, still sodden land, bleak under an overcast sky. The river was too deep to ford and he crossed the bridge that connected Shiloch with Huil. The branches, weeds and litter that hung heavily in the trees sprouting up from either bank added a desolate edging to the swollen waters below. He needed a change of clothes but, rather than head home directly, he took Sandancer through the village and up the north glen. He had felt a surge of excitement when, two days before, Becky suggested he apply for a passport. Now he felt a deep sense of guilt, which was only assuaged by Becky's assurance that he should have one just in case. He was still thinking this over when he arrived among the ghostly outbuildings of Lochanthrain.

Sandancer pulled up beside Aaron's pick-up, which sat, doors open, beside one of the workshop doors. Hugh tied the horse to a hook on the car and went in. Aaron looked up at him through the gloom. 'So the castaway has finally left his desert island.' He turned his attention back to the bench where he was working.

'It was tough leaving,' said Hugh, 'you know, a woman's appetites and all, but I thought you might be missing me.' He looked around. 'Everybody seems to be hanging about in workshops at the moment. When I went across to Shiloch Rebecca was busy on a lathe. You two should get together and start a DIY store or something.'

He walked forward until he was beside Aaron's shoulder, looking down at what he was doing. Six shot-gun cartridges were held by their shanks in a vice; Aaron was carefully gluing small blocks of foam to their metal tops.

'Except I don't think she was doing anything lethal.'

Hugh waited but Aaron kept working.

'What are you doing?'

'Watch.'

Hugh picked up a book from the workbench and noticed two large sweetie jars filled with small Styrofoam packing pellets on the bench. He looked at the book's cover: *David's Tool Kit: A Citizen's Guide to Taking Out Big Brother's Heavy Weapons.* He turned it over.

Learn how to:
- *Employ homemade explosives and detonators*
- *Construct Molotov cocktails*
- *Build effective flame-throwers*
- *Select accurate sniper rifles and scopes*
- *Place Claymore mines*
- *Generate smoke*
- *Use two-way radios*
- *Identify tanks, armoured personnel-carriers, thin-skinned utility vehicles, helicopters and jet aircraft . . . and take them out!*

Hugh hoisted himself onto the bench. He looked at the front of the book again. There was a picture of a man dropping a Molotov cocktail into a tank, which had its barrel pointed towards a woman and two children.

Then he raised his eyes to Aaron, who was bent over, concentrating on getting the small foam rounds placed exactly right. Hugh opened the book. There were pictures of sweetie jars filled with Styrofoam packing pellets.

Molotov cocktails are the devices plucky Hungarians used to destroy so many of Stalin's tanks. Modern tanks, however, are built with far greater fire resistance than those used at the start of WWII. Experts suggest that it will take a gallon or more of fuel to stall a modern main battle tank.

Below the pictures were the instructions.

Effective Molotovs must be of large capacity and employ some sort of fuel thickener . . . Lacquer thinner is used to help melt the Styrofoam and additionally vaporize the fuel load . . . Use of unleaded is recommended if one is dealing with environmentalists.

Hugh paused and looked up. 'What the fuck are you doing?'

'These?' Aaron smiled. 'These are just toys.' He picked up a flooring tack from the workbench and carefully pushed it through the foam until its sharp end hit the soft top of the cartridge's detonator. 'Bury these in a path and when somebody stands on them, *bam*, fuck up their ankle.'

Hugh gazed at his grinning friend. 'And these?' He reluctantly pointed at the jars.

'Molotovs, capable of taking out a tank.'

'Yes. So I just read. I presume you got this charming little bit of American culture from the Internet?' He lifted the book.

Aaron smiled easily. 'Amazing, isn't it?'

Hugh nodded slowly and got off the bench. 'No choral accompaniment?' he asked.

'I was just listening to *Finlandia* but it finished before you arrived.'

Hugh continued to flick through the book, coming to a chapter on 'Downing Military Choppers', then he put it down on the bench. He told Aaron about the Navy's visit to Shiloch, all the while walking around looking at the weaponry Aaron had collected. He found their old air-rifle, which Aaron had been given for his seventh birthday. He picked it up, cocked it and looked around for a pellet.

'Haven't seen this for a while,' he said, putting a small corner of paper in his mouth.

Aaron spoke without looking up. 'It took for ever to find. It was in our old fort – you know, the one in the attic. There were some old porn mags there as well.'

'I'm surprised it still works.' Hugh had chewed the paper down to a mushy, fibrous mess, pushed it into the barrel, closed the gun and fired at an old pair of sheep shears hanging on the wall. They clanged as they hit the wall, then fell with a clatter. 'Jesus. It does still work.'

'I've just put a new spring in it,' Aaron said. 'You could do something useful and attach the sights.' He pointed.

Hugh looked at the bench where the sights from one of the .22 rifles lay. He screwed the gun into the vice at his side and slipped the telescopics onto the small ridge that ran down its back. 'This isn't going to have much effect on those battle tanks you're planning to take on.'

Aaron flicked his head at a small brown-paper box. Hugh picked it up and opened it, looking at the rows and rows of small yellow feathers. He picked one out, studying the round's empty chamber and small needle point. In the corner of the box was a small bottle of clear liquid.

'Tranquillizer darts?' Hugh asked, looking up.

'Try one on that fucking nag of yours and see what she does.'

Hugh looked out of the door at Sandancer and then at Aaron. 'Nah, more interesting, and better for society, if I see what you'd do with one in your arse.'

'Die,' Aaron looked up. 'It's Immobilon – vets use it to top themselves. But it's fine on animals.'

Hugh, who had been about to open the bottle, carefully replaced it in the tray. 'I seem to have missed something,' he said. 'Just who are we going to war with?'

Aaron seemed surprised. 'War? We're not going to war with anybody.'

'Funny, I could have sworn that this place looks like an armament factory.' He finished tightening the bolts on the sights and took the rifle from the vice. 'We'll need to sight this thing. Perhaps we can use the porn mags as a target.'

Aaron took the gun, lifted it to his shoulder and pointed it out of the door. He dropped the stock and tested the telescopics to make sure they were firm. 'Thanks,' he said.

'No problem.'

Aaron had finished making his little landmines and began packing them in a low-cut shell box, end up so the primed detonator was clear. Hugh saw that he had been making them all morning: the last six filled the box.

'All my own idea,' he said. 'What do you think?'

'You win the Sick Fuck of the Year award.'

Aaron was turning the tray in his hand so that he could examine his work closely. 'It's going to be fucking great with the tourists, eh?'

They walked out into the faint light of day, and Hugh untied Sandancer then led her to the disused pheasant-breeding pen the two had patched up for her visits. Then he joined Aaron in the cab of the pick-up and they drove under Lochanthrain's great walls and down to the pier.

Hugh shook thoughts about what Aaron had been doing in the workshop out of his head, his initial concern fading now that they sat in their traditional positions. He felt comfortable, troubled only by the niggling guilt surrounding the passport: he was unused to keeping secrets from Aaron. But even this worry had left him by the time Aaron led the way to the boat and they began to row over to the island.

They were close, looking at each other, Aaron working the oars.

'So how did you get on?' he asked.

'It was great, really, really good.'

'She just keeps going?'

'Christ, I can't tell you how much my dick hurts.' Hugh looked away. 'And she's got some really bad habits.'

Aaron raised his eyebrows. 'Papist,' he said knowingly.

Hugh felt a grin emerging, the camaraderie catching him.

'So?' Aaron pressed.

Hugh told him what she did with her hands, her mouth, what she made him do. He was still talking by the time they were on the island, Aaron at the gate of the eagle's cage, one arm holding the black metal sill as he hung there listening. Hugh let his tongue trip to a stop, loving the shocked look on his friend's face.

'Fucking hell,' Aaron said, frowning, no longer looking knowing. 'Alison isn't like that at all, she just lies there looking scared. Maybe it's time I got more ambitious.'

'It's worth it, mate, I promise it's worth it.'

'You taken her up the arse?'

'Not yet.'

'Yet?'

'My birthday. Special treat.'

Aaron looked desolate.

168

Hugh saw that the cage had been painted. 'You've been working away here,' he said. 'It looks as good as new.'

Aaron was still considering Hugh's experience as he looked at the cage. 'I gave it two coats yesterday, while the sun was out. Our welding worked well – it's secure.'

'What are you planning to put in it?' Hugh remembered all the weapons and suddenly felt uneasy.

Aaron looked past him at the house. 'My mother.'

Hugh leaned against the cage. 'Bad few days?'

'Same old, same old.'

They began to walk around the island, looking up into the canopies of the Caledonian pines that towered twisting into the sky, their growth intentionally hindered years before by owners who preferred them gnarled and contorted. 'You should ring-bark one of these,' Hugh said. 'You'd probably get a couple of ospreys to nest.'

They both looked into the heights as if they might see great birds riding in on outstretched wings, fish hooked in their claws.

'It'd be a shame to kill a tree like this,' Aaron replied, patting one of the thick trunks. He leaned his back against the rough bark, expression serious. 'I'm afraid I'm going to have to teach Gus a lesson, something a touch more memorable than poisoning plants. Something he'll remember.'

Without taking his eyes off his friend Hugh picked at the tree, tearing small bits of bark off in his hands, waiting.

'The other night, when you rang – it feels so fucking weird you weren't there – he threw me out of the pub.'

Hugh still did not speak.

'He called me a shit, an "unpleasant and evil little shit". I think those were the words, and he threatened to hit me if I didn't get out. He told me not to come back either.'

169

Hugh didn't smile. Again he recalled the weapons Aaron had been building in the workshop. Three days, that's all it took, he thought. 'So what happened?' he asked finally.

'It's all that fucking Dane's fault, that stupid cunt student who thinks he's William fucking Wallace.'

Aaron walked a little further and Hugh followed. They reached the westernmost tip of the island where the bank dropped away to a small gravel beach, still covered under the flood-raised water. Under the heavy sky, the water's shifting surface seemed viscous in the low temperature while up in the distance only the white lower slopes of the Three Great Mountains were visible. Hugh suddenly felt their lives crushed into this sliver of atmosphere between land and sky.

'I had only just arrived at the pub.' Aaron paused; he had taken the shark's tooth from his pocket. He turned his gaze fully on Hugh. 'I hardly did anything. That Dane was wandering round the bar trying to talk to people in Gaelic, cheery as a puppy, not minding everybody telling him to fuck off and stuff. He sort of just took it all and pretended to take the piss. He didn't realize everybody was laughing at him, just kept telling everybody that they should be proud of their great heritage and if they thought him a fool for telling them to be proud, he was not ashamed. He said some gibberish to the Colonel and everybody asked him what he was saying; even people like Pete the Post who have the Gaelic said he had no idea what he was talking about, just to wind him up, you know, so he told the Colonel he had said, "I am not ashamed to tell you what a great man you are." Everybody was fucking laughing at him and said he should buy them all drinks if he thought them such good people.'

'Uh-huh, and where were you when all this was happening?'

'I was standing in the corner of the bar watching and then the twat turns on me, says that since I am the big landowner, a murderer of innocents – he said that, called me a murderer of the innocent animals – perhaps I should be buying all the drinks. He said it was time for a redistribution of wealth.'

'Uh-huh.' Hugh was picturing the scene, Aaron retreating like a burnt cat.

'Anyway, I keep calm, and I say there's not enough profit in killing innocent animals to buy for the house, so then he lays into me, tells them how I made him injure a deer, says I'm bad for the community and that in Denmark nobody would tolerate one family having the control the Hardings exercise. He said I didn't need the land, said I used it for nothing but the pursuit of my own pleasures. The thing is he wasn't angry or anything, sounded if he had read it in a textbook or something. But I was angry – I was fucking livid.'

Hugh didn't say anything, just watched his friend.

'Well, I just told him what I thought of him, that everybody was laughing at him and that he was a fool.'

'And Gus barred you for that?'

'Well, I might have told Gus what I thought of him for having this guy around.'

'Uh-huh. So how long are you barred for?'

'Until I apologize.'

Fat chance, thought Hugh. He could just imagine the scene, Aaron's inability to deal with others kicking in. Rather than the tall, gaunt figure he struck in his own landscape, inside, in a crowd, he curled into himself, his feral fear of entrapment hissing out. He could see Aaron in the corner, being told he shouldn't have the land, the only thing he loved, the only place he thought he could exist, by this stupid prick of a Dane. He could see Aaron spitting bile from the corner, not caring who was offended, no violence, just ugly words. He would have looked for all the world like a trapped animal.

'Oh, well,' he said. 'It was a shitty place anyway.' He laughed but it came out short. He thought he might have a word with Gus on his way home. After all, it was only a month until the new year and what the hell else were they going to do? 'So what revenge are you planning?'

'I haven't decided yet, nothing too quick. We'll follow the old advice and let a little time pass, I think.'

They walked back to where the boat was tied up.

'I might go home,' Hugh said. 'I've been wearing the same clothes for days.'

Aaron put a hand on his arm. 'Wait a while, will you?'

Hugh stopped and looked over at the big house, its rising walls masking a deep unhappiness that, with Aaron's request, suddenly grew more powerful. He looked at the door as if he could see into the vast space beyond, then picked his way over to the steps that led up to the eagle's cage and sat down, lit a cigarette and tasted the freshness of the clean air in the tobacco.

He reflected on how rare it was that they discussed the misery of Aaron's father or his mother's hatred of both husband and son. There was nothing left to say, all these years later, nothing that they didn't know about each other and the world in which they lived. Alienation had been acknowledged in their first years together, never really spoken of, somehow known. They were everything to each other, all that they had. All Hugh needed to do was sit there smoking silently and the landscape would reach in and hold them, comforting with the air, the smell, the sound, the heaviness of the sky above. The massive building across the water was so much stone piled up into a monstrosity of self-regard, just as much a cage as the one behind them, a repository for all the horror. Hugh inhaled and felt the nicotine work on him, easing the jagged edge of his feelings, and he wondered if he was betraying his friend in his dalliance with Becky. He dismissed the idea: they had to move with their lives and he felt sure that pleasure would carry them through to the right end.

The day moved on, its greyness unchanging, the boys sitting chewing through snippets of gossip, ideas, anything, sometimes lapsing into companionable silence, waiting. Aaron seemed relaxed, but Hugh could tell he was tense, the shark's tooth in a continuous roll between his finger and thumb. Their laughter from a small joke fell away when Aaron's mother, her face set, emerged from the front door with a travel bag, which she dropped on the back seat of her Jaguar. She paused for a moment to look across the water at her son, then she was in the driving seat and gone.

Aaron stood and walked down to the shore, stepped into the boat and sat at the back where he could watch the house, his eyes unreadable, darker than usual, changing to the colour of the water below, matching his surroundings. Hugh took the oars and pulled them back slowly towards the mainland.

On reaching the pier, Aaron pocketed the shark's tooth and jumped out onto the wooden planks, took the painter and tied the boat fast. Hugh stood up, turned towards the house, and found himself looking straight at Aaron's father, a tall but bowed figure in a fading tweed suit in front of his great mansion. Hugh noticed how his property, all that he possessed, rose up around him and served to make him look small, this quietly elegant man unhappily carrying his weakness, defeated by the weight of his own wealth. He stood gazing out emptily, not at them, Hugh realized, but at nothing. His expression was of long-endured failure, a growing doubt in the duty that ran him. Slowly he grew aware of the boys' eyes on him and he walked away up the edge of the loch.

Aaron and Hugh looked at each other. 'I may be up

for flighting a few woodcock later; you be around?' Aaron's voice was arid.

Hugh nodded. As he walked away he looked back and saw Aaron following his father.

Hugh returned to the pen where Sandancer was grazing and, to his relief, the horse gave herself up with ease. He saddled her then swung himself up, cantered down the soft surface of the drive and out through the gates. Once they reached the road he reined her back and slowed her to a walk.

The pub, an old barn, stood opposite the field where the games had been held, ten minutes' walk from the village, and Hugh rode round the side where Gus had added a quadrangle of rooms, motel-style. There was a round of grass at the centre with a hitching rail built especially for Sandancer's visits. Hugh dismounted, took the saddle, pushed his way through an old stable door and into the pub. He rested the saddle on one bar stool and took the next. It was still early and there was nobody about.

He sat for a while leaning on the Formica surface, looking at the bottles that lined the shelves, the notices for raffles, the ageing photographs of drunk punters. On one wall hung a framed copy of the Declaration of Arbroath and beside it a photograph of the publican himself at Stirling Castle. On the other wall was a factory's sign, but with Huil Inn written in a semicircle across its top. 'Days Without A Barring', it read in big black letters and under that, hanging from a nail, the number '3'. Below that it read 'Previous record – 524 days – Achieved 1940–1941'. Hugh stood up and looked at the new addition to the line of photographs below; Aaron's mugshot had been taken from a photograph of Huil primary-school pupils all those years before. He must have been about six, Hugh thought, and saw the edge of his own image where the rip ran down the left-hand side. Aaron hadn't changed much. Below the picture Gus had written, 'Sentence pending apology'.

Hugh looked back at the empty space behind the bar and lifted the flap. He took a pint glass from a shelf and placed it under the Guinness tap, pulling the little lever so that it began to fill. Then he went back into the open bar, returning to his seat. As he pulled himself up onto it Gus walked in. 'You should get a car and then I would hear you arrive,' the publican said, flicking the lever up and letting the pint settle.

'Nah, this way I've always got a designated driver.'

Hugh looked back at the notice on the wall. When he returned his gaze, Gus was ringing the pint into the till, his face tilted down in the mirror behind the bar. Hugh paid and Gus leaned back against the wall of bottles and put a heel on the sink in front. 'My mind's made up,' he said without prompting. 'I've had a bellyful of Aaron Harding.'

Hugh looked at his drink and Gus leaned forward, topped it up and slid it over. Hugh placed it carefully on a mat in front of him.

'He called me a "pigfucker", among many other choice phrases. So no. Probably not even if he apologizes and we both know he won't do that.'

Hugh, who still hadn't said a word, looked directly at the publican. 'Not now,' Hugh said finally. 'I can see that. I'm sure he was out of order but, Gus, you know, the New Year is coming up. Where else will we go?'

There was no wheedling in Hugh's voice: it was calm, reasonable and deadpan.

'You're welcome, but I'm not having him in here, no way.' He paused and looked down at his hands. 'He's worrying me, Hugh. He always was weird but he's an adult now, you're both grown up, and it's weird the way he's going on. He's becoming more removed from

175

the real world as time passes. Everything is an insult. Everything is an attack on him. Soon he'll make you paranoid as well. Hugh, you're a man but he's stuck in adolescence. Why don't you spend more time with that girl of yours? It would be healthier.'

Hugh felt anger rise in him, a flame against his skin. 'From what I hear, it wasn't entirely one-sided.'

'Bullshit. You hear wrong. Aaron's behaviour was out of order.'

It had flared fast, which was what Hugh had wanted to avoid: he had always been able to talk Gus down but right now he felt the suggestion of betrayal strongly.

'Aaron said that Dane, what's his name? Peter? was involved. Apparently he was spilling that bullshit you keep pouring into his head. What's with that, Gus?' Their gazes locked and stuck. 'What's your story there? He's a Dane.'

Gus threw up his hand dismissively and leaned forward to fix the position of some bottles. He had relaxed, even smiled. 'All hands are welcome, my friend, the revolution is inclusive.'

'So he tells Aaron that he should lose his land?'

Gus shot back up, hands palm down on the bar. 'Well, he fucking well should!'

'You know what he's like about the land, Gus, you know how he feels, you knew how he would react.'

'Aaron should damn well learn to live with other people, and until he does so, I'm not letting him into my bar. That is final.'

Hugh took a long draught of his pint, watching Gus all the while. He pulled the back of his hand across his lips and then he spoke. 'Well that's a pity.' Very softly said.

Gus was still looking, staring him down, anger kept under control but bubbling, churning away in the veins

176

beneath the surface. 'Don't be a fool, Hugh, don't try to cause trouble; you don't have the power.'

Hugh finished his pint, got up and picked up the saddle. 'Gus, I think you should remember that, for all your nationalist talk, this is the Highlands and my family has been here for a long, long time and you're still a newcomer.'

'Don't be a prick, Hugh. I haven't got any fight with the MacIntyres.'

Hugh looked at Gus for a long moment, then went through the door and out into the damp air.

A light drizzle fell as the bloodless day began to fade. Hugh and Aaron stood sixty yards apart, twenty feet or so away from the edge of the birchwoods to the west of Lochanthrain. Behind them open parkland, broken by rising oaks, elm and pine, fell away towards the loch. Both boys were wrapped up against the weather, shot-guns held low, watching the sky for the flutter of the small bird coming out of the woods to feed on the grassland in the coming night. In the distance Hugh could hear the faint sound of music fall away into the dark but he could not make it out. The atmosphere had an ethereal quality that left a slight chill on his skin despite his warm clothes. Out of the corner of his eye he saw movement and within an instant he had the gun up, but the bird was over Aaron. His friend's figure was a mere shadow, swinging freakishly until it pointed long towards the centre of the sky, spitting fire and forcing the tiny flutter to earth. Hugh held his hands to his mouth, blew on his fingers and turned his eyes back to the night above the trees' black depths.

TEN

'Lose the grin; you look like a chimp.'

Becky's sandy eyes studied Hugh from under the curve of her eyebrows. As he shifted his expression he examined the line, noting the exactness of where the silky hairs began on the rising ridge of the bone that led upwards from her nose.

'That's no use either.'

The air in the kitchen reeked of wax. Hugh looked over at the bulbous pot that sat on the range, its contents producing an occasional awful gasp. In its depths the farm's entire stock of candles now bubbled.

'I'll tell you when I want a profile.'

He turned back, frowning.

'That's good, keep it like that.'

'What if the power goes out,' he asked, 'now that you've used up all the candles?'

'I'm sure we can get the Navy to drop off more.'

She was standing at the kitchen table in a stained apron, her hair tied up in a bun at the back, the red that had originally marked it faded to leave it tawny and translucent. The sleeves of her denim shirt were rolled up, padding and protecting her elbows from the table, which was a mess of cooled wax and ruined kitchen implements. Her hands, which he thought so beautiful in

178

the way they worked, were on a large ball of wax that sat on a wooden bread-board. The ball was beginning to resemble the shape of a human head, the neck that held it already complete. In time it was her plan to make it look like his head, an idea that had intrigued him at first before the process had bored him. He asked what she was going to do with it when she finished.

'Treasure it.'

Leaning forward, he picked up his mug from the table and swallowed the tepid contents in large, noisy gulps. 'Perhaps you'll stick pins into it.' He put the mug down. 'One day I'm going to be riding the gorge and there will be a terrible pain in my head and I'll fall off into the water and drown.'

She smoothed the surface of a feature he could not see. 'That's a good idea, an insurance policy.' She picked up a fork, carefully running the point along a hidden surface.

'You better not be using that for drawing wrinkles.'

Her eyes flickered across her work. 'Oh, the arrogance,' she said. 'Your fresh face will decay soon, Hugh. It's all downhill from here.'

'I doubt it. Shortly I'm going to throw my hands to my head, pitch off the horse and into the water and drown. Then my father will find a note that will say, "Look for that witch Becky Hume and you will find the reason for my sudden demise."'

She looked at him closely this time, head cocked, then walked round the table, taking his chin firmly between her wax-smeared hands, one thumb pressing against the side of his nose. She went back round the table, reached into the soft wax and rolled a little ball between her thumb and forefinger.

'A spot,' she declared.

'Hang on. You're not going to put a spot on that, are you?' He reached up and touched the newly tender bit of skin. It felt oily.

179

'It's got to be realistic,' she was carefully applying the wax, 'and you should be grateful. After all, what better symbol of youth is there?' When she had finished she looked up. 'Stop grimacing,' she said.

When he had arrived the previous afternoon, after nearly three days of clearing windfall trees on both the farm and around Lochanthrain, he had found Becky once again in the workshop. She was honing her carpentry skills, having built a small buggy to drag logs for the fire. Hugh had left Sandancer at home and brought the farm's big Toyota Hilux filled with firewood. He worked into the night with an axe, Becky stacking the cut wood or leaning flirtatiously against the wall of the shed, Hugh pleasing her by saying she looked like a hillbilly. If he emerged from the back of the truck with a particularly gnarled or knotted piece of tree, Becky would demand that it be taken, still complete, to the workshop. She said she had decided to create something of real magnitude, some edifice that would assume all her anxieties and leave her a pillar of strength and conviction, and for that she would need everything she could find. Hugh had laughed but then she had found the stock of candles.

Becky sighed happily now and Hugh came out of his reflection. She was looking from sculpture to model then back again. 'Well, I've done enough for now, I think,' she said, walking over to shift the wax from the stove and then carefully removing the apron. 'What do you want to do now?'

For two days snow had fallen, thumb-sized lumps floating down from the dark heavens. Beneath the foot-thick covering the ground was wet, and although the skies had overwhelmed the land the melt had already begun. Aaron and Hugh stood in the woods, flinching as drops of water fell from the pines. They were both dressed in white overalls, the clothes packed beneath, swelling their frames into ludicrous caricature, rifles hanging from their shoulders, stocks and barrels hidden under strips of white linen. Hugh pulled on a white woollen hat. For once, against such a background, Aaron's hair showed a tinge of yellow, like urine.

Another freezing trickle of water rolled down Hugh's spine. 'Do you think we might get out of the woods?' he asked, a hand to the back of his neck to rub away the sickening chill. Aaron was studying the hillside through his field-glasses, and Hugh noticed the stains on his sleeves where blood had been bleached out. The large herd of deer on the flats below were clear against the snow, digging down into the heather for nourishment.

Aaron took one last look and then they were out on the hillside, moving quickly through a small gully that kept them out of the deer's sight. The snow had drifted and Hugh sweated with the effort of pushing through its thick depths. Although they stopped to look every few yards, they were careless relative to their usual efforts. From experience they knew the deer would fail to see them in this camouflage and within a short time they were close, a few of the beasts shifting, nervous. They lay flat on the edge of a hill where the wind had blown most of the snow clear, while above high clouds interlocked in myriad greys. Hugh felt the cold dig back into his flesh as soon as he stopped moving. He looked down at the herd: thirteen hinds and eight calves, the group still holding a stag although this late in the season he looked badly broken.

The boys lay and watched for a few minutes, judging which calf went with which hind, picking their targets. Finally they looked at each other and settled into their guns.

Hugh, who was on the left, felt the slight tap of Aaron's boot on his ankle. One, two, three.

Hugh started from the left, throwing back the bolt four times, watching his targets rear back in fright, looking for their fall. The cross-hairs fell on them and his hand clenched, a barren hind first, a calf, the calf's slightly fence-injured mother, another barren hind. They all staggered as the bullets tore home, and then they were down. With the last round ready in the chamber Hugh looked on to the scene, watched the victims kick their last in the snow. To the right two hinds and two calves were already on the ground, neck-shot by Aaron. The rest of the herd moved away a little then stopped and looked back. Everything they had aimed for was dead or dying, the last round unnecessary. Hugh slipped the safety-catch forward, hearing Aaron do the same. They stood up and those creatures that still lived moved off, their tracks breaking virgin snow.

'Neck shooting,' Hugh said. 'Very flashy.'

The killing-ground was only a short distance from the road. They gralloched the animals, moving fast from one to another, then dragged them across the flatlands, leaving trails of blood in the snow, and threw the carcasses into the back of the pick-up. They were soon on their way to Lochanthrain, Monteverdi on the stereo.

Hugh picked the CD case from among the cartridges, empty shells, string and keys between the seats. Claudio Monteverdi, *Vespro della Beata Vergine 1610*, La Capella Reial. A picture: a thin man with a chin-beard and moustache. Hugh looked at his friend. 'This is very silly music,' he said.

Aaron said nothing.

They pulled up outside the larder at Lochanthrain, Aaron reversing the pick-up to the door. Hugh led the way into the room, moving in among several more hinds hanging headless from a long rail of blocks and chains. They both stripped off their overalls, revealing brown and green camouflage, Hugh pulling up a draining tray and Aaron dragging the first beast onto it. They butchered the beasts fast, hauling the carcasses up onto the hooks and cutting away the vital organs. It was cold in the larder, the dark not far off, and Hugh walked over to a bench in the corner, poured a couple of whiskies from a large bottle and carried the glasses back to the centre of the room. They both downed the drink in one go and went back to work, the vespers entering through the door.

They were on the third hind when the singing stopped. Hugh and Aaron, both stained with blood and dripping with gore, turned to find the door-frame filled by the Rod of God. He blocked out the last of the light and the Monteverdi disc was raised in his massive hand. The grip tightened and the disc shattered. 'Meretricious idolatry,' he said, the syllables rolling down like a rockslide. 'I shall replace this at a later date with some good Gaelic psalm singing from Lewis.'

Hugh looked across at Aaron. They were still holding blades to their respective carcasses, suspended where they had been when the music stopped. Then Aaron smiled. 'I look forward to it,' he said.

The Rod was dressed in a black suit with a darker-yet shirt rising up to his white dog-collar. He pursed his lips as he looked over the deer. 'Well,' he said, his voice an assault on the granite walls, 'have you a knife for a man of God to do some honest labour?'

Hugh pulled a blade from a wooden rack and handed it to him. The Rod nodded to the draining tray and Hugh moved over to a hanging beast, both the boys now working the rail while the Rod prepared and hung.

They worked in silence, Hugh and Aaron turning every now and again to watch the craggy brute chop with terrifying speed then lift fully grown hinds with one arm to hang them. Hugh found himself pushed out of the way, his saw commandeered. He gave in without a murmur, picking up the hose-pipe to wash the floor of its viscera.

Night had come when they finished, and they washed the blades in the freezing water.

'You'll have a dram, Minister?' Aaron asked as they cleaned their hands under the pipe.

The Rod lifted an old, strapless digital watch from his pocket, pressing the button so that it showed the time in red: 16.07. 'Late enough,' he said. 'Quite late enough.'

They stood in the blood-scented air, nursing their drinks, their breath mingling with the soft steam of the animals. The Rod cast his eye over the line of carcasses. 'How many have you to shoot?' he asked.

Aaron quickly did the sums in his head. 'We've another three hundred and twenty-eight to get.'

'It's a lot.'

'The government. They've been threatening to come in if we don't cut back heavily but we've got plenty of time yet.' There was a pause. 'It's the trees, you know, the government likes their trees.'

The Rod patted one of the dead calves. 'And what do you think?'

'Ah, well, I don't know. I'd like to see more trees, I suppose, and if we get a hard winter I think we'll see starvation under our numbers.' Aaron looked at his filthy nails then returned his gaze to the minister. 'Are you here looking for some shooting?'

The Rod removed his hand from the calf so gently that it did not swing. 'A nice thought but, no, I'm on a parish visit.' Hugh creased his brow, noticed by the minister. 'MacIntyre still showing signs of doubt. That I expected, but I have high hopes for you, Aaron Harding. You haven't been to church lately, in fact not since that first visit of yours. I am here because I want to convince you back.'

184

Aaron stood up to refill the Rod's already empty glass. 'Well, I don't know about—'

'The trouble is, it's not very cheerful,' interrupted Hugh, trying to be light. The Rod's presence in such surroundings made him feel uncomfortable.

It was a mistake. The minister turned on him, forcing Aaron to lift the bottle fast to avoid spilling it. 'You want humour?' the Rod sneered. 'See how cheerful damnation is.'

Hugh shut up.

'Perhaps I had been mistaken but I thought you disapproved of me,' Aaron said, tone quiet and careful.

The Rod turned the glass in his hand, studying it before laying his attention on the potential convert. 'Your wealth is your problem. From all accounts it has brought you little but suffering.' This was said as fact and it caused Aaron to smile, but in the smile Hugh saw irritation and so, he thought, did the minister. 'But I think you understand the battle that now faces us, a battle against evil that in recent times has been gaining strength even here in Huil and now threatens to overwhelm us. If it wasn't beyond me I should begin to despair for the Lord's cause. The attacks have been so long and sustained – popery on the Continent, in England, and it now seems to threaten the very city power of Glasgow. Rolling before that idolatry comes agnosticism and atheism, even here in the very heartland of the reformed churches. Yes, I can see how people will despair but it is a test. Clearly the Lord is testing us. I have thought long and hard about this, Aaron, and it occurs to me that you may be one of the warriors we've been waiting for. You understand the dangers and you're not afraid of the mockery. We have to convince the young back into the Church.'

'But—' said Hugh, only to be cut off again.

'Don't you speak, boy, I know what you've been

185

doing.' The sudden attack flared on the Rod's face, a snarl burning up the skin of his neck and cheeks. He pointed. 'You have been mounting that Papist.' His voice was suddenly like a scalpel on the spine. 'You are in terrible danger, Hugh MacIntyre, and I'm not sure I can help you.'

'I am not exactly free from sin myself,' Aaron said, still quiet, the bones under his skin shifting. He was squaring up.

'What sin? What sin? Have you been with this woman too?'

'Hang on . . .' said Hugh, at the same moment that Aaron, clearly equally shocked, could only say, 'No.'

'Then you are no more sinful than usual, like the rest of us. You have to run from sin, run away from it, don't you see?'

Hugh was turning to walk out but Aaron's stance held him back: his friend's angular nature had become something hard-edged and dark, set against the granite minister.

'You mustn't insult my friend,' Aaron said. 'Don't do that. If he is going to Hell – or anywhere else for that matter – then I go too. You cannot change that.'

The Rod laughed cruel mockery in Aaron's face. 'Don't fool yourself, boy, he's already gone. You don't think this whore is going to leave him here, do you? He's left already, betrayed you, gone.'

'Get out,' said Aaron. 'Get the fuck out.'

The minister looked at each boy in turn then swallowed the rest of the whisky in one gulp, thanked them politely, put the glass on the table, walked between them and out into the night.

Later Aaron said he was determined to go to the church and burn it to the ground. He said he wanted to piss in the pulpit, cover the walls in paint and shit, leave the hearts of animals on the altar, smear the walls in

186

blood, break all the windows. That night Hugh had never seen Aaron so angry so he worked in balm with a soothing voice, and violence was avoided, or suspended at least, but only because he explained that their attack would be obvious, not least because of the tracks they would leave in the snow. He promised Aaron that they would have their revenge and reminded him of the rule that letting time pass was no bad thing.

Instead they went out into the night with a spotlight, up the edge of the loch where for a moment a full moon broke through the clouds and lit up the Three Great Mountains above them before the gap closed once more. Sometime after midnight they returned with the carcasses of two foxes and a pine marten. Aaron finally convinced Hugh at least to throw the dead foxes onto the path up to the church. The body of the pine marten they threw in the incinerator at Lochanthrain, a necessary precaution with the remains of a protected species.

Hugh sat up. For once, Becky was driving slowly. He peered out at the bleak high country. They were return-ing from a shopping trip and were now at the top of the hill. Outside the windows of the Maserati, the land was dark and ugly, like the stretched skin on a long-dead carcass. The snow had gone but its passing had set the country into the deep heart of winter. Light now was rare, the solstice fast approaching, the world congealing into the coming depression of January and February.

'Why have you slowed down?'

'Is there a rush?'

The engine burbled at the new calm. A group of stags, their coats whitening, lifted their heads and watched them pass. The dark green of a forestry plantation sat squarely to one side. 'Sometimes it's nice to spend time and look around,' she said.

He lifted an eyebrow in surprise.

The road meandered down the edge of the hill towards Huil, its path running along a slope that offered a view across the Kyle. Hugh, still looking out of his window, reached across to catch Becky's attention, her breast sliding under his hand. 'Pull in here,' he said, shifting his fingers to her arm. 'Pull in at the next passing place.' He felt the car slow.

'Are you making lunges at me?'

'Get out. Get out quickly.' He reached back for his jacket, fiddling until he found the pocket and his small pair of Leica binoculars. He turned back. She was still sitting there looking at him. 'Come on. Out.' He gave her a small push then swung the door open and stepped out into the day. There were still piles of snow at the edge of the road, piled up by the ploughs, their edges black and peppered with grit. He was looking up when she reached his side of the car. Above, two enormous birds, their outstretched wings censor stripes across the grey, swung easily in smooth curves. He lifted the glasses and focused on them, catching the otherworldliness of their flight.

Becky was looking up. He passed the glasses across and she asked what she was looking at.

'Sea eagles,' he said. 'The biggest bird of prey in Europe. They have just been reintroduced, those two are still young.'

He felt light looking up at these enormous birds, suddenly glad to be seeing them with Becky. If it had been Aaron beside him, they would now have been discussing the damage these creatures do, or perhaps their lack of fear, so unlike their cousin, the golden eagle. But Becky just gazed up through the binoculars. Above, the birds circled, their lazy arcs taking them slowly away towards the Kyle.

'They're beautiful,' Becky said, handing back the glasses. 'So elegant.'

Hugh looked at them again through the glasses. He could just see the big round tag on one of the wings as its owner banked, dipped then swung up and beneath the other, which in turn pulled in an extended wing to fall away from the mock attack. Its dive gave it speed, which lifted it in turn towards the aggressor and in a calm and fluid movement it made its pass.

'What are they doing?'

'They're playing,' Hugh said, feeling the joy in his chest. 'They're just having fun.'

They stood and watched the two eagles for half an hour as the game moved in a slow dance to the west, reducing them to black dots heading up the south glen. Hugh and Becky stepped back into the car and she reached across and placed a hand on his leg. 'You've got this big smile on your face. You really loved that and there I was thinking all you liked was killing things.' She started the engine.

They were more than beautiful, Hugh thought, as they pulled back onto the road, they were free. And then he felt foolish.

Becky was still driving slowly as she steered the Maserati down the Brae towards Huil, braking as they reached the junction for the north glen, the pub tucked into the corner. 'Shall we have a drink?' she asked. 'It's lunchtime.'

He nodded and they pulled into the car park. Three trucks were emerging from Huil, packed high with Christmas trees, their greenery compacted into a thick mat. As they passed the smell of the pine reached out to Hugh and Becky. Becky watched them go, and, once they had, kissed Hugh hard and happily on the lips. They began to walk towards the bar, but then Hugh stopped dead: he had heard the sound of the BMW coming down the north glen.

'Mac,' he said. Letting go of Becky's hand, he walked

towards the road. Coming down fast was the dark green car. He was aware that behind him Becky hadn't moved.

The station-wagon came to rest after a long, smooth deceleration. The window slid down and Mac looked out. 'Glad I found you,' he said, lifting a hand to wave at Becky. 'I'm looking forward to getting to know you at last.'

Becky waved back, confused. Hugh turned back to Mac, hearing Becky begin to approach from behind.

'I want you two to come up to the house on Sunday night, a little get-together. Aaron will give you the details.' A pause. 'OK?'

Hugh nodded.

'OK,' said Mac. He turned back towards the steering-wheel and the car pulled away, window rising as he went.

Becky reached Hugh's side. 'We've been invited to a party at Mac's,' he said.

'He has parties?'

'No,' said Hugh. 'This is the first I've ever heard of.'

He opened the pub door, allowing Becky in first, hearing the voices beyond quieten then resume as he passed beneath the lintel. Hugh nodded at the assembled patrons.

Gus stood with his hands on the bar-top. 'Nice to see you, Rebecca,' he said. 'And it's nice to see that man of yours with some decent company for once.'

Becky looked at Hugh and then at Gus. 'Is there something I should know?'

'Gus is refusing to serve a friend of mine so we've fallen out,' Hugh said. 'Unfortunately, this being a small community, we cannot avoid each other. He has the beer, after all. So perhaps you could ask him for a pint of Guinness.'

Becky looked back at Gus.

'He's lucky he gets served at all. I probably wouldn't if

190

you weren't here. He objects to the fact that this is my bar and I can choose who and who not to serve. Last time he was here, he was not far short of threatening me.'

'With what?' Becky asked, and then, 'Oh, a pint of Guinness and I'll have a pint of lager, thanks.'

Gus began to pour the Guinness.

'What did he say he was going to do?' Becky asked again.

'Bring down the vengeance of the MacIntyres on me, no less.' Gus moved to fill a pint glass with lager, watching Hugh.

'There was no threat.' Hugh used the most reasonable tone he could muster. 'I just said that I felt if Gus wasn't prepared to do me a favour then I might be forced to take that into account down the line.'

'And when would Gus need favours from you?'

It was Gus who answered. 'Ah, this is where you need to understand Huil politics, young lady. The subtext is that if I want the opportunity to run the bar at either the annual sheepdog trials or at the Huil games – they're both held on the MacIntyre farm – then I'd better reconsider the ban. Which I thought was a bit rich considering Hugh does bugger-all on the farm.'

'I don't believe that is what I said.' Hugh was still addressing Becky.

'But that's what you bloody well meant.' Gus was addressing Hugh.

Becky stepped between them, as if she felt the bar did not offer enough of a barrier. 'Now, Hugh, why don't you go and have a game of pool?' She lifted a palm to his face.

'Don't get involved, Rebecca,' he replied. 'Anyway, he hates the English.'

Becky put one hand on his chest and pointed through to the annexe where the pool table stood. The whole bar

191

had been listening to the exchange and the Colonel stepped forward. 'Hugh, rack them up. It's time I showed you that an old codger like me can still prove who's boss.'

Hugh reluctantly took his pint and made his way through to the annexe, searching his pockets for the coins that allowed him to set up the table. The Colonel joined him, picking up a couple of cues on the way, offering one to Hugh. 'Nice-looking girl you've got there.'

Hugh tried to look past the Colonel's whiskers, which marched up both sides of his face like infantry columns. Beyond, Becky was talking to Gus, a smile on her face, her hands stressing points. Gus was leaning against his counter, looking sceptical.

'Everyone has been saying how much better you've been looking now that you have a girlfriend, which just goes to show that I was right all along.' When the Colonel smiled his whiskers twitched as if they had been machine-gunned.

'About what?' They had started playing, Hugh already ahead but the Colonel producing an occasional flash of style. It isn't bullshit, Hugh thought, he probably is really good at billiards.

'That young men are at their best if they get a good bit of R and R.'

'You mean sex?'

'I wouldn't be so crude, Hugh,' he said, patting Hugh's shoulder. 'But I know that when I was in Malaya I always used to turn a blind eye to this sort of thing. Trouble is, they always got a bloody dose.' He paused in his shot and looked at Hugh. 'Not that I would suggest . . .'

'No,' said Hugh. He glanced across at the bar again. Becky was now listening to Gus, who was throwing one of his hands forward in a small chopping action as he spoke. Becky leaned on the bar, holding her head in her palms, eyes fixed on Gus.

Hugh took a shot, missed the pocket he had intended but scored on the rebound.

'Hell,' said the Colonel. 'How am I supposed to win against that sort of luck?'

Hugh took his follow-on but missed. They chatted for a while about the changes a landowner on the south glen was making to the fishing pools on his ground and whether they would improve the catch, Hugh's eyes flicking over to the discussion at the bar.

'So, have you thought any further on what I was saying about the Territorials?' the Colonel asked as he eased a ball home.

Hugh briefly tried to imagine himself spending weekends running around, giving and receiving orders. 'I don't think it's really my scene,' he said.

'I wish you'd do it. We need keen young men and I think you'd really enjoy it. You're exactly the sort of lad they are looking for.'

'Perhaps you should ask Aaron. He's good on a hill-side.'

The Colonel leaned on his cue and looked at Hugh. 'Aaron Harding is exactly the sort of man we are not looking for. He has no sense of responsibility.'

'Well, I suppose . . .'

'And furthermore,' the Colonel pointed the tip of the cue to make his point, 'he takes too much notice of that bloody Negro poacher up there in the mountains.'

Hugh walked round the table to take a shot that would leave him just the black to get. Becky was talking again, Gus looking more receptive.

'Mac Seruant's a Scot, Colonel,' he said, before dropping his ball. He missed the follow-up on the black.

'I don't bloody care what he is, I just wish the police would catch him at that poaching and get him out of

193

here. It's a disgrace that he still gets away with it after all these years. And he's getting worse, it's unhealthy him living all on his own. Sometimes I wonder if he isn't really quite dangerous. I wouldn't mind so much if he actually took part in the community, lived somewhere sensible, spoke to people. I think he's up to something. You know, I'm really not sure he isn't insane.'

'I'm quite sure of it,' Hugh said, and laughed.

But the Colonel was rolling now and wanted to push the issue. 'I mean it, you've got a girl now, and everybody likes her. You should spend less time with that man. And you'd be wise to tell your friend Aaron that too, although frankly I think he's too far gone.'

The Colonel paused as Hugh dropped the black, winning the game, then went on, his voice once again reasonable, 'You know, I'm only telling you this because I'm worried. You're a good lad and I'd like to see you do well.'

Hugh smiled. 'I know, Colonel. I know.'

Draining the last of his pint, Hugh looked at the old man and felt again the strong need to escape Huil. The Colonel was waiting for further assurances but Hugh gave none. Instead he thanked him for the game and walked back through to the bar where Becky sat smiling. Gus was wearing the look of a man who was about to prove infinitely generous. 'New Year's Eve,' he said. 'That's all. Just New Year's Eve. And if he causes the slightest trouble then he's out the door, without question – and for ever.'

Hugh looked at Becky, whose smile had grown into a grin. 'Yes, you should bloody well thank her. It's only because she's going to be away and she said she was worried about the sort of trouble you and Aaron might get into otherwise. But only New Year's Eve. After that we'll review the situation.'

Hugh smiled and gave Becky a kiss. 'Manipulated by an Englishwoman's charms, eh, Gus?'

'Don't push your luck. Anyway, as I keep telling you, it's not about the individual, it's about the mob.'

Hugh just grinned at him and ordered another pint.

Hugh leaned forward, the pool of water that had formed in the crown of his Akubra spilling out, splashing across Sandancer's neck and causing her to give a small, irritated whinny. Her ears swivelled back. 'Sorry,' Hugh apologized, straightening up.

The wind was coming in from the west, blowing the rain straight into his face, its force chilling him. He reminded himself that he was bound to Sandancer for life, in fair weather or foul, and any thoughts he might have of buying a car for winter were a betrayal. They trudged forward until past the gates of Lochanthrain, the wood offering limited shelter, Hugh sinking into the protection of the dripping pines, a soft, rotting world lying sodden around them. Aaron had not returned any calls for a couple of days and Hugh had finally grown worried enough to ride in unannounced. Strange music rose from the outbuildings as he turned into them, and he slipped from Sandancer, leaving her in the rearing pen. Then he walked over to the larder. The pick-up was parked outside, its doors closed, the strange and ethereal sound coming from within.

Singing.

A man's voice keening, asking for guidance from God.

Hugh stood in the doorway, looking at Aaron's back. A hind, intact except where the block had been pushed through the joints of its rear legs, hung down from the rail, chest facing both of them, head extended.

The music, coming from a CD player in the corner, strengthened in volume, rising in a babble of voices. Hugh, sensing a strange fear in the noise, stayed where he was, unseen. He looked at the beast and noticed no blood at its neck, noticed its untouched stomach still full, noticed the red smears running down from the wounds on its legs. Hugh stood still as Aaron lifted the sharp blade he was holding and sliced the creature open, blood at once bursting from the cut.

Hugh felt his muscles tighten, his neck contract, but still he watched, saying nothing, the voices masking all other sound. The falling rain continued to soak him but he made no move into the building or to put his hat on from where he held it by his side.

Aaron put the sharp blade in his belt and lifted the saw from beside his feet. Working quickly, he cut through the hind's sternum, the bones cracking, blood flowing down the creature's motionless neck onto its muzzle then steadily running to the floor. He prised the ribs apart, pinioning them with another block of wood, exposing the animal's lungs and between them its beating heart, contracting and expanding while on either side the lungs filled. Hugh felt the horror in his stomach. The babble of voices still filled the room. The blood was falling thickly now.

Aaron dropped the saw, his hands dripping.

He lifted the knife from his belt, reached in to hold the beating heart and cut it free. Blood burst thick and dark from the animal and its shell seemed to sigh in death. He held the heart in his hand, looking at it, watching its form deflate into his palm.

He turned towards the bleak day and looked at Hugh standing in the doorway, holding the heart out towards him as if in amazement.

The voices. Hugh suddenly heard what the voices from the stereo were saying. *Judge not.*

'What?' Hugh felt his words crackle inside him, and then he tried again, his face streaming in the rain. Bile was rising in his throat. 'Why?'

Aaron looked at him, he seemed dazed, and then at the muscle he held in his hand. 'Jesus, that was so intense.' He laughed.

Hugh still stood in the rain, not noticing the water running down his face.

'It was alive, Aaron. That thing was alive and you . . . you fucking well cut its heart out. Jesus Christ, man, that's sick. What's happening to you?'

Aaron was once again looking at the heart in amazement. 'So intense,' he said, seemingly to himself.

'Aaron!' Hugh shouted to get his friend's attention.

'Oh, stop moaning, Hugh.' Aaron was shouting too. 'Stop fucking moaning. It didn't feel a thing. I got it with a tranquillizer. It was out cold. What's happening to *you*?'

Hugh felt a pressure in his head. He held down the bile, digesting what he'd just seen. He walked forward, hands out. 'Aaron, that was fucking sick, really fucking sick.'

Aaron looked at him blankly then turned and skewered the heart on a peg. He went back to the carcass and began to clean it in the normal way. 'Well, I don't remember insisting that you come and watch,' he said, with a whine in his voice that Hugh had never heard before.

Judge not, sang the voice.

ELEVEN

'What to wear?' Becky moved around the bed, her newly washed skin flushed and alive against the white towel knotted above her breasts. She looked over at Hugh, who was lying on the bed. 'What does a girl wear to Mac's parties?'

Hugh had been looking at her bare feet, allowing his gaze to follow the gentle curve of her calves to her knees then up again to where the bottom edge of the towel covered her. He smiled at her long-suffering gaze and shrugged. 'We've never been asked with our girlfriends before. Wear anything.'

Aaron had been as baffled as Hugh by the invitation. The chill that had enveloped their friendship after Aaron's removal of the hind's heart had failed to withstand the need to discuss the coming dinner party, and Hugh had pushed the episode to the back of his mind. After Aaron had butchered the creature they had rowed out onto the loch in the rain and sat silently until they were ready to speak. A soaked Aaron had at last told Hugh that Mac had been just as brief when he visited Lochanthrain: a small get-together, he had said, bring the girls, just the five of them, and then he had driven off. So far Aaron had shown no desire to meet Becky and even less to be seen in public with Alison, so Hugh was unsurprised by his friend's near constant mutterings about the 'get-together'. To Aaron's speculation, he had suggested that maybe they were being too suspicious. Perhaps, he had said, Mac just wanted to meet the women, now that Hugh and Aaron were getting older. Aaron had looked both sceptical and disgusted at the idea, and continued to mutter.

'Wear anything?' Becky said. 'Helpful, thanks.' Now in knickers and a bra, she was sorting through her small wardrobe. 'A dress,' she said at last. 'I'm going to wear a dress.'

She pulled on a black cotton slip-dress that fell to her ankles. Then she lifted a black top off a hook and onto her shoulders. She twirled, stopped and looked at him. 'Simple yet elegant,' she said. 'Do you think it's too much?'

'Yes.'

She sighed. 'So what? I get out so rarely these days.' She sat down on the bed, leaning back against her outstretched arms, her legs curving away over the edge. He took one of her hands, leaving the other to hold her weight, and looked at the fingers, holding them up to the light, their tips black and encrusted under the nails. Seeing the subject of his gaze, she pulled away her hand and hung it and the other around his neck, letting herself fall and drag him into the covers. 'Dirty business, sculpture,' she said into his ear.

'It's as if people no longer existed.' Becky spoke with a quiet awe, the pre-moonrise night so black that nothing outside the windows was visible. Hugh turned the heater down a notch or two, and took the farm truck up into the high glen, beginning the gentle curve that would bring them to the track leading up to Mac's cottage. He watched the headlights pick out icy features in the night. After a while he spoke. 'When I was a boy looking up at these mountains I always thought they were where the mythical creatures lived. I would read books and my father would tell me stories and later, if we were out in the car, I would point up here and say, "That's where the wild things are," or the Lorax, or creatures of my imagination. I always believed there was a really exciting party going on. I've never been able to get out of the habit. That's why we're friends with Mac, really. My father has never been as down on Mac as everybody else in Huil, and when they come across each other on the road or in town they always speak. You can only imagine what I thought as a kid. Here was this weirdly put-together bloke who lived in these mountains, in a miner's hut no less, and he was the only real live black person I had ever seen. And for his part Mac sussed my little fantasy about what went on in these mountains and loved it, played the role to perfection. In my imagination he became the gatekeeper, the only law in this place where the adventures and parties were legendary.'

Becky had turned in the passenger seat to face him. 'I'd always seen him as basically Aaron's friend,' she said.

'Well, yes, that too. I mean, the two of us are always together so he would tend to see us both. I suppose it's true that he always seems more intrigued by Aaron than me, Aaron's more his sort, but in the beginning it was my father who brought us all together like that. Aaron's parents hated him to have any contact with Mac at all – they still do, as I think I told you.'

'The gatekeeper. I like that.'

'Well, there I was wrong, but by the time I realized that it was fine. By then I admired outlaws more than sheriffs and Mac fitted the new role pretty well too.'

The wheels of the truck rumbled on the bridge, and Becky lifted a hand to Hugh's neck as he drove. They said nothing more until they were outside the croft's small door, parking beside the BMW, Aaron yet to

200

arrive. Picking up the bottles they had brought, Hugh swung from the cab, meeting Becky in front of the car.

'That was a lovely story,' she said, inhaling the crisp air. 'I'm ready for anything now.'

'You might need to be.'

He knocked on the door, opened it and ushered Becky in.

Becky stopped almost immediately and Hugh had to nudge her inside before he could close the door behind her. Mac was not visible but could be heard moving through the kitchen. The heat embraced them, the smell of spices hung in the moist air. Hugh followed Becky's gaze and found himself looking at a Christmas tree, a small, exuberant affair that had been decorated with the broken gleaming bones of long-dead animals. Hugh walked over and was studying the way in which the smooth skeletal pieces were attached to the branches when their host burst in, lips pursing then breaking into a smile. Mac briefly dropped a hand on Hugh's arm as he passed and then placed both of his great fists on Becky's shoulders and, reaching up on the tip of his toes, kissed her on both cheeks. 'Rebecca, I'm glad finally to have the opportunity of inviting you to my little croft. I hope you will forgive me for it having taken so long, but autumn and early winter are such busy times.' He stepped back. 'You look wonderful, thank you so much for taking such trouble. Just the five of us.' He sighed. 'I have so few friends.'

Hugh was watching her take this in.

'Only the friends you choose, or so I hear, Mr Seruant.'

'Mac, please.'

'Mac. It's very nice to be here.'

They grinned at each other for a while longer, then Mac spun round to face Hugh, who was still holding one of the pieces of bone. 'Now, what will you have to

201

drink? I have made Bullshots. Will you both have Bullshots? It's a special recipe. Rebecca?' He swung round again.

'They're made with soup, aren't they?'

'Consommé, home-made, I'm afraid, but I use venison stock instead of beef. What do you think?'

Becky gave a ready-for-anything shrug.

Another turn. 'Hugh?'

'Absolutely.' Hugh smiled, and then, when Mac was about to head towards the kitchen, he held up the bone, a splintered piece of a deer's pelvis. 'What's with the pagan decorations?'

'You don't like it?' Mac had stopped mid-stride.

'It's good. But a little odd.'

'Well, I don't normally put up a tree but I felt I should, given our little get-together. But once I had put it up I didn't know what to use for baubles so finally I thought, What about my deformed-bone collection? I think it cuts just the right sort of image for some old-style St Columba Celtic Christianity. Look at the angel.' They did. 'It's the skull of a mink. If you look carefully you can see one of its teeth has grown straight through into its brain. It was already long dead when I found it, hardly needed to boil off its skin.'

Mac walked out of the room, lifting then dropping the curtain that hung over the doorway, leaving Becky and Hugh looking at each other.

'He's acting very weirdly,' Hugh whispered, concerned.

'He seems polite to me.'

'That's what I mean.'

Hugh looked again at the tree, noticing how many of the bones were twisted, buckled or broken. Then he walked around the room. The books had been stacked away. The floor was a mass of tanned leather rugs from several different animals, a goatskin lying in front of the

202

fire. He placed the needle of Mac's record-player on a disc without looking at what it was. The scratchy sound of a harmonica quickly came back at him.

Then Mac was at their side, the glasses lost in his paws.

'Junior Wells,' Becky said, smiling as she took the drink.

'And you didn't look?' Mac asked.

Becky shook her head.

'Not bad at all, but not too tricky, he plays so distinctively. I'll test you on the more difficult ones later.'

'I love the blues,' Becky said, reaching across for the album cover.

Mac picked up his own drink and sipped it. 'Yup, the Greeks may have invented tragedy, but it was Hart Wand that put music to it.'

'Hart Wand?'

Mac nodded. 'White guy, would you believe? Violinist from Oklahoma. Wrote a song called "Dallas Blues" in 1912 after a janitor in his father's drugstore heard one of his songs and said, "That gives me the blues to go back to Dallas", or so they say. Of course, the music, that four-four twelve-bar thing,' Mac made the beat almost silently under his breath, 'had been around for a hundred years before that so perhaps Wand just put the name to it. Before that everybody would have known what those ex-slave boys were talking about anyway.'

They all stood listening and as the song ended they heard the pick-up pull up outside, the sound of a large cathedral choir reaching them before it was suddenly cut off.

'The less cultured among us prefer the melancholy croak of ominous frogs.' Mac had spoken reflectively but Becky turned to him questioningly and he laughed. 'I can't abide Aaron's taste in music, but I am sure you feel differently, being a Catholic.'

She was about to respond but the door swung open

203

and Aaron walked in, tidy but for unwashed hair and blood under his fingernails.

'Harding,' roared Mac. 'Nice of you to come. Where's that woman of yours?'

'Still in town,' Aaron replied. 'We had a row and she wouldn't come.'

A brief flash of annoyance played on Mac's face before it died away. 'What a pity,' he said. 'Just the four of us, then. You know everybody, of course.'

Becky stepped forward. 'I don't think we ever did meet properly,' she said. 'I'm Rebecca.'

'I know.' Aaron looked at, then shook, her proffered hand. 'Hugh's new friend.'

There was a pause. 'Yes,' said Becky. 'I hope I'm not depriving you of his company.'

Aaron gave a dismissive laugh. 'You're welcome to him. Far as I can see, he's about all used up.' He turned to Mac. 'I could use a drink.'

Mac flicked his head towards the kitchen and they disappeared.

'You don't think I'm used up, do you?' Hugh looked at Becky, then straightened his back. 'I think I'm a young man in my prime.'

'You're not used up,' she replied. 'But I'm working on it.'

Hugh smiled and was about to lean forward to kiss her when the others emerged from behind the curtain, Mac stopping to hang the material from a hook so that the range beyond, with its line of large vats, could be seen through the doorway.

Mac smiled beneficently over the first uncomfortable silence.

'There's a lot of deer on the low ground,' Hugh said at last. 'Lucky I didn't hit one by the lochside.'

'An amazing sight all of them, and all those stags as well,' Becky added.

204

'We should really start killing them using the night-light.' Aaron had his hands wrapped around his glass and didn't take his eyes off it. 'Makes much more sense. We could take fifty or more in a night.'

Great, thought Hugh, he's going to be rude. He looked at Becky, who caught his eye, and he realized she would probably rise to the challenge.

'You like the deer?' Mac to Becky.

'They're beautiful, although the number of them takes away the mystique a little. It's hard to think of the Monarch of the Glen when there are five hundred standing around looking hungry.'

'Yes,' nodded Mac. 'That's why Aaron's thinking up ways to reduce their numbers.'

'I'm doing it because the government's telling me to do it.' Aaron's surliness seemed cartoonish. 'I like having them around.'

Hugh looked over his friend carefully, the hunched shoulders, the nursing of the drink. He knew that Aaron was uncomfortable, that even a crowd so small he found difficult and withdrew into himself, but he felt a growing annoyance too that Aaron wouldn't make an effort to be polite and would push him into a situation where he would have to take sides. He chose to shift the conversation.

'So what was the row about?'

Aaron's eyes flicked up. 'What row?'

'With Alison.'

There was a pause. 'I wouldn't let her stay at Lochanthrain tonight. I want to go after the foxes come twelve o'clock, so she said she'd rather stay in town.'

'Why don't you take her after the foxes?'

'I wasn't sure if you'd want to come or not.'

As if by reflex Hugh looked at Becky and when he turned back he saw that Aaron had registered the accord.

205

'I've got the truck,' Hugh said. 'I'll need to be fresh early in the morning.'

'You could drop Rebecca . . .'

'Not tonight, mate.'

Aaron shrugged.

The gap in the conversation coincided with the quietening of the stereo. A vehicle rumbled over the bridge. Aaron, Hugh and Mac all looked at each other, none recognizing the sound of the engine, all noting the cylinders' burnt-out groan. Becky watched them.

A door opened and shut.

The car reversed then pulled away down the track. Now the three men studied each other in surprise, the beginning of understanding on Aaron's brow.

There was a gentle, reluctant knock at the door.

No one moved.

'Shall I answer it?' Becky asked.

Mac went to the door, opened it and visibly relaxed when he saw who was on the other side. 'Alison,' he said warmly. 'I'm so glad you could make it.'

Alison, in a grey duffel coat set off by an orange scarf, shuffled round Mac and into the room, throwing nervous glances at each of the occupants in turn. Hugh smiled and said hello, in reply receiving a small smile and a grateful nod. He looked at Aaron, noticing that his withdrawal now seemed complete, that he had folded in on himself, so he stepped forward. 'This is Rebecca.' He tried to put a palm on Becky's shoulder but she had moved towards the newcomer, offering her hand, which Alison took briefly, instantly releasing her grip.

'It's nice to meet you,' Becky said.

Alison stood in the middle of the room, looking at the faces that surrounded her as she unbuttoned her coat, letting it drop to reveal a white shirt tucked into a pair of tight ladies' jeans. Hugh looked at her closely, a chance he rarely had. Her face was thin and very pale, touched by the faintest freckles. Her hair, which was tied back, was the colour of flax but lacked the plant's oily bounce. Everything in her looked frail except her eyes which, while frightened, were large and round and set slightly too far apart on such a narrow face. Mac took her coat and asked if she would like a drink. She nodded, and Mac smiled, pressed his hand reassuringly on her shoulder and went into the kitchen.

'I decided to come,' she said to Aaron, awaiting his judgement.

'Yes. Who brought you?'

'My uncle, Finlay.' She looked from Aaron to Hugh, seeking recognition of the name. 'He was on his way west.'

'You should have had him come in for a drink,' said Mac, reappearing from the kitchen with a glass.

Alison took it, examined it with surprise then tasted without comment. 'Oh, no,' she said, holding the glass exactly the way Aaron held his. 'Not here.' She realized this sounded rude. 'He had to be getting on. He works on the boats. Out of Ullapool.'

They were standing in the middle of the small room, its low ceilings crowding down from above, the thick stench of spice, oils and meats close around them and the stoked fire creating a heat that made their faces burn and brought a thin sweat to the brow. Hugh searched the others and noticed the moisture on Mac's upper lip and the dampness of his collar; once in a while he would run a handkerchief across his skull. Becky looked flushed but seemed able to take the heat and still glow. Alison, who from the start seemed to have only a tenuous hold on a delicate existence, appeared to wilt. Aaron seemed unchanging, his presence now reduced to that of cipher, although Hugh noticed he was drinking heavily. Hugh sipped, but found the drink no relief from the density of the atmosphere. He felt slightly faint. Becky, with Mac's assistance, kept the conversation polite and Hugh let the voices drift past him in the heat.

As the evening progressed he found his head thickening out from its earlier lightness. He noticed Becky moving into closer conversation with Alison, taking her away from the group. Mac asked Aaron about Gus Houston's behaviour and was careful to listen as Aaron emerged from the depths of his thoughts to list his complaints to this friendly ear. Hugh, the silent third, watched Aaron's grey eyes flick nervously towards the other guests then return to Mac, his need to air grievances increasingly animating him. Becky was chatting amicably to Alison over by the fire now, her gentle humour presented with an occasional touch. He was slightly suspicious of this meeting, but finally decided they were in light conversation.

With a grimace at the final details, Mac offered Aaron his sympathy then excused himself to the kitchen. Aaron turned and looked at Hugh. 'This is a fucked-up situation,' he said, shooting another look at the two women. 'They seem to be getting on.'

Alison whispered in Becky's ear and there was a burst of laughter. She seemed to grow stronger with Becky's pleasure, a smile rising to her wheyish lips before it fell away at a look from Aaron. Becky used a hand to retain Alison's attention, turning her gently so that her back was to her man.

Hugh kicked Aaron's foot. 'They're not talking about you, they're talking about Ironmonger John's erotic corner.'

'How do you know?'

'Rebecca was telling Alison about a trip we took to the shops. I was eavesdropping.' Hugh smiled, realizing this meant he hadn't been listening to Aaron. 'I've already heard your complaints about Gus.' He paused. 'Although they're justified, of course.'

Aaron's eyes moved once again towards Alison's back. 'I wish she hadn't come.'

'You surprise me.' Hugh laughed. 'What did you tell her, by the way?'

'I said it would be boring and that we'd spend the evening talking about stalking. But she keeps making a point of wanting us to go out as a couple.'

Hugh smiled, which prompted a hurt look from Aaron before the absurdity made both of them laugh. The women looked over suspiciously but before anything could be said Mac called them into the kitchen.

Aaron held Hugh back for a moment. 'Why did you ask what the argument was about earlier? You knew I couldn't say.'

'You were about to be rude to Rebecca.'

Their eyes were locked, unembarrassed, seeking the other's thoughts and then, at last, Hugh gave Aaron's shoulder an awkward squeeze. 'Unlike you, I like my girl,' he said.

Aaron stopped him again after only a couple of steps. 'You don't think they'd be talking about sex, do you?'

This time Hugh laughed loudly. 'I doubt it.' And then, to a continuing look of concern, 'They've only just met.'

Aaron nodded and stepped away towards the kitchen, looking grim. Hugh felt a burst of joy surge through him, recognizing a victory in Aaron's concern, the winning of some unimaginable prize.

The croft's kitchen was a room into which Hugh had rarely been invited. Any nourishment Mac chose to produce for a guest would normally be served in the living room, and even on the night when Hugh had come looking for Mac and Aaron he had only glanced into the kitchen before returning to the main room. At the time he had felt the urge to look over the entire croft, which extended to the bedroom beyond, but he had not been able to shake off the feeling that Mac might be somewhere inside, watching. Now when he walked into the kitchen he examined the interior in some detail.

It was almost exactly a square, a block built into the middle of the building's long, narrow length, but in here the roof rose away to that of the croft itself. On the wall facing into the mountain were two large ranges, one an old Rayburn stoked from three large coal scuttles, the other a shiny chrome block with SMEG written in black along its leading edge. This was fuelled by Calor-gas bottles that were lined up outside the building, their tops just visible through the windows. It was to this that Becky now moved, running her hand along it and turning to Mac in astonishment. Hugh was surprised to see Mac look self-conscious.

Three pig-iron pans of varying but great size sat in a line on the Rayburn's hotplates, while more hung from a butcher's rail on the roof. The rest of the roof space was turned over to a vast assortment of herbs, flowers and the occasional cured haunch of meat, all seemingly stained by the thick clouds that formed when Mac simmered his stock. Becky, who seemed to be taking in the room at the same pace as Hugh, was exclaiming at each new wonder.

On the opposite side were the butcher-block work surfaces, their expanse broken by two deep sinks, one stainless steel, the other porcelain. The room was lit by spotlights placed above the windows that ran down either side, which pointed directly at the cooking and preparation surfaces. An overhead light hung down from among the plants to focus on the starkness of the pine table that sat in the middle of the flagstone floor. Shelves lined the free space on the interior walls and on each shelf jars of spices, powders, sugars, dried fruits and pulses nudged each other for the limited space.

At the cooker Becky was shaking her head at Mac.

'This is all for soup?' Alison, who had moved up beside Becky, asked.

Mac laughed. 'For anything really, I just happen to like soup.'

They sat down at the table, Hugh opposite Alison, Rebecca beside him and opposite Aaron. Mac sat at the top. Hugh tried a reassuring smile on Alison.

'Eat,' said Mac, lifting a small spoon and dipping it into the shallow, clear liquid covering the base of a large bowl.

Each tasted and as they did so exclamations rose from around the table. Mac was set upon with praise, the loudest voice Becky's, a muttered exhalation from Aaron. Alison looked at her plate as if seeing the world anew. Becky turned to Hugh and asked him why he did not compliment the chef.

'Not bad,' Hugh said. He lifted another spoonful and looked at it. 'How come it's clear?'

Mac looked offended. 'What do you think this is, boy? Soup? This is no soup, it's the very essence of its ingredients, in this case two ptarmigan. Can't you taste the mountain-top?'

Hugh looked at the poacher and laughed.

When the next bowl arrived, it was filled to the brim with a rich, deep, bloody liquid, and with it Mac sent the first bottle of red wine around the table.

Hugh dug his spoon under the surface, felt it hit then move a mass of objects that rested at the bottom. He lifted and looked down at the small islands of cooked meat and crisp vegetables in their red sea. He put the spoon to his mouth, blew on the contents then placed them on his tongue. This time there was little delicacy, the sensations were immediate and deafening, a series of explosions, opening up flavours for those that followed. He looked again at Mac. 'OK,' he said. 'Brilliant. So good I feel emotional.'

Mac said nothing, taking another spoonful from his own plate and swilling it around in his mouth.

The company ate in silence, unable to take anything but the food in front of them, until one by one they cleaned their plates, soaking up any remains with cornbread taken from a basket at the centre. When they had all leaned back, Becky commented on the silence, suggesting it was due to the quality of the meal.

'It's soup that makes us live, not precious conversation,' Mac said.

Hugh frowned.

'Molière,' said the poacher, turning back to Becky. 'As you see, I live among savages.'

Hugh watched as Aaron drained his glass of wine and reached for the bottle. Mac casually uncorked another.

Becky made a forlorn bid to collect a recipe and was defeated, not by Mac refusing to offer up his secrets, but by his describing the exact way to butcher animals to allow the marinade its proper soak, causing her to grow squeamish. Instead he told her about the marinade itself. 'The secret is in the burning of the herbs,' he said, standing up, Becky rising with him, clearing the plates.

'Not bad, was it?' Hugh said to Alison.

'Not bad? It was . . . amazing.'

Aaron, as if emerging from a trance, gazed a little drunkenly around the room. 'There was Sika in that,' he said, spinning in his seat to look at an amused Mac. 'And red.'

'The red was only in the stock,' Mac said.

'And gall?'

'Again in the stock, the juice of a calf.'

Becky winced. 'Actually I don't want to know,' she declared.

Aaron nodded, pleased with himself.

'The key to the whole thing is access to fresh ingredients,' Mac said to Becky. 'Not something you find too readily in London. How much longer are you going to be here?'

'Oh, a few months yet.'

'And then?'

She shrugged. 'I'll go back south, I think. I'm afraid, in the end, Huil is just too far away from civilization for me. I miss the cinema, theatres, restaurants, you know.'

Mac took a tray with five plates of a pale soup from the fridge and offered them round. Taking one, Hugh found a thin slice of cucumber resting at its centre.

'And will you be taking our Hugh with you?'

Becky laughed and said it was up to Hugh what he did but she didn't mind having him around, so Mac turned to Hugh.

'Well?'

Hugh looked at Aaron and immediately regretted it. His friend was watching him, impassive, spoon resting in his palm. 'You know me, Mac,' he said. 'When I grow up I want to be a farmer. All I have to do is convince Rebecca to be a farmer's wife.'

There was no laughter around the table, and Hugh felt sure his expression told all there was to tell about his hopes and dreams. It certainly seemed to register with Mac. 'Oh, I don't think that's going to happen at all. London. That's where you'll be heading.' He winked at Aaron. 'Love. It's a beautiful thing.'

Becky slid back on her seat, turning the plate in front of her and picking up a spoon.

'Don't you think so, Aaron?' Mac said.

Aaron looked up from his glass. 'What?'

'That love is beautiful.'

Aaron looked round the table and then, with obvious distaste, at Alison.

'Love,' Becky said, watching, 'suffereth long and is kind.'

213

Aaron's attention swung towards Hugh. 'Do you know what the fuck they're talking about?' His hands were still on his glass. He had not touched the soup with the cucumber in it.

Becky was smiling expectantly, the drink having brought out a playfulness in her, and Hugh sensed that both she and Mac were looking at the increasingly soused Aaron as some sort of prey.

'Love, my gaunt and blond friend,' said Mac, 'we're talking about love.'

Aaron snorted. 'Women's work.' A pause for thought. 'Briefly.' He emptied his glass and noisily set about his soup.

'Good heavens,' Mac said to Becky, while refilling Aaron's glass, 'we've got Hamlet in our midst.'

Alison chirruped and it took a moment for Hugh to realize that the sound was supposed to be condemnatory.

Aaron looked at their faces for obvious signs of mockery, lifted his wine to lips now whitened by the soup, which smeared the glass. 'What are you looking at?' he asked Alison testily. She shifted her gaze to Becky, increasing his annoyance. 'And why are you looking at her?'

Hugh tried to calm his friend, his voice bringing the translucent eyes onto his, and then at last Aaron sighed. 'Why don't you all talk among yourselves? Leave me out of it.'

'Aaron's sensitive about love,' Mac said conspiratorially to Becky. 'He was conceived in a fit of passion. What we have here is a young man forged in the emotional cauldron.'

Becky remained insouciant in the face of such information. 'Really.' She leaned on her open palm, smile slight, its power in her eyes. 'I'd never have guessed.'

'I said leave me out of it.'

'Why don't you tell Rebecca about how you were

214

conceived?' Mac was refilling Aaron's glass again from a fresh bottle.

'Mac,' said Hugh. He noticed that Alison was now looking at Aaron with proprietorial concern, her eyes flicking towards Mac, willing him to refrain but her fragile body incapable of asserting any authority over the poacher.

Mac ignored Hugh.

Aaron looked outraged, his body stiffening.

'Can I, then?' Mac's face opened up into a grand smile.

'No. It's none of her fucking business.'

Mac made a show of looking deflated. 'But Hugh will only go and tell her on their way home.'

Aaron's whole body swung, and suddenly Hugh felt he was looking down the muzzle of a gun. He tried to reassure through the effortless telepathy they always used, but still Aaron's eyes lay fixed on his, the mind beyond already convinced of a forthcoming betrayal. For the first time Hugh felt their trust, so crucial to their unified front against the world, fail. He did not say anything.

'Of course he will,' Mac continued. 'Just like he's going to go to London with Becky. He's in love, Aaron, and he will fly away.' Mac thrust out his arms, elbows crooked, fingertips down, imitating an eagle. To Hugh he looked grotesque. All eyes were on him. 'He's your friend.' He slowly raised and lowered his arms. 'But friendship is love without wings.'

There was a long pause, then Mac turned to Becky, who was now looking carefully at him. 'Shelley?' she asked, trying to head him off.

Mac was having none of it. 'Aaron's the product of a familial violation, a seed of frustration,' he said cheerily.

Aaron's hand swept across the table, sending his soup plate spinning away to shatter on the flagstone floor.

Mac straightened.

'Why are you doing this to me?' Aaron said, raising himself drunkenly to his feet, hands still on the table.

'We're just having fun.' Mac wasn't smiling.

Aaron looked at him, then straightened to his full height and turned to walk out into the living room. They sat in silence for a moment, then Mac stood up and lifted a half-full bottle of Scotch from the worktop, raising his massive eyebrows as he walked past them to join Aaron. Hugh, Becky and Alison all sat listening quietly but not catching the meaning of the whispering from the next room.

Although Mac returned within minutes it took Aaron an hour, and the remains of the whisky, to reappear at the kitchen's open doorway. Alison, who had joined him, now stood behind him, seemingly distressed. Aaron allowed his eyes to slide across the faces of those looking up at him. He grinned and lifted a hand to his forehead to push back the dirty blond hair that hung down almost to his mouth, the weapon in his hand rubbing against his skull. Then he let the hand fall to his side.

'What are you doing with my pistols?' Mac asked, voice level.

Aaron raised both of the guns towards the roof in imitation of a highway robber, his thumbs resting on the flintlocks. Then he straightened his arms, pointing the barrels out towards the croft's separate windows. 'Let's have a duel.' He looked back at them and laughed. He pretended to fire, flicking back his wrists as if in recoil before letting the guns fall back to his legs.

Alison put a hand on his arm, which he shrugged off with an irritated scowl. His eyes slewed back to the table. 'So who'll take me on, or are ye lily-livered?'

Mac was leaning forward on the table-top, a thin, calculating smile reaching across his face. Becky seemed nervous. Hugh spoke. 'You haven't loaded them, have you?'

Aaron slowly raised a gun towards him. 'Nervous, are you? I'll clip your wings with one of these, my friend.'

Mac laughed and told Hugh there was no flint in the locks. Aaron looked disappointedly at the flash-pans then seemed to resign himself to the reality of the situation. He put the pistols on the table-top. Becky picked one up.

'You're all shites.' Aaron looked around. 'I finished that bottle, so I thought I'd come and see what was going on.'

Mac opened his hands, like Christ presiding over the Last Supper. 'What you see.'

Alison stood at Aaron's shoulder. Mac picked up the second gun and asked Aaron if he had filled it with powder and shot. 'Wasn't sure how much was needed.' Aaron's head rolled a little and he raised a hand to push away his hair. 'Thought you could do it and then we could have a duel. You know, twenty paces and turn.' He laughed at the thought.

'A little dangerous,' said Mac. 'Even in your state.'

Becky was looking into the inner darkness of the pistol she was holding. Aaron's gaze had shifted towards her. 'Like a cunt.' There was no slur in Aaron's words.

Becky glanced up at him, smiled and looked back down the barrel. Furtively Alison hit Aaron on the shoulder while Mac smiled paternally.

Hugh would have said something but he had seen a strange look come into Becky's eyes and it had stopped him. She reached into the small pocket of her cashmere top. Something in the movement caught everyone's atten-tion. There was silence as her hand emerged, holding two tampons. 'Lil-lets,' she said, with a smile.

Alison giggled but Mac, Hugh and Aaron remained quiet as she stripped the Cellophane from around the

217

first cotton slug. Then she picked up the pistol and slid the tampon into the barrel. The fit was satisfyingly snug. 'You're right, Aaron,' she said, voice high, the drink hidden within it. She pulled the tampon out by its little blue string. 'Just like a cunt.'

There was a stunned silence, then Mac slapped the table so hard they all jumped, his vast laugh filling the room.

'Oh, that's perfect, that is,' he shouted, face towards the aromatic herb garden hanging above his head. 'Just perfect.' He looked at Becky. 'Well, it can't be worse than a rubber bullet, can it?'

Aaron watched the tampon emerge with a hazy look of comprehension before turning to Hugh, who could only lean back against his chair and, once again, wait for those around him to wrench his life out of his control. He looked over his friends, at Aaron's drunken expectancy, at Alison's passive stare, at Mac's upturned laughter, at Becky's eye-heavy smile, and readied himself.

'So who's going to take me on?' Aaron said, still looking at Hugh.

'Can't we just have another drink?' Hugh's request was forlorn: he knew that there was now no possibility of this.

'I'll take you,' said Mac. Aaron looked at the poacher, suddenly uncertain.

'Actually, as it was my idea,' said Becky, her tricksiness becoming something hard-edged, 'I think it's my game.' She raised her eyebrows, causing the small white scar to crease.

'No,' said Mac and Hugh as one, but Aaron had begun to smile.

The risen moon was a mere sliver above their heads, snagged in a restless stream of clouds, white light illuminating the murky tendrils running fast towards Huil and the east. Becky stood tightly bound in her long coat, face to the wind, hair fighting free of a speedily knotted bun. She looked beautiful and cold.

'Don't do this, Becky, give me the gun. I'm used to this stuff.'

The wine had had its effect but there was something far deeper than drunkenness here. She laughed, unsettling Hugh. 'Stop trying to talk me out of it,' she said. 'Be a proper second and tell me what to do.'

'A proper second's job is to talk you out of it.'

Aaron was standing a few steps away, ignoring Alison, who was by his side. Mac was with him, priming his pistol and attaching the flint.

Becky was also looking at her opponent. 'Hugh, there's no danger. He's drunk. It's just a tampon. Tell me what to do.'

Hugh looked at her, scared.

'Hugh. Tell me.'

He gave up. 'Just aim it right at him and squeeze the trigger. Don't pull the trigger, clench your fist in one smooth movement.'

She put a hand on him and kissed him full on the lips. 'I'm doing this for you.'

'Don't . . .'

And then Aaron and Mac were at their side, Mac taking Becky's gun to prime the pan and set the lock. There was barely any light on the mountainside and Hugh began to hope they wouldn't be able to see each other.

'I never thought I'd see you take the other side,' Aaron said to Hugh.

Hugh saw a small smile touch Mac's lips. 'Well, I never imagined you'd try to shoot my girlfriend.' Hugh worried that the bitter cold had sobered Aaron. 'But I'm not taking sides, this is childishness.'

'Come now,' said Mac, offering Becky the now

prepared gun. 'Don't confuse romance with childishness, Hugh.' He looked at Becky and Aaron. 'You're sure you want to go through with this?'

Becky said she was ready and with a smile at her opponent, spun round and stood back to back with him.

'OK,' said Mac. 'Fifteen steps on my count, then turn and shoot.'

Mac gripped Hugh's arm and began to lead him backwards. 'Don't you feel the passion?' he whispered.

Hugh said nothing, feeling only a heavy sickness in his belly.

'*One* . . .' the poacher shouted, the wind swiftly carrying away the sound.

The rush of clouds above them made for constantly changing light. Becky glanced over at Hugh and blew him a kiss. Then she looked back to where she was going, taking comically long steps, fooling for him, not in the slightest bit nervous. The ground she walked on was uneven and she was leaping between the rocks. The wind was at her back and soon her appearance grew ghostlike.

'*Seven.*'

Mac, Hugh and Alison now had their backs to the Calor-gas tanks outside the croft. There was not enough light to see the vast cliffs that rose away in front of them, their absolute mass so dark as to appear a void.

'*Nine.*'

Aaron was by now merely an outline topped in white, the figure moving easily despite the effects of alcohol, reverting to an animal lope. There was an eerie sound on the wind and Hugh wondered whether Aaron was whistling.

'*Thirteen.*'

They didn't seem nearly far enough apart.

'*Fourteen.*'

Hugh felt like a coward. He should have forced the

220

gun from her. He heard Mac count the final number and found himself caught in a sudden indecision about which way to look, his eyes centring between the two figures. Then they caught on the first projectile, a swift flash of fire travelling towards Becky and then, hard by her shadowy outline, with one arm straight out, the fiery explosion at her hands and the streak of flame across the open hillside, a thump, a crash and a stream of brutal expletive.

'Well, what do you know?' said Mac. 'The tampons caught fire.'

Hugh knew Becky had escaped injury. With Alison beside him, he ran to where Aaron knelt on the stone, his body hunched over, holding his face and swearing bitterly. The pistol was by his side. 'Jesus, mate, are you all right?' Hugh was kneeling beside his friend, trying to prise away his hands.

He heard Mac arrive with Becky.

'It didn't get you in the eye, did it?' Hugh asked.

Aaron turned and looked at Hugh, his incensed eyes mirroring the whiteness of the moon. 'No, it fucking well didn't get me in the eye.'

Hugh could see the point of impact now, a soot-black mark absolutely dead-centre of Aaron's forehead. At first he tried to hold himself together but soon he began to laugh, and then came Mac, followed by Becky and Alison, the convulsions growing, voracious, delightful and utterly uncontrollable as Aaron sat looking up at them.

TWELVE

'There were days, they seem long ago now, when Sundays were my own.' Hugh steered the truck through the gentle turns, opening up a view down on to the washed-out yellow flatlands of Easter Ross. 'Now they all seem to belong to God.'

Becky roused herself from where she was curled sleepily against the passenger door and told him to shut up.

Mac's dinner party was now a week distant, and as Becky sank back into sleep Hugh allowed his mind to roll back over the romance, all the way back to the kiss on the rock. They were passing the ranging heights of Ben Wyvis, its peaks covered in snow, which seemed perfectly to evoke the Christmas that was almost upon them. The previous week had been difficult, Becky spending much of the time in the workshop.

On the morning after the duel she had retreated into the cold, dusty interior, demanding Hugh drive around the Highlands picking up materials with names like 'grog' or 'ludo', strange grits, sands and plasters straight out of a book called *The Materials and Methods of Sculpture*, which she now carried everywhere. She had been angry with herself for taking part in the gunfight at Mac's cottage, not from guilt, as Hugh first thought, but

222

because she felt she had lowered herself to Aaron's level. Although she did not say so directly, she made it clear that she thought Aaron a burden to Hugh and where in the past she had always accepted the friendship as part of Hugh's character, she now spoke of it in terms of a slowly corroding illness. If she did not disparage it openly, she felt free to express her distaste for the way Aaron treated Alison.

For his part Aaron ignored the subject of Rebecca when Hugh and he were together. Despite this, Hugh saw that her presence had started to gnaw at his friend. He had expected some comeback from the duel, for a livid bruise had blossomed at the point of impact, dead-centre of Aaron's forehead like some horrible medieval punishment scar. He had thought Aaron would withdraw from society completely to let the bruise fade but instead he had made a point of being seen in the village, allowing rumours to spread but scorning anyone who asked him directly about it. He seemed to feed off the mockery, and all the while Hugh felt his friend's character strain. Despite this, and apart from the detailed discussions of Hugh's sex-life, which still seemed to fascinate Aaron, Becky hadn't been mentioned until the previous evening when Aaron had told him, in a cold fury, that she had been speaking to Alison behind their backs. Thinking of this now, Hugh glanced over to where Becky napped in the passenger seat. He did not look forward to broaching the subject.

He slowed the car and turned onto a trunk road, his thoughts returning to the night before. If trouble beset him beyond the boundaries of Shiloch, he felt entirely at home within them. As he pressed down on the accelerator his mind wandered to the early hours when Becky, then in his arms, told him that they made great love, saying that for her it was only getting better and better. They fitted well, she had told him. He decided it would be simpler to keep his friend and his lover apart.

After several miles he turned off the main road and they left the flatlands, moving up a lush, steep-sided glen, the slopes holding ancient pines interspersed with the empty-branched oak, elm and beech. A thin but powerful river threw its froth towards them, the flurries passing under contorted silver birch. Hugh reached across, nudging Becky into wakefulness, and pointed to the frayed, outflung shoulders of a reddish-grey castle on the hillside above. Rubble spilled down the hill from the foot of its towers, the remains of the building's predecessors, which had suffered the periodic renewals of its once great clan. Once they were under the castle, the glen opened out, providing space for a large flat field, which in turn gave way to a village. Becky looked around in stunned and newly awakened amazement. Hugh pointed down to the open ground. 'That's where they would raise the standard and call the clan to arms,' he said.

'And they were Catholics?'

'Yes, and very brave.'

'They fought at Culloden?'

'Yes, fought everywhere. They were fighting the Germans half a century ago.'

'And they've gone.'

'The chieftains, yes, all gone.'

'It seems a pity.'

Hugh said nothing.

In the woods above the village two stone towers rose towards a bright, sunlit gap in the clouds, between them the steep sides of the roof tapering up to a vast cross. The road came low into the village so that the abbey was silhouetted above them, and as Hugh slowed to look up, the high-altitude winter winds pushed clouds home and the blue was gone.

Becky crossed herself, which made Hugh smile.

At the furthest edge of the village, a twisting driveway led up to the abbey, but Hugh pulled over to the verge and turned off the engine. 'We're half an hour early. I think we should walk up.'

Becky nodded and stepped out into the cold, pulling on her long coat and buttoning it tightly. Hugh joined her, easing himself into his canvas jacket. Becky took his arm and they walked up between the old trees that lined the route.

A little way in, walls emerged from either side across lumpen ground, meeting in wrought-iron gates, each bearing a large St Andrew's cross. On the other side, the ground was marked by the occasional mossy gravestone skewed from the upright by passing roots. They walked through the woods, pausing to read the names and look at the chipped symbols of death.

Hugh led Becky to where a burn cut deep into the hill. He looked up and down, judging his position, then made his way to where a small waterfall crashed down into a deep gully. He waited until Becky joined him then pointed at the wall half-way down the far edge of the chasm, its surface broken by a small path where the cliff turned to thick granite blocks. A door stood in the centre, weighty and long closed. He had his arm around her and he felt her tense under his grasp. 'Their mausoleum,' he said.

She freed herself and walked to the top of the waterfall, crossing the burn before making her way down the other side. Hugh stayed where he was, watching as she took the steps down onto the path and tiptoed along to the cave's cold exterior. A small round hole had been carved in the stone close to the top of the door and she peered into it before turning, unable to see into the depths. She looked over and shouted up at him, her voice breaching the sound of the waterfall, asking him how they were able to get the bodies inside. Hugh pointed up

225

to where the arm of an ancient oak overhung the gorge, its bark scarred by the metal stanchions of a pulley. She stood admiring the place for several minutes, then made her way back along the path and up the slope. Hugh joined her at the top of the waterfall, and there they turned back to admire the engineering.

'Tell me how it works,' she said.

'The chieftain's coffin would be hooked to the tree and pulled across the gully, straight into the mausoleum,' he said, gesturing with his hands. 'The priest would stand here, where we are, and pray with the clan standing on each side of the gorge. It was always at night, and as the body went into the cave the clansmen would throw the flaming torches they were holding into the pool below.' He looked at her and smiled. 'Or something like that.'

She looked at the ground underfoot and his eyes followed her gaze. The bare rocks had been well worn through the ages. 'We should be going,' he said and they turned up the hill.

Hand in hand they picked their way through the trees, past gravestones that grew increasingly ancient as they closed on the reddish stone of the abbey, whose walls now filled the gaps between the branches above. As they emerged onto the building's gravel surrounds, huddled groups of the elderly turned to watch them before disappearing into the abbey's depths. A van pulled up and disgorged five disabled. Hugh stopped to let them pass and they smiled up at him; an old lady with only half of her lower jaw used his offered arm to heave her way up the steps.

Inside the air was old. The parishioners filtered into the pews, forming lonely outcrops in such a vast space. Hugh shifted and found that Becky had walked away and he followed her to where she had picked up a small candle from a box, holding its wick to a dying flame

226

among those already burning, placing it among them. She looked at him and offered him a candle from the box and he did the same, placing his at the furthest, darkest corner of the frame. Becky put some money in a little box then took his arm again.

'Interactive religion,' he said, impressed.

They walked down the centre aisle towards the altar. Half-way along Becky, with one hand on the edge of a pew, genuflected and took the second seat in. Hugh, self-conscious, managed a small nod to the brass cross hanging on heavy wires from the ceiling high above. Then he slipped in beside Becky, who had knelt forward to pray. He took the time to look over the abbey.

Under the cross the altar was a thick slab of marble sitting on an even larger block of granite. An ageing attendant – the monks were long gone – lit the two candles in tall intricate sticks at either end. Twenty feet further on was another, smaller cross, its surfaces reflecting light, its form modernist on top of a pile of railway sleepers. Around the altar the building split off in four directions but Hugh was unable to see into the wings that made up the arms of the cross. He looked to the walls, the right holding the confession boxes, the left bearing plaques charting Christ's trip to Golgotha, then turned his attention to the fifty or so parishioners of whom only a handful could be described as young.

Becky had leaned back in her seat, her hand now resting on his leg, his flesh growing warm under her touch. Her fingers pressed into his thigh.

'I am the light in darkness.'

A priest was standing behind the altar, hidden voices were beginning to sing. A boy emerged from a door in the left wall holding a cross at the head of a choir of five. They walked slowly, singing their way, and Hugh noticed the priest singing with them, the assistant beside him, another boy entering holding a silver orb.

The priest filled the orb with incense, moving around the altar, shaking it. Hugh was too far away to smell the scent.

'Good morning,' said the priest.

'Good morning, Father,' the congregation replied.

'Imagine you see us lying naked, curled around each other on that altar,' said Becky.

Hugh's gaze fell on the cross behind the priest's head, and he could feel Becky's lips close to his ear, the scent of soap light on her skin. The pressure of her hand tightened and moved up his thigh, leaving the cloth of his trousers cooling where her touch had been. He looked at the altar, the candles burning at either end.

'Early,' she whispered. 'With the light just beginning to break through the stained glass, the incense, the cross hanging over us.'

Their heads were very close, cheeks almost touching. The priest was praying.

'How?' Hugh said quietly. 'Describe it.'

His eyes ran over the smooth stone of the altar, ran up the walls, over the windows, down the velvet of the drapes. He felt the heat of her hand, the taste of her in the air.

'No. You must help me, tell me what happens.' Her lips were touching his ear, and he turned his head to whisper back to her. Her hand tightened as she listened.

He searched for words but they were crass when they came. Effortlessly she took them and turned them into something beautiful, creating a place for him in her descriptions. The service moved forward out in front of them, the clustered congregation under Hugh's flickering eyes.

Her hand barely moved, propriety was preserved, yet her words were matched somehow by the feather-light sensations they described.

When he spoke again it was with more confidence. He

found himself joining in her fantasy. He no longer feared the gaze of others. Readings passed like shadows, the soothing voices of the choir comforting.

'. . . your touch on the crease of my back, lips on my neck . . .'

'Lord fill our hearts with your love,' the voices keened. The angel came to Mary and told her the Holy Spirit would bring her the inconceivable child.

As Hugh listened, as his hand reached out to her, he felt something change inside himself: his concerns, his youthful ineptitude left him, flew away beyond these great walls within which he was now free in the arms of her desire, where he was naked, he felt no fear, and while his eyes roamed and saw the congregation, the minister, the altar boys, he also saw Becky and himself at the heart, on the altar, together, the rest was timeless, the people around them necessary, worshipping them. Her fantasy was his.

His cheek brushed the soft down above her ears, his eyes on the freckled skin that lay across her collar-bone. At last the incense reached him. Becky sighed into him and her voice faded and she smiled her thin-eyed smile up at him. Then she lifted away from him, pushing down with her palm then lifting that too.

As the priest gave his homily, a disguised appeal for money, Hugh consigned the interior of the abbey to memory, a marker set down to remind him of his growing confidence.

Behind them a baby started to cry, the parents rattling the car keys in a vain attempt to keep the child entertained. Men wearing red sashes came down the aisles taking the collection. Hugh took a pound coin from his pocket and placed it in the velvet bag. Two women extracted themselves from a pew four or five back and walked up to shake Becky's and his hands, wishing them peace.

As Hugh and Becky left, they walked out past groups of people who watched them but made no move to speak, then found themselves under a sky far heavier than before. With only four days to go before the winter solstice, the day seemed to be collapsing in on itself; an ember about to die. It was just before one and the daylight would last little more than an hour.

The first drops of rain began to fall, forcing them down the driveway at a run, often pushed onto the verge by the parishioners' cars. Then they were through the gates and beside the truck, Hugh unlocking the passenger door, letting Becky in before reaching his own door to see her pulling open his lock.

'That was the perfect introduction to Catholicism,' he said, leaning over, laughing. 'Is it all like that?'

'Shush. We shouldn't have done that.'

'It'll make for an interesting confession.'

'Don't mention it ever again.'

He smiled and started the engine. 'Lunch?' he asked.

As it was Sunday only the village's grand hotel was open. There they fed on lamb chops served by an ancient waiter, his movements slow, corvine eyes hidden behind collapsed, bloodless lids. By the time they emerged the rain had set in, and Hugh felt its weight as he pushed the car through the gloom of the coming night. They sat in silence as they passed through Inverness then headed over the Grampians towards Deeside, the inanities of the radio their soundtrack. Occasionally he would point into the early night and describe beauty that was no longer visible in the gloom. As they struck deeper into the hills the static from the speakers became annoying and Hugh turned off the radio. They talked, about the Church and its grasping plea for money, about Huil and its residents, and about the imminent separation that would place Becky in the south for nearly two weeks while the year turned.

230

'You know I would have loved to spend Christmas and New Year with you,' she told him.

'It's fine. It won't make much difference here, just another day.'

'My mother wouldn't forgive me if I wasn't there at Christmas. She gets very lonely.'

'It's no problem. I'm sure Aaron will keep me amused.'

'And much as I love being up here, all my friends are going to be in one place for New Year and they haven't seen me since September.'

'It's fine,' he said, reaching out to touch her.

'It might be good for us to spend a little time apart. It's been quite intense.'

Even in the darkness, Hugh could feel the hills of Deeside close in around them as the car descended into the glen. Well-constructed fences caught the headlights, and the welcoming warmth of the houses they passed suggested a hidden valley, full of people untouched by the life and history of the counties to the north-west. This, the royal glen, seemed to have softened consciously for a southern monarch. He pointed out the bridge to Balmoral as they passed.

'From what I can make out, it looks lovely around here,' Becky said.

'Too nice,' replied Hugh.

Becky saw the small sign they were looking for as it flashed past in the rain and Hugh turned the truck, indicating onto the single-track road. Soon they were in a large farmyard, most of which had been turned over to a store for masonry. The sickly glare of the floodlights washed off the soft colours of the wet rock, the surfaces dappled by falling rain. Hugh twisted round and reached behind the seat for his and Becky's boots.

A man dressed from head to foot in yellow water-proofs approached as they stepped from the truck. 'Miss Hume?' the man asked, his face hidden in the shadows of his hat. His accent was American. When Becky nodded he looked up at the sky. 'Monster of a night,' he said, light playing for a second on his eyes. 'You should shelter yourselves under that shed over there while I get you your stone.'

'Do you want me to bring the truck?' Hugh asked.

'No, you're fine there.'

The man walked away into the yard as Becky and Hugh sought cover. 'This is annoying,' she said. 'I should have come in daylight. I wanted to see what else they had.'

In the distance, through the blurring of the rain, a machine, a rectangular box of a yellow identical to its driver's sou'wester, started up and trundled through the stacked stone. It stopped, complained and turned, clattering towards them with a square block of stone held at its snout. Hugh walked out into the rain and stood beside the flatbed of the truck. The machine came to a halt, lifted the stone high then rolled forward to Hugh's directions. Once the block hung square in the middle of the flatbed, it was gently lowered until the weight settled easily on the rubber inlay. The claws disengaged, lifted, and the machine backed away.

'The claw is my master,' said Becky, who was standing beside him.

Hugh looked round.

'*Toy Story*,' she said.

He continued to look bemused. Becky patted him on the back and went over to talk to the man, leaving Hugh to clamber into the flatbed, picking up the rope he had brought and running it around the rock. The man wandered over. 'You need a hand with that?'

'I should be fine,' said Hugh.

'Make sure it's real tight,' the man cautioned. 'You don't want that damn thing coming loose on your way home.' Then he motioned Becky towards the office, leaving Hugh to get increasingly soaked as he pulled the rope tight around the jagged edges of the vast block of pink granite, cursing as his fingers chilled to uselessness. He didn't even want to think about how they would get it off at the other end.

Becky came back from the office with the man, who leaned on the back of the truck and tested the cords. 'Nice job,' he said. 'You going back north tonight?'

Hugh nodded, water pouring from his head. 'Nice country up there, I hear. I've not managed a visit myself.' He suddenly noticed the rain running down Hugh's and Becky's faces. 'I'd better not be keeping you. Safe trip now.'

In the car they removed their jackets, Hugh started the engine and turned the fan to full in the hope it would hold off the steam that would soon rise and blot out the windscreen.

'Nice guy that,' Becky said. 'He's from Idaho. I asked if he had seen the Queen and he said he shouts, "Fuck George the Third," whenever he sees them go past. Makes him feel less homesick, he said.'

'What's he doing over here?'

'He married a Scottish nurse and she insisted on living near her family.'

'You found all that out just then?'

'He's an American. Friendliness is in their nature.'

With the heater going full blast, Hugh turned the car and started the return journey to Huil, feeling the weight of the stone on the rear axle.

They were within an hour of Huil when Hugh finally brought up the subject that had been eating at him. He had been trying to forget Aaron's claim of Becky's interference with Alison, but the thought had hung at the front of his brain, pricking at his enjoyment of the day.

'Aaron says you've been talking to Alison.' He saw Becky look across at him in the light from the dashboard.

'Yes,' she said, her voice level, unconcerned. 'I saw her in town the other day. We went and had a coffee.'

'You didn't tell me.'

'No.'

'Why?'

'She asked me not to.'

Hugh drove in silence for a while, bringing the car down a long slope to where the Kyle was obscured by darkness and rain. He wasn't sure what to say, so he said something stupid. 'Aaron feels you're interfering.'

'Aaron treats her very badly and, besides, if I was interfering I would have done so by talking to you about it.'

Again they fell to silence. Something inside Hugh was rebelling against the confrontation but he could feel Becky waiting beside him. In the end it was she who spoke. 'So what you're saying here is that I'm not supposed to talk to Alison, that although I met her at a dinner party I'm supposed to ignore her in the street?'

'But you didn't just say hello, you had a coffee with her and told her she should stand up to Aaron.'

'Well, she should. You told me the other day you thought she should.' Becky's voice remained calm but there was danger in it.

Hugh could tell he sounded as if he were pleading. 'It's difficult,' he said. 'It just makes things difficult between me and Aaron. He's sensitive to this sort of stuff, you know, and it's just . . . difficult.' He looked across at her before turning back to the road.

'Hugh, you can't just ignore the bad qualities in your friend. You can't just pretend they don't exist. I mean, where does this all end? So he treats this girl like shit – you do know she loves him, don't you? And, not that it makes any difference, do you have any idea how clever she is?'

He frowned, not knowing what she was talking about.

'No, you don't, do you? She's got six highers – that's what your Scottish A levels are, aren't they? And get this, they're straight As. Six highers and no confidence, thanks to your friend . . . and her family, but that's another story.'

'Really?' said Hugh, genuinely shocked. He wondered if Aaron knew.

'And on top of that you tell me you're worried because Aaron's planning to blow up tourists, telling me this like it's a big joke or something. And you say that he plans to get revenge against Gus, and what does that mean anyway, his revenge? And you don't know why he's doing up the eagle's cage and what he plans to do with it.'

'I'm sure he just doesn't want it to fall down.'

'Bullshit. You don't believe that. And what else, Hugh? I know he really shocked you the other day and you wouldn't tell me about that. What was that last thing, Hugh? What is it that you won't tell me?'

They had crossed the bridge over the Kyle and Hugh turned off the main road to take the smaller road up the side of the river. 'It was nothing,' he said.

'Right. Of course. Nothing. Hugh, I know you well enough now to tell that you're worried but you refuse to speak to him about it, don't you? That's what a real friend would do, talk to him about it.'

Hugh felt the sickness run through him. He sank into his seat and spoke in a monotone. 'Leave it. It doesn't matter.'

Becky gave a short laugh. 'No, of course it doesn't matter, not at all.'

THIRTEEN

Aaron emerged from the night having seen a light in the stable. Hugh was running his hand down Sandancer's face, not moving his gaze from the horse.

'You bonding?' Aaron asked.

'Yup.'

Hugh had wrapped himself up warmly against the cold. An optic clarity had settled across the northern sky, the icy stars whispering distance in cold flame. In the barn it was warmer but not so much that their exhaled breath did not vaporize around them.

'Let's get going. She'll still be here in the morning.'

Hugh stood looking into the slug eye that watched him. While waiting for Aaron to arrive he had found himself drawn down to the stable and now he adjusted the mare's forelock, aware of Aaron's impatience beside him. Then he put his palm to the softness of her muzzle and patted her gently, breaking the spell. She lifted her nose and he kissed it.

'Touching,' said Aaron.

Hugh looked at him. 'Wish Sandancer the best.'

'Why?'

'Because I want you to.' Hugh hadn't moved.

Aaron looked at the horse. 'Enjoy your evening, nag.'

Sandancer swung her head towards Aaron, who winked, turned and walked towards the door, Hugh following.

In the farmyard, Hugh felt the air burn his nose and lungs. He pulled his jacket and scarf tight, but the cold passed through the layers. As they walked his father emerged from the back door of the farmhouse and they joined him beside his car. 'You two coming to the party?'

They shook their heads.

'The pub,' said Hugh.

His father looked over to where Aaron had paused a few yards behind Hugh. 'Your parents going to the party?'

'They said they were.'

The farmer tapped the top of the car, gave an unhappy smile and, with a mutter, stepped down into the driver's seat.

As they walked towards the pick-up Aaron followed the departing car with his eyes. 'Is your old man growing sarcastic?' He had picked up the farmer's mumbled words.

'He doesn't like these things. I think he'd have preferred it if we had gone to the party with him.'

'He doesn't like these things because he's sensible.' Aaron looked up at the stars. 'I know how he feels. I fucking hate New Year.'

'Now, now, I know that's untrue. If it wasn't for that party you wouldn't exist, so let's go and celebrate the anniversary of your conception.'

Becky had left for the south shortly before Christmas, and with her departure Aaron's mood had eased. He and Hugh had fallen back into their old habits, spending day and night killing. It was the season where everything seemed to be on the move, and after they had spent a day culling hinds they would flight woodcock, duck,

237

snipe or geese. Hugh's failed attempt to censure Becky for interfering in Aaron's relationship had shaken him and now he avoided the subject, refusing to countenance the idea of talking to his friend about his behaviour. And with Aaron becoming calmer by the day Hugh's impulse to confront him weakened and left him. Despite this, and while Hugh and Aaron still moved across the landscape as companions, there were thoughts that hung unspoken. Even moments of closeness, so reminiscent of old, left sour traces. On Christmas Day, Aaron had fought with his mother and walked out of the family dinner at Lochanthrain. He had made his way to the farm, where his company was accepted without question, father, son and friend eating together. But even then the cheerfulness felt tense in its need for continuity. Hugh had caught their reflection in a mirror hanging above the sideboard: there was no longer a father sitting with two boys, just three men laughing, out of place, the certainties crumbling beneath them. Hugh had seen it in his father's eyes, seen the knowledge that this was probably the last time they would be together and that, come the next winter, everything would have changed. Even though his father had looked away Hugh knew he had witnessed a prophecy.

Yet these were uncomfortable reminders that Hugh felt could be overcome. Any real tension had been removed and so in time would these troubles. If anything irritated Hugh it was Aaron's refusal to acknowledge Becky's existence now that she was no longer there. Hugh would talk to her on the telephone but when he hung up he would shift to this separate reality in which his girlfriend ceased to exist. He had wanted to share her stories but, rebuffed, he had fallen back to the life he knew so well, crawling back into the cold womb from which he had so recently and tentatively stepped. He did not think about what would happen when she returned.

Now, with the new year almost upon them, Hugh sat in the passenger seat of Aaron's pick-up, stuffing his jacket behind him, noticing the Winchester repeater lying across the car's width. 'I thought you kept that thing hidden?'

Aaron started the engine. 'It is hidden.'

'Matey, it's New Year, Samson and Delilah might make one of their rare visits and you have an illegal semi-automatic in the car? They'll take away all your guns if they find it, you know that.'

Aaron peered back into the gloom behind the seats. 'Perhaps we should take it home and get the Parker Hale or something?'

Hugh noticed the shades of darkness on the fields beyond Aaron. 'Why don't we go out after a couple of foxes now, before going to the pub, and drop the gun off on the way back?'

Aaron took his foot off the clutch, and pressed a button on the CD player. As they passed the church they saw Aaron's parents' car slip by the other way, but left it unacknowledged. Hugh recognized 'O Domina Nostra' on the stereo. He settled back, feeling potential in the night.

A *ceilidh* band was playing in the back barn when the boys pulled up at the pub, several hours and two foxes later. They ignored the party, making instead for the bar where local people were seated at the tables around the fire, conversation stopping as they walked in. A number of revellers greeted Hugh, but there were sniggers over the fading bruise on Aaron's forehead. A keeper from an Arab-owned estate up in the south glen even made a joke, causing yet more laughter, ignored by Aaron.

'Well, if it isn't our for-one-night-only special guest appearance,' said Gus. 'So, Aaron, what will it be?'

Aaron ordered a pint, a bottle of alcopop and two

shots, without saying anything more, almost without looking Gus in the eye. He passed one of the small glasses to Hugh, smacking his own against it in salute. They swallowed the pepper vodka in one gulp and then, picking up their drinks, went through to the pool room. Aaron had taken change from Gus and now he lined it up along the edge of the table. In the corner a television mumbled away unwatched. Hugh glanced across, saw people he thought must be politicians.

They played a doubles game against those holding the table and when they won they played each other, following each of their drinks with chasers. People came into the bar for a quiet short then returned to the party outside, the celebratory atmosphere intruding each time the door was opened. Eventually Hugh grew bored of the pub's calm and suggested they see what was happening, and Aaron handed his cue to a waiting ten-year-old. As they walked out Gus called them over and they went to speak to him.

The publican had both hands on the bar. 'Peter's out there serving the drinks.'

Hugh smiled, saying nothing.

'People have already been complaining about him,' Gus continued. 'He's getting pretty good at the Gaelic now and maybe a little too smart. You know Betsy Lewis, the one whose sister's ill? Well, apparently he tried correcting her grammar. You can imagine how that went down. Anyway, a deal. Don't swear at him, spit at him, punch him, make him shoot anything or make a fool of him, and I'll let you compete in the clay shoot tomorrow.'

Aaron was quiet for a moment. 'I hadn't thought about the shoot,' he said, then nodded. 'I'll do my best not to upset him.' He turned to go.

Hugh remained. 'If you're getting tired of the Dane why don't you just tell him to piss off?'

Gus shrugged. 'It gives people something else to bitch about.' He went to serve another customer.

Hugh and Aaron pushed their way out of the door and into the courtyard. 'How did you manage to convince that bastard to let me back in anyway?' Aaron asked.

'Long story,' said Hugh.

Feeling the cold, they walked quickly across the gravel to the door of the barn, then inside. The smell of sweat struck them: the long room was heated by four or five gas burners and lit by a bare bulb hanging above the band. Faces strained in all directions. A box in the corner threw rotating colours on the crowd. A disco ball, almost collapsing in mould, hung from its long-held position among the rafters. Unlike the *ceilidh* those months before, the atmosphere here seemed edgy, menacing. Hugh nudged Aaron and pointed to the end of the barn where the Scottish flag hung. 'The bar,' he said, and began to push his way towards it.

The crowd thinned and then thickened again at the small worktop. The Dane was leaning forward to hear a customer's request and Hugh saw his eyes flick across to Aaron then to the bottles as he turned to get the drinks. Hugh stood in line while Aaron retreated to the corner. When Hugh's turn came, the Dane looked at Aaron. 'So Gus has let him back in.' The English was now perfect. 'The triumph of the landed rich.'

Hugh ignored him and asked for the drinks.

'I should spit in his drink.' The Dane swore in Gaelic.

Hugh let his eyes rest on the student but still he kept quiet.

The Dane poured the shorts carelessly and handed them to Hugh, putting a can of beer and a bottle of alcopop on the worktop. Hugh held the glasses in one hand and took a five-pound note from his pocket. As the Dane took it, he motioned him close. 'Listen, Peter, Gus asked me to be nice and I will be, but you behave

241

yourself too. I don't want to hear your snide remarks. In fact, I'm not even sure I want to hear your voice. We'll just do our business and then go our separate ways. OK?'

The Dane stood upright but Hugh had already lifted the drinks and walked away.

He found Aaron looking at the dancing bodies from a dark but calm corner. He handed him his alcopop and the vodka.

'Is Alison likely to be here?'

'Her whole family has gone to a party over the west. Her sister's expecting.'

Hugh downed his whisky and winced.

A thin woman broke away from the pack. Her hair was oiled back across her head, features revealing the concentration she required to keep the stagger out of her walk.

'Well, if it isn't Pamela McAnderson,' Hugh said, as she reached them.

'Don't say that,' her voice was high, smashed, 'you know I hate it.' She gave him a drunken shove then turned and tried to focus on Aaron, mouth puckering in distaste. She turned back to Hugh. 'So where's that English bit of totty you've been hanging out with, then?' She looked around and Hugh noticed the hardness of her bone structure, her cocked chin. 'Ay, I've heard she's a right cracker.'

'In England,' Hugh replied. He was careful with his smile: the ease with which she could move to insult hung threateningly in the air.

'England, eh? Gone off and left you, has she?' Her eyes were back on him. 'Left you, the English bit of totty, eh?'

'Just for the holidays.'

'Hugh?' This was Aaron.

The woman turned her loose gaze on him. 'Who was

242

talking to you? I think we were having a conversation here before you butted in.'

Aaron lifted his hands in surrender.

'Fucking freak.' She tried to focus. 'What the fuck happened to your head?'

Aaron said nothing, but pulled the shark's tooth from his pocket, turning it over as her attention returned to Hugh, who could see the effort she made to shift her sneer into a smile – it looked like a boot being pulled from mud.

'So you're all alone, eh?' She prodded him in the chest with her finger. 'Could be dangerous.' This was accompanied by a throaty laugh.

'I don't think so,' Hugh replied. 'I'm an honest man.'

This confused her for a moment. She looked at the floor. 'No such thing,' she said. 'Come and dance with me. Why are you standing here? Come and dance.' She grabbed his arm and began to pull him towards the dance-floor.

He looked round at Aaron in distress, but his friend grinned back at him.

The woman struggled through the crowd, nipping the occasional man, receiving smiles and bawdy exclamations in reply. Hugh thought she might have forgotten him and turned to flee, but she caught the movement and grabbed his arm. 'Don't you be thinking you're going to get away from me,' she said.

They joined a line in the middle of Strip the Willow and for some minutes they were able to dance without speaking, only her leer facing him. He was wondering what he had done to deserve this: she had never shown him the slightest interest in the past. This thought left him when he noticed her predatory look slip and leave her face pale. They spun and she stumbled, her complexion now white and then, on the next turn, green, and he hoped it might be the light from the colour box. They turned, hands crossed, and then she was on the arm of someone else and then back to him again, her head rolling, then to another man and, on the outside of the turn, she threw up. Hugh, who had been ready, stepped back, aware of his luck. She ended up facing him, the last of the puke dribbling down her chin, the bulk having sprayed everyone on the outside of the circle. She looked blankly at him as the cries rose and then she threw up again, this time onto the floor.

Hugh ran. Others closed to her aid, the victims assessing the damage to their clothes as Hugh hunkered down and tore through the crowd.

Aaron, who was standing where he had been left, led Hugh away through the back door. 'And there I was thinking you were going to fuck her,' he said, as they ran back to the bar. They stood facing the fire, attempting to suppress their laughter.

'You think that was funny,' said a voice from behind. 'You think causing a girl to be sick is funny? You're as big a prick as him.'

Hugh and Aaron turned to face the Dane, his expression so earnest that they tried, with difficulty, to appear serious.

'You are stupid. There are a lot of people out there who will be sending you their cleaning bills, but I think you should clean their clothes yourself.'

Gus had seen Peter arrive and, wiping his hands on a towel, was making his way over. Hugh fought to control himself, choosing not to lower himself by protesting his innocence, instead keeping his eyes steady on the Dane. 'Go on,' he said, nodding sideways, 'fuck off.'

The Dane straightened his back. 'You tell me to fuck off?' he shouted, before jabbing his finger at Hugh's chest, beating time with his next words. 'You Are An Asshole.' The last was said with such feeling that both

Hugh and Aaron straightened. 'You Two Make Me Sick.'

The staccato delivery was so perfectly timed that both Hugh and Aaron lost control and had to hold each other up.

'Peter?' Gus was at the Dane's side. 'Who's looking after the bar?'

'Assholes. You are assholes. Everybody says so.'

'Peter.' Gus grabbed his arm, wrenching his attention away from Hugh and Aaron. 'The bar? Who's looking after the bar?'

The Dane shook himself free in irritation. 'The bar?' He seemed to remember. 'The bar is closed. I closed it because of what these two did but I will reopen it in a minute.'

'You left it unattended? The bar? Unattended?' Gus's voice had lost its charm.

'It'll be fine until I'm finished here.'

'Fine? It'll be bloody well cleaned out by now, you silly bugger.' Gus grabbed his arm once again. 'Come on.'

The Dane looked at his patron in surprise, the anger leaving him as he turned to follow. At the door Gus looked back, remembering Hugh and Aaron. 'You two, out, and don't come back.' And then he was through the door.

They had left the pick-up on a forestry track and in the light of the moonrise picked their way along the edge of a stream, then through a gate in the heavy wire of a six-foot deer fence. Now they sat beside each other at the base of a tall pine, looking at the outline of the old manse. Hugh held a bottle of Scotch he had taken from behind the bar after Gus had left – he had left money with a regular – and handed it to Aaron, all the while studying the authoritarian permanence of the building that cut its dark outline against the night.

'You ever been inside?' asked Aaron.

Hugh shook his head. He felt drunk.

'Me neither.' Aaron took a gulp. 'Shouldn't be too difficult, though.'

They both looked away when an owl cried in the woods behind them.

'The ground will soon freeze,' said Hugh, reaching out to touch the earth around him. 'It'll show our tracks, so we should do it soon.'

'It shouldn't take long, it's just a check-out, look for a way to sort the bastard.'

'Good.' Hugh rubbed his eyes. 'Because if we cause any damage it's not exactly going to be difficult for them to work it out.'

Aaron said nothing. Instead he looked up at the walls. 'Big fucking house for a publican, isn't it?'

Hugh led the way to the back door, moving quickly along a path that cut through the large grounds. He tried the door-handle but it was locked, so he followed his friend across the manse's gravel surround, turning the corner, the building's large granite blocks sharp-edged in the moonlight. The windows were tall here, opening on to the reception rooms, but Aaron ignored them, continuing to the front door. It was locked as well. He turned and looked back. 'There'll be a window we can get in.'

Hugh gestured to the unturned corner. 'We should go round the house. There may be another way.'

The fourth side of the manse was pushed hard against a rhododendron-covered bank with only a small path between wall and bush. Half-way along they found the side door, which was open. Gently they pushed it back.

'Listen for an alarm.'

Aaron stepped onto a linoleum floor. The room's warmth reached out to touch Hugh as he followed, closing the door behind him. Excited now, the drink giving him courage, he pulled a torch from his pocket, switched it on and ran its beam along the walls. The hallway was sparse, doors leading off in several directions, the walls holding sketches of birds in flight. Aaron pulled a potholer's light onto his head and swung it up and down and from left to right. 'I think we're safe on the alarm,' he said.

'Unless it's silent.'

The light from Aaron's forehead trailed the edge of the ceiling.

'No motion sensors.'

'Pressure pads?'

Aaron laughed. 'What the fuck do you think this is? A bank?'

An open door led to a utility room, which in turn gave way to a modern, well-kept kitchen. Hugh and Aaron stood by the table and ran their lights over the room: the cabinets, work surfaces and cooking equipment seemed, if not new, unused. Aaron walked over to the range and looked down at the coffee-making equipment that filled a corner. He shifted along the cabinets, opening the doors and peering at the contents. At the other end of the room he opened the fridge, the interior light bathing his face yellow. Inside there was a four-pint carton of milk and a bag of coffee. 'Doesn't look like he does much cooking,' he said, closing the fridge door and walking over to join Hugh, taking a swig from the bottle of whisky.

'Likes his coffee, though.'

Aaron handed him the bottle and walked back to the wall, opening a cupboard and taking out a packet of salt, which he carried to the coffee-maker. He picked up the sugar jar, popped its top and slowly poured in a small quantity of salt. When he closed the lid he shook the jar to flatten the surface then put everything back where he had found it. 'It's the little gestures that make all the difference,' he said to Hugh.

Together they walked through into the dining room, their torches reflecting off the table, the candlesticks, the crystal, then joining on an enormous painting of Culloden moor. The sitting room, which seemed the best-used space they had so far encountered, was cluttered around the fireplace and the chairs were aimed towards the television. The bookshelf offered up history and assorted thrillers, a painting of the empty mountains hung above the fireplace, and another wall held a facsimile of the Declaration of Arbroath, identical to the one in the bar. Hugh walked through into the hallway, which offered access to both the front door and the stairs.

'Shall we?' Aaron asked, offering his arm.

'Let's,' said Hugh, and took it.

At the bottom of the stairs they froze, stopped by the sound of gears turning on the other side of the hallway. Worn chimes rang out, and they turned their lights to an old but polished grandfather clock standing in the corner. The gongs began, and the lights reflected off the gold face, both hands pointing straight up, cutting the Roman numerals for twelve in half. Aaron had one foot on the first step and his hand on the banister, Hugh standing right beside him. They waited for the last gong then turned to each other. Hugh transferred the light to his left hand so that he could shake his old friend by the right. 'Happy New Year,' he said.

They looked at each other and Hugh felt a great surge of affection.

'Onwards and upwards,' laughed Aaron, unhooking his arm and bounding up the stairs.

They moved swiftly through the spare rooms, which were empty, then into the master bedroom with its outsize ornate wooden bed. A painting of a woman

248

reclining nude hung above the headboard on a wall of dark green. Magazines were stacked under the side table and a couple of novels rested beside the lamp. A large wardrobe filled the corner between two of the windows and under the third stood a chest of drawers on which Gus kept various ointments.

Aaron disappeared through a doorway at the other side of the bed and Hugh heard him urinate.

Hugh took a swig of the whisky and turned to the side table, rifling through the magazines. He picked up a copy of *Penthouse* and tried to flick through it with the light shining from under his arm but the manoeuvre was difficult. He was about to lay it flat on the bed when his eye caught sight of a folder tucked further down the pile. He slipped it from the stack and opened it, aiming his torch. A naked woman was standing with her back to the camera, a waterbottle hanging near her shoulder and a tube passing down to the crack of her arse. She smiled over her shoulder, a speech bubble declaring, 'Nothing soothes like a *Waterflex Medical Product*.'

Hugh heard the toilet flush in the next room. He flicked through several more pages, smiled and walked through to the bathroom.

Aaron was standing in the corner beside the shower stall where an oversized hot-water bottle hung on the curtain rail, its trailing tube wrapped around the bar. 'What do you reckon this is?' he asked.

Hugh looked round the room: the floor was deeply carpeted, an old-fashioned enamelled bath sat on a marble block beside the window and along one wall stood a lavatory, a wash-basin and a bidet. 'He's got one of those things for washing your nuts,' Hugh said, smiling as he noticed Aaron peering at the scarred end of the tube.

There was an open Tupperware box on the floor of

the shower stall, which Aaron reached into, picking out two steel bits, each longer than a finger, one expanding in the middle before tapering away while the other opened out twice before it came to an end. He tried one on the end of the tube and, finding it fitted perfectly, pulled it off again, rolling it over in his hand. The finely ground smoothness clearly pleased him and he showed both bits, open-palmed, to Hugh. They were drilled hollow. 'It seems to be some sort of catheter,' he said, studying them, 'but there's no way in hell you could put those down your throat.'

'No,' said Hugh.

'So what are they?'

Hugh peered down. 'Do they smell of anything?'

Aaron lifted them to his nose. 'No, they've been washed, I think. They're slightly greasy, though.' He looked at Hugh, who opened the folder.

'Well, that one, which you just sniffed,' he pointed with the edge of the folder, 'is the Pleasure Plug and that', again he pointed, 'is the Two-humped Camel.' He held the brochure in front of Aaron so that he could see.

Aaron looked at the pictures. 'Oh, no.'

'Oh, yes.' Hugh turned the page. 'Look, you can become your own little human water pistol.' In the picture a woman on all fours shot a stream of water from behind her on to a wooden deck.

Aaron looked at the picture, then at Hugh. 'My hands!' he shouted, dropping the bits and scurrying to the sink, throwing away discretion by scouring his palms with soap. 'That's fucking horrible.' He paused. 'You bastard, you knew all along.' Another pause. 'He really shoves those things up his arse?'

'You are so innocent, Aaron.' Hugh was trying to keep his tone level, his laughter in check. 'Even the royals are into this sort of thing.'

As Aaron dried his hands on his jeans he looked over. 'Bastard . . . I was sniffing those things.'

'You're lucky I didn't get you to taste them,' Hugh said, walking over. He opened the first of two small caddies that sat on the shelf beside the basin. He sniffed at the contents then shoved it under Aaron's nose. 'Herbal tea.'

'Fuck off.'

He put it back on the shelf and opened the other. 'Coffee.'

Hugh put down the tin and flicked back through the brochure. 'He flavours them. Listen to this. "A warm camomile enema works wonders in helping you to sleep." '

Aaron took the folder from Hugh, read it and handed it back. He looked around. 'He puts that in the water?'

Hugh nodded, and Aaron smiled.

'I'm going to have that bastard. I'll be back in just a minute.'

With Aaron gone Hugh sat on the carpet and flicked through the pages of the brochure, his torch held at shoulder height. He read the pseudo-medical advantages of the process, took in the quotations from experts in the field, then looked over the pictures of nurses inserting tubes into their patients' orifices. The centre pages were dedicated to a first-person story of a man's bad wind having led to near divorce, then the discovery of 'irrigation' and the birth of a new, closer relationship.

He looked up as Aaron returned. 'I'm not going to be able to look at him without laughing,' Hugh said. 'This is really fucked up. What are you going to do?'

Aaron was standing above him. 'You found coffee, right? What's that supposed to do?'

Hugh flicked through the pages until he found his place. ' "Adding coffee to your enema provides a zappy way to start the day or prepare for an evening out." '

Aaron held up a tub of Madras curry powder. 'Well, things are about to get that bit zappier.'

'Wow,' said Hugh.

They were still laughing as they staggered out of the house twenty minutes later.

FOURTEEN

With January came the full horror of the annual darkness and, with it, a creeping despair that filled the soul. Hugh looked over the floodplain from Becky's bedroom window and listened to the wind hit its long whine, feeling the season close in around them. Becky, lying on the bed, talked happily of her trip, ignorant of the coming onslaught. Hugh turned to look at her, smiling sympathetically, and she paused in her story. 'Horrible outside, is it?'

He nodded.

'Well, stay in bed.'

He lay down beside her and she leaned over him, breasts curving away. She lowered her face to kiss him. 'It is so good to see you,' she said.

He slid his hand under her dressing-gown, touching her flesh and easing her closer, bringing his fingertips down the curves of her side, watching the movement of his hand then looking up into the eyes smiling back at him, small wrinkles cutting their edges. He pulled her close enough to touch her lips with his.

The phone rang downstairs and she slid away, stood up and kissed him once more before she left the room. He lay there for a while, then reached down to lift a large atlas from the floor. Carefully he flipped open the first few pages. 'Hugh, A world to romance your imagination, with love, Becky.'

He opened the book at random and found himself gazing at Scotland.

As he turned the pages he could hear Becky speaking, her voice hard and irritated. He was able to pick out only a few words, the indignant crests in the conversation, but he knew who she was speaking to – he recognized the familiarity of her displeasure. He was looking at Borneo when she climbed back into bed. 'Anyone interesting?'

She eased her weight onto her elbow, her eyes searching his face. He smiled, turning the page to a place he'd never heard of: Sulawesi.

'I ran into my ex when I was down south,' she said, pausing, but he held his smile, saying nothing. 'He's decided he still loves me. He said I seemed much more relaxed, more centred now that I've spent some time on my own, and he's decided he's made a big mistake and that we should be together for all time. He's been calling me and telling me this on an hourly basis.' She sighed and lay down again. 'All this from a guy who dumped me because he felt so threatened by my career.' She shook her head in amazement, but her eyes never left him.

He turned the page. 'So what are you going to do?' he asked, his tone flat.

She rolled back onto her elbow. 'Can I light a cigarette for you?' she asked, and when he handed the pack and lighter across she took one and lit it, inhaling before she spoke. 'I'm going to keep telling him to go fuck himself. I told him that you were one of the main reasons why I'm relaxed.' She handed the cigarette to him and, when he had taken it, ran her hand down his arm. 'I said that, compared to him, you are a model of maturity, and pointed out that physically you are in much, much better condition.' She laughed. 'He's an idiot. But I wanted you to know the situation in case he phones again, although I doubt he will after what I just said to him.' She smiled softly and closed in to kiss him. He didn't let her, and she stopped to look him in the eye.

'You are sure you don't want him back?' he asked.

'Yes, I'm sure.' Reassurance swam strongly through her eyes.

He closed the book, Iwo Jima catching his eye as the cover fell.

'So she's back,' said Aaron.

'Arrived last night.' Hugh stopped, two ducks held by their necks between the fingers of one hand. It was dark, although still well before five in the afternoon, and he was pleased with his victims: the gale had made the shooting difficult. 'Why aren't we shooting the pond up at Lochanthrain? And what's with the soundtrack? People say you're playing music up there.'

His friend was looking out into the gloom. 'None of your business.' Aaron, who had claimed three ducks but had only found two, pointed to a bush that stuck up from the water of the Kyle. 'Try Fi in there.'

Hugh directed his dog.

'So she was pleased to see you?'

'Absolutely,' Hugh said, lighting a cigarette and turning his eyes on his friend in the flaring light. 'We fucked all night, even standing up in the shower.'

The light died.

'Come on, Fi, pick it up,' Aaron shouted, hearing the splashing and barks of the dog. 'In the shower? Any reason?'

'She has her period.'

He knew, even in the darkness, that Aaron was looking at him.

'She lets you fuck her when she's on the rag?'

255

'Of course, likes it.'

'And you?'

'Yep, me too. It's not quite as smooth, it's got a slightly grittier feel to it.' He laughed.

'Grittier,' Aaron said seriously, and then, 'That useless mutt of yours is never going to find this fucking bird.'

'That's because you never fucking hit it.' Hugh shouted for Fi, who came splashing towards them, her speed showing her concurrence with Hugh's view.

'So why is it none of my business?'

'What?'

'The music at the pond.'

'It's a surprise.' Aaron picked up the birds he had let fall to the ground. 'Beer at yours?'

'Sure.'

Hugh emerged from Shiloch farmhouse and looked across the dark country. Days had passed, the month slipping away, and yet there was no change in the weather, the wind whipping at him, carrying rain in sheets across the yard, so cold that even Sandancer had lowered her haunches to protect herself. He patted her wet flank, walked over to the workshop and opened the door, flicked on the light, able to tell that Becky had been there recently. He shouted. No reply. He walked over to her car and laid his hand on the bonnet but the engine was cold. He was already soaked despite being head-to-toe in waterproofs.

He returned to Sandancer, untied her from the gatepost and swung himself up onto her back. Unsure where to go, he had Sandancer stand still, the powerful lethargy a result of knowing that movement would open up opportunities for the rain to find dry flesh. An old Mazda pick-up came down the road and rolled up alongside him. The shepherd wound down his window, they nodded at each other, and Hugh was directed towards the centre of the floodplain, a spot blocked from view by the buildings on his ride in.

Once past the shed and out on the edge of the plain he saw her. On a slight rise, in a wild array of colours, she stood hunched over a large lump of stone. Hugh cantered out towards her, Sandancer's hoofs kicking up mud.

She straightened and watched him come, her face just visible through the stinging rain, caught between the yellow of her hat and the silver of her long waterproof jacket. In front of her the block of granite sat on a strategically arranged plinth of twisted metal. In one hand she was holding a long cutting steel, its tip a series of heavy chisels, and in the other a hammer. She smiled as he reined in. 'Impressive,' she said as he slipped off the horse's back. She walked over to greet him with a kiss, their faces both chilled deathly cold by the rain. They made their way to the sculpture.

'Won't she wander off?' Becky said, looking back.

'If she does, it'll only be to the yard.'

He stopped and looked at the pink rock and the metal base, which seemed to be the stout legs of an old-fashioned wringer, bolstered by a selection of other material he could not place. The heavy granite block fitted snugly into the junk, just above waist height, its surface scarred. The tyres from the farm tractor had left gouges in the soft earth explaining the block's passage from the yard to where it now rested.

Hugh walked round the pile, his eye drawn to the way the rain was bouncing off the rock. He realized he was very cold, and did not feel like admiring a large, square rock sitting on a foundation of discarded metal. 'What is it?' he asked.

Becky moved forward to the granite, placed the cutting steel at a scratch and smashed the hammer into the other end. She repeated the move three times, then stepped back. She had left barely a mark.

'I don't know yet,' she said. 'It's an organic process.'

'A very long organic process.' Hugh ran his hand across the scratches.

'It's hard work but it's making me feel good.' She moved in and took a few more shots at the stone.

The rain felt heavier. Out on the floodplain there was no shelter and the wind whipped the water round to sting their faces even as they turned away. When the downpour eased, the air would clear enough for them to see another rolling squall surging in to break over them.

Becky showed no sign of wanting to stop, so after a few minutes Hugh asked how long she planned to go on. She took a quick look up at the sky. 'Oh, a while yet.'

'But it's horrible out here.'

She paused between strokes. 'If you don't want to be here then go inside. I'll be there when I'm done.'

He found himself looking over at the farm buildings. He felt left out. 'Well, can I do anything to help?'

'No. I really want to do this on my own.'

He searched for a place to sit but the ground was waterlogged. For a while he stood with his arms crossed, then circled the sculpture, trying to look interested. He tried to offer helpful suggestions but received warning glances in return. He felt an urge, which he suppressed, to stamp his feet. 'This isn't a very sharing experience,' he said.

She stood up straight and exhaled so loudly that even the wind could not drown the sound. Then she pointed to the house. 'Go on, make us some tea. I'll be there in a minute.'

Hugh made a show of sulking, walked out into the field to grab Sandancer by the bridle and led her back to the yard.

With Becky concentrating on her sculpture Hugh had time to spend with Aaron. Each day he would ride along the south glen until he reached a vantage-point from which, with the aid of his binoculars, he could see her working. He would watch for a while, then turn and ride back through the village to Lochanthrain. A week passed, his time with Becky restricted to the evenings. With January all but over he found himself standing in the woodshed at Lochanthrain watching Aaron attempt to heave a heavy roller from one of the outbuildings, a thick mat of several generations of unmolested weeds standing against him. 'For Christ's sake, Hugh, come and help.'

The wind had swung round to the north-east and the rain was turning to slush. Soon it would be sleet, and then snow.

Hugh shook his head.

Aaron put his shoulder to the handle of the roller but it would go no further. He looked over at his stronger friend, exasperated. 'Come on.'

'No.'

'Why not?'

'It's a crap idea.'

Aaron let the handle fall and came to stand beside him. They both looked over to the cleared bit of ground where Aaron had buried three of his landmines.

'What do you suggest, then?'

Hugh picked up a log from the pile beside him and lobbed it across the open ground. It landed perfectly: the cartridge exploded, blowing the log and a spray of dirt a foot high into the air. Aaron gave a high-pitched laugh of surprise, reached over and picked up another log. For the next few minutes they threw wood across the yard. Finally they hit and exploded the two remaining mines.

'Perfect,' said Aaron. 'They'll definitely work.' He walked over and looked into the still-smoking holes the detonations had blown in the soft earth. 'I've had this idea to stop the powder getting wet and give them a longer life.' He looked at Hugh. 'I'm going to wrap the cartridges in clingfilm before gluing the foam on top.'

'Smart,' said Hugh, his expression accommodating. 'By the way, just exactly what are you planning to do with them?'

'We, Hugh. We are going to plant them along the forestry walks the week before Easter. We'll go to one near Inverness. We don't want to mine any nearby – don't shit in your own woods and all that.'

Hugh nodded thoughtfully. 'You're completely fucking nuts, you know that?'

Aaron smiled innocently. 'It's going to be a hoot.' He looked around. 'Time to test a Molotov, I think.'

They walked out along a dirt road that led into the conifers. Aaron had tied one of the sweetie jars full of petrol to an axe-handle, which now rested on his shoulder. Hugh asked why he had glued a sheet of tinfoil around the glass.

'Protection. Gives me an extra few seconds to throw it.'

They came to the old dump, a deep hole cut among the trees in which Lochanthrain's rubbish used to be thrown. Lately it had become the last resting place of the cars that had given up life on the open road. There was an Austin Princess, an old Beetle and a battered truck of no obvious marque. All the vehicles' windows had been shot out, and bullet holes peppered the sides, the intensity increasing at the doors and around the fuel tanks.

'We never did manage to get hold of tracer bullets, did we?' Hugh was looking at the devastation.

Aaron laughed. 'I think we should manage to light them up this time.'

Hugh looked back down the track. 'Your parents away?'

'I told Father I was going to burn some junk.'

Aaron laid the Molotov on the ground, pulled a rag

from his pocket and reached over for the small can of petrol Hugh had been carrying. He soaked the rag and then, balancing the bomb on its shank, tied it tightly around the neck of the jar. 'Ready?' he asked.

Hugh nodded worriedly. 'Aim well,' he warned. 'I'll be pissed off if that thing hits me.'

Aaron gave him a big grin and splayed his feet, holding the Molotov straight out like a baseball player measuring up his swing. 'Flare me up, big boy,' he said, and Hugh, noticing the sleet turn to snow around them, put his lighter to the rag and jumped back.

Aaron spun on his heel once, twice, the bottle a sea of flames in front of him. Half-way through the second turn the jar tore away from the axe-handle and arced over Hugh's head to crash into the branches of a conifer, where it stuck. Hugh looked at it for a moment then ran at Aaron, who was staring up, open-mouthed. 'Run, you stupid fuck!' he shouted, pushing his friend in front of him, punching him in the back, Aaron's laughter adding to his violence.

They stopped and turned at a safe distance.

'Wait, wait, it's going to go!' Aaron said.

'Fucking arsehole!' shouted Hugh. 'I told you to make sure it was tight. That was way too close.' Just then the bottle exploded with a sharp crack and thickened petrol sprayed across several trees and the path where they had just been standing. The forest was on fire, billowing black smoke, with snow sheeting down into the flames.

'Beautiful, isn't it?' said Aaron.

Hugh watched the tree burn, watched the snow hit the wall of heat and disappear. The forest was too wet for the fire to spread. 'Yes, very pretty,' he agreed.

The Maserati pulled up, nose pointing out to sea, the passengers looking out into the gloom of the dying day.

Raindrops lashed against the windscreen, then joined to slide into the trough at the base of the glass.

'How much longer is it going to be like this?'

'It's February in a couple of days.'

'Is that going to be any better?'

'Probably not.'

Becky sighed. The darkness was beginning to weigh down on her. She turned to look at Hugh, a smile breaking through the strain. She had spent nearly three weeks now battering at the rock in the middle of the field and the work showed in her face. 'I don't know how much longer I'll be able to take it,' she said.

Hugh was gazing out to the west. 'It's worth it, come spring.' He tried to sound sympathetic. 'But I know how you feel. Sometimes in February you get crystal-blue skies. They make it all worthwhile.'

'How often does that happen?'

'One day, perhaps two.'

'Great.' Becky pulled herself together. 'So do you want to go for a walk or just straight to the hotel?'

He pursed his lips, then smiled. 'A quick walk?'

'Very quick.'

They leaped from the car, pulling on woollen hats, gloves and waterproofs. Then, led by Becky, they rushed down the wooden walkway to the beach.

The wind was whipping at the top of the waves, sending streamers of white spray across the sky. Sand rushed in small storms around their ankles. The tide was out and they ran into the gale. The shallow slope of the beach took the force from the waves, causing the water to trip over in its repeated attacks, each wave's progress accompanied by the explosion of its flanks hitting cliff walls further along. Where the rocks met the sea, the spray reached into the sky only to be caught in the wind and torn away across the salty vegetation.

'*Déjà vu*,' shouted Hugh, when they stopped. Becky

turned and he embraced her, kissed her theatrically, and then they held each other close. When they separated to look at each other, their eyes flicked back towards the car. They turned, and with Hugh leading Becky by the hand ran back to the Maserati.

'Hotel, then,' Becky said, when they both collapsed into their seats.

'Hotel,' Hugh agreed.

They checked into the inn and were led to a room overlooking the sea. The owner showed them around, asking what time they wished to eat. Then he handed Hugh the key and left.

'Not bad,' said Becky.

'This is one of the few good hotels in the Highlands. People drive from all over the north to celebrate special occasions here.'

Hugh was at the window, looking out over the lawn to where great sheets of white water rose above the cliff to hang against the black beyond.

'Like us,' said Becky, putting her arm around him.

'Like us,' replied Hugh, looking at her. 'Thank you for bringing me here.'

'It's a big birthday,' she said. 'You're a man now.'

'Not until tomorrow.'

'Well, then, maybe I should make use of you while you're still young.' She began to undress him, leaning back against the arms holding her waist.

Hugh felt a little self-conscious, standing at the bar. His shirt, a Christmas present from Becky, seemed to shimmer. He was wearing chinos, which had been purchased for special occasions but which had never been particularly comfortable. The martini Becky had ordered for him needed to be handled with care. He sipped at it and looked over her. She didn't look uncomfortable, she looked gorgeous, an image of effortless self-confidence and beauty. She smelt of soap, all warm, like honey.

'You're lovely.'

'Thank you.'

'I mean it, to die for.'

'I don't think that'll be necessary. Just sit there and listen.'

He looked at the smooth movements she made as she talked, telling him how she was going to pour bronze. She would need to borrow equipment from the ArtHigh foundry, she said, before explaining the method she planned to use; the lost-wax process of creating a cast.

The owner, now in a threadbare kilt, came into the bar and said that their table was ready. He led them out into a conservatory where the power of the weather rattled the glass with its full, fearsome force. He asked if they were sure that they did not prefer to be in the main dining room but they shook their heads. Two other couples were already in the conservatory and another would join them. Laughter from a large party could be heard within the main building. The owner poured their water. 'I always like this time of year,' he said. 'All the guests are local – well, except the couple over by the plant there and I think they may be here to buy an estate that's for sale near Kintail.' He put the top back on the bottle and set it down. 'The best thing is that everybody's celebrating something.'

Hugh and Becky smiled up at him. He frowned suddenly. 'You're not easily offended, are you?'

'I don't think so,' said Becky.

'Good, because those two, the ones buying the estate, seem to be constantly celebrating. I hope they won't bother you but if they do just shout.' The landlord poured the wine for Becky to taste, then left them.

Hugh studied the couple. She was leaning forward on her elbows, dark hair swept back from a widow's peak,

264

giving way to a strong-boned face. She was wearing a tight cashmere top that showed off her breasts and a firm waist. Her trousers were designed to reveal powerful, well-muscled legs, one of which was held straight, so her foot must have been resting in her companion's lap. If she was in her early thirties, he was approaching his forties. Lean and tough, he had gleefully predatory looks. His shirt was open-neck and showed off his Adam's apple as he held a shell vertically above his mouth, easing out the oyster with his tongue, all the time holding her gaze. She laughed, deep, rolling and filthy, as she lifted her napkin to wipe away the juice that had run down his chin.

'Oi,' Becky said, and Hugh turned his attention back to her.

'Amazing.'

She glanced with disdain at the couple. 'You've never seen Sloanes before?' she asked.

The first course arrived, langoustines for Hugh, gravadlax for Becky. He took a sip of his wine and Becky sighed with delight at her first taste of the salmon, offering some to Hugh. He broke into one of the little creatures on his plate. When he put the flesh to his lips, it was perfection.

'What's our next celebration?' asked Becky.

'You finishing that sculpture and returning to sanity.'

'Does it worry you?'

'You standing out there all day in the snow, rain, sleet and hail? Yes.'

'You know what I mean.'

'You turning that block of granite into an enormous pregnant belly? Should I be worried?'

Becky laughed. 'You shouldn't worry. I don't want your child.'

'I never even thought of that.' Hugh felt uncomfortable. He found himself avoiding her gaze, then bouncing

265

off the couple and back to her sympathetic smile. 'So what's next?' he asked.

'What do you mean?'

'With the sculpture, where does it go from here?'

Becky finished her salmon and leaned back, taking a sip of the wine. 'I'm drilling holes in the top of the granite so that I can fix a metal plate on the top. It's going to be very tricky. I might even require your help.'

'And what goes on top of that?'

'Something in bronze. I have no idea what it'll be as yet.'

They discussed the village's reaction to Becky's rising work of art – bafflement and suspicion – until the arrival of the main course. Then she asked what Aaron thought of it. Hugh told her he hadn't mentioned it, and she looked surprised, hurt. 'And you haven't either?'

'We don't really discuss you. He doesn't like it, gets all weird and wanders off or changes the subject.' He thought of his indiscretions over the wilder aspects of their sex-life, of the new experiences he would soon tell Aaron about, and felt faint guilt.

'I find it all very odd,' she said. 'Will he be there tomorrow night?'

'No. I'm shooting duck with him at dusk but he never comes to my birthday dinner. This year will be the first time it's not just me and Dad. It's always a bit uncomfortable, you know, given that it's also the anniversary of my mother's death.'

'And you're sure you want me to come?'

It was she who had insisted on an invitation but he did not point that out. 'Only if you want to. You're welcome, as long as you realize it's not going to be a bag of laughs.'

The hotelier refilled their glasses.

'So does Aaron still hate me?' Becky asked, when he had gone.

'I don't think he hates you. I thought he would after

266

you shot him in the head. I mean, it would have made sense, but in fact he seems to respect you for that. The mark's gone now but he certainly wasn't shy of showing it. If he's being weird it's because I don't spend as much time with him now.' Hugh paused and then went on, 'It's funny, you know, although he's very self-contained, he needs his audience.'

'You never did speak to him, did you? About Alison?'

'No.'

'Instead you help him set fire to trees.'

'Oh, I forgot to tell you. A couple of days ago we got that to work. He found that wire and tape help to hold the bottle on better. I think Mac suggested it to him. He managed to hit one of the cars this time. It was pretty impressive.'

Becky stopped eating. 'You did it again? After he nearly killed you last time. Jesus, Hugh, he could have covered you in burning petrol.'

'I thought the chances of him hitting me were pretty slight and he's not one to give up.' Hugh realized he should not have returned to this subject.

'It's not only stupid, it's childish.'

There was a silence, and Hugh noticed that the couple were looking at them. He caught the man's gaze, wanting to embarrass him into looking away, but the other's slow eyes held his until he had to break contact. He tried to pacify Becky by telling her that they had just about finished the deer cull, but she showed no interest. She ate everything on her plate then looked at him closely. 'You need to get out of here, Hugh. If you stay here you'll rot. You don't like the farm and you never will. God knows what will happen to Aaron. What if he doesn't get the property? He certainly won't if his mother outlives his father. I mean, I feel for him. He's a fuck-up. What is the story about his conception anyway? About his name? You never did tell me.'

Hugh put down his knife and fork. 'I don't think he'd want me to.'

'I'm your girlfriend, we don't have secrets,' she said. 'And, anyway, I'm hardly going to tell anyone, am I?'

Hugh protested for a while but she refused to let it go. He gave up, wanting the evening to be good. 'His mother's got lovers, always has had, and when she got pregnant she thought Aaron was the product of one of those affairs, right? So she started acting really nice to his father to cover it up. They hadn't had sex for years at the time and suddenly she's back into it. Well, he was so happy about it he admitted to her that after the New Year party that year, when she had been blind drunk, comatose even – she can get like that – he had taken advantage of her.'

'He raped her?'

'Well, I don't know about that. I suppose so – that's certainly what she accused him of. She told him she was going to get an abortion. She would have – I mean, she's told this to Aaron, this whole story, time after time since he was old enough to listen, it was our equivalent to the birds and the bees.' He smiled at his joke but Becky's expression did not change so he had to continue. 'Well, when she suggested the abortion she could tell his father thought it was a good idea, so she decided to have him instead, and Aaron was the first name she saw in the Bible by her bed. You see, Aaron's father doesn't like Jews.'

At first Becky didn't say anything. She sat silently until the plates were cleared and only then did she speak. 'All right, it's shit,' she said softly. 'It's worse than shit, it's really terrible. But are you going to ruin your life in some giant sacrifice to Aaron's unhappiness? He has my sympathy, Christ, my heart goes out to him but, Hugh, it doesn't change anything. You're too good to be wasted.'

She reached across with one hand to touch his cheek.

He did not move, just looked at her, staring into the sympathy in her eyes. 'So what, then? Just leave? Where would I go?'

'Why not London? Or Edinburgh? Or abroad even. Go round the world. Get a feel for it. Have you applied for your passport yet?'

Hugh shook his head.

'Tomorrow. You apply tomorrow. I'm going to take you to the post office.'

Hugh thought of the betrayal, and the ease with which Becky suggested it. The passport no longer bothered him: he knew Aaron already had one – his mother made him get it when she had once considered sending him abroad to be educated. Hugh would get a passport but also, at that moment, he realized that he would leave his friend if necessary. He wanted to be with Becky.

The owner arrived at their table to ask them about desserts. They ordered coffee and, at Becky's request, brandy.

'OK. We'll go and see Mrs Cameron tomorrow.' Hugh smiled at Becky. 'How about I leave with you when you leave?'

Becky reached for Hugh's hand. 'Perhaps. Perhaps with me. First I've got to decide where I'm going.'

'You could decide to stay up here.'

Her brow ridged. 'No, I don't think so. One winter is easily long enough.' She paused again. 'You promise me, whatever happens, you won't waste your life looking after Aaron?'

Hugh nodded, not at all sure of her. He must go with her. He would make sure Aaron was OK.

In the wake of the after-dinner drinks they were close again, touching hands across the table, smiling into each other's eyes, when the southern woman at the next table produced a vast roar of laughter. She even slapped her muscled thigh, the crack of a palm on healthy flesh.

'Beastie,' she roared, 'you're disgusting. That's why I married you.'

As the echo from her voice died away, it was replaced by his soft, moist laugh, 'Heh, heh, heh, heh, heh, heh.'

Becky looked at the other table, this time in disgust. 'Shall we go through to the bar?' she asked.

Hugh pushed back his chair to stand up.

The forest dripped on Aaron and Hugh as they followed the path down to the pond. They walked single file, guns resting on waterproofed shoulders, well wrapped, boots gripping the sodden earth. The wind had died, and above them the weight of cloud seemed slowly to dilate and contract. The trees thinned and the space began to fill with giant rhododendrons, the boys' footfalls sounding at first strong then swiftly lost, muffled in the weight of the air. The bushes grew higher and higher until they reached overhead to form an arch under which the light expired in gloom. Hugh paused briefly to light a cigarette, the flame revealing the thick, tangled branches of the great plants. It died and he continued after Aaron, soon turning a final corner and emerging into the darkening greyness beside an old granite boat-shed.

Hugh stood and waited, moving the gun from his shoulder to the crook of his arm so that he could shove his hands deep into the pockets of his jacket. He stood hunched, cigarette in his mouth, looking at the old, rotten walls of the building, his eyes slowly following the stonework up to the slated roof, its moss-covered pattern broken, split, cracked and lost, then along the lead topping to the landward end where a long cable emerged and rose up into the branches of an ancient oak before reappearing at the tree's other side, looping round a smaller pine then moving off into a beech. He could see other lines emerge web-like into other trees and turned his eyes back to the oak, where he could see the outline of a box sitting in the branches. The sound of oars made him turn, and a boat inched out from the front of the boathouse. Slowly Aaron, working the oars, emerged, and the bows turned towards the bank where Hugh was standing.

With Hugh on board Aaron turned towards one of the small islands that peppered the surface of the pond with thick, bulbous vegetation. As they passed the mouth of the boathouse Aaron held up a remote control, pressed a button and returned it to his pocket. He took up the oars again and pulled.

The bows cut into the water, leaving a smooth wound, the surface bleak, metallic.

From the great trees along the bank the first great exhalation of Fauré's *Requiem* moved like advancing dead across the waters, touching the young men in the boat under the hodden sky. The weeping of the voices surrounded them as the boat circled the island, coming in to land where a small patch of clear ground had been cut in the bush. As the keel rubbed against earth, Hugh lifted his gun and stepped out, turning to push the prow back out into the water. As the boat swung so did Aaron's form until they were face to face over the growing gap of air and water. Their smiles were those of friends, their eyes measuring all; in their growing distance lay the past and the present. Hugh broke the stare and looked down to his gun. He slipped the rounds into the barrels and closed the action, standing with his back to the rising vegetation and looking out into the dying day, the boat pulling away round the next island where Aaron would tie it up and take his own place waiting for the birds to arrive.

Hugh stood still. The pond had been left untouched throughout the entire season. Not once had they shot here, until this night, Hugh's birthday. This was Aaron's present: he had wired up the boathouse and the surrounding trees without Hugh's help, had played the *Requiem* every night to condition the birds, all for this moment. He listened to the 'Sanctus' break over the water, the rising power, 'Hosanna in Excelsis'. The first widgeon banked around the trees as the voice of the soprano, Arleen Auger, filled the air. The birds, out-stretched necks pushing forward, black against the bulging sky, the darkness between the beating wings eclipsed by the absolute darkness of the barrels that rose to follow their flight. The burning gunpowder flared from the muzzles and the birds tumbled and fell, then more came and fell too, or turned in confusion, and night crushed the already failed day, squeezed the life from this small liquid gap between land and sky, the guns fired and nature fell and the voices of a choir sang the departing day, and finally all was gone. And with the loss of light came a silent world but for the frantic scrambling of the dog.

There was the sound of oars, and the boat rounded the island. As it pulled in Hugh began to throw in the birds, counting twenty-eight. He picked up Fi by the scruff of the neck and stepped aboard, asked how Aaron had got on. His friend had taken twenty-five. He settled as Aaron turned the boat back in the direction of the boathouse, and offered his thanks for the gift.

As Aaron rowed Hugh leaned back and, to wash away the memory of applying for a passport, let the boat's movement slide him into a memory of when they were very young. There were plastic soldiers in great battalions across the vast stone floors of Lochanthrain. Armies moved towards each other only to fall prey to the guns of the opposition. More would arrive, set up to fall. Each of the boys, he could picture at once Aaron's face, wore a tape-recorder as a backpack, and moved against one another to the sound of great orchestras. He remembered the music. Aaron with Beethoven's *Ninth*, an awful twisted recording that Hugh subsequently found had been performed in Berlin during the war – still one of Aaron's favourites – while he had Elgar's recording of his own violin concerto with a young Menuhin in the lead. As he leaned back in the boat, listening to the silence, he closed his eyes and saw that day, saw them circle each other, lost in the music.

FIFTEEN

Hugh was waiting for the kettle to boil, thermos beside the range, when the telephone rang. He stayed where he was, listening to Becky's recorded voice say that she was unavailable, probably involved in some rural activity, and could the caller leave a message. The kettle fell quiet, the small pause before the boil and a man's voice, words softened with the hint of a Welsh accent, emerged from the machine. Beside Hugh the water began to bubble, steam rushing from the spout. He did not move. 'Becky, it's me. Don't feel like I'm pressuring you, just checking how your thinking's going, seeing if you've come up with any answers yet. I'll talk to you later. Don't get too cold.' There was a pause and then the man signed off. 'I love you. 'Bye.'

At last Hugh shifted, darting across the room to pick up the receiver but hearing only the dialling tone. He held it to his ear and listened until the sickness in his stomach subsided, only then putting it down and going back to take the kettle from the hob.

He filled the Thermos with tea, dressed for the weather and walked out into the farmyard, the cold at once tearing at his face. It was bleak, and the barn rattled with the wind as he walked past and on to the field. All was dead around him but for Becky who, padded and layered, her silhouette twisted further by the welding hat she was wearing, hunched over her sculpture. She seemed an ungainly figure in the wind and rain, the blue flame from the oxyacetylene torch the only live colour.

The light went out as Hugh approached. Becky picked up a large spanner and began to tighten one of the three bolts that emerged from the top of the granite belly. She put down the tool as he reached her side and waited for him to unscrew the top of the flask and pour her some tea. She held the cup in both hands and sipped. Then they turned to look at the stone, its shape rough but recognizable. The metal she had been welding formed a cone, like a dunce's or a witch's hat. 'Whatever I cast will fit over the top,' she said, her eyes wandering over her work and then on to him, noticing his thoughtfulness. 'What?' she asked.

'What decision are you planning to make?'

She gazed at him, and then turned to the sculpture. 'I need to decide how to finish this,' she said.

'That's not what I mean.'

Her eyes swung back to his, but Hugh, the cold digging through his flesh, the unbearable feeling heavy on him, turned and walked back towards the house.

When he reached the barn Sandancer looked up from her hay, complaining as Hugh led her out and saddled her. She tried to push him with her head but he shoved her away and she quietened at once. He led her into the weather and swung himself up, looking over the plain as he rode out across the yard. Becky was tightening the last of her bolts but watching him. Then she stepped back, threw the spanner across the field and turned to walk towards the house.

Hugh eased his heels into Sandancer's sides, sending her into a trot towards home. He was crossing the tributary when he saw the Maserati speed through Huil and up the Brae. He watched it go but kept Sandancer's pace a steady walk. He had left because he couldn't think what to say, he felt impotent in his efforts to influence her and, despite knowing that she was choosing their future, he felt there was little he could do. She would leave, that was obvious. His own future was less so.

She was waiting at the farm, emerging from her car, as he slipped from Sandancer. She reached him as he stood holding the saddle and bridle in his hands. 'Why didn't you tell me he'd called?'

Hugh went to the harness room while his horse walked away to her paddock. 'What's there to say?'

'Plenty.' She stood looking at Hugh over the saddle, now resting on its stanchion. 'Like what he asked me.'

He began to dry then oil the leather. 'I would have thought that was obvious, just as obvious as your decision to consider it.'

They were both soaked. The air in the room was cold, and they steamed. Becky walked away and spun on her heel. 'Look, I loved this guy for a long time, you know, most of the last decade. I thought we were going to be together for ever; I never even dreamed it would be otherwise. Then, as the years passed, I began to wonder why he didn't ask me, but he had always been down on marriage . . .'

'Is this going to make me feel any better?'

'Listen, just listen.' She unbuttoned the top of her jacket, which was tight around her throat. 'So then he leaves me, just like that. I'm devastated. I trash his flat. I take his car. I come up here, meet you . . .' She stopped and looked at Hugh, who felt those eyes hard upon him. He wanted to fall into them, away from the pain. 'But then he tells me that it was all a terrible mistake, a crisis. He tells me he was acting like a child and that he realizes that all he wants in life is to be with me for ever. He asks me to marry him.'

276

'And will you?'

'No.' She sighed. 'I don't know.' She looked at Hugh again. 'I mean, where is this going, Hugh? Where are we going? I always thought I wanted children. Maybe I want a life like other people. But you're young. When will you want that?'

Hugh thought. 'I just want you.'

Becky softened, and touched his face. 'Look, this is so bad for me. I don't know what I'm going to do, I promise I haven't made any decisions. All I want right now is . . .' she let out a short laugh '. . . a hot bath, a hot bath with you. Can we do that? Can we be nice to each other?'

Hugh felt cold and uncomfortable under her touch.

'Please,' she said, and at his almost imperceptible nod led him to the car.

'People of Huil, you are standing on the graves of your fathers and their forefathers, and their souls are burning in Hell today.'

The mourners stood huddled in small groups along the slopes of the graveyard, trying to avoid the bitter flurries of hail that ricocheted off the gravestones. Closer in, the shepherd from Shiloch stood with a straight back, a spade held into the mound of earth. On the other side of the grave stood Betsy Ross, her prayers unanswered, her sister in the hole. The Rod of God's voice rose over the sound of the river crashing through the falls. 'Which is where poor Mary is headed.' He looked into the grave, then took in the crowd, the majority of Huil's families represented. 'As are you.'

Hugh looked at Betsy, her body slightly hunched, her face stoic and expressionless. She would not be showing any grief today, her future a grave by her sister's side. For Hugh these moments always brought back the poem Mac would recite, written by some dead Gael, something

277

about life being so much black sludge. The recollection caused him to turn and look at the poacher, who stood outside the perimeter, leaning on the graveyard wall. Mac winked.

Hugh stamped his feet against the cold and looked over at his father, who turned and muttered to an old crofter sporting a giant dewdrop on the end of a great hooked nose. The crofter muttered a reply out of the side of his mouth, engendering laughter. The Rod looked their way. 'You stand in this graveyard now in apparent sympathy but it is mere guilt, I tell you. You think turning up at a funeral, at the burial of one sinner, will save you, but you are fooling yourselves.'

There was a stirring among the crowd. Hugh leaned over to Aaron, who was standing straight-backed in an old black suit from God knew where and a grubby white nylon shirt, a look that suited his yellow hair. 'The Rod seems a little more deranged than usual today.'

Aaron didn't reply. He stood watching the minister, blinking only when the wind threw lumps of hail into his face.

The Rod looked down into the grave again. 'One chance,' he shouted. 'One chance is all you have to save yourselves, otherwise all is darkness, all is pain. You must run towards the truth, run into the terror that is the Lord. But so few of you choose to do so. So few of you choose to stand up for what is right and face down the evil that encroaches upon us more each day.' Eyes, bright under lifeless skin, ran along the lines of people. 'Traitors,' he spat.

There was more uncomfortable shifting.

Hugh leaned over to his friend again. 'Why are we here? This is fucking ridiculous.'

Becky had wanted to come and see a Highland funeral but the shepherd had told her that Catholics were not welcome.

278

Aaron made no reply.

Hugh had been growing worried about Becky. She had spent the previous three weeks, nearly all of February, in her bed sketching her ideas for the pinnacle of her sculpture and allowing him to do everything for her. It had started with a bad cold and now she had decided that she wasn't going to deal with the winter any more. When she wasn't sketching, she spent her time reading the book on sculpture or talking to the ArtHigh foundrymen on the telephone. She was refusing to get up unless the sun began to shine. So far no luck.

He thought he had made progress when she expressed an interest in the funeral. At first she was intrigued by how bad it could get, but then her phone call to the shepherd to check on times had ended in this latest disaster. She said she was depressed and that Huil was a shithole, a view Hugh found it difficult to argue against.

'Soon,' said the Rod, 'the tide of filth will engulf us. Soon all that we have will be lost. We need to stand together against the future.' The minister's voice had risen to a howl, and spit now joined snow in the freezing air. 'Otherwise we fall. It is we who create God in our churches. Don't you realize, you people of Huil, that by staying away, by spending your Sabbaths lying in bed fornicating and reading the trash propaganda sent up from the south, that you weaken God?'

Hugh noticed Aaron smiling. The whole congregation was now concentrating on their minister.

'We will God into existence. Together, all of us, standing and believing, create a God who can move mountains, but as you all bleed away into your secular lives He grows ill and begins to die and when God is dead here in the Highlands, my friends, it is all over. Evil will have taken root and grown before you know what has happened.'

'Blasphemy,' Aaron whispered to Hugh, grin now

wide across his face. Hugh looked down to the shepherd, who had turned slightly towards the minister, clearly unsure how to act.

'Don't you realize that God is the champion of our cause? We have to make common cause and believe, my friends, believe in evil and fight it in strength. Our opinions as individuals are nothing compared to the will of God. All can be justified in his name.'

The shepherd reached across and tried to put a hand on the Rod's arm but it was shrugged off.

'God is nothing without fear,' the minister suddenly screamed. 'I am nothing without your fear. You are letting God die, you seed of Satan.' Having spat the last insult across the grave the minister staggered and was caught by the shepherd, who dropped the spade. The crowd stood unmoving as the Rod was led slowly towards the gate. Through the storm Hugh could hear someone whistling and turned to see Mac's departing back, but then Aaron had his arm, leading him towards the minister. The shepherd, supporting the Rod with his shoulder, looked up suspiciously as Aaron approached, watched by all.

'Do you want us to fill the hole in?' Aaron asked, and the shepherd nodded, thanking them.

They took a spade each and began to throw the wet earth into the hole as Betsy was led off, her face grey. Soon they were joined by others who had brought tools with them, all working without words, pulling a veil of dignity over the scene.

Hugh found Becky in the workshop, a blanket acting as a shawl across her shoulders, her figure crouched over the core. Two weeks earlier she had emerged from her bed to take up an invitation from ArtHigh to see a casting in action, reminding her of the process she had learned at school all those years before. Since then she had been twisting metal rods to her will and coating them with an earthy clay, half an inch or so every day. The upper trunk, head and upstretched arms of a figure emerged slowly under her hands. The room smelt slightly of molasses.

Hugh sat on the workbench, looking down. Becky glanced up. 'What do you think?'

'Breasts could be bigger.'

She laughed and ran her hand over the dried core. 'I think it's ready to take the wax now,' she said. 'Where have you been? I tried to call last night.'

'Stalking.'

'I thought the season was over.'

'It is. Aaron wanted to go up on to the Arab's land for a couple of days. He didn't tell me until we were crossing the march. It's not just out of season, it's poaching, so he knew I wouldn't approve.'

'Poaching?' She leaned back. 'Why did he want to poach? It's not like he's short of land.'

'The Arab doesn't keep control of his hill, and there are lots of muledeer – you know, cross-bred red and Sika. It's bad for the herd so Aaron wanted to take them out.' It wasn't too far from the truth.

Becky lifted a sheet of wax from where it floated in a small basin beside her. She began slowly and carefully to lay it against the core, pushing it into the surfaces.

'And do you approve?'

'No – well, I mean, he's right, but I think he's just got into the fun of poaching. Also, with the deer out of season, it has to be on somebody else's patch. Anyway, we were out there for a couple of nights, there's so little daylight.'

Becky looked out towards one of the small windows. Although the light was dirty, it was stronger than it had been during the darkest days. 'What if you'd got caught?'

Hugh smiled. 'Embarrassment. I'm not sure what

281

they'd do. It won't happen, though, we know what we're doing.'

Becky had returned to the sculpture. 'Did you get anything?'

'A couple.'

'What did you do wi—' She stopped again and looked up.

'It's another advantage of the Arab's place, it's close to Mac.'

'But there was no trouble?'

'No, the keeper's a drunk.'

Hugh didn't say that the trip was also revenge for insults the keeper had thrown their way in the pub at New Year, or that Aaron had insisted on completing the retribution by torching his byre.

Becky stood up and leaned over Hugh to pick up a small gas canister with a cooker attachment. She put it on the floor beside her and ignited the burner. Then she unwrapped a set of dentist's tools, picked out one and held it over the heat. Slowly she began to melt the sheets of wax together.

'Anyway, there's not much I could have said to Aaron. He was so keen, so excited. It's all getting pretty weird.'

Becky was concentrating, following the lines of the joins.

'He'd never have gone poaching before,' Hugh went on. 'Says it's because he now has the ability. We can work silently, you see, using the airgun with tranquillizers and then cutting the stags' throats when they're down.'

'I don't want to know,' Becky said.

Suddenly he wanted to tell her about the fire, the way Aaron had made it look like an accident, but he kept talking about the subsequent poaching trip. He lit a cigarette.

'I think he may have a point,' he said as he exhaled. 'It's a good idea, if you're going to poach in the first place, because it means it would be difficult for them to charge you; I mean, you're hardly going to shoot deer with an airgun, are you? But we had the rifle as well anyway, so . . .'

'And a couple of dead deer.'

'And a couple of dead deer.'

Hugh smoked his way down the cigarette while he watched Becky work. She was so different from when he first saw her: in those early days she had had an appearance of confidence, despite the alien location. Slim, pallid, urban, she had looked so glamorous and otherworldly to Hugh. Now, hunched over her sculpture, her blanket across her shoulders, she had taken on the appearance of a small creature newly emerged from an egg.

'I think you're right,' Hugh said. 'I need to get out of Huil.'

'Yes,' Becky said, not looking up, her voice matter-of-fact. 'You need to go.'

'With you.'

She said nothing, continuing to lay on the strips, melting each onto its neighbour. Hugh waited, then went to the house for tea, returning with a tray. The smell of molasses had been replaced by that of hot wax. Once the sheets were in place Becky began to mould the figure to the form she wanted. The shape began to flesh out. The woman's body, like the emergent half of a mermaid, arched backwards, her head thrown back, face to the sky she was reaching for. Standing now, eyes tight in concentration, Becky worked away at the tips of the outflung hands, pushing in at the small indentations of the nails.

'The shepherd's gone away,' she said, as if prompted by a private thought. 'Apparently he needs to do some course in Edinburgh, at the Free Church College. The minister's sick and he has to stand in.'

'The Rod's not sick, he's bonkers. It started at that funeral when he suggested he was God.' He saw her smile.

'I didn't think he sounded that sane before,' she said, looking up. 'But, anyway, it means I'm all alone out here for a day or two.'

They fell silent, Hugh watching Becky work. The progress of the sculpture weighed on him. Their compromise after the worries of a month before had been that decisions would be left until its completion. He presumed the man in the south waited too, to hear how she felt when this sculpture stood complete, throwing her hands out towards the northern sky as if in need of light, or insight. Warming the wax with her fingers, Becky eased in the joints of the fingers, moving down to the knuckles. Hugh had taken comfort from the sculpture, his part in the process, in the fetching and carrying. It gave him, he felt, the edge over all competitors. He watched her until lunch when he fetched soup from the house. Then, as she returned to her work, he slipped away, promising to return later.

The ride to Lochanthrain took barely an hour, and Aaron stood waiting for him in the gun room, the granite walls stacked with firearms of various types. On the table in the centre stood the box of mines, wrapped and ready to go. As Hugh walked in his friend disassembled the Holland & Holland shotgun he was polishing and returned it to its case.

'Are you really sure you want to do this?' Hugh asked, looking at the cartridges. The idea still made him feel faintly ill.

'Of course.'

As Aaron closed the gun case, tightening the leather straps around each end, Hugh decided to make a stand. 'Mate,' Hugh said, and Aaron looked over, 'this is shit. We're just going to injure some poor punter.' He could feel the disappointment, a betrayal already hanging in the room.

Aaron sniffed, then wiped his nose with the back of his hand. 'That's the idea,' he said, his voice calm but cold.

'But why? I mean, what's our problem with them? You had problems with Alfie and Gus, with the fucking stupid keeper, I can understand that, but you didn't actually hurt them.'

'Those are locals. We're talking about tourists here, Hugh, clogging up our roads, changing the place. Walkers as well. Jesus, Hugh, I shouldn't have to explain this to you. We've talked about this. They are . . . They are . . .' and here Aaron thought for a moment '. . . not us.'

Hugh snorted. 'They're not us? So we'll break their legs?'

'Exactly.'

Hugh was still thinking about this when Aaron spoke again. 'Look, it would probably just sprain their ankles, give them a fright.'

Hugh failed to look convinced.

'Imagine it.' Aaron conjured with his hands. 'It's going to be great. A family is enjoying their trip round the beautiful Highlands, the sun is shining, the woods smell beautiful, summer is in the air so they think they'll take a little stroll on one of the forestry walks, just perfect, right. They park their car and walk off into the woods, they're hanging out with nature, perhaps they're fond of birds and see a couple they like, perhaps they stop on a park bench and have a little picnic. The smell of pine fills the air, sun comes down through the branches. You know. Then they go a little further, the path leading them deep into the woods, to a waterfall, say, the day hot enough for them to think of going for a swim. Then, as they weave their way through the trees, at the furthest reaches of the path, *bang*! One of them falls screaming to the ground, clutching their ankle, a deep steaming hole blown where they just stood. They are all shouting, holding one another, trying to see the damage. What the hell was that? they want to know. What the hell was that?' Aaron's long fingers swept the air. 'Eventually they work out that it was a mine, a booby-trap, and there they are in the middle of a forest, miles from their car, one of them with a sprained ankle . . . in the middle of a minefield. Is that going to twist their minds or what?'

Hugh looked at his friend. 'Is that supposed to encourage me?'

Aaron sighed, the tension leaving his thin frame. 'This is the fucking trouble with you now, Hugh, you've lost your sense of fun. Six months ago you would have been well up for this. You're becoming one of them.'

'Mate, six months ago you would not have wanted to blow up tourists.'

Aaron looked at Hugh for a long time then turned to pick up the Winchester repeater from the table. He pulled back the action repeatedly, checking for any spare bullets that might have been caught in the chamber.

'OK, forget about it. Let's just fucking forget about it.' He let the action crash home and pointed the barrel at the floor, pulling the trigger to uncock the mechanism. There was a crack and the spines of both straightened in shock. Hugh stood absolutely still, his eyes on the bristling hairs that had sprung up on Aaron's neck.

The bullet ricocheted off the walls, its passage past them a whistle, its journey taking only a fraction of a second before it played itself out; a very, very long fraction of a second. They stood where they were for some time, and then they deflated, the tension leaving them like air from a tyre.

Aaron turned. 'Are you all right?'

Hugh nodded. 'You?'

They looked at each other wide-eyed, then sank to the floor. After a minute they began to laugh.

Finally Aaron, who had rested himself against the table leg and had been staring at the wall, looked back at his friend. 'Sorry.'

'That's all right. It's good to be reminded you're alive once in a while.'

Aaron pulled back the bolt on the rifle and peered into the breech.

'Clearly I shouldn't upset you while you're cleaning weapons,' Hugh said, slowly moving across the floor and picking up the shell casing that lay in a groove between the granite slabs.

'That's so fucked up.' Aaron removed the action of the Winchester and looked down the barrel, as if a malevolent genie might be hiding there. 'I never make mistakes like that.'

'Wouldn't they all laugh?' Hugh sighed. 'Aaron Harding ran out of things to shoot so he shot himself.' He looked around. 'Where do you think the slug went?'

They struggled to their feet, Hugh feeling unsteady on leg muscles stretched in fright. He looked in the corners of the room. There was nothing in the shadows. He checked the wooden surface of the table before Aaron called him over, taking an old side-by-side twenty-bore from the rack and carrying it across. He pointed to the stock and pulled the smashed bullet from the wood. 'That would still have done some damage if it had hit one of us.'

'Stung like buggery, I would imagine,' Hugh agreed.

'Well, I suppose if you're not prepared to go and plant landmines then we could go and sand this down.'

Hugh nodded and followed him from the room.

Hugh felt a sharp pain take root in his head. He stood holding the telephone to his ear listening to what Becky was saying, that the man who wanted to marry her, he wouldn't listen to the name, had arrived unannounced, flying into Inverness, hiring a car and driving up to Shiloch. 'I really didn't know,' she said.

He tried to get his thoughts together. He knew it was stupid but he couldn't help but feel this was his country. What the fuck was this man doing here?

'Where is he now?'

'In the bath. He said it was a long trip, a bad delay at Gatwick.'

In the bath. In the bath that he and Becky had shared so many times.

'I can't believe this. Why did you let him in?'

Becky sighed. 'Come on, Hugh, I couldn't turn him away. It would have been childish.'

The usual equilibrium in Hugh's head had been churned to the point at which he could hardly think. He had just returned from the ArtHigh foundry with the equipment Becky needed to finish the sculpture, and he tried to get this idiot thought out of his mind but it stuck, leaving him indignant. He had rung to tell her of his success. And now this.

'So what am I supposed to do?' he asked finally.

'Well, what do you want to do?'

He immediately thought of Aaron and was about to suggest violence but he realized he needed to appear mature. It was just that he couldn't think of what to say.

The pause was lengthening. 'Fuck's sake,' he said at last. 'Ring me when he's gone.'

He heard Becky sigh again. 'Come on, Hugh, it's not that big a deal.'

It was. Hugh didn't sleep that night, and the next day he found himself at the edge of a clearing in the woods that peppered the northern wall of the south glen. He took the Leica glasses from his eyes. It was still far too early for Becky to be out of bed, but he did not want them to leave Shiloch without his seeing it. Aaron sat with his back against the stump of a tree, and Hugh turned to look at him. His eyes fell to the long, thin, reinforced-plastic case that lay slightly to the side. Hugh had never seen it before but until then had been too preoccupied to mention its presence. Now he nodded at it. 'New case?'

'New gun.'

Hugh was surprised. 'You didn't tell me.'

'It's a surprise,' Aaron replied, his small smile suggesting pride.

'And you're so keen to show it to me you brought it on to somebody else's land?'

'Thought you might want to use it.' Aaron nodded towards the farmhouse on the plain below.

Hugh's first laugh since the phone call was short and bitter. 'It would have to be a fucking powerful gun.'

'It is.'

Hugh looked back at his friend. Aaron reached out and pulled the case over so that it sat between them. He flicked open the three catches and lifted the lid. The ugliest rifle Hugh had ever seen lay snug in its foam interior. Aaron lifted it out and handed the weapon across.

Hugh took it, feeling the grip of the reinforced plastic stock, a vile shade of scum green under his hand. The barrel seemed absurdly long, the bolt unconventional. Wedged onto the top was an enormous set of telescopic sights.

'Magnum 7mm. Laser sights,' said Aaron. 'It uses a little red dot.'

'Is this legal?' asked Hugh.

'Yup, and yesterday I sighted it for half a mile.'

Hugh looked back at the farmyard. 'It's more than that.'

'Hell, we're sporting people. We wouldn't want to do it without a stalk, would we?'

Hugh handed the rifle back. 'Very nice, very sick.' He raised the glasses again and looked out at the empty farmyard. 'Now, if you had a pickaxe handle, that might be a different story.'

But Aaron wasn't listening: he was using the rifle's laser sights to follow a car travelling west along the road below.

The phone call he received from Becky that evening was, if anything, more disturbing than the one of the night before. Hugh had spent the afternoon on the hillside watching her and this man – he could only make out general features over the distance, black hair, tall, that sort of thing – as they took a long walk up the edge of the burn where Hugh had found her fishing on their second meeting. Becky and the man had been in intense conversation, both gesturing as they spoke, but he had been glad to see that neither had touched the other more than to make the occasional point. Now Becky was suggesting he meet this guy. 'I think it might be helpful.'

'I don't.'

'It might make him realize that he's not the only man in the world. That he can't expect to come in here and for me just to take him back.'

'Has he tried anything?'

'Jesus, Hugh, don't you trust me?' She paused, waiting for a reply. There was none so she continued, 'He is sleeping in one of the spare rooms, of course. Do you want to come over?'

Hugh didn't.

Aaron had stayed with him throughout the day, never complaining, following the man's back with his laser sight as they walked up the river.

'Look,' said Becky, 'I want to cast the bronze

tomorrow. I'm going to need two men to help me pour the metal into the cast. It would be a good opportunity for you to meet. Why not?'

Hugh couldn't believe he agreed.

'Come over at about nine.'

And he spent another sleepless night beating himself up about it.

The man's eyes were hooded against the piercing light, the fresh end-of-winter sun leaching the sky of shadow, exposing the dead hills and glens to the possibility of a new life.

Hugh shifted nervously, eyes on Becky.

He had parked the pick-up a healthy distance from the fifty-gallon drum that sat on a large, flat rock beside the river, at the edge of Shiloch's home paddock. Becky had smiled when he had walked up, noticing the phoney arrogance in his step. He had peered into the drum, which Becky had turned into a furnace. The heat was intense, a glowing crucible at the centre of a high interior wall of firebricks. A fan-driven pump drove gas from two large cylinders into the depths, the flame hissing. Around the top, Becky had left several old bronze valve bodies and taps. Hugh looked over the field, as cold and white as the thin sky, the frosted floor melting away, sheep ignoring them from a distance. He joined the others and took his hands from the pockets of his camouflage jacket, holding them towards the heat. Then he lit a cigarette, looked at Becky and, quickly, at the man.

'This is ——,' she said and Hugh nodded, curtly.

The man studied him for a moment and then offered his hand. Hugh looked at it, left the cigarette in his mouth, shrugged and shook it.

They watched in silence as the furnace grew hotter, Hugh occasionally lifting his eyes to his rival and then, finding himself under a soft gaze, looking back to the twisting heat. The man had a thin face, the lips turned down, lines sliding away from his eyes. His hair was receding slightly but in a way that gave him a look of confidence, making Hugh feel like a child. He noticed that the index finger on the man's left hand carried a long jagged scar for its entire length.

Hugh returned to the pick-up and unloaded the heavy fireproof clothes he had collected from ArtHigh, carrying them over to the fire. He dressed, pulling on the heavy trousers and then the jacket. The man eased on the fireproof gloves and clapped.

'So, Becky, you're really about to cook up some molten bronze?' he asked, Welsh accent like pebbles in a stream.

Becky nodded and he laughed. 'I knew you'd go barmy out here. It must be in the water.' He grinned at Hugh, who felt suddenly sick.

Hugh shifted on his feet, aware of the ridiculous nature of the clothes he was wearing. He alone had donned the entire outfit. The man took off his gloves, laid them on the ground and walked over to check the furnace. Hugh asked Becky when the bronze would be ready. She told him it would be an hour yet and he tapped his legs with his hands. The man turned his head when Hugh began to remove the clothing.

'Jumping the gun a bit there, were you?' he asked.

Hugh didn't reply. He looked at the instruments that rested on the rock: a rake, some tongs and a pouring shank, which currently rested on three axle stands.

'So Becky tells me you're a farmer,' the man said. 'Interesting.'

Hugh looked at him, and at Becky, then turned and studied the sky. 'I'm going to nip home and drop off the car,' he said. 'My father' – he chose not to say 'Dad' – 'will probably need it and it's such a nice day, I should really give Sandancer a run.'

'Don't be long.' Becky nodded at the furnace. 'We don't want it to get too hot.'

Hugh walked back to the car, hearing the man laugh as he slid into the driver's seat, feeling his face go red for no reason at all.

When he returned he tied Sandancer to the rail in Shiloch's yard and walked out on to the field, the smell of sulphur strong in the air. The man was looking into the crucible while Becky stood back, the heat off the furnace now close to unbearable. Hugh hauled himself again into the heavy fireproof clothing and moved in towards the heat. The bronze scrap had gone from the top of the furnace. Becky smiled at him as he stood tapping nervously on the gas cylinders.

'Soon,' she said. 'We just need to get it a little hotter.'

The man stepped away from the epicentre. He was sweating, drops bubbling up from his forehead. 'Damn, Becky,' he said. 'Couldn't you have taken up painting?'

Her eyes were on the fire, the liquid alloy giving off a faint green flame.

To pass the time Hugh walked across to look at the mould. It was now a white, powdery cylinder, sunk into a sand-hole that had been filled in between several rocks. Only the mould's top showed, a large funnel-like hole where soon they would pour the bronze, the vents that would let the air out dotted around it.

Hugh looked across at Becky. 'Is this going to work?'

She came over and looked down. 'I hope so.' Then she gripped his arm. 'Thank you for coming back. I know how difficult this is for you.'

He thought about kissing her, in front of this man, blatantly, but she seemed aware of his intention because she turned and walked away. She looked at her watch then spoke to the man. He shook his head and pointed to Hugh, but Becky pushed the man towards the furnace.

Reluctantly he picked up the rake and, now watched by the others, pushed aside a little of the slag that glowed, even and red, across the top of the molten bronze. The surface reflected up at them, phosphorescence sparkling across the shimmer.

'It's ready,' she said, turning off the gas.

On Becky's instructions, using their fireproof gloves, Hugh and the man lifted the drum off the furnace, leaving the bricks and the crucible exposed. Then they picked up the tongs, one at each end. Hugh's rival looked serious. 'You're sure you're up for this?' he asked. 'We can't have any mistakes.'

'It's no problem with me,' Hugh replied.

'Hurry,' said Becky. 'It has to be hot.'

The man looked hard at Hugh, and then he straightened. 'OK, so what we're about to do is drop these tongs around the crucible, and lift it together. Then carefully, very carefully, we walk it over to the shank and put it down. Then we unclip and step away. OK?'

Hugh tried to look casual. 'No problem with me.'

The man kept his eyes on Hugh. 'I just want to make sure we understand each other because this is really fucking hot.'

'Come on, or it won't be,' said Becky.

Still watching each other, the two rivals moved the curve-edged grips over the crucible, lowered them and scissored the handles up so that the tongs fitted into place. They lifted slowly, the weight enormous, trying to keep the lip of the crucible horizontal, steady. With Becky clucking around them, they took short steps towards the shank.

On the ride across Hugh had fantasized about suddenly lifting his side, spilling metal all over the bastard, but now all he could do was focus on the superheated liquid with its surface froth. Nothing else should have existed at that moment, yet something still troubled Hugh. Earlier

294

Aaron had suggested lying up in the woods and shooting the man as he walked the metal home.

As Hugh looked into the crucible he heard Aaron's words in his head, the suggestion that when the body fell it would be covered by molten bronze, destroying all trace of the bullet. At the time Hugh had laughed, sure that it had been a joke. Now he desperately wanted to look up the hill, but found he could not take his eyes from the bronze, fear making its glowing, laval head omnipotent. Still, the thoughts ran through him: they were close to the woods here, easily within range of Aaron's new rifle, and Hugh wondered whether the alloy's density would slow a bullet enough to prevent it shattering the crucible. Hugh and the man stepped steadily across the rock, the heat terrible, and then they were over the ring at the centre of the pouring shank. For a moment Hugh thought he heard a shot, his body stiffened and the man cursed at his sudden movement, but he realized he had imagined it. They lowered the crucible into place and lifted away the tongs, the relief plain on both sides. The sound must have been the cry of a bird.

As Hugh stepped back he realized he didn't want this man killed, he just wanted him gone.

Becky cleared the scum from the top of the crucible with the rake, then pushed a small metal bomb deep into the liquid to get rid of any gases. She looked at her assistants and nodded.

'Same again?' said Hugh, and the man nodded.

This time they picked up the metal shank from where it rested on the axle stands. The two-pronged handle was at Hugh's end, meaning that he would have to pour. The bronze felt steadier carried this way and they crabbed sideways, towards the mould.

They were half-way there when a rifle-shot cut the air. There was no mistaking the sound of the real thing – its echo ricocheted across the glen. All three froze, the only movement the faint tidal rise and fall of the bronze, its clear surface reflecting the sky despite its great heat.

'They must be shooting on the hill,' said Becky, looking at Hugh, concerned.

'Let's finish this thing,' he said, moving as fast as he could towards the cast.

When the next shot came, Hugh kept going; he was watching the liquid.

Standing over the mould, shoulders aching, he gained the courage to glance up. His rival was hunched in concentration, face set hard.

Becky stood facing the pool of bronze in the crucible. She glanced at the hill and then at Hugh. 'Pour it slowly and steadily into that hole in the middle,' she said. 'Don't let too much in at once but don't go too slow either. Are you ready?'

The man nodded at Hugh, and slowly they tilted the vessel, letting the metal hit the top of the cast. With streams of sweat running down between his shoulder-blades, Hugh found himself suddenly, and bizarrely, enchanted by the beauty of the pouring liquid. It seemed to run with an ease unlike that of water, its colour and texture that of the sun, its arrival a shower of sparks, yet its mass sucked down and away. Slowly the cast filled, hot air rising from the ducts around the main hole. They kept pouring, kept pouring, kept pouring until the bronze bubbled up in all the holes. The pain, the tension was now excruciating, the only relief that Hugh was now sure Aaron had left his place in the woods, taken his rifle away, his joke played out.

On Becky's command, they centred the crucible, stepped to the side and emptied the last of the bronze into a hole she had dug in the sand. Carefully they tipped the crucible itself until it sat upside-down beside the wasted bronze, before walking the shank back to the axle stands and setting it down. Hugh and the man straightened and stretched their backs, easing the pressure off their shoulders. Hugh looked round at the various implements. 'What now?' he asked.

'That's it,' Becky said. 'Let everything cool. I'm not going to touch the cast for at least a day.' She laughed with relief. 'Shall we go and have a drink? I think we need one. That shooting came at a very bad moment.' They all looked up the hill, then Becky turned her eyes to Hugh. 'Any idea who it might have been?'

Hugh shook his head, watching the surface of the cooling bronze turn black, a yellowy dust forming on the top. She studied him, then walked over to the generator that ran the air pump, turning it off so that only the river now made any sound. Hugh and the man followed her as she walked across the field towards the farmhouse. Reaching the yard, Hugh stopped. 'I think I'll head home.'

Becky frowned. 'Come in for a drink.'

He was already saddling his horse. 'I want to give Sandancer a good run, probably take her up the hill.' He jerked his head in the direction of where the shots had come from.

'Call me later, then,' she said, as he pulled himself up into the saddle.

'Sure,' he said, easing the horse's head round. Sandancer was already beginning to move towards home.

'Ride safely now,' said the man.

Hugh didn't say anything, just burst out of the yard at a canter then galloped across the fields, feeling Sandancer powerful and alive underneath, his dead weight above.

SIXTEEN

Hugh threw down pitchforks of straw from the back of the pick-up. The muscles in his neck, all the way along his shoulders and down his back, ached from the work, but he did not falter. Then he caught his finger between wood and metal and cursed, nursing the bruised flesh in the warmth of his mouth, looking up at the sky, blue in the sunshine, and then at the grass, new shoots telling of spring. The world was turning under him, the home paddock always the first to respond to the return of the sun. Hugh felt his misery rise and bring with it tears, and he held them back, fighting the urge to let go. Then he went back to work, covering the earth with an even two-foot bed. But he felt tears water his eyes again and he spat in anger.

Still pained by the events of the previous days, he had been woken early by the sound of knocking. He had emerged from deep under the covers of his bed and walked down the hall in his underwear, pulling open the farmhouse door to find the pearl fisherman standing looking at him, dressed in black waders. He had caught the eyes at once, deep-set pools of sympathy, not just for Hugh and the news he was about to suffer, but for much more. At once Hugh had seen in those eyes an age of pain, of suffering, of watching others suffer, but he could make out no bitterness. He had been caught by the solid grace of the man, leaving him unselfconscious of his half-dressed state.

'Your horse,' the man had said.

Hugh recalled smiling, sleepily.

'What's she done now?'

'I found her dead.' The news fell through the air, softly, directly, turning over and over.

Thinking of it now, Hugh felt the shock again, and then the confusion. He had stared at the fisherman, unable to comprehend. 'Down by the river.' The man had turned and pointed towards the distant Kyle. 'She's caught up in the trees.' He had looked back. 'I'm very sorry.'

There had been a rushing in his head as the words enveloped him; he had felt the wood of the porch under his fingers.

The sound of the tractor reached him as he finished heaving straw into the hole, an increase of power as it pulled through a ford on its way into the yard. Hugh jumped down, drove the spikes of the fork into the ground and eased himself into the pick-up's cab, moving the vehicle out of the way. He watched the tractor, front-loader raised high, pulling its trailer round the steading, saw his horse's head lolling off the edge of the flatbed, her tongue hanging down. Hugh looked back into the deep hole below, Sandancer's last bed, and pulled himself together, setting his face hard. His father rocked slightly in his seat as the tractor moved into the ruts at the entrance to the paddock.

'By the river?' he had asked the pearl fisherman.

'By the river. I'll show you.'

Hugh had dressed without thought, pulling on jeans, leaving a shirt unbuttoned, all the while muttering, 'Let it not be her, let it not be her.'

When he had reached the back door again, the man

turned, beginning the walk down to the river, moving fast even in his waders, Hugh following, not speaking. They had walked down the gravel bed of the burn, using its width to avoid the thick brush that covered this length of the Kyle's bank. The branches of the trees were hung with floodplain debris; washed-out detritus giving way occasionally to the remains of a creature that had been caught and drowned, putrefaction everywhere.

As they had moved on to the burn's small delta the pearl fisherman had pointed. Caught in an eddy at the edge of the Kyle proper, snagged by an outcrop of thin birch, her back bent round branches, Sandancer's appearance seemed so ugly and unnatural. Hugh had stepped quietly through the hateful scene to lean down and lift his horse's cold head into his arms. 'Not this,' he said to himself, as he looked into the long since dulled eyes. 'Please not this.' Yet the weight was so real. There was no way round the dripping flesh. He had tried to pull himself together and had glanced upstream, catching the pearl fisherman's compassionate gaze. 'You didn't see anything?'

The fisherman had looked away sadly, saying no.

'I was fishing the shoal over there when I saw her. I remembered it was your horse from when she soaked me last year.'

Hugh had looked around again then back at the pearl fisherman who, looking troubled, chose to go on. 'It's not natural,' he had said. 'She hasn't got a broken leg or anything. I can't see any injuries.'

Hugh had looked down at his horse, hating her death so deeply, not wanting to think further. Seeing Hugh's scepticism, the pearl fisherman shrugged. 'It's the first day of the season,' he had said. 'It's bad luck.'

'You know horses, I suppose?'

The man had nodded, peaceful in the face of Hugh's sudden anger. 'A little. My people were horse traders, all

300

the way back. I've seen that horse of yours a few times, and she was in love with water. She wouldn't have made a mistake.'

Hugh had stilled for a moment, before shaking his head to clear the thoughts, making his mind up. 'It was probably a heart attack or something, she was getting old.'

The pearl fisherman had taken a tin of mints from his pocket and poked one into his mouth, not offering. He had sucked, grimaced, but said nothing.

Hugh's father brought the trailer to a halt alongside the grave. Hugh looked at his horse, her skin in a pool of water that swirled across the tarpaulin that covered the trailer. Jamie MacIntyre said nothing, just stared down into the hole as Aaron's pick-up rushed down the hill and pulled up in the yard, the sound of a Bach fugue quitting shortly after the engine. Aaron, who had been called by Hugh's father, stepped out, his face set. When he reached Hugh he dropped one hand in comradeship on his shoulder. 'I'm sorry, mate,' he said.

Hugh nodded.

'Where's Rebecca?'

'Off showing her bloke the west coast. Went early, before I found out . . .'

'Her bloke?'

Hugh shrugged.

His father tied ropes into the eyelets at the edge of the tarpaulin and handed one each to Aaron and Hugh, keeping the last for himself. They all walked round the grave so that the leads stretched across the abyss. Then they took the strain, pulling the body off the flatbed. She came hard at first and then, with the momentum up, slid fast and tumbled into the straw with a sickening thump and the crack of bones breaking under the weight. Dust rose in a cloud from the hole.

They watched as it settled, and then his father put his

hand on Hugh's arm, gripping tightly as they looked at each other. 'You want to say anything, before I fill it in?'

Hugh came out of his trance and shook his head. Instead he lifted the blanket Sandancer had always worn under her saddle, threw it open, then let it float down on top of her body. Once it had settled he walked away, followed by Aaron who let some dirt slip from his hand to the depths.

'The pearl fisherman who found her said he thought she was poisoned,' Hugh said to Aaron, once his father was out of earshot.

Aaron turned to take in his friend. 'It was a pearl fisherman who found her?'

Hugh nodded. 'It's ludicrous,' he said, his voice weary. 'Who's going to poison my horse?' As he spoke he saw the tranquillizer darts resting on the bench in Aaron's workshop and he hated himself for it. The mere suggestion seemed so unworthy, and he looked at his friend for reassurance.

'Insane,' said Aaron. 'What's a fucking tinker know about horses?'

They stood watching as buckets of earth were dropped back into the hole, Hugh's brain pushing against his skull. The weight was too much so he turned away.

Hugh heard nothing from Becky for three days after Sandancer died, although she said later she had tried to call. Aaron was a continual, unspeaking presence, despite Hugh's insistence on carrying out the worst chores the farm had to offer. Together they moved over the land, unblocking drains that had collapsed or filled during the winter, fixing fences, cutting the windfall trees. They worked until their hands were scarred and bloody and until they were falling with exhaustion. Then, on the fourth day, Becky rang early, her voice stronger than he had heard it for some time, asking him to come and see the finished creation. Hugh borrowed his father's truck and drove over to Shiloch.

Noticing at once that the man's hire car was gone, Hugh walked out between the steadings and on to the field. Her creation now stood as high as Becky herself, and as he closed on it its full scale emerged. Becky was standing gazing at her work; the scraps the sculpture's heavy granite belly rested on were now covered in beaten metal, offering the impression of kneeling legs, while the torso, head and arms, their form smoothly beautiful in their deep bronze, looked towards the sky, hands thrown up. Hugh walked up beside Becky and she looked over at him.

'It's good,' he said.

'Good?'

'Very good. Casting worked well.'

Becky looked at her hands, which were nearly as scarred as Hugh's. 'I've spent the last two days playing with an angle grinder, files and a wire brush. It took a lot of work.'

Hugh stepped forward and ran his palm down the metal until it rested on the extended belly. 'Despair?' he asked.

'What?'

'Does it symbolize despair?'

'Could be. Maybe hope? Ambiguity, heart of poetry and all that.'

Hugh slid his hand over the statue, bringing it to rest on the upstretched fingers. 'I like it,' he said.

'Come on, out with it.'

'What?' he asked.

'You have an objection, I can tell.'

'Well, it's kind of clunky, I mean the ambiguity, isn't it?' He was about to tell her about Sandancer, wanted her to reply so he could speak, but she said nothing. In the end he spoke again. 'It's a hell of an achievement. Truly.'

She smiled lightly and pulled herself onto the high stool she had used while waxing the finished bronze. 'I'll move on to abstract work shortly.'

She looked at him and they were silent. Hugh felt no urge to initiate talk of Sandancer, he wanted Becky to ask how he was. Instead, to break the quiet, he asked after his rival.

'He left two days ago.'

Hugh was about to ask another question, then felt the need float away from him. He felt tired and in need of comfort from this woman. He had stood by while she constructed this figure in the middle of the field. Here she was emerging from some self-absorbed, metropolitan idea of spiritual renewal, unaware of the reality that surrounded her. She had been spending time with her ex-boyfriend while he was suffering. On the way across Hugh had stopped at the small post office and discovered that Aaron knew that he had applied for a passport; the postmistress had let it slip several days before by asking if he would be needing one as well. Aaron had said nothing about this to Hugh, yet Sandancer had died. It seemed to Hugh that Becky was too self-absorbed to notice his distress, and he could only imagine he meant less to her even than the statue. He felt the awful yawning gap opening ahead. Something was about to happen and it was going to be bad. He stood and waited.

'Hugh,' she said, looking him straight in the eye, 'I think I'm ready to go back south.'

He tried not to move. 'To marry him?'

She looked away, at the ground. 'No.'

'He asked again?'

'Yes. But, look, that's not the point. It's just that I'm ready to go back. I understand myself better now, I'm revitalized. I have succeeded in what I planned to do.'

Hugh just looked at her.

'I am a creature of the city. I belong there among the people I have known all my life. That is who I am.' She paused and looked at the statue. 'You say this is . . . clunky, but these are my emotions, my ambiguities. I have placed them there. You may not see it, Hugh, but all those issues, those stupid, stupid issues, are there. I've freed myself from them, wiped them out by loading them on this, this . . . clunky statue. I'm going to leave them here. I want something, Hugh. I want a future where I'm not weighed down by worries, and now I feel I'm strong enough, free enough to go back and find it, on my terms. I lost most of my twenties and I'm not about to lose any more. The truth is that I was just kidding myself that I was ready to go out and do something different, open an entirely new life, drive new roads, plough furrows, whatever. It doesn't mean anything in the end, only ultimate unhappiness.'

Hugh said nothing.

'Don't get me wrong. I'm not being pathetic. I don't want you to get that idea. It is just that in my time here – with you, I know that, with you – I have pulled together the . . .' she started pulling together with her hands '. . . various bits of my life and examined each in turn, and what I realized by building this statue is that they are all one, that there are no real choices that should cut bits off me, tear me apart, but only decisions that will turn me as a whole in a direction where I should be going.' Her hands formed a globe. 'In essence it is about me and nobody else. You see, I cared too much about what others thought, about my place in the world, when in fact that's not the way to look at it at all. Fuck everybody else. It's me that's important. It's what I want. That is what I must grab. That has to be the route to take.'

Hugh finally broke his silence. 'And it's that man, the man who treated you so badly?'

'No. No, but I have to get back down there and start living my life and find out what it is that I want. Hugh, you have to step into my shoes here, it's really exciting for me. For the first time I feel none of the weight that nearly crushed me. I don't know where any of this will end.'

'Not with me, by the sound of it.'

She stood up and took each of his shoulders in her hands. 'Hugh, listen to me. You're young, you've got none of the worries I have. You can, Christ, you must leave here and seek what it is you want. What I'm saying for me goes a thousand, a million times for you. You should be excited, everything is out there for you to grab.'

'But can't we seek those things together?'

Her hands slipped away and she went over to the statue. 'No, I don't think we can. We're looking for different things. Your age shouldn't come into it but it does. I'm older than you and once you realize that – once you are out of this place you will realize that – I promise then you will want something else and I don't want to find myself in that position. I have already made one mistake. You have absolute freedom.'

Hugh tried to keep his gaze steady, tried to lay his sincerity onto her.

'But it is you I want.'

'You don't. I promise you don't.'

Hugh exhaled. He meant it so deeply, felt it inside.

'I do love you,' she said.

He spat out his reply. 'Christ, and I love you, I mean it. I want the ivy-covered cottage, the kids, all that. I really fucking do, so why are you doing this?'

'You don't. I know you don't really want that.' She sighed. 'Hugh, I don't think you could make me happy.'

And he felt his resistance collapse. The strain of the last week broke the fight in him. He turned and began to walk back towards the yard. She watched for several steps then caught up with him. 'Please don't let this come between us now. I want us to be good friends. I'll be there for you when you move south, we'll sort you out, it'll all be very exciting.'

They reached the truck and she held the door open as he sat down. 'Just have a think about this and you'll realize I'm right.' She leaned down and kissed his cheek before closing the door. The window was already down. He started the engine and she looked briefly around the yard. 'You didn't bring Sandancer?'

He thought about telling her, then just shook his head, slowly releasing the clutch. She lifted her hands and he pulled away.

Hugh reached the farm and telephoned Aaron, only to find he had spent the night over the hill with Alison and would be back later. Putting down the receiver, he left the house and walked down the burn to where Sandancer's body had been caught in the trees and sat there for several hours, eyes staring vacantly over the great sweep of the Kyle. His mind ran back to the first time he had seen Becky, how he had loved the grace with which she moved. She had become the future to him, encapsulating all that was missing. With her arrival, he had looked round, taken in this place that he knew, all that he knew, Huil, a Scots word that described the membranous sac containing the heart. In this country he knew so well had stood his means of escape and he had believed, really believed, she would take him by the hand and lead him away.

He would have betrayed Aaron. In the wake of Becky's rejection Hugh shuddered at how far he had strayed, his mind so turned that he had begun to believe that Aaron might have hurt Sandancer in revenge for a passport application. He crushed that thought now, deeming it blasphemous. His friend had stood by him, supportive as he fantasized about being whisked off to London in the arms of this woman. Aaron had no one else he could call a real friend, and for months now he had been faced with a comrade he didn't recognize, this metropolitan wannabe that Hugh had become. Hugh began to follow the love affair's course in his mind, flicking through the good times they had had, the falling in love, times that had allowed him to extend the space between his friend and himself. He now recalled her saying that it was time he left Aaron behind, and her attempts to drive a wedge between them seemed suddenly a grotesque incursion.

As Hugh sat unmoving, following the threads of his thoughts, a front brought clouds across the mountain-tops. He felt the anger eat at him, his foolishness disgust him. Time went with the passing waters and his fury burned stronger, and he allowed its irrationality to flame the firestorm within him. When finally he stood, the day beginning its slow, cloud-swept decline around him, he did not notice that the chill had stiffened his joints. He emerged from the woods to look up and see the Three Great Mountains exposed for a moment before the moist grey tongues slid in and surrounded them, and he felt his heart surrounded, enclosed and shielded by his anger. When he walked into the farmyard he found Aaron in his pick-up and, with barely a nod, joined him, taking his rightful place by his side.

Aaron started the car, glancing over. 'Are you all right?'

'I think we should go to Lochanthrain,' Hugh said.

Aaron pushed the car into gear, and took them out of the driveway onto the road. He looked at Hugh again. 'I had a bad morning too.'

There was silence.

'That Alison's a frigid bitch.'

Hugh kept his eyes out of the window, saying nothing,

so Aaron spoke no more, driving slowly, almost carefully down the Brae then up the north glen, reaching down to turn off the stereo, kill the sound of the Gaelic psalmists.

When the car was passing Lochanthrain's outbuildings Hugh gave a small grunt and Aaron pulled up.

'Your Molotovs in there?'

Aaron smiled and nodded.

'And the mines, are they up in the gun room?'

'No. There's two boxes here.'

Hugh stepped out of the car and walked to the workshop door, turned the handle and found it secure. Aaron followed, jangling some keys. He unlocked three different deadlocks and let them in. 'I've got two Molotovs. Enough?'

Hugh nodded and Aaron walked over to a cabinet, unlocked it and removed the two bottles, their shanks now tightly and professionally bound. He placed them, together with the small primer canister, gently by Hugh's feet. Then he slid two boxes of mines from the cabinet shelf, and put them on the workbench.

'Anything else?' he asked. 'What about the tranquillizer gun?'

'I suppose so.'

Aaron took out the airgun and a box of the darts, which he opened and laid on the table beside the mines. He slid his hands into a pair of rubber gloves, and took down a small bottle from the shelves. Hugh watched as he began to fill three darts with fluid.

Hugh walked round the room collecting things, building up a small pile on the table: the spotlight, two sets of gloves, the black paint they had used to fix the eagle's cage. He found a bag and started to fill it. Aaron finished his task, dropped a set of gardening tools and a rag into the pile, leaned an axe against the table then looked at his friend and smiled. 'Haven't seen you like this in ages.'

Hugh raised his eyebrows, then carried the bag and one of the Molotovs out to the car. Aaron watched him go, then followed with another load, putting the gun and the Molotovs behind the seats, the mines and the darts in the glove-box, the spotlight on the floor and the bag in the back, closing the grille on the top of the flatbed with a clang. Then he went back inside, emerged and locked the door. He got into the car and threw a couple of woollen garments onto Hugh's knee.

'Balaclavas,' he said. 'Found them in the attic. After all, I take it we're not planning to go to church?'

Hugh looked at them. A small, thin mushroom was growing out of one. Another idea sprouted. 'You never know,' he said.

Aaron started the car. 'Where to?' he asked.

Hugh gave him the first stop. 'How's your petrol?'

'Full tank. I just got back from town.'

Aaron pulled into the car park at the foot of the mountain just as darkness arrived, stopping under a high bank so the vehicle couldn't be seen from the single-track road below. At this time of the day and this early in the season, they were alone. 'Why here?' he asked, getting out and looking at the bleak surroundings. Seeing Hugh's expression, he raised his hands and answered his own question: 'Here's as good as anywhere. What do we need?'

Hugh lifted the mines.

Aaron dug around in the bag, and came up with the gardening tools, the gloves and the rag. 'We need to be careful about fingerprints,' he said, looking at his friend. 'I mean it, they're going to take this shit very, very seriously.'

They walked for forty minutes along the path, following a small river, coming out beside the loch. Even in this light Hugh could remember turning and smiling as Becky complained her way up, wearing the ridiculous silver coat. Up ahead he could see one of the places they had stopped to sit. Beside the path stood the now bare rowan tree that had been so covered in fruit. He thought back to her asking about the red berries, almost swallowing one, recalled the ageing man in Lycra passing them. Hugh noticed that the walk that had then taken more than an hour had taken Aaron and him half that time. He had enjoyed that walk.

Reaching the spot, he kicked at the clay and shale path. 'Here,' he said.

Aaron looked up the mountain, Hugh's eyes following. With the coming night the last light seemed silverish, blemishing where wedges of cloud dipped into the contours. 'Good, I don't fancy going much further.' Aaron pulled out a trowel and dug at the ground. 'Yup, this is good.' He pulled out what looked like a length of pipe with a cross-bar at the top. In the bad light Hugh could see 'TreeMate' written down its length. Aaron pulled on his gloves and drove the cylinder into the ground, excavating a perfectly round hole. 'This should be the perfect depth,' he said. 'I marked the barrel.' He pulled out one of the cartridges, now wrapped in cling-film, the foam glued to its metal top, and dropped it into the hole. It slid in perfectly. Aaron patted it down then turned to take a tack from the box, and squeezed it into the foam. 'Primed,' he said, grinning and looking up. 'You want a shot?'

Hugh took the tool and began making a small hole three feet further down the path.

As they walked back to the car, picking their way through the darkness, he could feel the energy and excitement off Aaron.

'Inspired, absolutely fucking inspired. Hill-walkers. Perfect.'

They reached the car and took their places in the cab.

311

'OK, where next?'

Hugh, feeling cleansed of a memory, spoke.

Again, the car park was empty. Coming down the track, Aaron swung the pick-up so that its lights barrelled across the sandy landscape, checking for other cars that might be hidden out in the darkness. Nothing. They stepped out and Hugh reached behind the seat for a Molotov.

'Want both?' Aaron shouted over the sound of the surf, picking up the second when he received an affirmative.

Each carried his weapon balanced on his shoulders as they scrambled towards the peninsula where Hugh had kissed Becky for the first time. The sea was calmer than before, but the tide was up and rollers were still crashing in, sending spray up the rocky walls. The going was tricky in the dark, so they moved forward slowly, careful not to break the bombs they were carrying. At last they stood on the grassy strip that led to the knoll where the two lovers had made the fire and watched the weather come in. Now, even under the heavy cloud, they could see the sea moving out in front of them, the cold wind salty and unchanging. The concrete bunker was a uniform shadow in the natural landscape, above it the windmill turning slowly against the very last embers of the long-gone day. The epic nature of the situation still caused Hugh to pause. He stood looking out, Aaron silent beside him. He felt real pain in this act, which would wipe clean a memory that had seemed so important. He flicked his head to dislodge the thought and turned to Aaron.

'OK, we're going to throw these out there.' He knew Aaron was looking out into the darkness.

'We're going to blow up a wind-generator?'

'We're going to burn everything on that peninsula.'

Even without being able to see, he could feel Aaron's smile.

'Fair enough, but can I ask why?'

So Hugh told him that Becky was ditching him, of her plans to return to London, that he thought she was going to marry the man. He didn't mention that he had felt he was being left behind, that his route out of Huil seemed blocked. Aaron knelt down and shoved the Molotovs' two rags into the primer before tying them round the bottles. Hugh took a lighter from his pocket and gave it to Aaron, the flames suddenly tearing up a rag. Aaron stepped back as Hugh swung the bomb around his head, letting go so that it sailed in a perfect arc over the short causeway to the knoll, landing on the weather-station roof and exploding outwards in a fountain of flame. Then he lit Aaron's Molotov and it, too, sailed over the land, crashing into the rotors of the windmill, shattering in a fiery burst that swamped the whole outcrop in thickened petrol, pools of flame floating briefly out to sea before disappearing behind the roar of the fire.

Both of them were caught now in the bright glare of the light, turning to look at each other then back at the tower of fire in front of them. The rotor still turned, with slow, rotating wings of fire.

Hugh watched his memories burn.

Aaron looked around: much of the near landscape was lit up. 'Perhaps we should get out of here,' he said.

As they drove away they could still see the burning peninsula: a lonely flame in the darkness.

They drove for some time before pulling in at a coaching inn perched high on one of the passes to the east, having put a good sixty miles between themselves and the beach. Hugh spoke to one of the men at the bar, a high-country farmer who was married to a distant cousin. He told him that they had been down in

313

Skye looking at a young horse to replace Sandancer, something his father would believe if he heard it. The inn's kitchen had opened for the season the previous weekend, and the two boys sat and ate, leaving soon afterwards. Once in the car Aaron asked where they were going next. Hugh, looking at the clock, asked how long the tranquillizer would work.

'Hind or stag?'

'Goat.'

Aaron thought about it. 'God knows,' he said.

'Probably won't want to do it for a couple of hours yet, with what I've got in mind,' said Hugh.

They were sitting in the darkness, which, once in a while, Hugh illuminated with the tip of the cigarette he was smoking.

'The goats,' said Hugh. 'There's some out on the Gairloch road and some up at Rogart. Gairloch's a possibility. It's quiet on that road and it's sort of on the way.'

'Where are they?'

'Just south of Ullapool.'

Aaron started the car and they drove south-west until they passed through the port of Ullapool and turned onto a single-track road, heading again towards the coast. Aaron found a turning into a forestry plantation and Hugh opened the gate. Once out of sight of the road Aaron stopped and turned off the engine. 'So tell me what we're going to do,' he said.

Three hours later they were heading east, a large, long-haired, ebony-and-white billy unconscious in the back.

To catch the goat they had driven down the coast road, passing several groups of the wild creatures as they grazed on the cliff edges lifting away to the landward side. They had finally chosen a target and turned the car round. Aaron had pulled up, reaching over to grab the spotlight, cursing as beer spilled from the bottle he was holding between his legs. Hugh stepped out, cocked the airgun and lifted a dart from the box.

'Careful!'

'I know.'

He had pushed in the dart without pricking himself, closed the action and looked up. Aaron turned on the light, sweeping the cliffside and zeroing in on the billy, which had launched itself up the small ledges and was now nearly twenty feet above them, Hugh aiming for its flank but not firing. 'It won't go through that hair, will it?' he had shouted. The goat was standing proudly, looking down on them.

'Fuck it. Try anyway.'

The billy, as if to insult them, had lifted its tail and sent down a stream of little brown pellets. Very stupid, Hugh had thought.

'Hugh, aim . . .'

'I know.'

He had fired and the dart plunged into the soft, brown skin of the goat's arse. It had given a loud bleat and leaped for the next ledge, missed and plunged down the slope, bouncing off ledges until it crashed to the road in front of them. Aaron had turned off the light and Hugh slid the rifle behind the seat, looking round, hearing a noise. Lights had swung over the water a quarter of a mile back. 'Car,' he had said, slipping into the passenger seat. 'Let's get this thing on board.'

To their surprise the goat was not dead, or even, it seemed, injured. Together they had thrown it into the back, each grabbing a handful of hair, packing it down so a car behind wouldn't see it through the grille. Then they were down the road long before the other vehicle had reached their position.

Now in possession of the details Aaron was excited, playing the *Messiah* loudly on the stereo, tapping his leg, singing along. Once in a while he would turn and ask a question. 'We can steal stuff?' he asked.

'Yes.'

'What are we going to write?'

'That we should decide.'

'What about the goat?'

'I haven't decided yet.'

'Hallelujah,' said Aaron. 'Or Rejoice?'

'What?'

'We could write "Hallelujah" or "Rejoice".'

'We could.'

'In goat's blood.'

'If you like.'

'God. This is fantastic.'

Hugh leaned back, feeling his friend's excitement, taking a slug of his beer, his mood not yet spent.

The approach was always going to be difficult. They drove slowly along the road, their lights off, turning the corner under the dark castle, seeing the lights of the village ahead. There was nothing coming the other way so they glided into a side road, pulling in on the other side of the small hut that served as a ticket office for the castle's visitors. The car would only be spotted if somebody came looking for it.

'Risky,' said Aaron, looking around.

'I think it's riskier going into the village at this time of night. There's bound to be some old insomniac who has waited all his life for this moment.'

They stepped from the car, and walked gingerly round to the tailgate. Hugh felt very sober as Aaron lifted the grille and lowered the back, pulling at the animal's leg. Nothing happened. Using the Maglite he kept in the car, he plucked the dart from its victim, and carried it towards the cab. 'You get to carry the goat,' he said, as he walked past.

Hugh pulled the animal towards him and then, bracing

himself, took the strain and hoisted it onto his shoulders, feeling its hair down the back of his neck. 'Fucking thing's going to give me fleas,' he said.

They made their way along the treeline of the park, using the glow of the village lights to judge their route. Aaron moved ahead, the bag in one hand, the other carrying the axe. He would look back and Hugh could tell he was finding it difficult not to laugh. Hugh tried to imagine what they would be charged with if they were caught. What would their excuse be? A goat and an axe? Spray-paint? Heading towards a graveyard? As they approached the village the abbey loomed above them, its two towers like shadows against the clouded sky. Hugh paused and waited as Aaron probed the graveyard wall for a place to cross and then, looking along the edge, saw an arch where the stream flowed through. Aaron had turned to motion him forward, but Hugh nodded in the new direction and his friend followed.

Hugh's back was aching from the weight of the goat, the load twice as heavy with the steep climb through the abbey graveyard. He no longer felt the full fury eating at him, his anger had been mostly burned away on the peninsula, but now there was madness in the moment, joy in the camaraderie of Aaron and himself against the world once more. There was beauty in this. As he passed the deep gorge where he had stood that day with Becky he reminded himself once again that he had been a fool to look for something new. He would survive her, she would soon be barely a memory, a mere education in sexual practice and a few cultural bookmarks. He laughed silently to himself as, the goat slung over his shoulders, he staggered out into the open at the top of the slope and looked up at the enormous building, the two crosses high above him. As his feet touched gravel he couldn't help but laugh.

*   *   *

317

'Inspirational,' said Aaron. He was sitting in the driver's seat, the pick-up parked in a lay-by on the road over the hill. It was Sunday, thirty-two hours after their attack on the abbey, and he had insisted they drive into town to buy the paper. 'Deciding not to kill the goat was fucking inspirational, mate. Who would have credited it?'

Hugh shifted slightly in his seat. 'So Gus is allowing you back into the pub?'

Aaron had told him this news a few moments before; he had not allowed Hugh to look at the paper until they were both able to give it their full attention. 'Yeah, but let me read this to you.'

Aaron lifted the paper, showing off the front page, with its enormous photograph of the trashed altar robbed of its trinkets, and then, beyond, on the wall, their words in dribbling, three-foot black letters.

'So why?' Hugh asked.

'Why what?'

'Why did Gus let you back in?'

Aaron looked at the paper. 'Hugh . . .'

'Just tell me and then we can get to the fucking newspaper. One thing at a time.'

Aaron crumpled the paper onto his lap. 'He apologized to me. He said that I was right about that fucking Dane. And . . . that if I wanted to come in for a drink that's fine.' Aaron looked at him. 'OK?'

'Why's he fallen out with the Dane?'

'I don't fucking know.'

'Has he sacked him?'

'Got him working in the kitchen.'

Hugh mulled this over while Aaron went back to the paper. 'Ready?' Aaron asked. ' "Satanists Defile Highland Abbey." ' He looked at Hugh again. 'You are ready, aren't you?'

Hugh nodded.

' "A suspected Satanist cult defiled St Magnus Abbey

in Lovat on Friday night, causing nearly fifteen thousand pounds' worth of damage, daubing the walls with paint, stealing valuable artefacts and releasing a goat that injured a senior member of the congregation. Last night the Bishop of the Highlands and Western Isles called for the 'perpetrators to hand themselves over to the police so that they can receive the help they so clearly need'." ' Aaron paused. 'Perhaps we should visit his house next,' he said.

Hugh was still thinking about Gus. When he didn't reply Aaron returned to the paper.

' "Police hunting the thieves have found a number of the crosses, candles, urns and other sacred works scattered across the Highlands, sparking the belief that the attack was motivated on quasi-religious grounds. 'Given that we have already recovered nearly half of the material that was stolen, including an expensive set of silver candlesticks, it now seems likely that greed was not the overriding motive,' said Detective Chief Inspector Thomas Rankin of the Northern Constabulary. 'But we are not ruling out anything. We are still missing a very valuable foot-high gold cross.'

' "Mrs Francis Fraser, 68, a widow, who was the first to enter the abbey yesterday morning, came across the scenes of devastation including a wall daubed with the words, 'This is our creation. Do not weep. Rejoice in your fear.' She was frightened by a blast from the organ. 'I looked over and there was this huge goat standing on the keys and eating the velvet curtain,' Mrs Fraser said, from Raigmore hospital in Inverness where she is recovering from shock. 'The beast saw me at the same time as I saw it and it leaped off the organ and came charging towards me. I turned and ran thinking it was the Devil himself.' " '

Aaron punched Hugh on the arm. 'As I said, the goat was fucking inspirational.'

Hugh gave him an indulgent smile. He was wondering what had got to Gus.

' "The vandals destroyed a religious scene that had been built by the village children for Christmas and one left faeces on the altar where the Host is usually placed. For a while police were hoping to use it for genetic identification but last night it was confirmed not to be human.

' "So far police have failed to find a pattern in the distribution of the articles stolen from the abbey. 'We have found the Darkanst cross, the ancient brass cross that hung from the ceiling, hanging on the Bonar Bridge,' said DCI Rankin. 'And the stainless-steel modernist cross was tied to the front of a Lochinver fish lorry. We questioned the driver, but it is clear he was asleep when it was attached to his vehicle and that he knew nothing about it. The two candlesticks were in the branches of the old oak of Ardnashellach, their candles still burning.' "

'That's good, isn't it? They were still burning.'

Hugh muttered that it was indeed good.

' "The goat, believed to have been part of the herds that roam Scotland's west coast, had been left unharmed by the cult members, and was later subdued by five members of the town rugby club. Animal-rights activists said they were disgusted by the people who abandoned the goat, and its survival is put down purely to its will to protect itself. 'It put up quite a fight,' said Lovat rugby captain and former Scotland prop John Mackinnon, who helped subdue the billy. 'It hit harder than Finlay Calder on a cold day.' " '

Hugh couldn't imagine Gus apologizing.

' "People in the village reacted in outrage at the attack on their abbey. 'I know exactly who did this,' said one member of the community, who preferred not to be named. 'It was those bloody Protestants. They won't let us live in peace.' Another, shopkeeper Claudia Humphreys who is originally from Bristol, said, 'We may not have seen who it was but God will have, and I am sure His retribution will be terrible.'

' "The police are looking for more immediate results, however. 'They have left so many clues we will get them in the end,' said one policeman at the scene. The Devil Came Visiting. More reports pages five and six." '

Aaron sighed happily. 'Brilliant. I'm in awe, Hugh. You're a natural showman.' He looked at his watch and then started the car. 'Pub's open.'

To reach the pub they had to pass the church, and Aaron slowed when he saw the small crowd of parishioners standing by a stream that ran past the kirk's western wall. At their centre was the shepherd from Shiloch, a baby held in his arms, a sullen mother looking on, an ageing grandmother by her side. There were maybe seven people in all, and as Aaron began to accelerate the Rod of God broke from the group and lurched onto the road, with both his hands held up. Aaron braked hard, and following the Rod's instructions parked on the verge.

'Fuck,' said Hugh. 'We should never have done this. He'll know.'

Aaron climbed out and Hugh followed. The Rod seemed curved, like a stretched bow, his eyes extended, white phlegm in the corner of his mouth. One of the old crones veered outwards, bustling over to lead him back to the chair that had been set up for him, pulling him from his place in front of Aaron, whom he had managed to grasp by the shoulders and shake, eyes excited and quite insane.

The shepherd waited until the boys had joined the congregation before he continued his prayer in a soft accent: 'We were praying to you, Lord, for the future. We know you are testing us, we know that our inability to pay our debt to the bank, the Church's decision not to support us through our troubles, is nothing more than a hiccup, a reminder that we will just have to fight harder to worship you. We know that our minister's madness is grown out of a seed of doubt, a weed that has taken over his brain. Lord, we beseech you to heal Roderick and return him to us whole. O Lord, we understand that we were becoming soft in our comfortable pews, relaxed and content in our churchly splendour. Lord, by having bailiffs come and bar the door to us we see that you want us to worship like our forefathers did, on the humble earth that you created . . .'

Hugh looked over at the door of the church, noticing that it had a plank nailed across its heavy façade and a bailiff's notice hammered into the wood. He thought of Becky, packing for her trip south, and realized how much he would miss her. He felt calm now and he looked down the glen, the spring morning prompting him to wonder what the future would hold. Perhaps things were changing.

He turned back to the group and saw that the shepherd was looking into the eyes of the baby in his arms, the baby he was christening. 'Lord, we ask and hope you will watch over this beautiful child . . .'

The Rod staggered to his feet. He grabbed the child, cradling it lovingly in his arms, tears starting down his haggard features. 'Lord, we look at this beautiful baby,' he said, in a small voice, the quietest Hugh had ever heard him use, 'this beautiful, wonderful baby with her lovely innocent face . . .' The Rod's voice almost caught on itself. Others who had closed in on him stayed back, silenced by the emotion in their minister's voice. '. . . The young baby, the most beautiful thing in the world . . . but I tell you this, its heart is filled *with sin*!'

As the minister's sudden shout fell away the mother stepped forward and grabbed the child. The Rod

322

shrugged off his guards and came and stood next to Aaron and Hugh. The shepherd, throwing a look in their direction, held the baby once again, continuing the service.

The Rod, between them now, drew their heads together with his great veined, bony hands, close to a fresh dribble that surged down his chin. 'Thank you, boys,' he said, with a quiet, intense and conspiratorial sneer. 'The Lord thanks you, thanks you for the cross.'

'What cross?' said Aaron, but not convincingly.

Hugh was wondering how to escape, thinking the Rod might try to kill them.

'The gold Papist cross you left in the bell-tower.' He wiped his mouth. 'Blasphemous, of course, but God will forgive you. Once it's melted down and sold we'll have enough to pay off the bank. Aaron, I told you that you had been sent here for a reason.'

With that he patted them hard on the back and staggered over to his chair. The boys looked at each other and, without even a nod to the shepherd, headed for their car.

PART THREE

PROLOGUE

As Mac winched the carcass back into the eaves, Aaron started to wash the surfaces clean, picking up the pail and pouring away the beast's blood, flushing the floor and watching as the water cut its route out under the heavy curtain and down into the mineshaft. He filled the bucket with the beast's innards and hoofs, set it down by the door and turned to wait. Mac lowered himself to the floor and used the pole to close the hanging doors above, then looked around and grunted. 'Good.'

'Wouldn't they search this place?' asked Aaron. 'I mean, if they wanted to bust you?'

'They don't think they'd find anything. I convinced them long ago of my invulnerability.' The poacher took the lamp from its hook while Aaron lifted the bucket, and they let themselves out into the night.

They walked along the path in silence, the cliffs reflecting the light until a cloud scraped across the moon. The bucket rubbed softly against the cloth of Aaron's trousers, his footfalls sounding through the silence.

Mac entered the croft and put a flame to the candles, looking to see if Hugh had moved anything. Finding nothing changed, he went through into the kitchen with its thick scent of fats and herbs. Aaron watched as the poacher slid another large stockpot onto the hotplate and took the bucket, emptying the contents into the pot, reaching in to extract the hoofs. With a knife he skinned the beast's lower legs as if peeling carrots and dropped the bones into a skillet to brown. He selected vegetables from a basket beside the stove, cut them up and added them to the pot. Then he pulled a length of muslin from a drawer and reached up to cut away at the dry herbs, selecting stems and leaves with speed, laying them on the cloth and tossing the waste into the bin. He crushed the leaves between his fingers before pulling the corners of the cloth together and tying a piece of string around the neck, dropping the package into the stockpot and pouring in cold water.

'So you need a plan,' he said, taking a jug from the cool box and pouring a thin soup into two mugs, handing one to Aaron who was leaning against the table. 'This woman? Rebecca? That's right, isn't it?'

'Yes, he calls her Becky.'

'Do you think she actually loves him?'

'I doubt it. I think she's probably just using him. But, as I said, she's a little fucked up.'

Mac turned the cup in his hand. 'She probably thinks she loves him,' he said contemplatively. 'To justify herself. That means you'll have to be very careful of her.' He looked up at Aaron. 'Because she will do everything in her power to destroy you if she thinks you're a threat. She won't understand your friendship, they don't, women. But she'll know love and think it justifies any atrocity.'

'But . . .'

'Just listen for a moment.' Mac eased himself forward, spat into the rubbish, then stared at Aaron. He pursed his lips and took a swig of the soup, his other hand holding the bar on the range behind him. Finally he leaned back against the heat. 'You don't want to go into open battle with a woman. She'll rather destroy both of you than lose. A man should fear a woman when she loves. Yes. If you want to win, you can't ask Hugh to make a choice. Even if he did drop her in the face of losing your friendship, he would never forgive you, never trust you again.' A pause. 'You understand?'

Aaron nodded.

'What you need to do is bind him to you while making him less attractive to her. You need to draw him in.' He was looking at Aaron again. 'You should start to act a little strangely, a little out of the ordinary. I don't know, take offence at a couple of people, Alfie or that wife of his, for example. Alfie gave you shit during that casting competition, didn't he?'

Aaron nodded, although it was more of a shrug.

'Once you've done that, start a vendetta. Decide what you're going to do to him, then draw Hugh into the plan. Probably best to wait until the very last moment so he can't try to talk you out of it. Knowing Hugh, he'll follow along for the ride, see how it'll turn out, he's indulgent that way.'

Aaron was nodding.

'So then you do something nasty to Alfie, nothing too unpleasant, small, so as not to worry Hugh too much but enough for the two of you to have a live little secret to share, something he won't be overly keen to tell this sophisticated Londoner.' Mac turned to the stove and dropped the browned bones from the skillet into the stock, replacing the pot's heavy lid. 'Then, a few days later, you do something else. A little more serious this time. I'll leave it to your imagination. Pick on someone or something else and draw Hugh in. Make him part of the decision-making process, bond him close, choose something that might amuse him but something he won't be able to talk to anyone else about but you.'

Aaron was smiling now.

'And so it goes on. Take it as far as you like.' He

329

paused. 'The best thing, of course, is that eventually, if he loves this girl enough, he'll confide in her and she will quickly develop some serious concerns about her Highland boy, just you see if she doesn't. And these will grow until she leaves him. And then who will he come to?' Mac pointed at Aaron with a large wooden spoon.

'That's a plan,' said the boy.

Mac gave him a wide, fatherly smile. 'More broth?' he asked.

Aaron offered his mug.

On the stove the stock began to warm.

SEVENTEEN

'Hidden roads leave trails like angels, lost cities fly right past. Her heart's the place that I possessed before all fell away to dust . . .'

Hugh could feel the sun, not long up, throwing out warmth. The smell in the air was of renewal, the barren land breaking open. Life pouring through.

'Signs pass without meaning, hurtling through . . .'

Still he felt the chill of loss lie crystalline along his spine. He stood in the dust of Shiloch's yard, leaning on the car with the horrible misery of it. It seemed so far beyond what he had expected, this real taste of love leaving. Hugh now understood how much he had changed, how much something new had lodged itself within him, warming him and leaving in its wake cold misery.

'It never was going to last . . .'

Becky emerged from the house with a last bag and reached into the Maserati to switch off the stereo. He watched her.

'I thought that was quite appropriate,' he said.

She left her shoulder-bag on the driver's seat and walked up to him, standing close, lifting his chin with one finger. They looked at each other, unspeaking, Hugh finding the sympathy in her eyes difficult to stomach but not wanting to ruin this last moment by turning away.

'I'm not deserting you, Hugh,' she said. 'I'm deserting Huil.'

Sympathy, lies and pity.

She wanted him to move to London. She would look after him until he found his feet, she said. 'You are going to follow, aren't you? You're not going to get stuck here? Tell me you're not going to get stuck here.'

Hugh moved his head so that her finger was no longer under his chin. She was not asking him to go with her as a lover. He was being treated like a child.

'Hugh?'

'I'm not going to get stuck here.' He said it quickly, layering the comment with irritation, trying to show how much remained unsaid.

'And you'll ring me and tell me what you're doing?'

He looked at her shiftily, looked into those compassionate eyes, and nodded.

Becky stepped forward and wrapped him in her arms. He couldn't help himself, he dropped his head on her shoulder, feeling her hair on the side of his face, the pain in his chest.

'Thank you so much, Hugh. I couldn't have had a nicer time in all the world.' She moved back to arm's length, hands on his shoulders. Her eyes. 'It's been extraordinary. I owe you so much.'

'I love you,' he said.

'I love you too,' she replied easily, as if it was nothing, the friendly exit. She leaned forward, kissed his cheek, and got into her car, closing the door and rolling down the window. 'Take care, my Highland boy, you're some kind of a guy.' She blew him a kiss.

He lifted one hand as she drove out of his life.

Hugh watched the car move away along the uneven track, cross the bridge and turn on to the road south.

From the distance he could hear the engine accelerate. He stayed where he was for a long time, facing the emptiness, not moving. At last the shepherd's Mazda swung into the yard, pulling up next to him.

'You won't be moping around here too long, will you, MacIntyre?' the shepherd asked, his satisfaction obvious. 'We're expecting tenants in later and that face of yours would put them off their holiday.'

Hugh looked down and then, without replying, turned and walked over to the second-hand estate car his father had given him two days before, sat down behind the grey *faux*-leather steering-wheel and started the engine. He was only just out of the yard when he started to weep, for Becky, for Sandancer, for himself. The tears stung as he shook with the misery of it.

Aaron found him a day and a half later, back where Sandancer had died. He was sitting on the river bank holding the chalice they had taken from the abbey, looking into it as though some truth might be hidden in the distorted reflection. Shotgun in hand, Aaron asked him whether he wanted to destroy the sculpture.

Hugh put down the cup and looked up at his friend. The idea hadn't occurred to him and, now suggested, distressed him. He shook his head.

Aaron pursed his lips and looked up and down the river. Hugh turned his attention back to the depths of the chalice. He had wedged it between his legs, perfectly held to reflect his image. As he sat gazing into it, there was an explosion above him and then a shouted exclamation from Aaron. A heron smashed into the ground between Hugh's legs, its beak shattering bloodily on impact with the stones an inch from the flesh of his right leg, the chalice now hidden under its crumpled grey body.

'Shit,' gasped Aaron. 'Sorry.'

Hugh realized he hadn't even flinched. One moment he had been looking into the silvery depths and then . . . He laughed and stood up, grasping the bird by its neck and handing it to Aaron. Then he leaned down and picked up the chalice. It had been dented in the impact, the reflection warping as he turned it over in his hand. 'I think I'll bury this above Sandancer,' he said, and looked at Aaron. 'Then we could go and check out your new-found freedom in the pub.'

Aaron, heron in one hand, gun in the other, nodded.

Aaron went through the door of the pub first, walking straight towards the pool table, failing to acknowledge the other customers. Hugh followed more slowly and turned towards the bar. He nodded to three locals, all brothers, all ancient. Gus was sitting on a stool behind the counter reading the newspaper. He folded it up when Hugh approached. 'You haven't been beating up on the Papes, have you?' he asked. The story of the attack on the abbey had not yet died.

Hugh sighed and Gus looked sympathetic. 'Sorry, I heard she left. I wondered when we'd see you, thought you might decide to drown your sorrows.'

'I don't really feel like it.' Hugh sounded very tired.

'I understand. Tomorrow you'd have both depression and a hangover to cope with.'

Hugh lit a cigarette and leaned on the bar. He ordered a pint and a double whisky for himself and shouted to Aaron to find out if he wanted an alcopop. Gus began to pour. 'And get yourself one.' Gus nodded his thanks.

Hugh waited until Gus had taken the money and given him the change, watching the Dane come through the kitchen door carrying two plates of food for a couple of early tourists sitting beside the fire. The Dane, seeing

Aaron and Hugh, stood tall, walking through the wide gap between them, ignored by both.

On Hugh's offer Gus poured himself a whisky and carefully picked up a selection of little brown pills from a number of cups behind the bar. He swallowed them, gagged, and took a gulp of the Scotch. 'Homeopathic medicine,' he said, to Hugh's unspoken enquiry. 'I've managed to develop irritable bowel syndrome.'

Hugh winced. 'Sounds painful.'

'It is, I assure you.'

Aaron had begun to play against one of the youngsters in the bar. Hugh nodded across at him. 'So you decided to let him back in?'

'Time passes.' Gus began his habitual cleaning of glasses.

'He said you apologized.'

The publican laughed. 'Hardly. I just said I was coming round to his way of thinking about the Dane. The bastard won't stop drivelling in Gaelic. He's even started berating me because I don't speak it. And he's giving me a hard time about not being sincere for the cause.'

'Well, he does have a point, doesn't he?'

'No, he doesn't have a point. He doesn't seem to realize that it takes a measure of cynicism to be a good nationalist.' He paused, then continued. 'I suppose Aaron didn't tell you he also apologized?'

Hugh coughed on his whisky.

'Well, as much as can be expected. He gave me the first spring salmon he caught. A beautiful creamy silver six-pounder. Delicious. We filleted and fried it.'

'That's an apology.'

'I know. I actually feel rather warmly towards him – although I'm sure it won't last.'

Hugh laughed, picked up his drinks and wandered over to the pool table where Aaron was now waiting. He looked back briefly, lifting the glasses. 'Keep 'em coming, will you, Gus? To hell with the hangover. I think I'll get stocious.'

Gus raised his glass in salute.

Hugh drove slowly up the north glen, examining the expensively engineered blandness of the estate car's dashboard. Nothing offended him but as his eye roamed down the central column to the cheap velour that rose up around the tinny metal gearstick he felt disgust grow. He dropped one hand and ran it along the unnatural fabric of the seat. It was oppressive.

He looked up as the tyres ran onto the gravel edge. Up ahead the Three Great Mountains sparkled in the clarity of mid-afternoon, their surfaces dotted with patches of as yet unmelted snow. He was approaching the gates of Lochanthrain and on impulse he pulled up onto the bank, stepping out into the day. He breathed in and felt the constraints of the hateful vehicle slip away.

Pulling on his jacket, he began to walk down the long drive, passing between the stone eagles that glared out towards the world. Among the pines, the birch, elm and beech had begun to green for the coming summer. He found the air caught in the driveway and the easy light that filtered through the high tops calming; the chill still caused his breath to show. He walked onwards, grabbing what little comfort he could from the first faint stirrings of recovery.

The drive twisted and turned through the woods. He passed the pheasant-rearing pens that Aaron's father had built years ago and stopped to look out from the shooting stands, using the small binoculars he kept in his pocket to seek out the songbirds he heard among the trees. He was pleased to see a chaffinch in a stand of mature birch, singing in a place where its kin had once been exterminated in a competition between two ten-year-old boys. In another spot Hugh remembered Aaron shouting at him to bring down a kestrel, remembered his guilt when he had. It was a moment he felt that high-lighted the difference in their bloodlust.

As he walked, Hugh felt the countryside coming alive around him, felt deep down its constant renewal, and at once he saw Aaron and himself a part of it. This was their country, the place they understood like no other. Here they could exist, it would look after them, absorbing their actions as part of the greater nature, Aaron's cruelty no different from so much else. He remembered the eagle looking down on them as they stalked the year before and realized that they fitted into the tableau it had seen spread out below. They were men now, and this was their home.

He had been a fool, but that was no crime. As he walked he came to understand that Aaron's behaviour of late had been the result of his own actions. He recognized that rather than the intensely solitary creature he had believed his friend to be, Aaron was reliant on him, if on no one else. It was natural, he reckoned, that in such a place Aaron could only believe in his own existence if it were reflected off another. Together they were a movement away from the norm, but alone they were mere freaks that others could only fear or ignore. Now that Hugh was not entrapped by Becky, Aaron would return to normal. Aaron had been there for Hugh, and had been right, and Hugh now knew that the terrible longing for Becky would slowly release its grip. He would do his best to be there for his friend. They would have to get a grip. The night before the radio had reported that a mountain biker had been blown off his bike by one of their landmines. At the moment they were safe, the police were blaming the local landowner, who was notoriously anti-rambling, but it was too much: the cyclist was in hospital with a broken collar-bone and half his nose missing. The radio had said he scraped along on it for several yards. And so, while still heavy with the pain of Becky's departure, Hugh walked steadier out of the woods and into the shadows of Lochanthrain's outbuildings. He was sure he was better prepared for the future. Like the trees around him, he was emerging after a long winter, ready to suck life from where he stood. He did not need Becky's help. He was a man in his own environment.

The sound of the clarinet hit him as he rounded the last building and was about to emerge on to the lawns of Lochanthrain. He stopped and listened as a piano kicked in. The volume filled the gardens with sound and Hugh noticed speakers lining the battlements. Aaron's parents were away, had been for close on a week, and Aaron had been left to his own devices owing to Hugh's self-absorbed misery. Hugh felt a shiver run slight and cool down his back. He knew the music, it was Messiaen, a quartet written from a prison camp in the depths of the Second World War, its score preceded by the cry of the Angel of the Apocalypse in the Book of Revelation. Aaron played it only occasionally, usually when his mother was screaming at him. Now Hugh stood and listened, waiting, the light buttery around him. Then he slipped off the road and crouched down into a tunnel the two boys had cut years before in the massive rhododendrons. It was overgrown but still navigable, leading to a vantage-point from where he could look over the entire gardens without being seen. Without much thought, but with grim prescience, he pushed his way through.

The music covered all sound but still Hugh was careful not to shake the branches as he clambered forward. He was filthy by the time he found himself looking out at the house, the lawns and the loch. Right in the middle of his view stood Aaron, his body straining against the weight of a bound, struggling hind. Slowly, using the rope holding the beast's legs together, he dragged her towards the jetty, the animal straining its neck back in terror. Hugh took the glasses from his pocket and looked over towards the island. The cage stood at its centre, gleaming from its renovations, empty but secure. He turned the glasses back to Aaron then passed quickly over the hind, appalled by its terror. Aaron stopped and Hugh dropped his glasses and froze. His friend looked around and then gazed directly at the bushes where Hugh was hidden. He smiled and looked again at the island, dragging the struggling beast behind him.

Hugh thought of stepping out into the light. He couldn't tell if Aaron knew he was there but his emerging dirty would require explanation. He decided to stay, the desire not to interfere winning, the need to see Aaron's plans taken to their conclusion. He remained crouched as his friend lifted the hind into the boat, and rowed for the island shore.

The oars cut the water without leaving a mark, and through the glasses Hugh saw Aaron's gaze level, focusing at comfortable distance, at nothing. Every few seconds, the animal's head rose above the gunwales, its snout held up towards the sky in desperation, its neck muscles showing its urge to thrash itself out of the tight bonds. Hugh watched then dropped the glasses. He chose to let the details lose themselves in the distance as the trip was completed, the ethereal, avine music turning the day's crisp optimism into shadow, the notes forming a rolling, menacing beauty. One knee on the damp earth, his back already aching, Hugh found himself held and helpless, a prisoner looking out.

Aaron dragged the hind from the boat, and pulled it up the shore. For an instant Hugh hoped his friend just planned to lock the deer in the cage but this idea fell away quickly – Aaron did not keep pets, not even a dog. Hugh watched as he moved forward amid the dark, tangled Caledonian pines, watched him pull the animal to the gate of the cage, a cage that until then had been a talking-point, its ugliness all in the past, but then the lenses in Hugh's Leicas converted the cage to bars. The gate opened, all sound drowned by the Messiaen, and Hugh thought of a silent movie, felt his distance from the events grow until he heard the loud, thin cry of a bird cut back towards the speakers. The hind ceased her struggle and stilled; even Aaron waited before, in a two-armed throw, he hoisted the beast onto the cage's concrete floor. Hugh watched through the glasses as Aaron pulled out his gralloching knife and cut her bonds.

The freed animal leaped up and bolted to the far corner of the cage where, shivering, she watched as Aaron retreated and locked her in. Then she turned her attention to her damaged flanks, licking where the skin was raw, her head darting nervously at every movement from her jailer, who leaned against the cage watching her. After several minutes the intensity of the music relaxed and Aaron stepped away backwards, watched carefully by both the deer and Hugh, who saw a length of string unravelling from his friend's hand. The hind, now that her tormentor was almost at the jetty, walked along the back edge of the cage until she came to the door of the small house it adjoined. Her movement caused another thin cry to cut the air. She turned and bolted, leaping up against the bars, only to fall back on to the concrete. As she staggered to her feet, Aaron pulled on his rope and the door opened.

For several minutes nothing happened.

Then, one after another, two golden eagles stepped out and rose up to perch on the bars that crossed the aviary's higher reaches. There they sat, looking down at the hind who was circling the cage below in increasingly frantic circles. One of the eagles, the male, extended its wings and hunched once again. Hugh remained utterly still, finding himself caught in the tension of the scene, the players now in their places, the victim running round and round, the eagles watching, Aaron standing by the jetty, body held in a posture of one caught mid-stride by the unexpected. Hugh had talked with Aaron so often about this, this grim use to which the cage had been put a hundred years before for the amusement of the residents of the castle. Now it was being played out before him, here and now. Aaron had captured two eagles.

The Messiaen came to an end and began again, programmed on a loop, and all remained the same, all caught in their places until finally the hind could run no longer. Dribbling foam from her nose, she staggered to a halt and stood panting, head down, legs slightly apart. Casually, the female eagle opened its wings and swooped low over the animal's head, sending it once again into the bars, the bird rising to alight on a crossbar. The hind, recovering, was running, and running until time forced her to stop once more. Then the other eagle swooped. The birds took their turns.

Nothing interfered with the slow display, the sun moving round its southern axis, softly lighting the game.

The panting deer was close to collapse. She stood now, only stepping away as the rush of the birds' wings rolled over her. Her fight was done, her commitment to her part was absolute and now she waited stupidly for the end.

When it came the female eagle rolled off the crossbar and this time the claws came forward, tearing into the hind's flesh so that, in pain, she ran once more up against the railings, stumbling and falling, struggling for her feet, but in that moment the male was off its perch and down to pluck her eye from her head, and then the bird was rising, trailing the long white nerve from its beak. The eagles set about their harassment in earnest, running the creature until they had taken its sight completely and she was down for ever, and as they dug deep into the flesh of the still living beast, their claws red, their beaks holding gore, Hugh found himself slipping backwards and away, his last view that of Aaron leaning forward, looking on. The sound of Messiaen, now on its fourth loop, hung over Hugh as he emerged from the bushes and ran from the scene, through still air caught in the avenue, intense with the smell of pine, finally reaching the car that would take him away from such cruelty.

Hugh regained his balance as he sat and looked at the gates of Lochanthrain. He tried to work out where all his plans lay in the wake of the events he had witnessed. His optimism had evaporated. Something fundamental was happening to Aaron. His friend was now in a fantastic landscape where he could not – did not want to – go. It was important that Hugh try to make Aaron recover his sense of reality but, rather than confrontation, he needed to find a way of getting to him without provoking the accusation of betrayal. The actions he had seen his friend take on the island were clearly not the act of the loner at one with his environment. Hugh, blaming himself, felt guilt engulf him. He decided he needed to act fast, and for strategy he would ask the master himself. Starting the car, he pulled past the gates and headed up towards Mac's eyrie.

He parked alongside the BMW, stepped out into the cold spring wind and looked up to the cliffs. At this height the air seemed cleaner than in the valley below where Lochanthrain and Huil, with its thin tendrils of smoke rising up to show life, were telescoped into insignificance. Hugh could see his world, his existence, entire except for Shiloch, but that no longer played any part in his life. He turned and walked over the loose shale, the cast-off slag from the mine, towards the croft's front door. Everything seemed to shine brighter in the sunlight.

He was about to knock when he heard the shout of greeting from behind the croft and walked along the path that led around the side, passing the woodshed and the neatly stacked pile of empty gas cylinders, seeing Mac looking at him from the burn. The poacher waved and Hugh raised his hand in greeting. As he drew closer he saw Mac was adding to the small dam that funnelled water down to the croft. He was stripped to the waist and filthy from packing peat against a length of blue plastic sheeting. There was a pile of rocks to one side that he was using to create the dam's outer wall. He straightened when Hugh arrived, putting one hand to his back.

'Repairs?' asked Hugh.

'Winter nearly washed it away,' Mac said. 'Thought I'd make it stronger while the weather was good.'

'Want a hand?'

Mac looked down at his work. 'Why not?' He stepped to one side as Hugh clambered down into the riverbed beside him. 'You can pack the stones on behind me. Try to match the edges so there are no real gaps.'

Hugh looked at the work already in place, all the pieces carefully and exactly placed. He picked at a couple of rocks until he found one that he thought fitted, leaned over the wall and pushed it into place. Mac watched him out of the corner of his eye, and when Hugh was done the two smiled at each other. 'Not bad,' said Mac. 'Try to keep it up.'

They worked without speaking, Mac moulding the peat over the plastic while Hugh gave it a crazy-paving finish, enjoying the exactness of the work. He picked up speed and followed Mac a shade too quickly, in his haste scratching the poacher's fingers with a piece of granite.

'Easy,' said Mac, shaking his hand. He looked at the boy, and decided to push for the questions he knew would follow. 'So, let me guess, you want to know how to heal a broken heart?'

Hugh waited until Mac had finished his latest bit of packing before he said no.

Mac looked at him without surprise. 'I heard she'd left.'

'You heard right, but that's not the problem.' They looked at each other. 'I'm fine, I promise. Anyway, I'm hardly going to come to you for advice on girls, am I?'

Mac snorted in mock-exasperation. 'Such innocence,' he said. 'So what is it, then?'

They continued to pack the earth as Hugh told Mac what he had seen at Lochanthrain. He felt embarrassed to admit that he had crept up on his friend but Mac seemed not to notice. Instead he just kept at his moulding, his expression weary. Finally he shook his great head in irritation. 'So what?' he said. 'He's bored. Once you spend some time with him he'll go back to doing his own killing.'

Mac had reached the other side of the watercourse and now stood wiping his hands off on a towel while Hugh finished his part of the job. As Hugh fitted the last pieces together he wondered if he should say more, deciding as the final rock slipped into place that Mac, of all people, wouldn't react in a dangerous way to the little projects Aaron and he had been carrying out. He stepped out of the riverbed and sat down beside Mac, taking a cigarette from the packet in his pocket, turning down the offer of soup. 'You don't know the whole story,' he said, and told him.

Mac showed no surprise beyond a reflective expression. 'Nice touch that, not killing the goat,' he said.

Mac fell quiet as he considered the situation.

Eventually he stood up and pulled his shirt over the weighty flesh that covered his shoulders. They began to walk towards the croft. At the top of a rise Mac stopped to take in the view, the sweep of their existence. 'So this woman,' he said, 'what's the story?'

'She left. What's more to say?'

Mac was standing on a rock above him so that when Hugh looked up the poacher's head eclipsed the sun.

'Are you going to follow her?'

'I doubt it.'

'That's what she wants?'

Hugh kicked at a stone and looked at his feet. 'She thinks it'll save me. She doesn't want me. I don't know what I want.'

'She's right, you need to see the world.'

Hugh could tell Mac was nodding because the corona of the sun shone beyond his skull, offering brief warmth to Hugh's face. He looked up but was blinded by the halo around Mac's head. He pointed into the glen. 'All this . . . ?'

'All this is nothing,' Mac interrupted.

'What about Aaron? I can't leave Aaron, especially when he's like this.'

The poacher began to walk and Hugh followed, listening.

'No, you can't leave Aaron.' Mac was speaking loudly because Hugh was behind him, unable to see his face. 'You must take him with you, show him there is more to the world than this. That is the way to bring him back. Remove him from Huil and Lochanthrain. Go on a vast adventure, a tour, maybe even abroad. Sell it to him like that . . .' Mac's head now blocked out the view of the village below. 'An adventure, a chance to see the world.'

And as Mac spread out the idea before him Hugh

could see them abroad, in far-off places, travelling together, them against the world. It was perfect – his responsibilities, if not his desires, answered, and best of all Aaron might just go for it. Together they would strike out beyond the hills and prosper.

EIGHTEEN

They crossed Lochanthrain's western march just after two in the afternoon, walking into a gale. The air was waterlogged, rain moving in waves across the mountainside, packing up in front of the gusts to douse Hugh and Aaron as they forced their way forward. Hugh was dressed to stay dry, but rivers were flowing down his Goretex jacket and leggings, his boots slipping on the waterlogged peat, his gaiters muddy. With every step the pack on his back seemed heavier, pulling at his clothing, offering the streams that formed in his hair access to the dry interior. His shoulder was rubbing from the weight of the two holstered guns hanging nose down under his left arm. He felt the burning in his legs and tried, as Aaron advised, to feed on it.

He was walking with his head down, looking at the ground although they were now on the other side of the law, moving into the wilderness that surrounded the Three Great Mountains. While the thick tangle under his feet, the arctic plants, the mosses and bog cotton he trampled belonged to others, the weather was so bad he did not search the landscape. Only Aaron could have chosen to continue on a day like this and he looked up at his friend, who walked head up against the immense whiteness that covered the sky to the front of them. The rain gave way briefly and Hugh looked out in awe: Aaron struggling forward, a sliver of a man bent into a visibility of zero, backlit by the lost sun, which caused a translucent whiteness so bright it could have been the approaching apocalypse.

Hugh stared. Another sheet of water rushed in to wash against his open-mouthed face, and he felt it roll from his lips and drip from his chin, yet he could not help but look on, feeling the immensity of the vision. Aaron glanced back, his joyful expression caught under his streaming blond hair, confirming that he too was caught in the moment. Hugh raised his hand in greeting and Aaron, pointing forward, bade them on. As he stepped Hugh looked into the glowing sky and staggered, his feet sliding on the treacherous peat. Laughing breathlessly, he turned his eyes back to the ground, pushing forward with the occasional glance to take in this impossible future.

As they climbed, the light grew stronger, blinding, and the peat gave way to granite and shale, the heather smaller, broken by pastel lichens clinging in the fissures of the rock. Aaron, his face whitened by the rain, slowed to let Hugh come alongside. 'We should keep going,' he shouted. 'We'll chill fast if we stop, and this weather gives us good cover to get deep in and out of danger.'

Hugh spat out the water that had swilled into his mouth. 'Fair enough.' He couldn't see any features to tell him where they were. 'We in the Butcher's now?'

Aaron looked out into the whiteness. 'Not yet, the mountain should be coming up on the left.' He pointed. 'Amazing, isn't it?'

Hugh held one eye half closed against the driving rain. 'You feel that if you keep going you'll break through into some other place,' he yelled. 'Some other world, you know?'

'We will, Hugh, another world. Just you watch.'

They climbed on for more than an hour, the ground flattening off into the Butcher's Pass, the weight of the second of the Three Great Mountains darkening the sky to their left. Rocky crags appeared and after weaving along their edge, Aaron cut in and they climbed a series of small waterfalls, rocks giving way under their feet and falling soundlessly against the storm. With freezing hands clawing his way, Hugh scrambled out of the wind and under an overhang, the immediate silence shocking. Aaron smiled and slipped the 7mm from his shoulder, Hugh gingerly doing the same with the dartgun and the twelve-bore. Then they dropped the packs on the ground. It was all Hugh could do to stagger to a ledge and ease himself down while Aaron stood the guns in a corner and began to look around.

'I can't believe you managed to find this place,' Hugh said. 'You're like a goat.'

'That's why you'll never get by without me.' Aaron was scrabbling up into the darker recesses of the rockface. 'You don't listen to the land, don't let it speak to you.'

'The land spoke to me all right,' Hugh said, as he examined his raw hands. 'It said "Fuck off." '

Aaron dropped down from the ledge, his arms full of sticks and dried peat. Hugh looked up in amazement. 'When did you put that there?' And then he realized. 'This is one of Mac's hideouts, isn't it?'

Aaron smiled indulgently.

'Don't tell me,' said Hugh, 'there's some soup stashed some place around here.'

Hugh removed his waterproof outer clothing and opened his pack to find firelighters. Together they started a fire in a corner where the blaze would be hidden from the outside even if the storm hadn't already closed them in. The smoke wound its way up a natural chimney in the rock, its rain-wet surfaces hissing from the heat.

Aaron disappeared out into the gale, which still cried overhead, its passage sucking at their small, calm hideaway as Hugh pulled bottles of whisky and vodka from the packs and sat down beside the fire. He watched his friend return with a couple of rusty old utensils: a triangle and a pot.

'You really have been spending quality time with Mac, haven't you?' Hugh looked out at the storm. 'I still hope the weather clears. One night out here will be enough.'

Aaron put the cooking equipment on the ground and took a swig of vodka. 'It'll clear,' he said happily.

The storm distanced itself as the heat from the fire filled the space. With the wind cresting the edges of the mountain behind them, the granite walls offered a protective arm. They laid out sleeping-bags on the natural shelves, Hugh glad to find his pack had held out the damp, then turned back to the fire, placing the triangle over its now white depths. Aaron sat the pot on the surface, emptying the contents of a screwtop Tupperware container into its depths. 'I don't believe it,' said Hugh. 'Soup.'

He felt himself relax as he sipped at his bottle of Scotch, Aaron squatting over the flames. Always preferring the comfort of his home, he had never enjoyed these extended trips, which Aaron would take once in a while, but here he felt fine, the fire, the alcohol creating an atmosphere perfect for the suggestion he planned, worth the journey into the mountains. He looked at Aaron, who was concentrating on the coals, and wondered if at these moments he was thinking or whether he was merely lost in his own private eternity. He found himself worrying that Aaron would refuse to go.

They drank the soup out of tin mugs they had brought, picking at the meat in the depths with their gralloching knives. When it was gone Hugh passed his mug for more. Later, sated, he leaned back and yawned.

He could see out of the cave to where the wind blew through a deep darkness.

Aaron flicked the triangle from the fire and began to build the base so that flames once again darted up towards the natural chimney. The early evening flowed past in easy conversation. They discussed the police investigation into the attack on the mountain biker, which had faltered and seemed set to peter out, then talked over Aaron's parents' recent return from America, which, he said, had done nothing to improve his mood. When Hugh had driven up to Lochanthrain that morning he had looked over to the eagle's cage to find both the gate of the cage and the door of the birdhouse open, the eagles gone.

Aaron asked suddenly about Becky, as if the conversation had rubbed too close and he wanted to turn it away. Hugh told him that she had rung when he had been out but that he had not returned her call.

'Unlike you,' Aaron said.

'I need to move on.'

They paused for a while, both sitting with their backs against the ledge. Then Hugh decided he should make his pitch. 'But I think taking a trip might be a good idea.'

Aaron didn't move, but the bottle he was holding stopped two inches from where it had rested, caught in its rise towards his mouth. 'To see her?' The tone was calm, friendly.

'No, not to see her. That's all over.'

The bottle completed its journey, then fell back.

'Where, then?'

'Oh, I don't know. Somewhere interesting. America, Africa, Asia.' He waved his bottle in a circular motion. 'Hell, Australia. Somewhere.'

'Australia?'

'Why not?'

Aaron laughed, and Hugh was encouraged. It seemed that the failure of Becky to enter the plans had taken him off-guard.

'Abroad,' Aaron said. 'Why bother? We have everything we need here.'

Hugh looked out into the filthy night. He decided this was the moment to be inclusive. 'It would do us good. See the world. You know.'

Aaron laughed. 'I'm not going anywhere.' He looked around. 'Why do I want to see the world? It's full of people, and further south it gets hotter and they all start becoming more . . .' he grasped for words '. . . like animals. The heat makes people rot. I know as much about the world as I need to.' A smile at Hugh. 'And so do you. Fuck it, we need to stay here.'

Hugh found they were looking into each other's eyes, and in contrast to the slur that was causing Aaron's words to drift a little, the irises were hard, blue and still in the textureless eyes. He noticed that Aaron had failed to pull his shark's tooth from his pocket. He felt a chill but he was not prepared to give in. 'We wouldn't go for long,' he said. 'Just see some of the outside world.' He decided to appeal. 'I need to do this, mate. I really do. And I think we should do it together.' He took a slug of Scotch. 'It's been a weird few months. It might steady us.'

'That's what we said when we went to see the Rod of God.'

Hugh put the bottle down. 'I really want to do this,' he said. 'And I really want you to come.'

Aaron scratched the rocky floor with a stick he had picked up, forming a figure eight. 'Would you do it anyway? If I didn't come?'

Hugh pretended to think. 'I hadn't thought that far ahead.'

'Well, think. Would you?'

Hugh didn't say anything, just took another swig of whisky.

Finally Aaron threw the stick into the fire. 'OK,' he said.

Hugh felt the surprise shock him, the pleasure sear up his neck. 'Brilliant,' he said. 'Fucking fantastic. It'll be brilliant, we'll have a great time.' He saw the future open up and realized he had never really believed it was going to happen. Aaron had granted his wish. The mountains outside seemed kinder and more hospitable now that their hold on him was no longer absolute. 'Fantastic. Where should we go?'

'I don't know. You decide.'

His lack of enthusiasm made Hugh pause for an instant but he sprang back, still ecstatic. 'New Orleans? I've always wanted to go to New Orleans.'

'OK.' Aaron screwed the top onto his bottle of vodka and leaned forward to settle the fire. 'New Orleans it is. I think I'll sleep now.'

Hugh woke to hear Aaron moving about shortly before dawn and roused himself. He felt the clarity of having slept out in the open break the back of the hangover; the whisky's remains caught only in his muscles. He inhaled through his nose and felt the phlegm break away from his throat in a solid block, falling onto the back of his tongue, and he struggled out of his sleeping-bag, dancing in his bare feet across the cold stone to the fire where he gobbed the mucus lump into the flames. It hissed horribly, and he sighed in the relief of being able to breathe, only to find that the chill, fresh air sent him into spasms and he was on his knees coughing. More mucus came from his lungs and he spat that into the fire as well.

Aaron was crouching to his left where he had been building up the fire's base for their breakfast. He looked at Hugh in disgust. 'Ever think perhaps you should pack in the smoking?'

Hugh, who was lying on his side moaning, opened his eyes and looked at his friend. 'No,' he croaked. 'Couldn't. It impresses women.'

Aaron asked whether he was finished gobbing up his lungs because he wanted to start cooking. Hugh nodded and rolled onto his feet. He stood up and went over to his pack, took out a cigarette and lit it. He coughed a little at the first inhalation. 'See?' he said, blowing a smoke-ring.

'No,' Aaron replied, cutting two slices of black pudding and setting them down at the bottom of the pot.

'That's because you're not a girl,' Hugh replied.

The day had barely dawned when the boys emerged from under the overhang, the morning's empty hours still ahead. They had washed and hidden the cooking equipment and spread the ashes of the fire. Now they stood on the edge of the mountain looking down into the pass. The storm had disintegrated and given way to a light drizzle held up by barely a breeze. They squatted and searched the high country from one end to the other for any sign of life, each crossing the entire area so as to miss nothing. It was empty, except for midges which, in the last week, had made their annual reappearance. Hugh took a canister of spray from his pack and covered his arms and face.

'I think we should keep going over the watershed,' said Aaron, pointing to the west.

They were standing at the top of a small cliff where a thick ledge ran down to their left, leading away in the direction they wanted to go, offering a route that would not immediately take them on to the floor of the pass. Aaron looked over the landscape again. 'The deer will be over the other side. We might as well have the shotgun out in case we see ptarmigan.' He looked at Hugh.

'Don't give me that look, they haven't started breeding yet.'

Hugh did his best to look unconcerned.

'I'll shoot,' said Aaron. 'I'm happy to take the gun.'

Hugh shook his head. 'I'll do the shooting.' He handed the tranquillizer gun to Aaron and took the shotgun out of its sleeve. He checked the barrels and slipped two cartridges into the chambers. 'After all, I carried the bloody thing up here.'

Aaron shrugged, and with Hugh walking slightly ahead of him they picked their way along the edge of the mountainside.

Below them, the pass spread out in a patchwork of rocky flats and small, shallow waterholes. Hugh stepped along the cliff edges, planning his route far into the distance while careful to select the safest footholds for his boots. To the front the pass fell away into the horizon, the other two mountains rising to the left and to the right, but at its centre was only the sky, as if they were at the point where the land fell away into the void at the edge of the world. Hugh carried the gun in his right hand, away from the mountainside. Above them the clouds were cracking, and insects rose from the heather.

Hugh moved nearer to the side of the mountain, picking his way up through a small gap between a rocky slope and a boulder-strewn buttress that guarded the western end of the pass. He ran his eyes over the hillside that revealed itself on the other side and began to push down the scree slope. With a cry of alarm, a ptarmigan rose from the rocks, its body grey with coming summer, its white wings beating fast before extending to take it in a long, fast glide over the mountain's extended ridge. Hugh watched it go before he felt the shotgun, still hanging from his right hand, taken from him.

'I should have known,' Aaron said, checking the cartridges.

'They're so beautiful,' said Hugh, content to see it fly. 'That one has already lost its winter coat.'

Aaron didn't say anything, just stepped ahead with the gun, pocketing the shark's tooth that had been between his fingers. Hugh lifted the two rifles and slung each, barrels down, over his shoulders, making a superstitious gesture to himself that they would not frighten up any more of the birds.

Slowly they began to descend, traversing the mouth of the pass to circle the wall of the voluminous corrie that sat between the three mountains. They stopped, sitting for nearly an hour, watching. The sun was breaking through, dappling the heather and grasses below in moving spotlights. Once in a while sunspots reached the real depths at the heart of the bowl, reflecting off the slate or corrugated-iron roofs of the cottages that nestled there. Aaron leaned over and they discussed approaching the herds of deer they saw moving up the slope that led towards the greatest of the three mountains, its peak still tightly held in cloud.

Aaron slipped the shotgun back into its sleeve. 'Do you see any walkers?' he asked.

Hugh shook his head. 'We should get in there, then, before they come.' And soon they were moving again, across the rough ground, keeping high.

Aaron shot the stag from the buttress that stood sentry over the northern end of the pass. The boys had climbed into its heights, picking their way between the scarred pillars of granite to find a protected ledge from which they could look down and along the cliff-face that acted as the mountain's first line of defence. There they had waited for the deer to come to them, the animals following a route that took them round the buttress and into the pass. Aaron had watched them approach, the sun now shining down on them from a sky still harbouring great white galleons while Hugh had scanned the unrestricted view of the bowl for signs of hill-walkers making a bid for the peaks this early in the season. His eyes followed the path leading through the cottages below but he saw nothing.

Aaron had removed both the dartgun and the sniper rifle from their covers and stood them against the rocks. The distance to the path below was extreme for the airgun but Aaron was keen to try. As the beasts followed each other in single file he would track them through the sights of the 7mm, looking for a target he liked. At last he had nudged Hugh and pointed, Hugh following the directions until he caught sight of the stag. He had looked at it through his binoculars. It was beautiful, one of the most lovely creatures he had ever seen – young, weight perfectly set, its antlers still short and covered in a white velvet that gave off a halo as it moved through the shafts of sunlight. It looked almost mythical, as if taken from a fairy-tale. He had leaned close to Aaron's ear. 'I thought you were looking for bad stock,' he had whispered.

Aaron hadn't responded.

'Why don't you wait for—'

'If I'm going away I'd like my last beast to be a good one.' Aaron's voice was level but filled with warning. 'OK?'

'OK, OK.' Hugh drew back, placing a hand on his friend's shoulder. 'That's fine.'

Aaron had watched the line of animals pass beneath him and slowly cocked the airgun, the primed dart already in the breech. He curled round the protective rock so that he had a clear line to the path and fired, the dart catching but then falling away. The beast jumped and looked around nervously. Aaron reloaded and fired

357

again. This time the dart had stuck, then the stag was in difficulty, then it crumpled. 'Good shot,' said Hugh, but Aaron didn't reply, only plunged the gun back into its sleeve. He picked up his pack, scrambled back the way he had come and down to where the beast had fallen, sending the other deer, which had barely registered the stag's troubles until that moment, scattering in shock. Hugh watched as Aaron stuck his blade into the beast's neck, bleeding it to death. By the time he joined him at the foot of the cliff, Aaron had gralloched the animal. He looked at the corpse: all its beauty had drained away with its blood.

Aaron tied the rope round its head and forelegs and began to pull it down the path. 'Keep a watch for walkers,' he said. 'We'll need plenty of notice.'

It took an hour for Aaron to exhaust himself out of the worst of his ill-temper, and then they took turns to haul the beast towards the village below. The path veered wildly between the escarpments, the footing often perilous, the incline requiring the two of them to hold the beast by both fore and hind legs. Hugh could now see the folly of where they had killed: they would need to drag the creature all the way round the second of the mountains to reach Mac's croft at its opposite side, a distance of six or more miles. When the land finally flattened and trees began to pepper the edges of a stream that had taken its place at their side, the afternoon was more than half gone.

'We're going to be out here another night,' Hugh said, sitting down on a rock in an effort to get his strength back. 'We'll never get to Mac's this evening. A lot of it's uphill.'

Aaron stood beside him. 'We'll stay in the Heights tonight,' he said. 'It'll be comfortable.'

Hugh acquiesced, wishing himself at home.

The sun, burning deeply, was falling towards the

horizon as Hugh, sweat soaking his clothes, pulled the beast past the first cottage. Aaron barely muttered, his angular form locking forward against the weight behind. Both now had a hand on the animal's rope, pulling with their shared exhaustion. Hugh took a brief look at the cottage. Its windows and doors were gaping black holes, its corrugated-iron roof had rotted away and folded in on itself, sagging into the centre, offering up the image of a caved-in skull. The walls of an old garden could barely be made out in the overgrown tangle of high-country weeds.

The stream had grown in size and now meandered beside larger birch, the inside edges of its curves marked by pebble beaches. The path followed its edge, heading away only where the water fell into a big pool and then, with tranquillity restored, rejoined its companion on the slow decline. Hugh and Aaron paused and looked about them, turning to each of the houses that lay scattered at various points across the landscape. Most were in the state of the one they had passed, but a couple, with slate roofs, had yet to collapse. Aaron pointed up at a cottage set off from the body of the village, its position surrounded by several ancient pines that had blown over in a gale years before, all now pointing in one direction in great walls of brown needles. 'That one?'

Hugh looked at the others and concurred: the cottage would offer a good view of the path both in and out of the village. They began dragging the animal again, turning up a track worn by centuries of use and covered by years of neglect. The building, a two-room cottage, with another two rooms under the awnings of the roof, had a weathered wooden board fixed in one of its windows, giving it a permanent wink. They dragged the dead deer towards it.

They left the stag at the door and peered into the gloom. The floor was shelved up to one side with the shit of generations of animals escaping from the weather. An old range still stood in one corner, Nu-Rex written on its chimney, its lower oven now hidden by dung. Several bottles stood on a shelf above, their labels faded but some still readable: Hay's lemonade, Barr's Irn Bru, Famous Grouse. The other downstairs room was caught in darkness because of its sealed-up window, but when Hugh's eyes adjusted he could see that the floorboards had been ripped up and used either for firewood or to secure the room against animals. He turned and followed Aaron to the upper floor, careful not to rest too much weight on any step. The banister had long gone and he was amazed to see that the animals had made it to the upper floor, their muck lying scattered about.

One of the rooms had been trashed while the other, still with a door leaning against the frame, was almost complete, the air stale, the acidic smell of bats mixing with the musty reek of rotten wood. Gingerly Aaron tested the floorboards, finally turning to where Hugh was standing in the doorway.

'This should be all right,' he said.

'Perhaps, but it gives me the creeps,' Hugh replied. 'This whole fucking place does.'

'It's the best we can do.'

They concealed the stag among the fallen pines then walked down to the stream, stripped off and dived into the deep pool at the bottom of the falls. The shock of the cold water caused Hugh to gasp in pain, his head seemingly caught in a vice, but then the joy of pushing the thick sheen of sweat from his body asserted itself and the pain from the temperature became pleasure. Aaron rose out of the depths and back-paddled slowly to the pebble shore. Half in the water, he lay drying himself as Hugh swam into the force of the flow and was beaten down by the falling water from above. Soon the cold was threatening his muscles and he let himself float down to the tail of the pool where he clambered out onto a rocky ledge and sat sunning himself, cursing at the sky when clouds moved heavy hands of shadow across the landscape. The heat, after the freezing water, made him sneeze.

Aaron sat staring at the waterfall, waiting until Hugh regained control. 'Paradise, isn't it?' he said.

Hugh, drinking a handful of cold water to calm his throat, looked about. 'Refreshing anyway.'

Aaron did not say anything more, just sat looking up at the waterfall and the mountains beyond. He was still sitting there when Hugh, by then dry and dressed, went to look around.

The next morning Hugh swam again. Having made short work of an eerie mist that filled the corrie at dawn, the sun now burned down from a cloudless sky while Hugh washed away the filth of the rotten room and the effects of the whisky he had drunk in necessary preparation for sleep. As he swam he thought about Aaron's mood, which had continued into the night, with him listening as Hugh spoke of their forthcoming trip, not contributing until he had steered the conversation to the sexual acts Becky had encouraged Hugh to perform. Now Hugh could barely recall the end of the discussion, the effect of the whisky had been so strong. Yet despite the intoxication, he could remember justifying his final indiscretion through her desertion and telling everything. He had hoped the intimacy would draw Aaron out of his gloom but instead it had sent him deeper into himself. With the sun hitting the back of his head, he winced at the unsteady memory and dried himself with his shirt before pulling it on. Then he made his way back towards the cottage.

By ten Hugh and Aaron were traversing the slope of the mountain, aiming towards the hidden path that would lead them along the series of cliffs and into the corrie where Mac's cottage lay. They were pulling the deer together, in silence, the pain from the previous day's work long gone from their muscles. Once in a while they rested and Hugh scanned the ground for activity, fearful the weather might bring walkers, but as time passed they grew more confident: they would soon be among the rubble of the weathering mountain and out of danger. As he pulled through the thick heather, Hugh looked up at the cliffs that rose by his side, blinded by the flames of the sun, which crested the upper edges, the shadows only a few feet to his left. He used his free hand to shield his eyes and saw a dot move out from the core into the blue and watched it until his vision returned. He saw it was an eagle, circling back into the sun.

'What?' Aaron asked.

Hugh realized he had stopped. He was about to point up but chose instead to apologize and take the weight once more.

They were a quarter-mile from the start of the hidden path, where they would have to hoist the carcass up twenty feet of ankle-breaking scree, when a brace of red grouse crested the horizon, flying towards them and seeing them, griping their disapproval and breaking away to the right. They had been pulling the beast up the edge of a deep peat-hag and, with the passage of the disturbed birds, they let it slip back. Someone was beyond the horizon and they lowered themselves deep into the heather, using a knoll as cover, waiting, ignoring the flies that landed on their faces, Hugh feeling the tension of possible discovery play inside him. At last a head bobbed up, gaining height against the horizon. The sharp features and earnest look of the Dane.

'Jesus Christ,' whispered Hugh. 'This is getting out of hand.' He turned his head to Aaron, who was looking at the newcomer through the scope of the 7mm.

Aaron did not speak so Hugh went back to his glasses,

noticing that the Dane was wearing the same canary-yellow jacket he had the year before, only now it was tied by its arms around his waist. He was coming towards them.

'Why can't this fucker stick to the paths? Where does he think he's going?'

Aaron shushed him quietly.

Hugh looked again through the binoculars. The Dane stopped and let his small rucksack slip from his shoulders and fall to the ground. Without looking around he unbuttoned himself and began to urinate, Hugh watching the concentration on his face.

The force of the blast spun the Dane like a top, his hands coming away from his penis, flailing as he turned and pitched backwards into the heather. Hugh had seen the passage of the 7mm slug spit bone and blood into the air behind the Dane before the unexpectedness of the blast had caused him to jerk away and lose his focus. When he had recovered enough to look at Aaron, the screaming from beyond had begun.

'Winged him,' said Aaron and laughed. 'Must have been nervous.' He carefully removed the empty shell and put it in his pocket. Then he fitted another cartridge into the breech. He smiled open-faced at Hugh, all darkness gone from his features.

Hugh stood up. The screaming had an unbearable plaintiveness, its tone gasping and desperate, filled with fear. Dazed, Hugh looked around, even up to the sky. The eagle circled.

Aaron had also risen, and was now walking slowly across the heather towards the scream. He had hung the 7mm over his shoulder and was taking the shotgun from its sleeve. He broke it and Hugh noticed the box of cartridges in his other hand, which Aaron opened. He slid two cartridges home, the SSG buckshot he carried everywhere. Hugh began to walk after him, towards the voice, which had fallen to deep, bloody-lunged sobs, which gave way once more to fear when the Dane saw who was standing over him.

'Murder,' the Dane cried, gasping for air to make his shout. 'You tried to murder me.' Hugh heard this, picking up the incongruity of wrong inflections, the sudden lumpenness of the second tongue, accuracy gone. He drew up beside Aaron and the Dane's eyes swung towards him. 'And you.'

He was twisted in the mat of heather, his legs bent at the knees, body turned away from his hips, one hand picking at the torn clothing where the bullet had hit, its impact through the top right of his chest, hence the flying gore. Hugh noticed his penis, thin and anaemic, still hanging from his trousers, and, seeing his gaze, the Dane moved his other hand to cover himself but made no further effort to tuck it in. Hugh thought his arm must be all but useless.

The gesture seemed to bring home the reality of the situation to the Dane because between the gasps his tone softened and he began to plead. 'Please get help. I think I am bleeding badly. I need a doctor.' He looked from one to the other of the boys standing over him. 'This is all a terrible mistake, yes, yes, a mistake. I know you are not murderers, a terrible, terrible mistake. Please, please get help.' He started to cry, a horrible crackle between the gasps. 'Please,' he said.

He coughed and a reddish foam bubbled from between his lips. A strand of heather was caught in the hair beside his ear. 'Please. Please get help.' He was talking softly.

Hugh felt a nudge at his shoulder and he looked across. Aaron was holding out the shotgun, but Hugh ignored this and studied his friend. The blue of his eyes had all but evaporated: they were sickly and translucent. Aaron seemed intrigued, as if a long-fought-over question was about to be answered. The gun was still held at arm's length. The Dane had gone quiet but for the occasional cough.

Hugh took the gun and Aaron smiled.

'Hugh, please, I know you are not like him. Please.'

The words were coming hard now, requiring fits of blood to lubricate their way. Hugh looked down at the Dane, knowing he was already dead, that time no longer held any meaning in his life. All that was left was Hugh and Aaron.

'Please, Hugh, please. Get a doctor.'

Hugh looked at Aaron and saw the first signs of disappointment on his friend's face, as though those long fingers were about to take back the shotgun. Hugh looked into the translucent eyes and saw the first faint stirrings of regret. He forced himself to smile.

'Please.' The Dane might be able to speak but he no longer existed for Hugh.

He was dead. They were alive.

Hugh looked at the safety-catch and then noticed a small stream of urine squirting rhythmically from between the Dane's fingers. He flicked the safety off, swung the gun up to his shoulder and fired, splitting the Dane's head open from above the bridge of his nose in an almost perfect semicircle. The remainder of his brain caught in the shattered skull shone in the sunlight, perfectly smooth, reminding Hugh of the liquid metal he had helped pour from the crucible. There was a steaming hole in the heather. Hugh fired again, removing one side of the face. Then he handed the gun back to Aaron and threw up, wiped his mouth and looked around, suddenly aware of the landscape again. He checked the sky. The eagle had gone. A great calm drew over him like a shroud.

After stripping the Dane, they took turns with the shotgun to fire into his body. It took the entire case of buckshot as well as the case of seven-shot they had brought for ptarmigan and grouse to turn the body into unrecognizable mince. Hugh knelt and checked the remains for anything humanlike, using his hand to search the mush and, finding nothing, wiping the viscera off with heather. They picked up their victim's clothes and belongings and made their way back to the stag. Neither had spoken. Hugh felt no need to say anything. He felt calm, as if oil had been spread over the waters of his soul, and he made no reply to the agitated glances Aaron threw his way. It was as if he had withdrawn from the usual stuff of life and now nothing could touch him. He was without thought, serene, and in this state he walked back to the peat-hag, packing the Dane's belongings with his own. They lifted the packs onto their backs, Aaron hopping in his excitement. Hugh turned to him as he picked up the rope attached to the stag. 'We never talk about this,' he said. 'We leave on our trip tomorrow.'

Aaron gave him a nervous, excited grin, but he nodded.

The effort of dragging the stag no longer troubled Hugh and they moved across the bleak landscape quickly. On reaching the scree slope they pulled the beast up to the first ledge without so much as a grunt, and there they paused to look back. Hugh couldn't make out any mark of their passing and the bowl was still devoid of people. Soon carrion would discover the remains and, still hungry from the long winter, would make short work of the mess. He looked at Aaron, whose eyes were back to their normal blue, sparkling in the sunshine. 'You OK?' he asked.

'Never better,' his friend replied, grinning. 'Never better, brother.'

'Let's get home.' They began dragging the carcass along the hidden path.

*   *   *

Mac was waiting for them, watching their arrival from the small walled garden behind his croft. A previously agreed sign had meant all was well and he pointed them towards the mineshaft as they came in from the cliff path. Ridding themselves of their packs, they dropped the beast off in the room where it would be butchered, and returned to the garden, half of which was covered by a new glasshouse. Mac was outside working on his collection of arctic herbs.

'Interesting time out there?'

Hugh looked at Mac, aware that Aaron was grinning beside him. Mac kept his eyes on Hugh, a small, knowing smile on his lips.

'Long way to go just to get a stag,' said Hugh.

Mac turned down one corner of his mouth and spoke. 'Still, nice to get out,' he said. 'Anyway, it would allow the two of you to spend some quality time together.' His eyes were still on Hugh but suddenly they flicked across to Aaron. 'Right?'

'Right,' said Aaron.

Mac dusted off his hands and pulled several banknotes from his back pocket. He handed them to Aaron. 'So,' he said, expectantly, 'anything else happen? How was the cave?'

'Oh,' Aaron exhaled, 'the cave was great. The cave was fine. The big news is that we're planning to go abroad for a while. Not long, just a while.'

'Abroad,' said Mac slowly, as if it meant the moon. 'Interesting.'

They stood in a circle, an awkward silence between them. Finally Mac spoke. 'So you'll want a lift down to your car, I suppose.'

'That would be great,' said Hugh.

After they had said goodbye to Mac and begun the trip back to Lochanthrain in Hugh's car, Aaron was still itching with excitement. His head kept turning in agitation but Hugh stayed silent, the calm covering his nerves so comforting he did not want to disturb it with talk. He was aware that his lack of communication meant that Aaron would be back up to Mac's cottage the moment they parted, but this did not trouble him. He felt sure no further damage could be done by an indiscretion in that quarter. The moment he had seen Mac he sensed that the poacher knew everything, that those bruised eyes had looked down on the killing from the hidden reaches of the mountainside. He could not gauge how the poacher would react, only that it was imperative that Aaron and he depart first thing in the morning.

He pulled up to Lochanthrain and sat for a moment without speaking. Then he turned in his seat. 'We'll leave at ten tomorrow. We mustn't wait.'

Aaron nodded and stepped out of the car.

Hugh had expected to hear from Aaron later that evening. He had thought that his friend would not be able to pass the time on his own, but there was no call. Instead Hugh prepared for his departure, took a bath and went to bed, at once sleeping deeper than he could remember.

NINETEEN

Hugh woke late, emerging as if from the depths of the sea, gasping at the air until he gained consciousness and felt the comforting descent of tranquillity. He sat up and shivered at the brief proximity of fear, which had pricked at him between darkness and light, waiting until he felt sure that all recollection was with him before swinging his legs over the side of the bed. As if for the first time, he noticed his surroundings: the room with its old wall-paper of charging horses chosen so long ago, the chest of drawers full of toys, the Airfix planes hanging from the ceiling, an airgun by the window. He checked the clock, with its blood-red read-out, and found he had time for a shower but little more. He stood and scraped his foot on the buckle of his belt, drawing his gaze to the floor, allowing it to wander outwards again over the debris of his life, the years moving away in concentric circles, his earliest childhood possessions stuffed in the furthest corners. He checked the side-table and saw the envelope he had addressed to his father resting against the lamp. He picked a towel off the floor and headed for the bathroom.

Washed and dressed, he made himself tea, mixing it in an American-style carry-cup. He tightened the cap and rested it on the kitchen table, returning to the bedroom

369

to pick up his hold-all. On his way back he left his bedroom door open, picked up the tea, walked down the corridor and out into a day so beautiful the farm seemed to exist within a rainbow, an effect muted for Hugh by the deep-seated sense of balance that now held him, allowing no lifting of the spirits. He walked to the car, threw his bag behind the front seat and covered it with a jacket. Once behind the steering-wheel he took a sip of the tea, rested the mug in the well, started the engine and began the drive up to Lochanthrain.

With the sun half-way into the sky behind him, he drove through the gates of Lochanthrain, crossing the shadow of one of the stone eagles, its form thrown long so as to cover the entire width of the road. He passed through a darkness under the overhanging trees and then the outbuildings and round the budding purple of the rhododendrons. As soon as he reached the driveway he saw the two police cars sitting at the house steps and would have stopped but for the uniformed officer watching his approach. Tranquillity readjusted to numbness but the change in effect was almost imperceptible. He drove on.

As he pulled up he recognized the officer, Whingeing George from the town across the hill. The other police car belonged to Simon Galvary, the police sergeant. Hugh parked and stepped out, watching the constable walk towards him.

George greeted him by name, and Hugh recalled the year they had spent together at Huil primary school. He saw no reason for any quarter on the policeman's part.

Hugh nodded back and George spoke. 'You seen Aaron?'

Hugh looked over to where the pick-up was parked. 'I was looking for him myself.'

The policeman made no move towards Hugh, instead

looked into his car. His gaze snagged on the coat-covered bag but then moved on.

'What do you want him for?'

George did not say anything, just gazed towards the house, his face showing the struggle not to gossip.

When he looked back Hugh nodded at Galvary's car.

'Samson and Delilah,' he said. 'Must be serious.'

Hugh studied the policeman, his gaze settling on his acne-scarred forehead. George raised his hand self-consciously, then spoke. 'The sergeant's here but Delilah,' he corrected himself, 'Morag, is in Inverness, at Raigmore, in the ICU, looking after Alison MacGilvery.' His relish for the story was obvious. 'It's more than serious, Hugh. We're talking GBH and rape, and a few other things as well. The bastard tied her up, tortured her and beat her almost to death.'

'Which bastard?' asked Hugh.

George all but sneered. 'Your friend Aaron. Which bastard do you think I mean?'

Hugh looked at the policeman, the news forcing re-adjustments under the heavy blanket that lay across his emotions.

He saw Samson walk down the steps and George, catching his shifting gaze, turned too. The sergeant towered over Aaron's mother, who was at his side, talking intensely, using her hands. When she saw Hugh she began to scream. 'You're responsible for this, you little shit,' she yelled. 'You get off our property now, right now. Sergeant, that is the boy you should be arresting. It was him who put all those ideas into Aaron's head, him with that stinking whore of his. Get off Lochanthrain, you filthy little – little, orphan—'

Samson was trying to calm her, but she was ignoring him so he came down the steps in giant leaps and was across the gravel in seconds.

371

'I should never have let him near you or any of you inbred Highland filth, you – you no-neck – cunts!'

The sergeant was by his side. 'The woman's a loon,' he said, under his breath. 'Hugh laddie, get in your car and drive to the other side of the workshops and I'll be there in a mo. Go quick now.'

'MacIntyre, you don't deserve to have a mother—'

'Oh, and, Hughie boy, don't be disappearing on me now. I'll find you and lock you in a cell with Delilah for an hour or two, you understand me?' He closed the car door and watched as Hugh drove off, then sent George over to try to calm Aaron's mother.

Hugh pulled over by the pheasant cage where he used to leave Sandancer and stepped out into the day. Looking across at the workshop, he noticed that the door stood open. He walked across and peered into the dusty gloom: all signs of Aaron's bomb-making had gone. The tools, bottles, cartridges, petrol and books no longer existed. He looked over at the cabinet, but it, too, stood open, its metal doors hanging. He heard the police car pull up and turned to meet it, stopping to watch Samson squeeze himself through the door-frame of the Metro, the driver's side of the car bouncing up as his feet took his weight, a problem usually counteracted by Delilah's presence on the other side.

They met half-way.

'He's not in there,' the sergeant said, nodding towards the workshop. 'We've already looked. He's away on the quad bike, we think.'

Hugh nodded.

'You really don't know where he is?' Samson's eyes were on his, ready to catch the slightest indication of hidden knowledge. Hugh had guessed but, for the first time, he found it easy to lie. 'I was looking for him myself.'

Samson seemed to accept this and looked away. 'I take

it George showed his usual crime-busting cunning and told you everything?'

'Aaron beat up Alison.'

'Broke three of the bones in her face, several ribs and a few other things beside. There's the question of rape, and buggery and, Jesus, Hugh, it's really very bad. He left her tied up and she wasn't found until just after seven. She could have died.'

Hugh felt a distant disgust.

'I need to warn you that she told Delilah that this had been coming for a while. Apparently he would arrive and demand she do certain things and when she complained he would lose his temper. He told her they were perfectly normal things and that you and that English bird you were seeing got up to them all the time. He tell you any of this?'

Hugh shook his head.

'Well, what you got up to is your business, of course, but it could play badly. You might want to take a holiday.'

'Go south for a while?'

Samson nodded. 'First I want you to try and find Aaron, though. I want you to listen very carefully to me now.'

Hugh showed no expression so Samson continued, 'If someone else gets to Aaron before us he will probably be lynched, you understand? Within hours the county will be in uproar and they'll be looking for him. They hate him anyway, I don't need to tell you that. He'll only get away with his extremities intact if he hands himself in pronto. You as his friend are going to help me find him and convince him to hand himself over. Then you go. OK?'

Hugh stared at Samson. He thought for several seconds, the sergeant waiting. Then he gave his assent. 'I'll go and look for him.'

'Good lad.' Samson relaxed. 'Don't worry about trying Mac's. I'll go up and see him myself.' He turned and walked back to the Metro, leaned on the open door and then looked back. 'You hear about Roderick MacLeod, the Free Church minister?'

Hugh shook his head, another slight ripple in the blanket.

'I had to arrest him yesterday. He'd been in to see Rob the Bank and tried to pay off the Church debts with the gold cross stolen from that Catholic abbey.' Samson winced in reply to Hugh's feigned amazement. 'He won't speak any sense either. Fell to his knees in the lock-up and, get this, shouted, "St Augustine, I have a confession to make," which I thought sounded hopeful, but then he spent the entire night praying in this weird gibberish.' The sergeant sucked his teeth. 'It's been a bad couple of days. Can't wait for the next disaster . . .' He paused and, caught by the horror of an idea, pointed. 'Hughie my boy, I'm relying on you to make sure it isn't the lynching of Aaron Harding.'

Hugh watched the sergeant push himself back into the small car, turn in the seat and begin to reverse back up the road. Then he walked over to his own vehicle and started the engine.

Hugh drove down the glen and turned up the Brae, checking the mirror as he swung off the road and into the forestry plantation. He drove fast along the white dust track, switching left and right as he came to junctions. Finally he slowed, stopped and reversed into a gap in the trees, turning off the engine once the car was hidden from all but ten feet of road. He wanted to see if he had been followed.

Here in the dusky light beneath the thick pine the air seemed to fill with life. He looked out at it on the other side of the glass, watching the constant evolution in this small universe, a momentary visitor, soon to be gone. He looked through the windscreen and watched as a large horse-fly landed and walked around, looking for a place to break through, wanting his blood. Then he thought that even the omens seemed to mock by their cheapness and, with a small laugh, his position expanded out to its proper place and he felt the world exist around him, waiting for him, his future resting on the choice he had just made. He had but one duty, one obligation, an act of loyalty that he knew he would now perform. Content that he was alone, he started the engine and turned back onto the track, picking his way through the maze of roads.

He pulled up again, this time reversing far into an ill-used dead end and parking in a small hidden clearing. He stepped out and, for the first time, locked the vehicle, pocketed the keys and followed a small deer path through the trees and up to the forest's top fence, where he hunkered down and slipped through a hole in the wire. Out into a new plantation, he followed a ridge of young trees, only so tall that they reached his calves, then climbed a second fence and began to walk over the open moor.

The sun was hot on his back now but he carried nothing and moved quickly to a high ridge where he could see the wilderness open up in front of him. To the west the Three Great Mountains were grey presences hardly visible through the haze, their forms fast evaporating. The layered hillsides darkened as they tumbled closer, finally emerging as shadows. Hugh turned and checked behind him, but nobody followed so he moved down the slope towards the long slate waters of the Coronach. No trees grew on any of the precipitous slopes that led down to the loch, and the land seemed to become darker and less hospitable the further he went. Only one building marked the shoreline, and that was the small boat-shed that rusted at the eastern end. Beside it stood the quad bike, its trailer attached, while a boat sat offshore, a dot in the desolation. Hugh had guessed correctly, and as he walked he remembered, inconsequentially, that it was here the Dane had been fishing when they had met on that stalk so long ago.

Aaron must have seen his approach because the boat turned and began to move towards the shore, reaching the rocks as Hugh made the water's edge. Aaron swung in the seat and looked at him, the spark barely alive in his pale, unslept-in face. At his feet were several laundry-bags tied tightly shut and a pile of heavy metal objects – an old lawnmower roller, a sump from an engine – taken from Lochanthrain's dump. Hugh stepped into the boat and sat down, his feet among the bags.

Aaron turned the boat and began to row towards the centre of the loch, his eyes searching the hillside behind. He said nothing until they were a hundred yards from the bank. Then he said he thought Mac was watching, hidden.

Hugh turned and looked, his eyes searching for shape among the ridges and gullies of the slope, the sun now at a height where it reached down into the depths and mottled the landscape. He could not see any movement.

Aaron turned his eyes on Hugh. 'I told him,' he said.

'I knew you would.'

He looked back out to the hillside. 'He didn't seem to care. Told me he was busy and didn't have time to talk to me.' His eyes still searched the ground, almost with desire. 'He sent me away.' The oars cut the water without a sound. 'So why is he here now? And why doesn't he show himself?'

Hugh said nothing and they moved further out into the loch. The weight of the blanket of calm still settled him. Nothing mattered now but that everything work as he planned. He saw the boat's priest hanging from its hook under the rowlock and he leaned over to pick it up, examining its ten inches of antler and lead. He swung it into the palm of his hand, feeling the weight hit home. He hung the leather strap from his wrist and kicked one of the bags by his feet. It was soft.

Aaron caught the movement and brought his eyes back from the hill. 'The Dane's stuff,' he said. 'I let myself into his room at the back of the pub this morning and cleared it out.'

Hugh peered into the bag then sat up, momentarily disturbed by the sight of the personal effects.

Aaron ceased to row and rested the oars along the gunwales. He leaned down, tied a bag to a weight and pushed it over the side. It sank, leaving a trail of bubbles. Hugh looked over the water. Streams of bubbles were rising all around. He felt Aaron's eyes on him.

'I suppose you've heard?'

'About Alison?'

Aaron did not move his head, or blink.

'Samson and George were at Lochanthrain when I arrived.'

Aaron tied up another bag and launched it over the side. Hugh sat there, his back against the stern of the boat, as if thinking.

'It's going to be tricky trying to get down the road,' Aaron said carefully. He was waiting for a sign of betrayal, waiting for the argument for surrender.

Hugh looked back, his gaze steady, his interest mildly raised by what might happen if he were to make that argument. Instead he chose to be reassuring. 'We'll work something out,' he said.

Aaron smiled and tied the last bag to an old five-kilogram grain weight. He looked at the hillside again. 'Mac,' he said softly. Then he picked up both bag and weight and, with a spin, sent them out across the water.

He was still watching their fall when the priest came

377

down on his head. Hugh felt his friend's skull cave at the blow and the jarring release as the antler shaft snapped in his hand. Aaron fell forward into the slats at the bottom of the boat and spasmed. Hugh tied the remaining weights to his legs before heaving them overboard. For a moment the boat hung at a dangerous angle as Hugh lifted his friend and pitched him over the side. He drew breath as he watched the blond hair disappear into the darkness, reminding him of the innumerable times they had dived into hill pools and lochs during a lifetime of summers. For several minutes after he disappeared Hugh watched the bubbles rise from the bottom of the deep, deep loch. As an afterthought he threw in the broken priest and carefully checked the bottom of the boat for blood or debris. He noticed a reflection among the slats and reached down, rising again with the shark's tooth in his hand. He rubbed it between his fingers, then put it into his pocket and looked over the bottom of the boat again. There was nothing more. Everything had gone.

Still the blanket lay over his consciousness, despite his duty being done, his obligation to himself paid in full. He waited for feeling but there was nothing, and he sat down in the rower's seat, taking the oars in his hand, heading, without needing to look, for the boathouse. He relaxed back into his place and eased the boat from among the streams of bubbles, their small geysers holding his eye until they became too small to see. At last he felt the boat rub the gravel bank and he turned to see that he had hit land perfectly, arriving at the boat's slip. Mac stood on the shore waiting for him, grinning, the expression on his dark face solicitous and appalling. Hugh stepped out and pulled the boat up to its latch, all the while keeping his eyes on the poacher, who suddenly started to sing. 'Boy, you'll be a man soon.' His voice was soft, inveigling.

Hugh clipped the boat home and stood up, looking at Mac, his expression causing the poacher to burst into vast laughter. Hugh looked beyond, at the hillside, at the quad bike. He felt the heat of the sun, saw the poacher's bulk, his laughing face, and he pushed past, feeling the solid weight give as their shoulders connected. Mac let him through, the laughter roaring then dying as quickly as it started. As Hugh made the last few steps to the quad bike, Mac started to shout. 'You should thank me, MacIntyre . . . All your obstacles are gone . . . I've given you freedom.' He began to laugh again, the words choked through the hilarity as Hugh pulled himself onto the bike. 'I've made you into a man, MacIntyre, a man, a man . . .'

Hugh turned the key and reached for the starter button. Mac's last words broke through just before the engine roared into life: 'Don't be downhearted, Hugh, even the best misunderstand themselves.' And then the bike was in gear and he was away. He did not look back, his face determinedly on the south.

Hugh brought the bike through one of the lesser-used gates at the top of the plantation and drove it deep into the forest, close to where he had left the car. He covered its tracks then walked back to the clearing, unlocking the estate and reversing onto the track, picking his way slowly back to the road.

By the time he reached the church he found his paranoia was playing at him, and he pulled up, leaning over to check the glove-box, sighing with relief at the sight of his passport. When he looked again at the road he saw Gus's van coming the other way. It slowed and the window went down. 'You look pale,' Gus said.

Hugh shrugged and told him that Aaron had beaten up Alison.

'Ah. That's why Samson was up the glen. So you been looking for him?'

'Samson's worried about him getting lynched.'

'Fair worry. Say, by the way, you haven't seen Peter, have you? He's disappeared.'

'The Dane?' Hugh looked interested. 'You lost him?'

Gus looked at the sky then back again. 'All his stuff has gone. He said he was going hill-walking but he must have just used it as an excuse to light out on me. It's odd – I owed him money – but we were falling out.'

There was a pause while Hugh looked over the landscape, the fields of his family farm, the boarded-up church. 'Perhaps he's with Aaron,' he said.

Gus laughed, looking in his mirror, and saw a tourist car coming up behind him. 'Well, I'd better be getting on,' he said. 'I'll catch you later.'

Hugh gave a short wave then let the foreign car pass before he pulled away.

He was soon down the hill and passing the farmhouse on his left. He took one last look and saw his father kneeling over a sheep in the home paddock, the passing car catching the farmer's attention, causing him to stand up and raise a bedraggled placenta-covered lamb above his head in greeting, its mother taking the opportunity to scramble for freedom. As his father dived for the sheep, Hugh raised his hand in a small gesture of recognition and felt the blanket tear, the tranquillity shatter, the calm splinter in one long and terrible rush.

WHILE THE SUN SHINES

John Harding

At fifty the guarantee runs out . . .

Obsessed with sex, increasingly cocaine-fuelled and
gripped by a crippling fear of death, Professor Michael
Cole finds his life spinning out of control. He's supposed
to be writing the definitive biography of his literary hero,
John Donne, yet barely manages a few hundred words a
week. He knows he really shouldn't seduce his prettier
female students but it's hard to stop because they're only
young once. And the failure of a colleague to succumb to
his waning charms is a challenge he could well do
without. Throw in a fight for promotion, a wife to lie to
and two small children to look after and it's no wonder
his blood pressure has soared to life-threatening heights.
Something has to give.

But Michael is a creature of habit and old habits die
hard, especially the bad ones. It's only when he's caught
in the act of adultery by his grandmother that he sees the
writing is on the wall. After all, she's been dead for
twenty-five years . . .

Funny, compelling, tender and truthful, *While the Sun
Shines* confirms John Harding as a wonderfully shrewd
and provocative chronicler of the human condition.

0 552 99966 0

BLACK SWAN

THE BOOK OF THE HEATHEN

Robert Edric

'MORE DISTURBING EVEN THAN CONRAD IN HIS
DEPICTION OF THE HEART OF DARKNESS'
Peter Kemp, *Sunday Times*

'RELENTLESS . . . AN IMPRESSIVE AND DISTURBING WORK
OF ART'
Robert Nye, *Literary Review*

1897. In an isolated station in the Belgian Congo, an Englishman
awaits trial for the murder of a native child, while his friend
attempts to discover the circumstances surrounding the charge. The
world around them is rapidly changing: the horrors of colonial
Africa are becoming known and the flow of its once-fabulous
wealth is drying up.

But there is even more than the death of a child at the heart of this
conflict. There is a secret so dark, so unimaginable, that one man
must be willingly destroyed by his possession of it, and the other
must participate in that destruction.

'MANY RESPECTABLE JUDGES WOULD PUT EDRIC IN THE
TOP TEN OF BRITISH NOVELISTS CURRENTLY AT WORK
. . . AS A WRITER, HE SPECIALISES IN THE DELICATE HINT
AND THE GAME NOT GIVEN AWAY'
D.J. Taylor, Spectator

'STUNNING . . . EVOCATIVELY BRINGS TO LIFE THE
STIFLING HUMIDITY AND CONSTANT RAINFALL OF THE
CONGO'
John Cooper, *The Times*

'A VERY GRIPPING STORY . . . THE READER IS DRAWN IN
INEXORABLY TO DISCOVER WHAT HORROR LIES AT THE
HEART OF IT . . . AN APOCALYPTIC FABLE FOR TODAY'
John Spurling, *The Times Literary Supplement*

'RENDERED IN PROSE WHOSE STEADINESS AND
TRANSPARENCY THROW THE DARK TURBULENCE OF
WHAT IS HAPPENING INTO DAMNING RELIEF. IT WILL BE
SURPRISING IF THIS YEAR SEES A MORE DISTURBING OR
HAUNTING NOVEL'
Peter Kemp, *Sunday Times*

0 552 99925 3

BLACK SWAN

A SELECTED LIST OF FINE WRITING
AVAILABLE FROM BLACK SWAN

THE PRICES SHOWN BELOW WERE CORRECT AT THE TIME OF GOING TO PRESS.
HOWEVER TRANSWORLD PUBLISHERS RESERVE THE RIGHT TO SHOW NEW RETAIL PRICES
ON COVERS WHICH MAY DIFFER FROM THOSE PREVIOUSLY ADVERTISED IN THE TEXT OR
ELSEWHERE.

99915	6	THE NEW CITY	*Stephen Amidon*	£6.99
99921	0	THE MERCIFUL WOMEN	*Federico Andahazi*	£6.99
99820	6	FLANDERS	*Patricia Anthony*	£6.99
99619	X	HUMAN CROQUET	*Kate Atkinson*	£7.99
99860	5	IDIOGLOSSIA	*Eleanor Bailey*	£6.99
99917	2	FAY	*Larry Brown*	£6.99
99922	9	A GOOD HOUSE	*Bonnie Burnard*	£6.99
99824	9	THE DANDELION CLOCK	*Guy Burt*	£6.99
99854	0	LESSONS FOR A SUNDAY FATHER	*Claire Calman*	£5.99
99979	2	GATES OF EDEN	*Ethan Coen*	£7.99
99686	6	BEACH MUSIC	*Pat Conroy*	£7.99
99912	1	BIG SKY	*Gareth Creer*	£6.99
99925	3	THE BOOK OF THE HEATHEN	*Robert Edric*	£6.99
14698	6	INCONCEIVABLE	*Ben Elton*	£6.99
99587	8	LIKE WATER FOR CHOCOLATE	*Laura Esquivel*	£6.99
99827	3	IN COLD DOMAIN	*Anne Fine*	£6.99
99966	0	WHILE THE SUN SHINES	*John Harding*	£6.99
77109	0	THE FOURTH HAND	*John Irving*	£7.99
99859	1	EDDIE'S BASTARD	*William Kowalski*	£6.99
99873	7	SNAKESKIN	*John McCabe*	£6.99
99785	4	GOODNIGHT, NEBRASKA	*Tom McNeal*	£6.99
99959	8	BACK ROADS	*Tawni O'Dell*	£6.99
99817	6	INK	*John Preston*	£6.99
99645	9	THE WRONG BOY	*Willy Russell*	£6.99
99809	5	KICKING AROUND	*Terry Taylor*	£6.99
99819	2	WHISTLING FOR THE ELEPHANTS	*Sandi Toksvig*	£6.99

All Transworld titles are available by post from:
Bookpost, PO Box 29, Douglas, Isle of Man IM99 1BQ
Credit cards accepted. Please telephone 01624 836000,
fax 01624 837033, Internet http://www.bookpost.co.uk or
e-mail: bookshop@enterprise.net for details.
Free postage and packing in the UK.
Overseas customers allow £1 per book.